"A great read concerning A.D. 59/60 and the Boudiccan rebellion in Britain. Not only will you meet and learn of the Druids, you will share in the ordinary lives of Britons and Romans. St. Luke and St. Paul move across the scenes, and we hear of the Christian faith spreading. This is a novel and the events may not all have been so, but it is well researched and gives you a feel of what it was like in the first century A.D. This is a good story—enjoy it."

David Adam
Author, *Cry of the Deer, Eye of the Eagle,* and
Fire of the North

"The conflict of Christianity and pagan religions, the clash of cultures, and a hint of love will keep the reader turning pages."

Susan Titus Osborn
Director, the Christian Communicator Manuscript
Critique Service

"Andrew Seddon's liberal use of historical characters enriches *Imperial Legions*, making us feel that every character portrayed did live this story of the Roman conquest of Britain. We believe that each scene is absolutely authentic because of his meticulously detailed description. His ability to write from the viewpoints of the conquering Romans—both political and military—and the resistant Britons allows insight into the emotions and motives entwined in this desperate struggle."

Mary Carpenter Reid
Author, Backpack Mysteries series

"*Imperial Legions* is a compelling story of faith and sacrifice during one of England's most fascinating time periods, when the Roman, Celtic, and Christian worldviews struggled for hearts and minds. First, Dr. Seddon convinces his readers he has done his homework, and then he draws us into his tale with a web of intriguing, convincing characters. Even his antagonists—one destroyed by revenge and one who simply refuses to see the truth—have their own honor."

Kathy Tyers, author of *Firebird* trilogy

IMPERIAL LEGIONS

{ A NOVEL }

IMPERIAL LEGIONS

NDREW M. SEDDON

BROADMAN
&HOLMAN
PUBLISHERS

NASHVILLE, TENNESSEE

0-8054-2180-7

Published by Broadman & Holman Publishers,
Nashville, Tennessee

Dewey Decimal Classification: 813
Subject Heading: FICTION
Library of Congress Card Catalog Number: 99-088716

Scripture quotations are from the Holy Bible, New International Version, © 1973, 1978, 1984 by International Bible Society.

Library of Congress Cataloging-in-Publication Data
Seddon, Andrew M., 1959–
   Imperial legions : novel / Andrew M. Seddon.
      p. cm.
   ISBN 0-8054-2180-7 (pbk.)
   1. Great Britain—History—Roman period, 55 B.C.-449 A.D.—
Fiction. 2. Christian saints—Great Britain—Fiction. 3. Boadicea,
Queen, d. 61—Fiction. 4. Paul, the Apostle. Saint—Fiction. 5. Soldiers—Rome—Fiction. I. Title.
PS3569.E3145 I48   2000
813'.54—dc21
                                                            99-088716
                                                                  CIP

1 2 3 4 5 04 03 02 01 00

To the memory of
Rev. Edwin C. Speare
(1924–98)

Those who are wise will shine like the brightness
of the heavens, and those who lead many to righteousness,
like the stars for ever and ever.
Daniel 12:3

ACKNOWLEDGMENTS

Thanks to:

Mary Carpenter Reid, whose insightful critiques have helped make me a better writer.

Colleen Drippé, for insisting that a Druid have a larger role, and for reminding me of "the tip of the iceberg."

My parents, Ernest and Cynthia Seddon, for reading many drafts of this novel and suggesting improvements.

Leonard Goss of Broadman & Holman for taking an interest in my excursion to the past and for encouraging me to make it better.

Luanne Pfeiffer for helping me out of computer-related difficulties.

The many excellent employees of English Heritage, and particularly the caretaker of the Roman fort at Letocetum, who allowed me in on a "closed" day.

Rev. John Naumann and the good people of St. Stephen's Episcopal Church, Billings.

Thanks also to Kathy, David, Mary, and Susan.

And especially "him who is able to do immeasurably more than all we ask or imagine . . . to him be glory (Eph. 3:20–21).

DRAMATIS PERSONAE

Romans

NOTE: Male Roman citizens typically had three names: a forename (*praenomen*) used at home, a family name (*nomen*), and one or more additional names (*cognomina*). Common forenames were typically abbreviated by the first letter. Men may be known by either the *nomen*, the *cognomen*, or both. For simplicity's sake, I have capitalized the name most frequently used in this novel. An *H* indicates a historical person.

Marcus SERGIUS Lysias, a young military tribune,
    son of APPIUS Sergius Rufus and LYDIA Pomponia
QUINTUS, his aide
Gaius VETURIUS Longinus, his best friend
H Gnaeus Julius AGRICOLA, military tribune
H TITUS Flavius Vespasianus, military tribune,
    son of the future Emperor Vespasian
H Gaius SUETONIUS Paulinus, governor of Britannia
H Decianus CATUS, procurator of Britannia
H PAULLUS, Christian apostle
H LUCANUS, ARISTARCHUS, Paullus's traveling
    companions
H Quintus Petilius CERIALIS, commander of Legio IX
    Hispana
Porcius CRISPUS, commander of Legio II *Augusta*
Gellius MARCIANUS, commander of Legio XIV *Gemina*
Virius FALCO, commander of Legio XX *Valeria*
H Lucius Annaeus SENECA, philosopher and advisor
    to NERO
H Sextus Afranius BURRUS, advisor to NERO
H NERO Claudius Drusus Germanicus, emperor of Rome
Sextus FUSCUS, centurion of the procurator's guard

Alypius JUBA, financial advisor to CATUS
Sextus Didius PERTINAX, cavalry prefect
Helvius ADVENTUS, chief centurion of Legio XIV
H POENIUS Postumus, camp commandant of Legio II
Ofonius NEPOS and Junius BASSUS, centurions
Septimus JUSTUS, a junior tribune

Britons

H PRASUTAGUS, king of the Iceni
H BOUDICCA, his wife
AIFE and CINNIA, their daughters
AILIDH (Ay-lee), daughter of CATHAIR, an Iceni noble
EGOMAS (Eck-o-ma), a dog-seller
LOVERNIOS, a Druid judge
AIRELL, WEYLYN, and BAIRRFHIONN (Bear-ee-on),
    Iceni nobles
CARA, an Irish wolfhound

*They [the Romans] create a desolation
and call it peace.*

Attributed to the British chieftain Calgacus
by Roman historian Tacitus

Roman Britain about A.D. 60

Oceanus Germanicus

Oceanus Hibernicus

Brigantes

Parisi

Deva Flumen

Mona Ins.

Llyn Cerrig Bach

Segontium

Deceangli

Deva

Mediolanum

Pennocrucium

Vernemeton

Lindum

Viroconium

Letocetum

Mancetter

Venonis

Ratae

Durobrivae

Venta Icenorum

Iceni

Ordovices

Cornovii

Tripartium

Bonnaventa

Catuvellauni

Trinovantes

Camulodunum

Cononium

Lactodurum

Maglovinium

Caesaromagus

Demetae

Dobunni

Glevum

Durocobrivis

Verulamium

Londinium

Tamesis Flumen

Silvres

Pontes

Tanatus Ins.

Sabrina Flumen

Atrebates

Calleva

Regni

Duroveruum

Durobrivae

Rutupiae

Portus Dubris

Portus Lemanis

Cantiaci

Belgae

Durotriges

Noviomagos

Dumnonii

Isca

Oceanus Britannicus

Fretum Gallicum

	Major Roads
•	Towns and Places
■	Forts and Fortresses
Britain	*Tribes*
	Maritime Features

See the Glossary for modern place name equivalents.

PROLOGUE

The Festival of Lughnasadh
Augustus 1, 802 a.u.c.
(August 1, a.d. 59)

Ériu (Ireland)

With his long, uncalloused fingers clasped behind the small of his back, Lovernios waited on the periphery of the oak grove for the speakers to the gods to summon him.

Servants sat on the grass at a discrete distance, and from time to time Lovernios caught snatches of subdued conversation. But he ignored it, as he tried to ignore a rodentlike gnawing in his vitals.

He breathed deeply of air tangy with the scent of shrub and moss and tipped his neck to gaze upward at a square of blue sky imprisoned in a leafy frame. At the apex of its great arch, the noonday sun exulted in the freedom of the summer months. In winter, the sun struggled to maintain his place, but today he blazed brightly.

It was a good sign.

For today was Lughnasadh, the festival celebrating Lugh. It was a time of joy and prayer for the coming harvest; a plea that the fields would sway with golden heads of grain.

Lovernios sighed. He enjoyed the long days of summer. And out of all the gods, he felt a particular affinity with Lugh—Lugh the fair one, the lord of arts and crafts, the sun whose name no man dared utter.

If only he could have come to celebrate.

Lovernios glanced to where a narrow track wound between the shadowed trunks of the ancient oaks into the invisible depths of the grove. At the end of that track the speakers to the gods made their preparations. And at the thought of those preparations the rodent in his belly intensified its gnawing.

1

What gnawed at him had to be, had to be.

Because of the Romans.

Curse them! Curse every son of that accursed city!

For it was because of the Romans, not to celebrate Lugh, that he'd taken ship to Ériu from his home on Albu. For Ériu was clean, untainted, blessed by Lugh. Whereas Albu . . .

For seventeen years now, the Roman invaders had stalked the length and breadth of the island they called Britannia, dealing out death and defilement, grinding one tribe after another into the dirt. Those who resisted, perished. Some tribes, like his own Iceni, made peace. But one thing always resulted: Wherever the Roman conquerors placed their thrice-cursed sandals, they sought and killed the Druid. Now, only in the fringes of the world could the remnants of the Druid gather in safety.

Lovernios let his arms fall to his sides and clenched his fists.

Romans! Their twisted tongues couldn't even pronounce the names of those they slaughtered. He hated the very thought of them. But lately, no matter how hard he tried, he couldn't escape thoughts of Romans.

He made an effort to relax and closed his eyes to enjoy the sun's warmth on his face.

No Roman foot had ever trod in Ériu.

The gods willing, none ever would.

"Master. Master!"

Lovernios opened his eyes at a tug on his sleeve. A boy in the first order of wisdom gazed up at him. "Yes?" he answered.

"The speakers are ready for you, Master," the boy whispered.

Lovernios nodded. The knot in his stomach tightened. He fingered the golden rod tucked into his belt.

As a nobly born youth, he'd aspired to join the ranks of the gutuatri—the speakers to the gods. But he lacked the gifts, and gifts couldn't be earned or learned. So he had taken a different path, one that had led him to the highest reaches of knowledge and scholarship. He became wise in the law. His golden rod contained the power of life and death. He could judge between kings. He could order armies to stay their swords, and he would be obeyed.

He became ollamh, a master of the Druid way.

Then, in his thirtieth year, he—Lovernios the giftless—had dreamed.

2

Not as in the bull feast, when a Druí influenced by incantations dreamed who would be king. Nor as a seeker of visions who meditated beside a waterfall while wrapped in the hide of a newly slain bull. Nor had he slept on a bed of rowan branches in a quest for enlightenment.

The dream had come unbidden and was the more powerful because of it.

But he hadn't understood its meaning.

First, he'd told his dream to seers of his tribe. Surely the fáith of the Iceni would reveal its meaning. But no.

No interpretation came—not from the flight of birds, the entrails of a bull, the casting of hazel wands, or the roots of trees. The cloud diviner spread empty palms before the sky, and the astrologer pronounced the stars mute. The Three Rites of Prophecy failed.

With hushed voices, the fáith told him of the only way to learn the message of his dream.

"There must be a sacrifice," they said.

Lovernios took their meaning. Something inside him cringed. "It's not worth it."

"There is no alternative. The dreams of those with oak knowledge require explanation."

And because he was a prince of the Iceni and a Druí, he couldn't blame his dream on weakness of mind or the weight of rich food and drink.

The seers insisted. In this matter, their authority overrode his. Lovernios was forced to concede.

Romans. He knew the dream had something to do with the Romans.

"Master?" The boy's tentative query penetrated his reverie. "Are you all right?"

Lovernios shook off his hesitation. It was discourteous to keep the speakers to the gods waiting.

He patted the boy on the shoulder. "Wait here."

"But master—," the boy's face fell.

"This is not for you to see," Lovernios said firmly.

He shrugged down his knee-length léine and tightened the criss belted around his waist. A long woolen cloak hung over his shoulders, secured by a gold brooch. Lovernios touched his fingers to his lips, then to the brooch.

Then he gathered the folds of the cloak and followed the track into the grove. Rich loam cushioned his steps, and the oaks clustered together like silent seers themselves. Their leaves hung motionless in the breathless air.

He laid his palm against a gnarled trunk and could almost feel the spirit beneath the rough bark.

The trees parted, and Lovernios stepped into a clearing.

In front of a massive oak, the tree of life, stood a small shrine. Four roughly hewed corner posts upheld a thatch roof. A carved wooden effigy occupied the place of honor beneath the roof. A curl of fragrant wood-smoke from a fire flickering on a hearth tickled Lovernios's nostrils.

He paused before an array of robed and hooded men. Their eerie silence made his skin tingle.

An elder, gray-haired and wrinkled, acknowledged Lovernios with a slight inclination of his neck. He was undoubtedly the senior priest, the sacerdote in charge of the correct performance of the rite.

The priest rasped, "By truth the earth endures."

Lovernios replied, "The truth against the world."

"Who seeks insight?"

"Lovernios; son of Kirwin, son of Henbeddestr, son of Gwri; ollamh of the seventh level of wisdom; a judge of the tribes." Despite the occasion, he couldn't avoid a moment of self-congratulation.

The priest made no answer. Lovernios removed his golden rod, crossed to the shrine and laid it alongside the effigy, then he returned to face the priest.

"Speak, Lovernios."

"I have dreamed."

"Tell us your dream."

Lovernios took a breath. Even if he'd wanted to, he couldn't forget. Multiple tellings had seared the vision onto his mind. He began, "My dream was threefold. I saw a large dark bird with a cruel beak, wings that blotted out the sun, and talons of iron."

"What type of bird was this?"

"I don't know. In form an eagle, by voice a raven."

The priest shushed a murmuring from the assembly with a slash of his hand. "Continue."

"It carried a wren in its claws. As the bird neared the earth, it released the wren, which fell to the ground."

"Dead?"

"Wounded. It tried to hop away, dragging its wings."

The priest's expression remained unreadable.

Lovernios swallowed. "Next, I saw a woman riding a horse. She was tall and longhaired, finely dressed, her bearing fierce and regal."

He paused. "The bird stooped upon her and knocked her from the horse. She fell and did not move."

"The third portion?" the priest asked.

"The horse wasted until its belly swelled and its ribs stood as a palisade about its chest. But it didn't die."

The priest's eyes seemed to retract into his withered skull. His lips compressed into a narrow, bloodless scar. After a long moment, he deemed, "Truly a dream of portent. You were wise to seek us." He stared at Lovernios. "Truth is the foundation of speech."

"All words are founded upon truth."

"Your account is accepted." The priest raised his arm. The sun reflected off a gold wand clutched in his hand. "Bring the condemned!"

Two junior priests escorted a man into the grove. Lovernios guessed him to be in his midtwenties, with coarse features and a lumpy, misshapen nose. Dark brows surmounted the unfocused eyes of a man drugged with a narcotic. His wrists were bound behind his back, and he was naked. He smelled of stale sweat and urine.

"This man has killed," the senior priest intoned. "His trial was fair; his punishment is just."

Lovernios gave a slight nod. Better a convicted criminal than an innocent or an honorable prisoner of war. To make the execution—sacrifice—legal, the law required a Druí judge's supervision. Though he hadn't tried the man, Lovernios's presence would suffice.

The junior priests conducted the prisoner into the shrine and forced him to his knees. Quickly and efficiently they bound him to the effigy with sturdy ropes. They backed away.

Lovernios fought down a renewed spasm of anxiety. As a judge, he'd condemned men and women. He'd supervised executions. Why the worry?

He wanted to know the meaning of his dream.

Or did he? He wiped his damp hands on his cloak.

The chief priest laid his wand next to Lovernios's and slid a knife from his criss.

Lovernios followed every move. To think that a knife should be the instrument of knowledge!

The fáith, the inspired ones, began a low, chanted incantation.

The knife hilt's crimson enamel glistened. The bronze blade glinted in Lugh's light like a thing alive, hungry for the soul of man.

The priest raised the blade. "Souls are everlasting, and among the shades is another life."

The blade flashed.

The condemned man screamed as the keen metal buried itself in his back. The priest twisted the knife and yanked it free.

Lovernios tried to jerk his eyes away, but they remained fixed on the tableau of knife and flesh. His stomach heaved. He dared not vomit, though he knew he would feel better if he did.

The speakers to the gods leaned over to study the flow of blood and the man's death throes.

It was over quickly. The man slumped across the effigy. His breath rushed out. He lay still, his open eyes staring into a horrified distance.

The chant crescendoed to a climax.

Into the sudden emptiness came the moaning of the gutuatri. They swayed in slow, snakelike movements. One slumped to the ground.

Lovernios stood still, half-afraid to breathe. He raised a hand to his beard, and then to his mustache to try to ward off the reek of fresh blood.

Would this sacrifice yield an answer?

Romans, surely the dream concerned Romans. What else could an eagle represent? *Please,* he pleaded inwardly, *let the sacrifice be sufficient* . . . .

Finally, a gutuatros ceased his rocking. His eyelids snapped open. He ran his tongue over his lips. His gaze fixed on Lovernios.

Lovernios felt pulled into that gaze, into the blackness of a cavern, into the night sky, into a depthless void so infinitely remote that he dared not attempt to name it. He chilled. He could never have been one of the speakers to the gods.

"What?" he whispered, surprised that he could even speak. "What does it mean?"

The gutuatros's words, flat and uninflected, barely sounded human. "It is a hard burden you must bear, Lovernios, son of Kirwin."

Aquileia, Italia

Lydia Pomponia rested her back against a fluted marble column and watched a beam of morning sunlight shaft through the rectangular colonnade onto the arching fountain in the center of the courtyard garden. The silvery spray splintered the sunbeam into a myriad of miniature rainbows and flung them onto statues of dancing women and playful animals. Beyond the fountain and the beds of flowers, the blue Adriatic Sea twinkled in the distance. If Lydia looked in the opposite direction, from the forecourt, the city of Aquileia spread out in a jumble of white marble and red tile.

She loved this hillside villa. This courtyard was her favorite spot, especially on hot days when the warm sunshine and cool water invited contemplation, and flower scent relaxed the mind.

A figure knelt on the grass in the sunshine beside the fountain. Lydia studied her son and frowned.

Marcus Sergius Lysias wore his informal, loosely belted household tunic and light sandals. The clothes didn't concern her—her son dressed casually when he wasn't tramping the city's underside as one of three men in charge of Aquileia's capital crimes police. And she thought him the only one who took his responsibilities seriously. Casual dress simply indicated his lack of plans for the day.

But his posture . . .

She turned to her husband, who stood in the shadows beside her, leaning on a staff to take the weight off his one remaining leg.

"He worries me."

Appius Sergius Rufus shrugged. "It's a phase. He'll grow out of it."

"Are you sure?"

"It's natural for a young man to experiment with different gods, to find where his true allegiance lies. Don't worry."

"But this fascination with a Jewish cult seems to have obsessed him."

"It's not illegal," Appius consoled.

"But it's not an approved religion, either," Lydia countered. "The emperor hasn't condoned it."

"Nor condemned it."

"Do *you* approve of it?"

Appius scowled and shifted his weight. "The Jews are always causing problems. Claudius was wise to banish them from Rome." His nose wrinkled. "Mark my words, we'll have to subdue them properly one of these days."

Lydia related, "I heard of riots in Ephesus a while ago. The followers of Diana objected to a Jewish teacher."

Appius gestured, "On the other hand, from what Sergius has said, the teachings of this Christus fellow sound harmless. Would you rather Sergius followed Cybele?"

Lydia shuddered. "Gods forbid. But these people meet after dark. Is there . . . something shameful about their practices?"

"Sergius has more sense than that," Appius reassured. "Can you see our son involved in degrading rituals?"

"No, but . . . I'm *worried,* Appius."

"I've heard," Appius said slowly, "that there are followers of Christus among the Praetorian Guard."

"So? You know better than I what soldiers are like."

Appius sighed. "All right. I'll have a talk with Sergius. Tell him it's not fitting for a young man of his rank to consort with lower-class individuals."

"Thank you."

"But it's the same as with women. Once the infatuation strikes—"

"He hasn't shown much interest in that area."

"Give him time."

Lydia shook her head. "He's so much like you."

Appius chuckled. "Thirty years ago, perhaps. And look what happened to me." He indicated the garden. "Villa, wife, and children." He sobered and held up a papyrus, rolled in its container. "This just arrived for him."

Lydia covered her mouth with her palm.

Appius beckoned with the hand that held the roll, "Come."

Lydia followed her husband as he limped across the courtyard, his weight supported by his thick staff.

At the clack of the staff on paving stones, her son rose.

Lydia smiled. Sergius was the image of her husband on their wedding day. They shared the same squarish head, fine brown hair cut short, matching brown eyes, firm chin. Just shy of his twenty-second birthday, Sergius even had his father's stocky, muscular build, as Appius had been before wounds and inactivity robbed him of his vigor.

"Son," Appius called, "a letter from Rome for you."

Sergius jumped to his feet and brushed grass off his knees. His heart skipped a beat at the sight of the bronze bound canister his father held out. "Thank you, Father."

He took it and turned the roll over in his hands.

"Open it," his father urged.

Sergius pried off the canister's top and slid out the papyrus. He traced a finger over the official seal, then broke it and unrolled the papyrus.

"It's from army headquarters." He read quickly, then looked up.

His mother chewed on a fingernail. His father waited with the patience that had outlasted Germanic barbarians. But that was the way life went—his mother always worried. Sergius wondered what she had been like before his father's injury. He'd been a child at the time; he'd never known his parents to be any different.

He shared, "I'm assigned as military tribune to the legions in Britannia, under command of Suetonius Paulinus."

"Britannia?" his mother gasped.

His father nodded. "Just the place for a young man to grow up. Suetonius is one of our finest generals. You'll learn much."

"So far away?" his mother protested.

Appius swung to face his wife. "He won't learn *anything* here in Italia."

"But the Britons are barbarians! They're cannibals! They—"

The slap of Appius's hand meeting the bare flesh of his stump stopped her in midsentence. "Don't blather to me of barbarians, Wife!"

Sergius started at the harshness of his father's tone. His mother bowed her head, her cheeks pink.

"Assignment under Suetonius is exactly what the boy needs. Would you rather he served in Armenia or on the Parthian border? *They* are barbaric."

Sergius comforted, "Britannia is fine, Mother." He looked to his father. "The legions there were stationed on the Rhine, like your legion."

"You'll be a boy among men, Sergius."

Sergius straightened. "No I won't. I'll be an inexperienced man among experienced ones. And experience can be gained."

Appius clapped him on the shoulder. "Bravely spoken."

His mother asked softly, "When do you leave?"

"Immediately. I'm to ride to Gaul, and take transport to Britannia from Gesoriacum." Sergius frowned. "I wonder if Veturius received his assignment. Do you suppose he'll be going to Britannia too?"

"If so, he'll be good company for you," Lydia hoped. "You can look out for each other."

"Your posting won't be easy," Appius warned. "Suetonius is a tough commander."

Sergius grinned. "And you aren't? Sometimes the Rhine runs through this villa."

His mother coughed into a hand. "Show respect to your father."

Sergius gazed at his father's weather-beaten face, imagining him barking orders that had once sent thousands of legionaries into battle against hordes of Chatti, Chauci, and Cherusci tribesmen. Sergius stated, "I would never do otherwise."

Rome

"Four legions?" The emperor Nero's small, petulant lips pursed and his forehead wrinkled beneath a fringe of wavy hair. He tapped an elegantly manicured finger on his knee. "Why am I paying for four legions in Britannia, when other provinces don't require any?"

Lucius Annaeus Seneca closed his eyes and as quickly opened them again. Nero pouted like a spoiled child—which he was, despite his twenty-one years. Seneca thrust away the thought. He could never, ever, express such an opinion. Not unless he desired summary execution. Nero's anger wouldn't spare even an old and valued teacher.

To his left, Sextus Afranius Burrus, prefect of the Praetorian Guard, studied the intricate mosaic on the palace floor. Burrus was looking old, but no more so than himself, Seneca thought with resignation. He detested the strands of gray that had crept into his hair and mustache and the deep furrows that crevassed his cheeks. Restraining the worst excesses of Nero proved to be a demanding task. A dozen counselors couldn't have thwarted all Nero's schemes.

But there were just two, himself and Burrus, because of all men, Seneca trusted only Burrus to aid him with the emperor.

"*One* of you answer me," Nero barked.

Seneca cleared his throat. "The Britons are a fractious people, Caesar."

"Four legions fractious?"

"Unfortunately, Caesar."

Nero leveled a finger at Seneca. "Tell me one, *one* return we've had for our investment." The emperor's aquamarine toga swirled as he surged to his feet. His voice became a high-pitched, mocking imitation of Seneca's diction. "Appoint Quintus Veranius as governor. He's a wise and able man. He'll obtain gold and silver and copper! He'll make Britannia into the jewel of the Empire!"

The emperor snarled, "And what do I get? Worthless slaves, inferior wool, and packs of flea-bitten hunting dogs! Am I a dog to be trifled with?"

Seneca lowered his gaze. "No, Augustus."

"*No!* And then the wise and able Veranius has the unutterable gall to die in office! Can I punish a dead man?"

"Unlikely, Caesar," Seneca murmured.

Nero glowered. "I'm deprived even that simple pleasure. Instead, I have to choose a new governor for that miserable backwater. And what does Suetonius Paulinus do? Two seasons of warfare!"

"He wins victories," Burrus lightened, looking up. He wore his full dress uniform; his scarlet cape hung in sharp folds over his mirror-bright engraved breastplate.

"Seneca here could win victories against that rabble," Nero undermined scathingly. He slumped back into his throne and massaged his tiny, upthrusting chin, as smooth and hairless as a boy's. "Perhaps we ought to abandon Britannia entirely."

Seneca stiffened, conscious that Burrus had done the same. He chose his words carefully. It was never wise to remind Nero of something he'd forgotten. Even a conversation that had taken place five years ago, when Nero was new to the throne.

"It would set a bad example to other rebellious territories, Caesar. If they saw that Rome couldn't control an area of her empire . . ."

"*Can* we control Britannia?" Nero asked. "Or are my legions inadequate?"

Seneca winced at the scorn in Nero's voice. He could imagine the effect on Burrus. He spoke quickly. "Britannia is controlled, Caesar. Suetonius's actions ensure the security of the province."

"The legions aren't the problem, Caesar," Burrus added.

Nero pounced. "Then what is? My advisors, perhaps? Should they be replaced?"

Seneca tried to remain calm. "Suetonius Paulinus is able, ambitious, and popular. Allow him to complete his campaign."

Nero mused. His eyes glittered. He ran his thumb along the side of his nose. "Ambition is the cousin of folly," he quoted in Seneca's direction. "So you have told us."

"Suetonius's victories enhance your reputation, Augustus," Seneca soothed. "He seeks only your honor."

"Really."

Burrus added, "Julius Caesar and the Divine Claudius both gained reputations at the Britons' expense. The same could happen to your most illustrious name."

Nero assumed a thoughtful expression. "The empire of Nero Claudius Drusus Germanicus Caesar would be greater than that of my adoptive father Claudius. *He* has temples built to his honor."

Because he's dead, Seneca nearly said, but caught himself before the words slipped out. "It's only a matter of time before the gold and silver begin to flow."

Nero snapped his fingers. "It's the fault of the Druidae."

Seneca sighed. "It seems as if every malcontent in Gaul has fled to Britannia and found sanctuary with the Druidae."

Nero required, "Suetonius is to deal with them as well."

Burrus cleared his throat. "The Empire has always shown the utmost respect for local gods, Caesar."

This isn't the place, Burrus, Seneca thought. He illumined, "The situation in Britannia is different." He faced Burrus and ticked off on his fingers, "The Druidae are a center of disaffection, and they control the flow of gold in Britannia. As long as they retain their influence, we will never have the control we need. The power of the Druidae must be broken."

"Caesar," Burrus appealed, "the Empire has never set itself against a nation's religion. Change takes time. Generations—"

"We don't have time!" Nero flared. "Britannia drains the imperial coffers. Am I made of money like Seneca?"

Seneca flinched. The only things that exceeded Nero's lust were his greed and jealousy.

"I wish I had his hands," Nero mused. He leaned forward to peer at Seneca's fingers. "Everything he touches makes money." He raised his eyes. "Would you give me your hands, Seneca?"

Seneca held them up. "They are at your service, Caesar. But I prefer they remain attached to my body."

Burrus spoke stiffly. "May I suggest caution regarding the Druidae, Caesar? Rashness begets mistakes."

Nero sulked, "Seneca says one thing, you another. But somehow, you two always get your way." Nero gripped the arms of his throne. He spoke to Seneca. "See that Suetonius knows what's expected of him. The Emperor of Rome will not be opposed by a clutch of savage priests."

"I will, Caesar," Seneca accepted.

"And tell Procurator Catus that I expect the Britons to pay well for the trouble they're causing."

Seneca bowed his head. "As you require."

"Leave me."

The door to the emperor's audience chamber closed behind them, leaving Seneca and Burrus in the corridor outside.

Burrus rubbed his forehead. "What a day! First I have to listen to Paullus, that long-winded Jew that Festus dumped on us, and now this. Abandon Britannia? I can't tell anymore when Nero's serious and when he's not."

"Having his little jest, I expect."

"You taught your pupil too well, Seneca. He leans on us less and less. Who's using whom, I wonder?"

Seneca took a deep breath. He glanced to make sure nobody loitered within earshot, and moved away from the door.

Burrus followed, complaining, "He's likely to be the death of us. I'm sick of playing these games."

Seneca nodded, "Yes, though if anything goes wrong, at least he can't say he wasn't warned. But you played your part too well, my friend."

"Who says it was a part?"

Seneca ignored the comment. "Tell me your candid opinion of the situation in Britannia."

The Praetorian prefect fiddled with the clasp of his cape. "Suetonius will break the back of the Briton resistance. But mark my words, Seneca, interfering in religion will cause nothing but trouble. Suetonius is a soldier, not a diplomat."

Seneca spread his hands, "I see no way around the difficulty. For all his immaturity, the emperor understands that the Druidae hold the key to control of Britannia."

"Then it is a key that you will turn, Seneca, for I shall not."

"We've planned this for years, since Suetonius proposed his actions. The groundwork is laid. To change plans now would be even more expensive."

The two men walked down the hall. Minor functionaries stepped aside and nodded respect to Seneca in his white toga and the uniformed Burrus. A slave carrying a tray of delicacies for the emperor scurried past.

Seneca said, "It's only the Briton priesthood that's the problem, not the religion."

"Your distinctions are too fine. Worthy of your role as a philosopher, perhaps."

"If it makes you feel better, think of the Britons' human sacrifices, their cannibalistic rituals—"

"Sheer hearsay. Scare your grandchildren with them. If you believe those stories, you probably believe that the circus games are rigged."

"What I believe isn't the point. And only barbarians and criminals face the circus."

"It's a pretense."

Seneca laughed. "All politics is pretense. That's why we're still alive. Come, I have a new Aminian vintage I'm certain you'll enjoy. A glass of wine will sooth the headache I see gathering behind your noble brow."

Burrus nodded.

"The west of Britannia is the crux," Seneca mused. "What an infernal pity that Veranius died! He could have subdued the tribes with diplomacy."

"That's what I don't understand," Burrus began. "With what you have at stake—"

Seneca stopped short. "Don't *you* start."

Burrus shrugged. "You're the one with the golden fingers. You won't find me risking money in Britannia."

Seneca gestured. "They're old loans, made while Claudius was on the throne."

"No matter," Burrus sniffed. "You could lose it and not miss it."

Seneca laughed mirthlessly. He struck Burrus on the arm. "I could lose it, my friend, but I *would* miss it."

"So would Nero," Burrus added pointedly.

In a plainly furnished room in a house on the outskirts of Rome, Lucanus dipped his pen in ink. He smoothed out a sheet of papyrus on the table, thought for a moment, then began to write.

> In the second part of my work, most excellent Theophilus, I gave an account of the acts of the apostles and how the gospel was spread in Judea and the provinces of Asia, Greece, and Rome.
>
> Paullus remained in Rome two full years, proclaiming the kingdom of God and teaching the facts about the Lord Jesus Christ. He spoke freely, without constraint.
>
> At that time, he was called to present his case before Caesar and his chief advisors.
>
> Nero said to Paullus, "Felix and Festus and King Agrippa determined that you are guiltless of crime against Caesar. But you have appealed to Caesar, and

Caesar will hear your case. Where are those who accuse you?"

Burrus, one of Caesar's advisors, answered, "This case involves aspects of Jewish religious law. None of those who accuse this man are here."

Nero announced, "I have read the charges against you, Paullus. You have our permission to speak your defense."

Lucanus paused, trying to think how to condense the account of the trial that Paullus had told him. Nero could have appointed a special prosecutor. Instead, he heard the case personally. But after a while Nero's interest waned, and he left Burrus to decide the verdict.

Lucanus smiled. God had provided a judge who wasn't afraid to uphold the law. The case against Paullus had always been specious.

The house door swung open and admitted the clamor of the street: soldiers, hawkers, children, dogs—and the smells: baking, horses, humanity, and smoke. A breeze, hot and humid, curled the sheet of already limp papyrus.

Lucanus raised his pen before movement blotted what he'd just written. He studied the tall, dark-haired man who entered.

"Are you writing again?" Aristarchus's eyes twinkled beneath thick eyebrows. He shook his head, "I don't know who's wordier, you or Paullus—"

A third man, short and stooped, followed Aristarchus into the room. He wore an often-mended, dust-stained toga. Streaks of silver slashed through black hair cut longer than current fashion dictated. "Who's talking about me now?"

Lucanus laughed. "We were discussing the writing of letters."

The older man squinted. "Another letter? Save your ink. We're leaving Rome."

"Leaving?" Lucanus laid his pen aside and weighted his papyrus with his inkhorn so it wouldn't blow off the table. He rose. "Where are we going?"

"I've seen a man from Britannia."

"Oh." Lucanus paused. He exchanged glances with Aristarchus. "In a vision? As you saw the man from Macedonia?"

Paullus lowered himself carefully into the chair Lucanus had vacated. "No. I was in the flesh, not the Spirit."

"You, Paullus? In the flesh?"

The apostle ignored the joke. "His name is Caratacus. He's a Briton chieftain."

"*Was* a chieftain," Aristarchus corrected. "He was defeated and captured years ago. Claudius granted him the freedom of Rome."

Paullus said, "He and his family have received the gospel—"

"Your point?" Lucanus interrupted.

"Caratacus asked me to visit his people. As I've said before, I've long desired to preach to the westernmost ends of the Empire."

"But you're free! Nero has acquitted you. The church in Jerusalem—"

"Can abide longer without seeing me—in the flesh, as you put it. They have letters to read."

Lucanus squeezed the other man's shoulder, feeling the sharp edge of bone beneath a thin covering of skin. "Your zeal is admirable, Paullus. But as your physician, I object. Your health is poor. Your vision grows worse daily. Britannia is a hard journey—"

"Hard? To one who's been shipwrecked, stoned, lowered down city walls, bitten by snakes?"

"Exactly."

"What are the forests of Britannia in comparison?"

Lucanus looked to Aristarchus for help. The younger man gave a resigned shake of his head.

"You're no longer young, Paullus," Lucanus pleaded. "It's time to rest. Preach here in Rome. But no more travel, I beg you."

"I appreciate your concern." Paullus turned away. "But my mind is made up. Caratacus tells me the Britons are eager for the gospel. The Lord will sustain me in the work I do for him."

Lucanus sighed, "When do we leave?"

"When you and Aristarchus have arranged passage."

Later, when Paullus had gone to rest and Aristarchus departed to the docks, Lucanus retrieved his pen. How many more chapters in Paullus's life would there be? He began to write.

PART ONE

Autumn, 802 A.U.C.
(A.D. 59)

ONE

Sergius Lysias awoke to a dull, lifeless dawn. He lay on his back with dense gray clouds seemingly poised a mere handbreadth above him. He stretched, winced as stiff muscles in his neck and back protested, and clambered to his feet. His night-chilled fingers fumbled to tighten his cloak against a damp sea breeze that crept through both the thick wool and his linen tunic underneath.

The liburnian galley pitched and rolled, and Sergius fought for balance. He chose a moment when the galley hung poised on a wave crest and reeled to the port rail, somehow managing not to step on any of the legionaries sprawled across the deck in a grotesque parody of battle's aftermath. He gripped the stout oak rail and braced himself.

The regular splash of oars and the slop of water against the hull broke the early morning stillness. The liburna's lateen sail tugged against creaking and groaning stays.

Sergius filled his lungs, hoping the brisk breeze and salt spray would clear the heaviness of a poor night's sleep from his head. His mouth tasted stale, and he wished he'd thought to bring a wineskin on board with him. He rubbed crust from his eyes.

The gauzy, mist-dimmed sun shot tentative rays over the horizon like an archer unsure of his target. But it was enough light to reveal four other galleys wallowing on parallel courses. In the distance, the masts of a small flotilla of merchant ships punctured the horizon. The fat-hulled, lumbering cargo ships made slow progress compared to the light, fast galleys.

Westward, beyond the galley's high prow, a lighter patch rose from the sea, extending to the clouds. Was it cloud, or—God be praised—land?

"Ggghah!"

Sergius started. Not five feet away, another figure leaned against the rail, bundled in a thick cloak the duplicate of Sergius's. "Gaius! I didn't see you."

"You nearly blundered into me." Gaius Veturius Longinus's voice was thick.

"Are you eager for a first glimpse of Britannia?"

"Sick from eagerness." Veturius leaned over the rail and retched.

An oarsman below muttered an oath.

Sergius squinted in the half-light at the green pallor of his friend's narrow face and aquiline nose. Discolored, puffy bags hung beneath bloodshot eyes. Rumpled hair stuck out at odd angles.

He clapped Veturius on the shoulder. "Only a few more hours. We'll be ashore before you know it."

Veturius gave him a bleary glare.

Sergius gazed at the horizon. "Think of the glory, my friend. The adventure."

"In Britannia?" Veturius folded his arms on the rail and pillowed his forehead on them. "I want sunshine, wine, and beautiful Syrian women, not dirty painted savages. I bet you can't even buy decent wine there. And they say the sun never shines."

"Surely you don't believe every traveler's rumor you hear."

"I'm sure as Hades not going to believe the recruiting tales the army tells me."

A rent in the clouds opened to spill a golden sunbeam toward the distant shore. The towering cliffs lit up, sparkling white, reminding Sergius of a temple perched on one of Rome's hills.

He nudged Veturius, "Look."

Veturius raised his head, grunted, and lowered it again.

"Come on, Gaius. Has wine blinded you? It's beautiful."

"Women are beautiful. Cliffs are rock."

"You, my friend, need a new view of life."

"Not that I'll get it from a friend who's made it his mission to hold me back from life's scant pleasures."

Sergius snorted, "You're headed for a life of debauchery."

"At least it's a life."

Sergius sighed. "Be that way." He allowed his body to fall into a gentle sway, moving with the ship.

He was grateful he hadn't succumbed to seasickness like Veturius and most of the troops. His sleep had been interrupted countless times as cursing legionaries heaved their guts over the rail. In contrast, he'd felt no more than a momentary unease before his stomach had settled down.

The convoy of five ships had put to sea from Gaul the previous day, leaving Gesoriacum on a calm, moonless night when starlight twinkled silver on ebony waves. Four ships transported legionaries and auxiliaries drawn from all across the Empire. The other carried materials and supplies.

Sergius was no mariner—life spent voyaging up and down the Mediterranean like his uncle Publiu didn't appeal to him—but a night's sail from Gaul to Britannia? Hardly a matter to upset a newly appointed military tribune on his way to join his first command.

Sergius glanced at his friend. Veturius seemed to have lapsed into sleep, still draped over the rail.

The slowly rising sun burned aside the low-lying morning clouds. The sea transformed from ashen gray to azure blue, and the cliffs shone as alabaster. Seagulls flocked to the liburna's wake, plunging into the turbulent water to emerge with struggling fish. Their harsh, insistent cries drifted across the waves.

A century ago, Sergius thought, the great Julius Caesar had surveyed these same cliffs, determined to give the natives a taste of Roman military might. Perhaps it had been a morning just like this, when you couldn't tell if those were trees on the cliff tops or armed savages with murder in their hearts. . . .

A thrill shivered down his spine.

The liburna drew closer to the towering cliffs. The sea surged against the solid wall of rock.

"Are we there yet?" Veturius moaned.

Sergius recalled the historical event, "Caesar's troops almost didn't make it ashore. They had to jump into deep water in full armor, under a hail of spears."

Veturius sighed, "Not the *Gallic Wars* again! Don't you have anything else to read?" He rolled so he faced the sky. "What happened?"

"The men panicked. But the standard-bearer of the Tenth Legion jumped into the breakers with his eagle. He shouted a challenge to the troops. They followed him. Once ashore, a charge flung the Britons into retreat."

"Inspiring," Veturius muttered. "Did he live?"

"The standard-bearer?" Sergius paused. "I don't know."

Veturius cocked an eye, then closed it again. "Probably didn't matter to Caesar."

"You're a cynic as well as a debaucher."

"I am a cultured young man who has no desire to see his blood shed at the hands of barbarians in a godforsaken land on the edge of the earth."

Sergius chuckled.

Rome had tried three times to invade Britannia. Julius Caesar's expedition a hundred years ago had amounted to little more than a raid.

Twenty years ago, Gaius Caligula's mad attempt had ended in a seashell-gathering spree on the coast of Gaul. Caligula claimed to have conquered the ocean. Two years later, he was assassinated.

Seventeen years ago, the third, successful invasion by the emperor Claudius almost foundered when troops commanded by General Aulus Plautius balked at being ordered to venture beyond the bounds of the world. Only the personal intervention of Claudius's representative persuaded the legions to cross this narrow strip of water.

Sergius shaded his eyes. Behind Britannia's cliffs he imagined a fertile land of green valleys, forests, and fields. Britannia couldn't be as bad as rumor maintained. Claudius had claimed the credit for his general's successful invasion, and—except where women were concerned—Claudius had been no fool. Besides, if Britannia was so terrible, then why would the emperor Nero want to annex more of it?

Sergius aired, "I'm glad to be away from Rome."

"Why?"

"My parents suggested I marry the abominable Claudia."

Veturius shuddered. "A fate worse than death."

"My sentiments exactly."

"I thanked the gods that your parents took more initiative than mine."

Sergius stared. "Your parents had plans?"

Veturius nodded, "They did."

"I would gladly have renounced any agreement in favor of my best friend."

"Who would have fallen on his sword," Veturius said gloomily.

"A man of two minds," Sergius chided. "First he doesn't want his blood shed, then he does."

Veturius scowled.

"Think of it." Sergius teased, "If you married Claudia, your aunt Drusilla would prepare one of her famous banquets. We could have a jellyfish and eggs appetizer, a main course of sow's udders stuffed with salted sea urchins, or perhaps boiled tree fungi with peppered fish-fat sauce— I know you like that—"

"Enough, Sergius!"

"Followed by dormice stuffed with pork and pine kernels, or boiled flamingo with dates for your mother—"

Veturius hung over the rail and heaved.

The ships angled to the north, following the line of the coast. As if sensing the end of the voyage, though short, the oarsmen picked up pace. The sleek liburna cut through the waves.

A swift clack of soles on the deck sounded and the liburna's captain stood beside the two tribunes. He gave an affable nod and pointed at a promontory. "There it is. Rutupiae."

"Gods be thanked," Veturius muttered.

The transport turned shoreward.

The captain peered into the water. "Shingle banks," he explained. "It's dangerously shallow in places." He bellowed an order to the helmsman, and the liburna edged away from an underwater outcropping.

Sergius elbowed Veturius in the ribs. "Open your eyes, idiot. Set an example for the troops."

Veturius pulled himself erect and shook the creases from his cloak.

Sergius looked at the shore. The buildings of the supply base clustered on the promontory's summit. Guards patrolled the timber ramparts while porters carted goods up the slope from the shoreline wharfs. Smoke curled into the air, and even from a distance the air rang with the sounds of human activity.

The captain gave a last glance into the water, said, "Excuse me," and hurried aft.

The liburna lost way and eased toward a dock. Waiting dockworkers readied mooring lines.

On the bow a centurion bawled orders and laid into the legionaries with his twisted vine stick. "On your feet, you lazy scum! Move it! I've seen dancing girls in better shape than you!"

The vitis cracked over heads and shoulders.

"Lucilius II," Veturius snickered.

Sergius chuckled. Everyone remotely connected with the army knew the story of the centurion Lucilius—old "Fetch Me Another." If he broke one stick of office over the back of some dim-witted legionary, he'd cry for a second or third stick. But finally, he'd fetched once too often, and enraged troops had him lynched.

"This one had better watch out," Sergius agreed, glad that tribunes didn't answer to centurions.

The grumbling legionaries struggled to their feet and stood swaying on the deck.

Sergius took in their ashen, green-tinted faces, dark-circled eyes, and unsteady postures. If Caesar's troops were as unseaworthy as these foot-sloggers, it was a wonder he'd won any battle at all. Perhaps his men had feared the Britons less than the sea. Or maybe less than they'd feared Caesar.

The centurion cursed and threatened and finally chivied the legionaries into the semblance of a formation.

The ship grounded against the dock. Lines swished through the air to waiting hands, and boarding planks clattered into place.

Sergius bounded across onto the dock and jumped to the stony beach. Britannia at last!

The air was heavier and saltier than the perfumed air of Aquileia yet lighter than the thicker air of forested Gaul. A feeling of unreality washed over him.

His mother worried, but why fear Britannia? The Britons had no leader worthy to oppose the legions. Not anymore.

As a boy of fourteen, he'd seen the last Briton hero, Caratacus, paraded before the emperor Claudius. Claudius's triumph was as vivid in his mind as if it had happened yesterday.

He and his parents had journeyed to Rome for the occasion. Citizens had turned out by the thousands to view the rebel Briton who had escaped Plautius and fought on for years before being betrayed by his people. The elite of Rome, row on row of animated spectators, watched beneath the burning sun.

Long lines of chained prisoners snaked sullenly along the decorated streets, scowling at the hoots and jeers of the crowd. The bravest or crudest spectators leaned out to spit at the captives. Carts laden with spoils of war—gold and silver ornaments, decorations, bronze and iron weapons—clattered over the cobblestones. Ranks of legionaries, all bright steel and bronze, their polished helmets and armor almost as bright as the sun, marched in unwavering formation. Their standards and eagles gleamed. Near the end of the procession came Caratacus's family.

Last of all the Briton warrior himself, striding erect and dignified, oblivious to the abuse heaped upon him, his multicolored shirt and trousers an anachronism in a sea of tunics and togas.

Sergius had slipped away from his parents, scurried through the crowd, and followed the procession into the forum. The legionaries formed into a square, facing the dais where Claudius, enthroned in his royal purple toga, waited behind an armed phalanx of the Praetorian Guard.

Caratacus stepped forward.

Claudius held up a hand to still the multitude.

Sergius wormed his way through a knot of sweating bodies to where he could hear.

Caratacus raised his chained arms. He spoke clearly in heavily accented Latin.

"If my success in battle had matched my lineage and rank, I would have come to this city as your friend rather than your prisoner. Nobly born, the ruler of many tribes—you wouldn't have spurned a peaceful alliance with me. As it is, humiliation is my lot, glory yours. I had horses, men, arms, and wealth. Does it surprise you that I am sorry to lose them? If you want to rule the world, must everyone else welcome enslavement?"

Sergius gasped. He covered his mouth. Any moment, Claudius would raise a hand, and a soldier would lop Caratacus's insolent head from his shoulders.

But the emperor didn't move a muscle.

Caratacus continued, "If I had surrendered without striking a blow, neither my downfall nor your triumph would have become famous. If you execute me, they will be forgotten. Spare me, and I shall be an everlasting token of your mercy."

Claudius leaned to his side. His lips moved as he spoke to his wife Agrippina. Her face twisted. She gestured thumbs-down.

Claudius rose. "S-Silence!"

When the crowd's noise subsided, the emperor motioned to the guard commander. "S-Strike off his ch-chains!"

The soldier hurried to obey.

The stooped, almost comical emperor said to the tall, muscular Briton, "F-For your brave words, I, Tiberius Cl-Cl-Claudius Nero Germanicus, implacable toward the rebellious, but m-merciful and generous to the defeated, p-pardon you, Caratacus, and your f-family. Henceforth live in p-peace among us."

"What are you doing?" Somebody cuffed Sergius's head. "Get out of here, boy!"

"Sergius! *Sergius!* Have you gone deaf?"

Sergius blinked. The vision of the forum faded.

Veturius beckoned. "Are you going to stand on the beach all day?"

Sergius scuffed across the shingle. "I was just remembering."

"Dreaming, more like. Do it some other time. I need a bath and then a meal. A *light* meal."

Sergius spared a last look for the ships, hoped his armor, weapons, and horse wouldn't get misplaced during unloading, and then followed Veturius to the wharf gate. A guard gave their documents a cursory inspection, saluted, and waved them inside.

The base swarmed with controlled activity, and it smelled like an army installation. Sweat of men and horses, acrid fumes from the armorers' shops, the fragrance of worked leather, dust—all blended together. They whiffed none of the tarry, salty smells of the navy.

When first built, Rutupiae would have been a simple, economical affair of earthen ramparts and wooden sheds. But as the Occupation progressed, the base expanded. Now, it sprawled across acres of ground, a panorama of granaries, barracks, stables, workshops, storehouses, and officers' quarters. Anything the Roman Army in Britannia needed could be found at Rutupiae.

The two men paused to gain their bearings. At the far end of an arrow-straight street, the main gate presented an imposing barrier to arrivals from land.

In theory, the base should have been laid out on the same plan as a legionary fortress, in which case the headquarters ought to lie at the T-junction where the via principalis joined the second main street, the via praetoria. But Rutupiae degenerated into a tangle of branching passageways.

"We could ask," Veturius suggested.

"Let's try over here." Sergius pointed to a timber and stone building off to his right guarded by a pair of sentries.

Veturius reached for the door, but it was flung open from inside, and he jumped back. "Watch where you're going!" he snapped at the uniformed young man who hurried out.

Sergius extended an arm to bar the man's progress. "Pardon me, but is this the principia?"

The young man halted, ran a pair of shrewd eyes over them, and queried, "Newcomers?"

Sergius nodded. "How could you tell?"

The man pointed at Veturius, "Skin color."

Sergius snickered. Veturius frowned.

"I mean," the young man covered quickly, "that you haven't lost your tans yet in our bleak northern climate."

"Give us a chance," Veturius quipped.

A broad purple band on the man's cloak identified him as of senatorial rank, the same as Sergius and Veturius. Sergius guessed him to be younger than himself by a year or two. An intelligent forehead surmounted pink cheeks and a prominent chin. His straight brown hair was slightly lighter than Sergius's. His accent hinted at an origin in Gaul.

Sergius introduced himself and Veturius.

The young man returned the greeting. "Julius Agricola, senior tribune of Legio II *Augusta*. Welcome to the emperor's Britannic province."

Sergius said, "As you noticed, we've just set foot off ship. We haven't received our appointments yet."

"And you won't. Not here at any rate." Agricola gestured to the door behind him. "This is the principia, but I wouldn't go in there unless you want to find yourselves guarding grain." He lowered his voice. "Lots of clerks and other civil servants, and you know what they're like."

"But the commandant—," Veturius began.

"Is so buried beneath administrative details he won't even notice you're here. And if he did, he wouldn't know what to do with you. Believe me, Praefectus Scaurus won't miss you."

Agricola turned on his heel. "Come with me. I'll show you where to eat. I have some errands to run, and then we'll meet at the bathhouse, and I'll fill you in."

Sergius and Veturius fell into step beside him.

Agricola continued, "My legion, the *Augusta,* is based at Isca in the southwest, where the Britons are quiet at the moment, so Governor Suetonius has assigned me to headquarters staff."

"Were you detailed to meet us?" Veturius asked.

Agricola laughed. "Not a chance in Hades. I'm here because the chief armorer's been tardy in shipping munitions to the frontier stations. He has this fear that if he sends his precious swords to active regiments we might actually use them."

Agricola snorted, "He won't acknowledge that metal breaks and leather wears out and armor dents and we aren't about to fight bare-handed. My task is to put the fear of Suetonius into him." Agricola's lips twitched. "But I'd hoped to meet you, so you've saved me the trouble of looking."

"Glad to oblige," Veturius said.

They circled the principia. Agricola indicated the adjacent building. "This is the mansio. Contains everything important, including officers' quarters."

Agricola halted outside an arched doorway. "Have lunch. After, meet me at the bathhouse—around the corner, third door on the left." He waved and plunged back into the maelstrom of activity.

"What do you make of that?" Veturius asked.

Sergius shrugged. "I don't know. We can't expect Britannia to be as orderly as Rome, I suppose. Agricola seems to know what he's doing. I guess there's no harm in relaxing for a few hours."

Veturius bared his teeth. "Then let's get a drink!"

Later that afternoon, after a plain meal of fort food, Sergius and Veturius headed to the bathhouse. They undressed, stowed their clothing in lockers in the apodyterium, and entered the bathhouse proper.

"Come on in!" Agricola beckoned from the steaming waters of the caldarium.

Sergius lowered himself gingerly. His skin tingled, and he let out a breath through narrowed lips.

"Too hot for you?" Agricola gibed, already submerged.

Beside him, Veturius let out a contented sigh, and slid down until his chin touched the water. "This is the life." He splashed water over his hair.

"We may live among barbarians, but that doesn't mean we have to live like them," Agricola reveled.

"Where's the governor?" Sergius asked.

"Up north, inspecting the Ninth Legion. We're to meet him in Camulodunum in a few days."

"He didn't send orders for us?"

Agricola massaged his legs below the water. "He likes to meet new officers first. Once he's met you, he'll decide where you're to be posted. We've lost several tribunes recently."

Veturius opened his eyes. "Were the tribunes we're replacing, uh, killed?"

Agricola raised an eyebrow. "Recalled. Tour of duty ended. On to greater things, no doubt."

"Good," Veturius relaxed.

"Are you worried?"

"I can hardly wait for a good fight," Veturius said, deadpan.

"We're not likely to see much action, in my opinion," Agricola replied. "Unless, of course, the emperor's orders are to expand the frontier."

"There was an Imperial courier on our ship," Sergius commented.

"There's been a steady stream of them. Some for Procurator Catus, others for Suetonius. But if he's received orders, he hasn't discussed them at staff meetings."

"What are the Britons like?" Sergius investigated.

Agricola shrugged. "About what you'd expect. Definitely in need of civilizing influences." He raised himself out of the water. "I'm hot enough. Who's for a plunge in the frigidarium?"

In his palace at Venta Icenorum, in the heart of Iceni territory, Prasutagus, king of the Iceni, coughed. The deep, rumbling cough tore through his chest and left a trail of fire from his collar bones to the bottom of his rib cage. With a trembling, blue-veined hand he wiped away the spittle that clung to his lips. Streaks of crimson mixed with the yellow-gray phlegm.

"Drink this." A white-robed Druí physician held a silver goblet out to him.

"Bah!" Prasutagus shoved the Druí's arm away. The goblet slopped amber liquid onto the bed. "No more of your foul-tasting poisons! Out of my sight, charlatan!"

"But, King—"

"*Out!*" Prasutagus shouted. His voice broke, and he fell back in a fit of coughing.

A woman's voice guided, "Leave us, physician. Return when the king is in a better mood."

Through watery eyes Prasutagus watched the Druí leave. He closed them while he waited for the spasm to stop and the pain in his chest to subside. When he looked again, his wife stood beside him.

"Gods spare me from such as he."

She chided, "You shouldn't speak to the Druí so."

"Bring me wine. And don't put anything in it."

She reached to a low table. He heard liquid gurgle, and then she handed him a goblet.

Prasutagus swirled the brick red wine, sniffed it, then sipped. The warmth spread through him, warming him more than the bearskin on the bed and the brazier near the wall. Gradually, the cough-induced throbbing in his head lessened.

"He means to heal you," she continued.

"There's no healing for me," Prasutagus resigned. "I'm a dead man, Boudicca. Before the winter is out, you'll be laying the turf over me."

He waited for an answer, for her to argue and tell him not to be foolish, that he had a common illness that would run its course and fade away. When she didn't reply, he patted the bed. "Sit."

She complied, and her waist-long, tawny hair splayed across the bearskin. Prasutagus stroked the tresses that he loved more each year. In the prime of his life he'd married this she-wolf. He had never tamed her—not when he was young and virile and certainly not now when he was old and sick—but they had somehow existed together in a condition of mutual respect.

"Is there news?" he asked.

Once, nobles of the Iceni would have brought him word. Once, his audience room would have overflowed with graybeards and young hawks, with wise advisors and crawling sycophants. Now, Boudicca and the Druí physician alone entered his presence. As strength left him, other faces became unbearable. He banished his daughters for fear they might catch his lingering illness.

Boudicca nodded, "A letter from Decianus Catus."

"What does the Roman leech want now?"

"Seneca is recalling his loans."

"How much?"

"Everything."

Prasutagus started, "Forty million sestercii?"

Boudicca nodded again, "At once."

"That's absurd! Surely there's been a mistake!"

"No mistake. Catus insists."

"And they call him a financial officer? The only finance he knows is how to rip it from us. Repaying the loans will ruin us!" Prasutagus leaned on an elbow. He swept his other hand around the room. "This has cost me dearly."

He lay back again. He didn't need to explain to Boudicca, but some inner urge compelled him. "When I became king of the Iceni, Venta Icenorum was like any other king's settlement, a cluster of squalid huts. But to be a client king, the Romans told me, you must have a fine house. You must have luxuries so that all men know your importance. To be on equal terms with Romans you must be *as* Romans."

He coughed. "But to be a Roman costs money. I didn't want to borrow, but they forced their loans upon me. And I built this house in the Roman style and bought Roman furnishings and Roman luxuries. I lie on Roman cloth and drink from Roman goblets and walk on Roman mosaics. And as the king did, so did the nobles."

He fought for breath. "And this . . . this is how they repay one who has been their ally. Cartimandua, Cogidubnus, and I—we were the ones who made peace. While other tribes fought and lost, we have lived in prosperity. Why would the Romans strip it from us now?"

"It's their nature," Boudicca rasped. "They're a people without honor. I've never trusted them as you have."

Although the brazier gave a steady glow, Prasutagus shivered. "I can't fight now, Boudicca. Death calls, and I must answer him alone. Pay what we can. Tell Catus we will repay every sestercius, but we must have time."

"He won't accept that."

"What more can I do? Send him word. Perhaps he'll listen."

"If you believe that, you're a fool."

"Or the governor—"

"Catus doesn't answer to him. Suetonius lives for victories, not loans and taxes. You dream, Husband."

"Then let me dream. When I'm gone, the Iceni will belong to you and our daughters."

"I?" Boudicca blinked.

"Who better?" Prasutagus asserted. "The tribal assembly will elect my successor from among my kin. The assembly may be slow-witted at times, but not stupid. Our daughters are too young, and there isn't a man of the tribe who can match you. You will lead the Iceni, Boudicca."

Boudicca rose to her feet.

Prasutagus had to look up into her finely chiseled face. She stood tall and shapely as a goddess, clad in her multicolored léine and cloak secured by a gold brooch. *A goddess.* Prasutagus smiled. That was what he'd thought the first time he had laid eyes upon her. She sat astride a horse, sword slung from her criss, a lance in her hands, and he thought he saw the goddess Epona.

Tall, beautiful, and armed: the perfect woman.

And, an arrogant warrior who'd seen one wife die in childbirth, he'd chased and won the young goddess.

"You smile, Husband?"

"I remember." Prasutagus sighed. "You have the future to face, Boudicca, while I have only the past to console me."

He coughed again. This time, there was more blood.

Conversation among the delegation of nobles who waited in the courtyard outside the palace ceased abruptly as Boudicca came through the door. She halted and faced them.

"Well?" demanded a gray-haired man in the front row. "What did the king say?"

"We do as Seneca wills, Airell. We pay."

The man spread his hands. "How?"

"We sell what we have."

"I won't," a younger man declared. His hair strayed in waves to his shoulders, and his long mustache drooped. He touched the gold torque around his neck. "Are we to sell the very emblems of our rank in payment of these debts?"

"I agree!" a third man exclaimed.

A swell of acclamation rumbled through the crowd.

"And you?" Airell demanded of Boudicca. "What will you sell?"

Boudicca clenched her teeth. "As long as the king, my husband, lives, we will obey him."

"The debts were not entered into fairly!"

"I know, Airell. I loathe paying the Roman extortioners as much as you do. But I am loyal to the king, and I will pay." She touched the hilt of the longsword that dangled from the criss around her waist. "Any man who disobeys the king has my sword to face!"

Airell held up a hand. "Prasutagus has been a good king. He's just and fair. There's not a man here wouldn't give his life for him. But he's ill."

"His mind remains sharp."

The younger man put his hands on his hips. "Our quarrel is not with the king but with the Romans."

Boudicca said, "Listen, Weylyn. While the king lives, we follow his commands. But when he dies—"

"A new king may decide otherwise!" Weylyn burst.

Boudicca's sword whispered from its scabbard. The young man stepped back. Boudicca lowered the shining blade until the tip touched the dirt. "That may be."

Airell nodded slowly. He beckoned to the nobles. "We have heard sufficiently."

"But—," Weylyn began.

"Later," Airell silenced him.

Grumbling among themselves, the nobles filed away.

Boudicca watched them leave. Then she sheathed her sword and returned inside to where her husband tossed in uneasy sleep.

"Fools," she muttered under her breath. "Young fools and Roman fools."

She sat down and listened to Prasutagus's labored breathing.

Bright shafts of moonlight stabbed between the trees like sword thrusts through the night-black foliage. Lovernios bent low over his horse's neck, wincing as an overhanging branch plucked at his hair and scraped along his back.

The trackway was a dark thread running through the forest, visible only intermittently in the moonlight. Unable to discern the twists and turns, Lovernios trusted his horse to guide him. The whisper of leaves and muffled clop of hoofs on packed earth accompanied his progress.

The trackway meandered through Catuvellauni territory, north of the Roman road that cut like a scar across Albu. Lovernios gritted his teeth. He'd traveled like this—alone, on horseback, at night—since returning from Ériu. After a brief stay on Mona, the Druid island off Albu's west coast, he'd made his way cross-country, heading toward Iceni land.

To think that he should have to journey like a fugitive through the country of his ancestors, lands that he should have traversed with honor!

But a Druí was a marked man and would be killed on sight by the Romans. He dared not ride by day, risking detection by a Roman patrol. He avoided centers of population. He kept to the forests, to the tracks that only the Britons knew.

He endured the humiliation and the rage that smoldered within.

He longed to raise the sword as his father had done and ride screaming, down the throats of the invaders. Kirwin his father, prince of the Iceni, had joined with Caratacus and Togodumnus to oppose the Roman invaders. But Kirwin had perished alongside Togodumnus, taking Roman legionaries with him into death.

A true warrior's end!

Lovernios hadn't been there. But he'd heard tales and listened to the bards sing Kirwin's praises.

Lovernios grimaced at his enthusiasm. He'd been chosen from his youth for service as a Druí and had never borne arms. His weapons were his mind and his spirit.

He entered a clearing and halted, gazing at the steel-bright stars over-head. The gutuatri of Ériu had hinted of the evil the future held.

He shivered.

The immensity of his appointed task gave him pause. The Romans could not be allowed to win. They couldn't continue to oppress the people, to expand their empire at the expense of others. The Romans were ravening wolves, never satisfied, never content with what they possessed. Always they sought more.

But how could the might of Rome be opposed? How could he, one man, make a difference?

The gods alone knew.

But it lay to him, Kirwin's son, the recipient of a vision, to find a way.

He'd begin that task among his own people, the Iceni, and their allies, the Trinovantes.

Lovernios urged his horse on into the night.

TWO

The door to Sergius's small guest room thudded and rattled. "Wake up! Time to ride!"

Sergius jolted to awareness. Without the distraction of seasick troops, he'd slept well. Possibly too well. "Be right there," he called.

Rather than fumble for a lamp, he swung himself out of bed, crossed to the small window, and cracked open the shutters. A stream of pallid daylight filtered into his room. He threw on a clean tunic, belted it, then opened the door.

Julius Agricola stood outside, wearing full armor and carrying his helmet under one arm.

"It's too early," Sergius yawned as he ran a hand through his hair.

"There's a cavalry wing heading for Londinium," Agricola explained. "If we hurry, we can ride with them."

Sergius nodded, "All right." It seemed far better to ride with a cavalry detachment than to march with a cohort of heavily laden infantry at a twenty-mile-per-day slog. "Did you wake Veturius?"

"First. I figured he'd take longer to get going."

Sergius gave Agricola high marks for character assessment. He wrapped his scarf around his neck, then pulled on his breastplate. He turned to allow Agricola to fasten the lorica's hooks. "Are the roads dangerous?"

"Three of us could probably travel without harm, but there's no sense taking chances."

"Bandits?"

"The same as everywhere else—lower-class elements looking for an easy target."

Sergius's traveling cloak went over one shoulder, his greaves to guard his shins. He jammed his helmet on his head. "Ready."

Veturius put in a belated appearance, and fifteen minutes later, five hundred horses and riders trotted through Rutupiae's main gate. They clopped through the canabae—the civilian settlement of traders, entrepreneurs, and riffraff that clustered around every military post—and onto the broad causeway that threaded across a marsh and linked the semi-island to the mainland.

The weather, a conglomeration of cool temperatures, low skies, and threatened drizzle, should have been discouraging, but instead made for pleasant riding. Sergius's horse, a gift from his father, cantered at a steady pace along the highway, seemingly at peace with its task. Sergius leaned back in his saddle to enjoy the gently rising terrain. Streams and rivers, some bridged, bisected the undulating hills. Patches of forest contrasted with swaths of cleared ground and panoramas across open countryside.

After a brief rest stop at the crossroads village of Durovernum, the cavalry wing reached Durobrivae by dusk. The small town lacked a fort, and so the senior cavalry officers secured rooms in the posting station while the troopers bedded down in lofts and sheds and fields. The three tribunes found accommodation in a house owned by a businessman from Pompeii.

The second day was a virtual repeat of the first. The only incident occurred on their arrival at Londinium. They approached from the south and rode onto the long bridge that spanned the river Tamesis, connecting the sparse south bank outskirts with the town center and garrison on the north. Sergius's initial impression of Londinium was of a rickety, hastily built town. But ships dotted the river, and a forest of masts sprouting from the docks indicated active commerce.

"Make way!" somebody shouted.

Sergius started and jerked too hard on his reins. His horse staggered sideways and pinned his right leg against the bridge rail. Pain shot from his calf to his thigh. For a long moment, as his horse leaned over, he thought he was going to be pitched into the river. With the weight of his armor, he'd have sunk like a rock. But his horse regained its balance, the pressure on his leg relaxed, and he swayed back into an upright posture.

A mounted escort forced its way past the file of cavalrymen.

"Watch where you're going, idiots!" Agricola yelled, shaking a fist.

The leading escort officer saluted. "Apologies, Tribune."

Sergius held his horse still. One man—the escort's obvious charge—caught his attention. A gaudy cloak and white toga covered a corpulent, middle-aged figure. One heavily ringed hand held reins lightly, while the other pressed a small bouquet of flowers to a red, fleshy nose. He wore no weapon, and his sneering expression roused Sergius's immediate distaste. The man paid no attention to anyone around him.

Sergius twisted in his saddle to watch as the escort filed past.

"Who in Hades was that?" Veturius demanded.

"Decianus Catus," Agricola answered, urging his horse back into motion. "Procurator of this fair isle. The financial offices are here in Londinium."

Sergius rubbed the side of his leg. His greaves had prevented a hunk of flesh from being torn out. He'd only have a scratch and a bruise. Hardly the sort of wound to write home about.

He dismissed the procurator from his mind. Since the governor and chief financial officer functioned essentially independently, chances were he'd have no contact with Catus.

They spent the night at Agricola's house near the governmental headquarters. Agricola's taste ran to a plain, functional style. Sergius doubted the young man lacked money, but he saw little sign of affluence.

The following morning, with a smaller escort and rest breaks at Caesaromagus and Canonium, they covered the remaining forty-three miles to Camulodunum.

Agricola provided a running commentary.

"We're in Trinovantes land now," he said as Canonium fell behind. "There's a couple of dozen or more Briton tribes. They fought with each other all the time before we came, just like the Germans. Now, those in the province proper—like the Trinovantes, Atrebates, Dobunni, and Regni—are fairly tractable. The western ones are different. It's taken us two years to subdue the Silures and Deceangli."

Camulodunum, he explained, had been the Trinovantes capital until first the rival Catuvellauni and then the Romans annexed it. The name meant "the fortress of Camulos." Agricola laughed: "A Celtic war god who obviously didn't help his tribe."

Agricola swept the coastline with his right hand. "Farther ahead are the Iceni, a client kingdom of contentious nature. They're an isolated people, with a nose for spies, so it's not always easy to know what's happening. But word has it their king, Prasutagus, is ill, and his wife is ruling."

"A woman?" Veturius exclaimed.

Agricola shrugged.

Shortly before dusk, Camulodunum came into view. The setting sun glinted off buildings perched on a distant hill. Mellow stone shone yellow in the fading light.

"At last," Veturius moaned. "I swear this horse is made of iron."

Agricola glanced at Sergius. He jerked a thumb in the direction of Veturius. "Horseflesh doesn't sit well with him?"

Sergius grinned. "Nor he on it."

The road skirted a series of earthworks that extended out of sight but formed a roughly rectangular pattern. The grassy mounds enclosed acres of ground, fields, forest, and irregularly scattered clusters of huts.

"The Trinovantes tribal center," Agricola explained in response to a question from Sergius.

"What a dump," Veturius muttered.

Sergius guessed the rectangular collection of earthworks to be at least three miles per side. Perhaps they impressed the Briton mind, but they hadn't impressed Plautius's invasion army. Camulodunum had fallen easily to his troops, providing Claudius the pretext for his triumph. Not that the emperor had stayed to enjoy it—a mere sixteen days in Britannia had been ample for Claudius to decide he preferred the amenities of Rome to receiving the submission of conquered chieftains.

A score of conical huts—thatched roofs surmounting wattle and daub walls—huddled near the edge of the primitive defenses. Horses grazed both inside and outside the earthworks. Meat dried on racks. Dogs barked and chased after the travelers.

Sergius wrinkled his nose. The tribal center reeked of poverty and other, equally unpleasant odors. He saw several individuals engaged in menial tasks. Sergius realized they were the first true Britons he'd seen. Both sexes dressed alike, in brightly colored shirts and trousers, with cloaks to ward off the chill.

Men in trousers?

No wonder they needed civilizing.

The road bypassed the tribal center, ascended another low hill, and passed a cemetery. A stone-chiseled centurion stared coldly at Sergius from a rectangular tombstone protruding above uncut grass. He wore full armor and gripped his vitis. Sergius slowed his horse and leaned over to read the inscription.

Marcus Favonius Facilis,
son of Marcus of the Pollian tribe,

centurion of the Legio XX.

Erected by his freedmen Verecundus and Novicius.

Here he lies.

Sergius grimaced. *Marcus.* The first tombstone he saw, and the man bore the same name as himself.

On the next, a cavalry officer sat bolt upright on his horse, the animal's hooves trampling the prone figure of a Briton.

Longinus Sdapeze,

son of Matycus, duplicarius of Ala Prima Thracum,

from the territory of Sardica.

Aged forty in his fifteenth year of service.

Erected by his heirs in accordance with his will.

Here he lies.

Aged forty. Sergius wondered: Had he died naturally or fallen in battle?

On the fringes of Camulodunum the riders passed the neatly planned homes of the Colonia Claudia, a retirement community for veterans. Men who'd saved enough money during their years of service could afford homes like these—not fancy, but comfortable—on individual plots of land. Beyond Colonia Claudia, low, grass-covered mounds surrounded Camulodunum proper. Sergius pointed them out.

"What's left of the old legionary fortress," Agricola disclosed. "The Twentieth Legion, the *Valeria*, was quartered here right after the invasion. All that's left is a small garrison of two hundred men."

"No walls?" Sergius exclaimed.

Agricola gave him a look he couldn't interpret. "None."

Sergius waited for the senior tribune to explain, but Agricola made no further comment.

The road pierced the neglected rampart. Where the main gate ought to have been Sergius glanced around for sign of a sentry, but they entered Camulodunum unchallenged and unnoticed.

For all the lack of attention to security the inhabitants showed, Sergius thought, Camulodunum could have been located in central Italia rather than Britannia. Agricola didn't seem concerned, however. Sergius rubbed his chin. What had he expected to see—Briton war parties scouring the countryside in chariots? If all the Britons were the same as the pitiful folk in the Trinovantes village, he'd be more likely to die of boredom than enemy action.

The horses' hooves rang on cobblestone streets. Toga-clad citizens and commoners wearing ordinary tunics and cloaks moved through the shadows cast by timber and stone buildings. Few spared the three riders more than a cursory examination.

Well-built stone villas bordered the street. Most had their shutters closed for the evening, to barricade the interior life from the outside world. In contrast to the Briton settlement, Camulodunum exuded a contented affluence.

In the forum and the marketplace shutters banged and doors slammed as shopkeepers ceased business for the day. A giant bronze statue of Victory brooded over homebound shoppers and workers.

The trio rounded a corner. A three-foot-high wall enclosed a vast building that dwarfed Camulodunum's other structures. Columns ringed its walls, and a partially completed roof tapered to an elegant crest.

Sergius guided his horse into the precinct, halted beside the massive stone altar at the foot of the temple steps, and gazed at the stark inscription chiseled into the marble facade above the portico.

DIVO CLAVDIO PROVINCIA BRITANNIAE F

The Temple of the Divine Claudius, Sergius acknowledged the title. Lights winked into existence between the columns as a temple functionary worked his way from one stanchion to the next. In minutes, the temple glowed with the warmth of flickering torches reflecting off alabaster and marble. The heavy wooden doors stood open, revealing the statue of the emperor inside.

"Impressed?" Agricola asked.

Sergius wasn't sure whether he detected a hint of mockery in Agricola's voice or not. Despite his chatter, Agricola hadn't voiced either his political or religious convictions.

"Expensive," Sergius calculated.

"Very."

A knot of Britons emerged from the temple and trudged off.

"The devout," Veturius remarked.

"Construction workers," Agricola corrected in the same ambiguous tone of voice. "Cuts the cost if they're slaves."

A movement in the dusk caught Sergius's attention. A stocky figure strode along the outside of the precinct wall.

Dark shadows beneath the figure's eyes and nose resolved into a beard as the man passed beneath the torches at the precinct entrance. He wore a long white robe with a cowl thrown back onto his shoulders. It was draped differently from a toga, which only Roman citizens could legally wear.

As he passed, he stared directly at Sergius.

A shiver ran down Sergius's spine.

Despite the uncertain light, the man's eyes burned like twin coals. Perhaps it was only a trick of the temple torches, but Sergius felt suddenly uncomfortable, as if he confronted a malevolence he couldn't name.

But why? Why should this stranger give him a look of hatred? Or did he imagine?

The man hesitated but then hurried past, angling rapidly toward a side street, his steps pattering on the pavement.

Sergius interrupted another Agricolan monologue and pointed. "Where's he from?"

The senior tribune broke off in midsentence and followed Sergius's outstretched arm. "A Druid! What's he doing here? Come on, let's get him."

The Druid disappeared around the facade of the basilica.

"Who cares about an old Druid?" Veturius disregarded. "Let's find somewhere to stable the horses and bed ourselves."

Agricola looked disappointed. "I'll alert the urban cohort. They'll track down the devil."

They wheeled away from the temple and rode through the town center. Guards were posted outside the villas designated for the governor and procurator when they visited Camulodunum, but lights shone only at the procurator's. They passed the mansio and the town council chamber and reached the garrison. The duty guard saluted and waved them in.

At the stables, several attendants were busy brushing and grooming animals. Veturius abandoned his horse with alacrity.

Sergius dismounted slowly. He handed the reins to one of the attendants, along with a few coins. "She's a good horse. Take care of her."

The man ran an appraising eye over the horse, patted her neck and haunches. "That she is, sir. Fine stock. You're a man who knows his mount." He led the horse away.

Agricola slid to the ground. "I wonder what that Druid was doing in Camulodunum?"

"Looking for a human sacrifice, perhaps," Veturius laughed nervously. "Maybe you could help him out, Sergius."

"That's not funny," Sergius snapped.

"Sorry," Veturius mumbled. He exited the stable.

Agricola fell into step beside Sergius. "What's that about human sacrifice?"

Sergius pulled a face. "Sometimes Veturius's humor leaves a lot to be desired."

"You don't belong to some strange cult, do you?"

"I'm a follower of the Way." At Agricola's raised eyebrows, he continued, "We follow the teachings of Christus, the Son of God who came to show us the way to God."

"Son of God?" Agricola laughed. "The world is full of them. But I never heard of that particular one."

"He lived in Judea."

"Oh my shades and spirits," Agricola moaned, "that explains everything. But get to the part about sacrifice."

"Rumors say we practice human sacrifice."

"Do you?" Agricola's eyes narrowed.

"Of course not! It's a claim made by the ignorant and superstitious."

"Which includes most of the world's population. What do you do, then?"

Sergius spread his hands. "We have a simple ceremony of bread and wine and sing hymns."

"That doesn't sound so extreme."

"And we worship one God."

"Only one?" Agricola chuckled. "How do you know which one to choose? Aren't you afraid the others will be offended if you ignore them?"

"There is only one God," Sergius said. "The others are human fabrications."

"You're not serious!" Agricola seemed to digest Sergius's comment. "I'm not religious myself," he disclosed, "but I don't see how you can dismiss the entire gamut of gods offhandedly."

"You can if they're not real."

"I'm a student of philosophy," Agricola shared, "but I've not encountered this 'Way' of yours."

"Perhaps we can talk sometime."

"Perhaps."

They entered the officers' barracks.

"Vale," Agricola said, appropriating a room to himself.

Sergius undressed and prepared for sleep. But he lay awake long into the night, his thoughts centering on a man in a strange, white robe.

Why should he worry about a Briton Druid?

His father had told him tales of the dark Germanic forests, where savages nailed their enemies' severed heads to trees and committed unspeakable atrocities by smoky torchlight.

Appius had even brought home a Germanic god—a crude, carved wooden head with large ears and bulging eyes. It had given Sergius nightmares when he'd seen it as a child, and his mother had insisted that it be disposed of. Sergius hadn't laid eyes on the carving for years. It probably gathered dust in a storage shed on the estate.

Suddenly, Britannia seemed less of an adventure and more of a descent into the black depths of horrid superstition.

Stout walls protected him, and sentries patrolled outside. Sergius told himself not to be stupid.

After sighting the Roman officers, Lovernios blended into the shadows that descended on Camulodunum. He listened for the clatter of pursuing horses but didn't hear any.

He moved from doorway to doorway, cautious this time to avoid patches of torchlight.

He'd been careless. Lost in thought, he hadn't realized that he'd arrived at the temple until it was right in front of him. And to have three Roman officers stare at him . . .

He clenched his hands into fists. They'd alert the city police, certainly, which meant he'd have to be even more circumspect in his movements.

He'd come to talk to men of the Trinovantes, warriors who now slaved in the quarries for the Romans. The Trinovantes weren't a force any longer, not since they'd submitted to the Romans. But he needed to know the temper of Camulodunum, and these slaves were his eyes and ears.

This monstrosity of a town sickened him—this town built on Briton land of Briton blood. The white marble disfigured the hills like a sore.

Lovernios slipped past the abandoned ramparts and into the countryside.

Let the Romans search for him. They wouldn't find him.

THREE

I n the morning, Sergius checked with the garrison commander only to learn that Suetonius Paulinus and his staff hadn't yet arrived. "They'll be here any day. I'll let you know," the commander said. Without duties to occupy his time, he decided to explore Camulodunum.

"Take a look around," Agricola urged. "I've work to do, but you're free until the governor arrives. Have some fun—it might be your last chance for a while."

In contrast to the previous evening, the forum and the marketplace thronged with activity. Retired Roman soldiers, with their wives and children, dominated the crowds, but Britons comprised a sizable minority. Some affected Roman fashion, with short hair and tunics. Others retained native fashion and dress, wearing brightly colored shirts and trousers, their hair straying in savage shoulder-length curls. Here and there, Sergius spotted foreigners: conservatively attired Greeks and Jews, a pair of dark-skinned Africans wearing eye-searing, flowing cotton robes, and a blonde giant almost certainly a Germanic tribesman attached to an auxiliary cohort.

The scents of oils and perfumes mingled with the homelier smells of freshly baked bread, meat, and fish. An appetizing aroma came from smoke shops selling cooked food ready to take out. Add a haze of wood-smoke, and the result was a brew almost as heady as that of any great city of the Empire.

Languages, too, fought for dominance. The cadences of educated Latin and the rhythms of Aramaic and Greek contested with the guttural growls of Gauls and the unfamiliar syllables of the native Britons.

Sergius drank it all in.

He even passed a trio of street musicians playing cymbals, pipes, and lyre, soliciting for their efforts. He dropped a handful of sestercii into the wicker basket provided and received a thank-you from the lyre player.

Camulodunum was no Rome, not even close. Its population of fifteen thousand ranked it smaller than Aquileia, too. But it attempted a cosmopolitan life, as the capital of a province should.

Sergius wandered idly, waving off the attentions of a made-up young woman searching for business even in the morning, the gabbled sales pitch of a goldsmith hawking "the best jewelry north of the Alps," the cries of a perfume dealer selling irresistible aphrodisiacs, and the pleadings of a potter extolling locally made items as if they were the finest Arretian or Samian ware.

The crowds fascinated Sergius, and he studied the faces and dress of all he passed. Nowhere, however, did he catch a glimpse of a Druid. He wasn't sure whether to be pleased or disappointed.

He passed through the forum into the temple district. The spirit of Claudius wasn't the only claimant for the reverence of the provincials. Temples to Mars and Jupiter and Apollo of the Romans, Mithrates of the Persians, and Minerva and Athena of the Greeks rubbed shoulders. Small doorways led into lesser buildings dedicated to Cybele or Isis or any of a hundred other deities.

Sergius wondered if the Way had reached Britannia. If so, when believers met in homes and not prominent temples, how did one locate them? He could ask, but . . . . Even Aquileia boasted only a handful of believers.

That morning, Veturius had stated his intention of making offerings to as many gods as possible, starting with Silvanus, the god of the woods, and finishing with an encompassing plea to all genii loci, the unknown and unnamed spirits that dwelt in hills, rivers, or swamps.

"I have every intention of surviving this miserable island," he elucidated.

"Do you really expect these offerings to help?" Sergius challenged.

"I don't care if I have to build a hundred altars in fulfillment of vows. I want to return home unscathed."

"I've told you there's a better way."

Veturius glanced around, as if expecting to find a deity eavesdropping over his shoulder. "I'm not relying on one god. Not a chance. You can, if you want to."

Sergius sighed, then remembered that he'd once felt the same. As recently as two years ago, he'd been ridden by superstition, half-afraid to pass a temple without making an offering. As bad as the most fearful legionary, scared to venture from camp without a favorable augury.

He turned away from the temples, returned to the forum, and meandered along a row of booths. He passed a pottery shop boasting cooking ware from the factories of Felix, Aquitanius, Licinus, and Momino. Another sold Samian ware from Primus. Next door, a wine shop carried amphorae of Falernian, Aminean, and other vintages from Italia and Gaul. An importer displayed amphorae of dates, figs, plums, and olives.

Sergius was studying drinking ware at a booth—in particular a hideous rhyton with a grotesque head and large mouth that might appeal to his father's tastes—when a commotion erupted outside a booth across the street. Men shouted; dogs barked; a woman screamed.

Sergius hurried over and elbowed his way through the throng of bystanders, pushing aside those who blocked his view.

A middle-aged, paunchy Briton, wide nosed and heavy jowled, had both hands wrapped in the tunic of a slightly built, though taller, younger man. He shook him as a cat shakes a mouse; or a dog, a rat. Sergius couldn't place the second man's country of origin.

In the partial shadow of the stall, six or seven chained dogs barked and howled and strained to join the action. Behind the Briton, a young woman of about nineteen held a hand to her cheek.

Sergius opened his mouth, but a male voice cut across the commotion.

"What's going on here?" a short, portly man, toga clad and balding, fronted the Briton.

The Briton didn't loose his grip. "Who wants to know?" he demanded in passable Latin.

"Speak civilly, slave!" The balding man spoke in a precise, fussy manner. "I am Balbus Celsus, decurio of this town."

The crowd quieted to hear the town councillor. The woman bent to hush the dogs. The yapping subsided.

The Briton's pockmarked face was purple. "My name is Egomas, seller of trained hunting dogs. This thief tried to steal one of my animals."

Sergius pronounced the Briton's name—Eck-o-ma—silently to himself.

Balbus spoke to the other participant in the argument. "Is this true?"

The tall young man spoke quietly, his calm in stark contrast to Egomas's anger. "No. I was merely passing by and inadvertently trod on the dog's tail. It snapped at me." His accent sounded eastern—Greek probably.

"Liar!" the dog-seller shouted.

Sergius studied the offending animal, a big wolfhound whose weight probably matched that of the slender Greek. The dog's ears pressed back against a thick coat of rich brown. Its tail drooped. It gazed with large, pleading eyes at the young woman, as if conscious of having committed a wrong.

Egomas shook the Greek harder. "You owe me the cost of a dog for the trouble you've caused!"

Balbus hesitated, his perplexity palpable. Sergius sympathized with the councillor's puzzlement over the preeminence of a Greek stranger's story on the one hand and a Briton's claim on the other. Whom to believe?

Balbus licked his lips. "I think—"

The young woman interrupted him. "The Greek speaks the truth. He walked too close to the dogs. I shouted 'cave canem'—beware of the dogs!—but too late."

"I heard her," one of the bystanders interjected.

Egomas whirled. "Shut your mouth, insolent daughter of a fox!"

He removed one hand from the Greek's tunic and aimed a back-hand swipe at the young woman. The wolfhound stiffened and snarled.

In one swift movement, Sergius lunged and gripped the dog-seller's fleshy wrist.

Egomas's eyes widened. "Let go of me!"

"Don't hit her," Sergius warned.

"I will discipline my daughter as I see fit!"

Daughter? Sergius hesitated. What right had he to interfere in a family matter? He was new to town; he knew nothing of Briton customs. . . .

Egomas tried to wrench free.

Two pairs of eyes—the young woman's and dog's—decided Sergius's mind for him. He shifted his grip and twisted.

Egomas howled. "You're breaking my arm!" He let go of the Greek and beat his other hand on Sergius's shoulder.

"Your word that you won't hit her."

"This is intolerable! I—"

"Your word."

Egomas's knees sagged. "I promise," he snarled through clenched teeth.

Sergius released his grip.

Egomas scrambled to his feet and rubbed his arm. "You see how I'm treated!" he screamed to Balbus. "I'm a free man!"

Sergius ignored him. He turned to the young woman. "Are you all right?"

She nodded.

"I demand my rights!" Egomas fumed. "I demand this dog snatcher be arrested and appear before the praetor!" He glared at Sergius: "This ruffian too!"

"A charge of theft is serious," Balbus said, scrutinizing the crowd, as if to judge where the onlookers' sympathies lay, "but nothing was actually taken—"

"Not for lack of trying!" Egomas yelled. "By the gods, he tried!"

Sergius defended, "The young woman—," he glanced at her.

"Ailidh," she supplied.

Sergius tried to copy her pronunciation: "'Ay-lee' says the Greek was not at fault."

"Then she lies too!" Egomas raged. "She's in league with this thief!"

The Greek raised a corner of his robe to reveal a jagged rent in the fabric. "The animal attacked me."

As the man held up his robe, Sergius noted that the clasp was made in the shape of a small fish.

"My animals are trained!" Egomas stated. "That tear could have happened any time."

Balbus cleared his throat, "The praetor will decide."

"I don't think that's necessary," Sergius said. "It sounds to me like an accident and a misunderstanding."

"Who are you?" Egomas demanded.

"He asks rightly," Balbus reluctantly supported. "Who are you to interfere?"

Sergius addressed himself to Balbus. "I am Sergius Lysias, a senior tribune assigned to the governor." He thought it best not to mention that he hadn't even laid eyes on Suetonius Paulinus and as of yet had no official status.

"This is a civil matter, Tribune," Balbus said respectfully. "No concern of the army."

"Exactly!" Egomas punctuated.

Sergius turned to the Briton. "You say you want the price of the dog?"

"I want this thief punished."

"But your stories conflict. What if the praetor believes his? Neither of you are citizens."

Egomas glowered.

"How much for the dog?"

Egomas pursed his lips. He looked to the wolfhound—now lying quietly on its belly, licking its paws—and back to Sergius.

"I'll give you the price of the dog," Sergius offered, "and let that be the end to the matter."

"That is very generous, Tribune," Balbus commended.

"For the army, two thousand sestercii," Egomas simpered. He smiled, an insincere, merchant's smile. "Worth every one of them."

Sergius tried to contain his surprise. Two thousand sestercii equalled five hundred denarii, more than double a year's pay for a legionary. Granted, officers were often independently wealthy, but . . .

What was a hunting dog worth, anyway? At home, he'd never priced them. But he could be sure that by the time an animal made it to Italia, middlemen would have raised the price considerably. So perhaps Egomas's demand wasn't exorbitant.

Egomas leaned forward, as if sensing a sale.

"She's worth half that," a soft voice said.

Sergius glanced toward its source. The girl knelt beside the dogs, scratching silky heads. A soft smile played on her lips. A scarlet welt splayed across her cheek, but alluring green eyes sparkled beneath a shoulder-length mane of reddish auburn hair. Fine cheekbones framed a turned-up nose neither too large nor too small.

"Quiet, girl!" Egomas surged toward her.

Sergius's upraised hand restrained him. "Are you a cheat, dog-seller? I'll give you two hundred fifty denarii."

Egomas spluttered, "You're mad! The finest blood lines. The months of training. You won't find a better animal anywhere."

"Two hundred fifty denarii," Sergius repeated. "Is that fair, councillor?" he asked Balbus.

The decurio licked his lips again, then nodded. "It is."

Sergius reached into his purse and found a gold aureus. He pulled out four more and jingled them in his palm. "I have half here and will send the remainder. Well, Egomas, what's it to be? Payment now, or the uncertainty of a hearing before the praetor?"

The dog-seller's eyes glittered with mixed greed and suspicion as they fastened on the sparkling coins. "What if you don't pay? If I never hear from you—"

Sergius balled his free hand: What gall for a provincial to doubt the word of a future senator! "My word is good. Councillor Balbus is witness to the transaction."

"Very well." Egomas held out a hand. "The dog is yours."

Sergius dropped the coins into the fat, sweaty palm, which closed like a trap.

"Give him his dog, girl!" Egomas snapped.

Ailidh untangled the chain and held it out for Sergius. As he took it, their fingers touched. Again, he noticed the flash in her eyes. "Thank you," she mouthed. Out loud she said, "The dog's name is Cara. It means 'friend.'"

Sergius looped the chain about his wrist and returned her smile. "I hope I have more than one cara in Camulodunum."

Color rose into the curves of her cheeks.

"Let's be about our business, then," Balbus dismissed. He waved his arms at the bystanders. "The show is over."

The crowd began to disperse. Egomas turned aside to secrete his money. Ailidh returned to the dogs.

"Come, Cara," Sergius directed the wolfhound. "Let's go to the barracks."

"I must thank you, Tribune."

Sergius had almost forgotten the man who had unintentionally caused the fracas. The Greek stood next to him. Sergius beckoned him away from the dog-seller's stall. As he walked away, Cara trotting obediently at his side, he caught Ailidh following his progress, but she glanced away quickly.

"That man is an animal himself," Sergius expressed.

"He's a creation of God, as are we all. A poor creation, perhaps."

Sergius concealed a smile.

The Greek held a hand, back first, toward Cara. The wolfhound sniffed it, then gave it a quick lick. "She seems to bear me no ill will," he said.

"I didn't catch your name."

"Aristarchus of Philippi."

"Aristarchus?" Sergius mused. "I've heard of an Aristarchus. He travels with companions named Lucanus and Paullus."

"I am he."

Sergius stopped and gripped his arm. "Then we're brothers! I saw your ichthus."

"Praise be to God." Aristarchus touched his fish clasp. "Truly the Lord's ways are past understanding. Normally, I wouldn't wear adornment, but a local silversmith made this as a gift. I couldn't refuse."

Sergius inquired enthusiastically, "Is Paullus here, in Britannia?"

Aristarchus nodded. "Indeed. And Lucanus."

"Then you're meeting. Where?"

"In the house of Genialis the silversmith."

"Tonight?"

"Yes. After the evening meal."

"Then I'll be there. Good day, Brother."

"The Lord be with you," Aristarchus said, "and your dog." He gave a bright, disarming smile. "I'd willingly buy her myself, but she's too expensive for me."

Cara tugged her chain.

"Besides," Aristarchus continued, "Paullus isn't fond of animals. They make him sneeze."

When Sergius arrived back at the barracks, he contemplated contriving a story, realized he could never keep a straight enough face to deceive Veturius, and told his friend the truth.

Veturius laughed until his eyes watered. He clutched his sides. "A dog? You're here one day, and you buy a dog?"

"I didn't intend to," Sergius protested. "It's not as if I went looking for one."

"You didn't intend to," Veturius mocked. "Tell that to Suetonius: 'Have dog, will serve.'"

"She seems to be a very good dog." Sergius ruffled Cara's ears and ran his hand along her square muzzle. The big wolfhound stretched her neck and rumbled contentedly.

"She's probably half wolf. And she takes up half the floor, by Mars! What are you going to do with a hunting dog?"

"Hunt, I suppose."

Veturius laughed harder.

To turn the conversation, Sergius reported, "I saw a girl, Gaius."

"As well as the dog? You had your eyes open today, my friend."

"Gaius, you should have been there. Even your jaded senses would have been impressed."

Veturius feigned a scared expression. "Don't tell me Claudia followed you to Britannia?"

"Not the abominable Claudia, idiot! Ailidh."

"A Briton?" Veturius frowned.

"A beautiful Briton."

"He buys a dog and falls in love on the same day."

Sergius flushed. "She was the dog-seller's daughter," he explained stiffly.

Veturius swallowed the wrong way and coughed. "Dog-seller's daughter? Your mother would have a fit. I can see her face now. 'Marcus, my boy,'" he warbled, "'is it wise for a boy of your station—'"

"Enough, Gaius!"

Veturius abandoned his falsetto, "Tell you what—you watch the dog, and I'll pay attention to the girl."

"I know what you're like." Sergius refused, "No thanks."

"If you need help, call on your best friend."

"Why are you so eager for the dog-seller's daughter? You've not even met her."

"Because if she caught *your* attention, she must be something."

In early evening the forum gradually emptied. The last weary shoppers concluded their purchases, and the fatigued sellers closed up shop.

Ailidh watered the unsold dogs, scraped up their piles, and prepared to return the animals to the kennels.

A Roman retiree shoved his hands in his toga and departed, unswayed by Egomas's offer of a reduced price for immediate sale but promising to return after consulting his wife.

"We'll never see that one again," Egomas grumbled. "His wife will convince him to buy some useless luxury—a new necklace or earrings." He hefted his coin purse. "And as for you—costing me a thousand sestercii!"

Ailidh loosened an overtight collar. "You were trying to cheat."

"I was trying to make a decent profit! In case you hadn't noticed," Egomas sneered, "the young fool was senatorial rank, probably dripping with more money than you or I will ever see." He scowled, "fresh off the boat, too, I don't doubt." He shoved his purse into a pocket. "But of course you noticed. Don't think I didn't see those doe eyes you were making. Bah!" Egomas spat on the ground. "If he knew more about you, he wouldn't give you a second look."

Ailidh froze. "That was unkind."

"But true. Don't cross me again, girl, or I'll give you the beating you deserve."

Ailidh straightened. "If you lay a hand on me one more time, you'll regret it. I'll leave."

The color rose into Egomas's face. His hands clenched. "You wouldn't dare, Daughter!"

"I'm not your daughter. If I left, where would Egomas's reputation be?"

"I could manage," Egomas faltered.

"Hah!"

"Where would you go? One word from me, and you'd find yourself without a friend in the world. You owe me, girl."

When Ailidh didn't answer, Egomas said, "I suppose you're going off again tonight."

Ailidh nodded, "I won't be late." She paused. "Come with me."

Egomas guffawed. "Not a chance! I wouldn't be caught dead with that group." He pointed a finger at her. "Alien cults like that have caused all our problems. Return to the old gods, that's what I say."

"Old and worn out."

"Don't mock, girl. Tell me one thing this new religion has done for you."

Ailidh collected the dogs' chains. When she looked up, her eyes flashed. "It's prevented me from slipping a knife between your ribs."

Egomas's jaw sagged.

Sergius declined an offer to go drinking with Agricola and Veturius. Instead, when nightfall had called a finish to the day, he knocked on the door of a silversmith's shop in the northern quarter of the city. After the second knock, the door creaked open, and a middle-aged matron filled the gap. She wiped her hands on an apron. "We're closed. Come back tomorrow."

"I'm here for the meeting," Sergius explained before she could shut the door.

Her eyes jumped to the sword slung by its baldric over his left hip, visible beneath the folds of his cloak. Sergius had abandoned his armor, but he never went unarmed at night in a Roman city, and he certainly wasn't going to abandon the practice in Britannia.

The woman stood still.

Sergius turned the collar of his cloak to reveal a small fish brooch. "Please."

She edged aside, and Sergius eased past her into the dim interior. He adjusted his cloak, clasped over his left shoulder, to conceal the sword.

"In the back room." The woman pointed to the rear of the shop. She called, "Genialis! The army's here!"

Sergius made his way through the clutter of Genialis's establishment. The back room, to judge from stains on the walls and metal shavings underfoot, served as a workshop in the daytime, but now it had been cleared, the silversmith's tools consigned to a corner, and low wooden benches brought in. Lampstands set at strategic places glowed with warmth, and beeswax candles flickered in a pair of candelabra. The low hum of conversation emanated through the open door.

A dark opening led to a set of stairs to the building's upper floor.

An elderly man with a fringe of white hair met him at the entrance. His face wore a wary expression. "Tribune, why does the army interest itself in my poor shop? I pay my taxes. If there's jewelry you wish to see, or a special commission—"

"I'm a follower," Sergius replied. He displayed his ichthus again.

The man's eyebrows twitched together. His posture radiated suspicion.

"Baptized by Apollos," Sergius said.

"Well, then . . . ," the frown changed to a smile, "then you're welcome, Brother. I'm Genialis."

Sergius gripped Genialis's bony arm. "Thank you."

"Please, be seated. We're full tonight, but there are a few spaces left."

As his eyes adjusted to the uneven light, Sergius spotted Aristarchus half-turned, talking to a woman whose back was toward him. Sergius crossed over. "Good evening, Brother; Sister."

Aristarchus sprang to his feet. "It's good you've come." He indicated the woman. "We have a mutual acquaintance."

The woman turned.

Sergius gasped. "I . . . I had no idea. . . ."

The candlelight accented amber flecks in Ailidh's green eyes. "Did you think only Romans worshiped?"

"I . . . Of course not! But . . ."

Aristarchus indicated the bench, "Join us."

Ailidh scooted over to make room for him, "Please."

Sergius hesitated. Sit in mixed company? Society must be different in Britannia. He swallowed his uncertainty.

Shifting his sword to an unobtrusive position, Sergius settled into place between Ailidh and Aristarchus, who resumed his seat.

"How's your new friend?" Ailidh asked.

"She's fine," Sergius answered. "And you?"

Her face darkened for a moment. Her hand crept to her bruised cheek. "All right. Thanks to you."

"I was glad to help."

The stairs that led to the upper level creaked, and two men descended. Both wore tunics of Roman cut, plain and unadorned. One was of medium height, full without being fat. His cheerful face bore the creases of an outdoor existence.

"That's Lucanus," Aristarchus whispered.

Sergius scanned the eager faces in the room. "Where's Paullus?"

"Next to him."

Sergius blinked. Beside Lucanus stood a stooped, frail figure, whose head perched forward. He peered around in a near-sighted manner, as one who'd read too many books. That couldn't be Paullus! Paullus had stood before procurators, King Agrippa of Judea, and the emperor Nero himself. Paullus was a giant, a man of intellect, a fire-breathing preacher who carried the gospel around the Empire. Paullus couldn't be this shriveled, near-sighted husk, a skinny old man that a breath of wind would blow over.

"Him?" Sergius croaked.

Aristarchus shrugged as if he'd encountered similar reactions before. "You were expecting a laurel-crowned athlete?"

"No, but—"

"Man looks on the outside," Aristarchus said, "but God looks on the inside."

"Grace to you, and peace." Paullus shuffled forward to stand between the candelabra. "Welcome to any newcomers." He cleared his throat. "As I walked through Camulodunum, I saw many temples dedicated to the gods of Rome, of Greece, and of distant lands. Long ago Jeremiah said, 'The people of Israel feel ashamed—they, their kings, their princes, their priests, and their prophets, who say to a block of wood, "You are our father," and cry "Mother" to a stone.'"

A sweep of Paullus's arm took in Lucanus and Aristarchus. "We don't bear witness to idols of wood or stone but to the God who created the world and everything in it. He is Lord of heaven and earth. He doesn't live in tabernacles made by human hands. . . ."

As the apostle spoke, Sergius leaned forward. Paullus's voice resonated with power. It was as if, indeed, the voice of God emanated from this infirm body. If Sergius closed his eyes, he could imagine himself in the presence of a giant.

Aristarchus's company on his left, and even the warmth of Ailidh close on his right seemed to fade away. He had senses only for Paullus. The apostle spoke until the candles guttered low and Genialis's wife replaced them. The people sitting across from Sergius yawned, but he had never felt so awake.

"God has overlooked the age of ignorance, but now he commands men and women everywhere to repent. He has fixed the day on which he will have the world judged in righteousness by a man whom he has designated. He has given assurance to all by raising Jesus Christ from the dead."

The apostle paused. He scanned the room. "Many still living saw him and can testify to the truth of what I speak." He raised a hand to touch the dull orbs of his eyes. "I saw with the Spirit, in a vision granted me from heaven. But others saw with their own eyes. . . ."

When the aged apostle had finished speaking and the crowd dispersed, Aristarchus drew Sergius across the room.

"Paullus, may I introduce a friend of mine, Sergius Lysias? Sergius is a military tribune."

"I'm honored," Sergius mumbled. "I've long wanted to meet you."

The stooped figure pushed close to him, head tilted back, the faded eyes seeking Sergius's. "A soldier, eh?"

"Yes, sir."

Paullus's nose nearly touched his. The old eyes continued their scrutiny. Sergius felt as if the aged apostle's vision penetrated right through him.

Paullus's leathery lips twitched. "I think not."

Sergius stiffened.

"You wear a sword," Paullus continued, "but are you truly a soldier?"

Sergius bit back a short remark. What was the old man talking about?

"What do you hope to gain by force of arms, young man?" Paullus spoke in a low voice as if speaking to himself.

"Military service is required. There are certain duties I have to fulfill in order to achieve a higher station," Sergius said patiently.

"Yes." Paullus reached out a calloused finger to touch the ivory hilt of Sergius's sword. "But what have you given up? What have you sacrificed?"

"Sacrificed?"

"Think and pray, young man." The apostle turned aside. "Aristarchus, I must rest. Grace, Tribune Lysias." His eyes met those of Ailidh, who had come to stand beside him.

Aristarchus nodded a good-bye to Sergius and Ailidh and led Paullus from the room.

"What did he mean by all that?" Sergius wondered.

"I have no idea," Ailidh replied.

Sergius shook his head. "May I escort you home?"

Ailidh pursed her lips, then nodded. She shrugged into a goat's hair birrus and arranged the hood to cover the back of her neck. "I'm honored."

She slid her hands into her sleeves as they entered the darkened streets. Sergius picked up a torch from beside the door.

"Do you always carry a sword?" she asked.

"I didn't know how safe Camulodunum would be at night," he conveyed.

"Safe enough." She extracted a hand and parted the birrus enough to indicate her belt. "A dagger's sufficient."

Sergius chuckled. "Where do you live?"

"We travel frequently. Home is actually about five miles away. But I'll show you the quarters we rent."

"We? You and your father?"

"Egomas and I—but he isn't my father."

"No?"

"My mother was a woman of the Trinovantes. She died giving me birth. My father belonged to the Iceni. He was killed by the Catuvellauni in a raid. I was the only child of my parents. Egomas is my mother's brother. He took me . . . several years ago. So he's been almost a father to me."

"Not a good one, I gather," Sergius said.

"He's not so bad, except when his temper gets the best of him." She sighed. "Some days, if it weren't for the dogs . . . . Do you realize that Egomas's dogs are known across Britannia? You bought a fine animal today. Cara was one of my favorites."

Sergius grinned. "Egomas may have the fame, but I'm sure you do an excellent job of training the dogs."

"Me? What makes you say that?"

"Egomas hardly seems to have the patience necessary to train dogs. Whereas you—I saw how you handled them. They responded to you."

"Dogs are often more human than people," Ailidh said. "You're correct. I do the training. In general, Egomas is good to me. He knows that without me his business would die." The torchlight illuminated her smile. "He'd be most upset if he knew you were escorting me home."

"Why? Because I bought a dog at the proper price?"

"Because you're Roman. I should hate you."

"What for?"

Her smile faded. "You need to ask? Because you came to our country uninvited. Because you take our lands, tax our people, treat us as children."

Sergius swallowed, wishing for a way to change the subject.

"We're barbarians," Ailidh continued. "Aren't we?"

"In Rome's eyes, yes."

"The tribes you call the Celtae once ruled from Ériu—what you call Hibernia—to Galatia. Did you know that?"

"I—"

"But now Rome's way is the only way."

"Rome doesn't oppress people—"

Her voice dripped scorn, "Rome desires to make all peoples into Romans."

"True. In a sense."

"You're honest, at any rate."

Sergius frowned. "To civilize the world is Rome's destiny."

Ailidh snorted, then changed it to a laugh.

Sergius bristled. "What are you laughing at?"

"I intend no offense. But you should hear yourself, Sergius Lysias."

"Why?"

Ailidh responded with a moment of silence, then, "I've said enough."

"No. I want to hear what you have to say. Don't be afraid to speak your mind."

Her eyes bored into him with the same intensity Paullus had shown. "Who wrote, 'Forget not, Roman, that it is your special genius to rule the peoples; to impose the ways of peace, to spare the defeated, and to crush those proud men who will not submit'?"

"Vergilius," he replied without thought. Every Roman boy learned those lines in school. But to hear a Briton recite them . . . .

They reached the southeastern outskirts of the city. A district of wood-framed buildings pressed close together with barely inches between them.

Ailidh paused outside of one, no different from the rest, and laid her hand against the door. "Did you hear Paullus say 'There is no such thing as Jew and Greek, slave and freeman, male and female; for you are all one person in Christ Jesus'?"

"I did."

She leaned close to him. "Think about that, Roman."

The wind blew strands of her hair onto his neck.

She opened the door and as quickly shut it behind her.

FOUR

A wet rasp across his face started Sergius from sleep. He wiped his lips with the back of his left hand. He tried to fend off Cara with his right, but her large, shaggy body refused to budge. Sergius groaned, rolled over, and received a second wet tongue across his face.

"All right. All right! I'm coming."

He wiped sleep and dog slobber from his eyes. Cara stood beside him, her chain dangling from her mouth, her tail lashing back and forth.

Sergius dressed quickly, laced on his second-best pair of caligae, and opened the door. Cara bounded out—by heaven, she was strong—and forced Sergius into a jog to keep up. The activity and the crisp morning air rapidly brought him to full wakefulness.

Should he attempt to see Ailidh again? He'd turned the question over in his mind all night long. They'd parted on strained terms, but she hadn't actually rebuffed him.

He wished he knew more about Briton attitudes toward Romans. As a member of a defeated people, would Ailidh refuse to associate with one of the conquerors? Or, on the other hand, would she feel unable to refuse for fear of repercussions? If he gauged her age accurately, she'd grown up under Roman occupation, which ought to make a difference.

A brisk walk through the headquarters neighborhood decided him. He was ignorant of dog care. What harm could there be in asking for advice? He could assess Ailidh's attitude. If she wanted nothing to do with him, that ought to be obvious.

He angled his steps toward the marketplace. Despite the early hour, the shutters of the dog-seller's stall stood open, framing Egomas's flabby figure. When the dog-seller spotted Sergius, he gripped the wooden slats as if he'd like to slam them shut. Ailidh crouched inside the stall, brushing out the tangles from a dog's ruff with a wide-tined bone comb. She laid down the comb and stood up as he approached. Cara whined and pulled to reach her.

"What do you want?" Egomas snarled. "I don't give refunds."

Sergius shook his head. "Simply a question. What do I feed Cara?"

"Meat, of course," the dog-seller growled. "What did you think? Fricassee of roses?"

Sergius didn't answer, more interested in the welcoming gleam he thought he detected in Ailidh's demurely downcast eyes. Her bruise had lost its red and now glowered a dull purple on her cheek. When she stood, he noticed details that had escaped him the previous day—how she matched him for height, the way the healthy skin of her arms glowed over firm muscles, and how her tunic and trousers, though loose and coarsely woven, enhanced her figure.

"Be off with you!" Egomas barked.

"Uncle," Ailidh rebuked, "be polite to the customers." She turned to Sergius. "Let me explain. A good dog demands the proper care." She beckoned to him. "Come inside."

Sergius edged past the scowling Egomas into the stall.

"First," Ailidh instructed, "feed her just once a day. And don't let her be greedy and eat too much, or she'll become fat and lazy."

Like Egomas, Sergius thought.

"Next, she needs plenty of exercise. . . ." Ailidh fondled Cara's ears while she continued with more basics of dog care. Sergius listened intently.

"Do you have all that?" Ailidh checked when she'd finished.

"I think so. For the moment." Cara seemed to be laughing at him with her mouth open and tongue lolling. "Will you be at Paullus's meeting tonight?"

Ailidh paused, then answered. "I expect so."

He couldn't read anything in Ailidh's green eyes. "Perhaps I'll see you there."

Egomas ignored Sergius's good-bye.

Sergius spent the day loafing, talking with Veturius and Agricola, and lingering in the bathhouse to chat with officers of the local garrison.

Veturius ribbed him when he departed that evening. "To listen to your apostle or to see the girl?"

Sergius smiled, "Wouldn't you like to know?"

"By Cupid," Veturius chortled, "the man's besotted!"

"I hardly know her."

"A dolt could read the signs—the bright eyes, the nervous movements, the bead of sweat on your upper lip—"

Sergius let the door bang shut on Veturius's laughter.

Ailidh arrived late at Genialis the silversmith's and sat across the room from Sergius. Paullus spoke at length before Aristarchus led the gathering in a closing hymn.

Ailidh didn't refuse, however, when Sergius asked to walk her home. Neither brought up the subject of Roman-Briton relationships.

As the door to her house shut and he turned to make his way home, Sergius reflected that, had this been Rome and Ailidh a Roman, he'd have been invited inside. Most young Roman women considered that the way to a man's heart was through his bed. Sergius took Paullus's teaching seriously. Perhaps Ailidh did too.

Or maybe Briton women were like the Germanic tribes who had a reputation for chaste behavior—warranted or not, Sergius didn't know. He'd never thought to ask his father's opinion.

The next day, he returned to Egomas's stall to inquire about grooming. He silenced Egomas with a loudly made comment in the presence of several interested shoppers concerning Cara's worth.

"Had I the means," Sergius stated, "I would buy six more like her. I've never had a better dog."

Egomas glowed and turned his effusive attention to the shoppers.

Sergius winked at Ailidh.

"Have you ever owned a dog before?" she whispered.

"No."

She stifled a laugh.

Sergius feigned an innocent expression.

The next day he had questions about training, and Egomas, while surly, at least grunted a hello.

After the evening meeting, Sergius and Ailidh ambled through Camulodunum's deserted streets.

"How did you learn about the Way?" Sergius asked, voicing a question that had occurred to him during Paullus's talk. "I wasn't aware of any churches in Britannia."

Ailidh's answer, after a long pause, came in a hesitant, jerky manner. "It was before Egomas took me in permanently. His wife was still living. She became ill. . . . I had certain skills and came to nurse her. I also helped Egomas with the dogs. I heard about the Way from a girl of my people named Jana. She was the slave of a praetor's wife and had converted to the Way in Rome. Her mistress loved dogs, and so I met Jana frequently. She had almost as many questions as you do."

Her tone was bantering; Sergius relaxed.

"And you?" Ailidh returned.

"My father sent me to Corinth to learn Greek," Sergius said. "One day, I heard a man named Apollos preaching on the steps of a temple. The crowd jeered him unmercifully, but what he said was different from what I had always been taught. It had a ring of truth to it and made sense in a way other teachings didn't. If not for the Way, I might have become a dissipated, depressed sensualist like my friend Veturius. You'll have to meet him."

"Would I want to?"

"He complains endlessly, but he has a good heart. We've known each other since we were boys playing mock battles with wooden swords and stick spears."

"He's not a follower?"

Sergius sighed, "No. He always has an objection."

"There aren't many of us."

"But there'll be more, God willing. Paullus has the energy of ten men—," Sergius broke off. He halted so abruptly that Ailidh clutched his arm for support.

"What's the matter?"

"Over there," Sergius whispered harshly. He pointed into the shadows near Egomas's rented dwelling.

"I don't see—"

"Leaning against the wall. It's a Druid!"

He glanced down the street. As usual, there wasn't a member of the urban cohort in sight. What did the city police do with their time?

He could arrest the Druid himself. . . .

He hesitated, and as he did, Ailidh took the torch from his hand and raised it higher so the flickering flames threw light across the street.

"What are you doing?" Sergius grabbed for the torch. "You'll scare him away!"

Ailidh relinquished the torch. She scurried across the street. "Lovernios!" She opened her arms.

A twinge of envy and dismay shot through Sergius. He stood unsure whether to advance or to retreat in silence. But something drew him across the street, and he followed in Ailidh's wake.

The Druid turned. His arms remained by his side. Ailidh came to a stop and slowly lowered her arms.

The Druid remained silent.

Ailidh introduced, "Lovernios, meet a friend of mine, Sergius Lysias."

The dark, glowing eyes fixed on him.

"We've met." Sergius held the Druid's gaze.

"When?" Ailidh began.

The Druid threw back his cowl. Sergius, who'd had only a poor glimpse of the Druid's face previously, expected an old, withered haglike face, scarred and diseased. But Lovernios appeared about thirty, with combed ginger hair to his ears and a neatly trimmed mustache and beard. Other than a few pockmarks on his cheeks and forehead, his skin was unblemished. In fact, Sergius thought he could have passed unnoticed in a crowd but for the intensity of his hazel eyes.

Lovernios's lip curled, "Who could miss the three Roman tribunes riding their proud horses through the marble streets of their city?"

He turned to Ailidh. "Walking with a Roman, Cousin?"

Ailidh straightened. "He saved me from a beating at Egomas's hands."

Lovernios seemed to digest the words. Then he nodded at Sergius. "For that I thank you, Roman. Ailidh is a flower that should not be harmed."

He spoke softly, but Sergius detected a warning between the poetic words.

"Enough!" Ailidh held up a hand. "I can take care of myself."

Lovernios shrugged his cowl into position. "We'll talk later, Cousin. Vale, Roman."

"Wait!" Sergius reached for his gladius.

Lovernios halted.

Ailidh gripped Sergius's wrist and tried to urge the sword back into the scabbard. "No."

Sergius pushed her hand away. "It's the law."

"*Your* law," Lovernios clarified. He spread his arms. "Slay me, if you dare."

"Let him go, Sergius—" Ailidh pleaded, "for me."

Lovernios folded his arms across his chest. "Choose your friends wisely, Cousin." In one swift motion he blended into the shadows and disappeared.

Sergius stared into the dark. He slammed the gladius back into the scabbard.

Ailidh said softly, "Thank you for not arresting him."

Sergius snapped. "I neglected my duty."

"Lovernios would never harm anyone," Ailidh assured. "He's a very gentle man."

"You know him well?"

She opened the door to the house. "We were to be wed."

With a smile that managed to be both bright and sad, she slipped inside.

Sergius gulped.

The next day, the governor arrived.

Advance riders warned of the approach of Legatus Augusti pro praetore Gaius Suetonius Paulinus. The garrison turned out to meet him. Centurions chivied their troops into arrow-straight ranks in front of the praetorium. Sergius, Veturius, and Agricola donned full armor polished to mirror brightness, cloaks folded into precise lines, and helmet plumes stiffly erect. They joined the troops standing in ranks near the praetorium.

"The governor prefers efficiency to show," Agricola informed, "but it still pays to put on a good appearance."

A troop of cavalry and a body of infantry preceded several tribunes and a trio of legates.

Agricola leaned slightly toward Sergius to whisper the names of the legionary commanders. "Petilius Cerialis of Legio IX *Hispana*, Porcius Crispus of Legio II *Augusta*, and Gellius Marcianus of Legio XIV *Gemina*. Virius Falco of Legio XX *Valeria* must have remained on station."

Sergius studied the men as they dismounted. Cerialis, slender and dark, moved with quick jerky movements. Crispus, average in all respects, seemed slower, as if years of warfare had taken their toll. Marcianus, short, stout, and round faced, needed help to reach the ground with dignity.

After the legates came Suetonius. A governor could have an unofficial staff of friends and advisors, a cohors amicum, but Suetonius appeared not to have indulged the luxury. Instead, only a mounted bodyguard accompanied him.

Suetonius wasn't a large man: he appeared lean rather than stocky, yet his presence dominated all others. Even if Suetonius had lacked the distinguishing scarlet cloak of a commander in chief, Sergius could have picked him out simply on the basis of his gravitas. The man who had crushed the tribes of the Atlas Mountains moved with the authority and assurance that came from knowing his every order would be obeyed instantly.

Suetonius swung himself to the ground with the suppleness of a younger man, handed the reins to a waiting stable attendant, and strode up the steps into the praetorium.

"He didn't even notice the turnout," Veturius grumbled. "What was the point of dressing up?"

"He noticed," Agricola corrected; "even if it didn't seem like it. He was watching. Believe me, if a man was a few inches out of line, his centurion is going to hear about it."

A senior tribune, well built with a lumpy, thick-browed face, vaulted to the ground and ambled across. "Agricola!"

"Titus, you dog."

The men clasped arms.

Titus studied Sergius and Veturius. "Newcomers?"

Agricola introduced each of them, finishing, "Meet Titus Flavius Vespasianus. He's not bad in a bloodthirsty sort of way."

With an exaggerated movement, Titus sniffed. "They smell all right." He winked at Agricola.

Agricola burst into laughter.

Veturius flushed. "What's that supposed to mean?"

"His father's a legate," Agricola explained through laughs. "Once this officer, a real prig, comes to Vespasian to ask for a promotion. Straight from the baths, mind you, and you never smelled such an awful perfume in your life! I swear he'd bathed in sweet violets. Vespasian said—"

Titus finished, "'I'd rather he stunk of honest garlic.'"

Agricola held his side. "Vespasian threw him out. After that, no perfume dealer ever got any business from his legion again."

Sergius couldn't help but smile. "We pass?"

"You pass," Titus bared his teeth. The movement unnerved Sergius. Even if Agricola hadn't mentioned "bloodthirsty," he thought that the mocking curve of Titus's lips and a glimmer in his eyes bespoke a streak of cruelty.

"How's your old man doing?" Agricola asked. "Any news?"

"Living quietly," Titus informed.

"Lying low, more likely."

Titus faced Sergius. "Is it really true about Agrippina?"

Sergius nodded, "She's dead."

"At last."

Sergius raised an eyebrow.

Titus enlightened. "My father was close to Narcissus. So when Agrippina rose to power—"

"I understand,"—Sergius followed. Nero's scheming mother had no use for freed slaves, especially Claudius's advisor Narcissus who'd arranged for the murder of Claudius's adulterous third wife, Messallina. Against Narcissus's wishes, the widowed Agrippina then set her sights on the newly available Claudius. Agrippina prevailed, convinced Claudius to adopt her son Nero, then poisoned him and imprisoned Narcissus. Despite Narcissus's subsequent suicide, stigma attached to any of his associates.

The wise ones, like Titus's father, chose obscurity over death. Agrippina never forgot a grudge.

"Maybe now your father can regain his position," Agricola posed.

"Did Nero really try to kill Agrippina by building a ship that fell apart?" Titus wondered.

Sergius nodded. "After she escaped the collapsing bedroom, the boat sank but she swam ashore. Nero's minions hacked her to pieces. He accused her of the usual crimes to justify it to the Senate."

"Was there an outcry?"

"What do you think? Nobody valued life so lightly as to protest in public."

Veturius added, "But I hear that someone hung a leather bag on a statue of Nero."

Sergius chuckled. "I hadn't heard that." The punishment for killing one's father was to be sewn up in a leather bag along with a dog, a cock, a viper, and an ape, and to be thrown in the water to drown. Somebody thought Nero rated the same punishment for eliminating his conniving mother.

Titus snorted, "Anybody who gets rid of an Agrippina can't be all bad."

"Just wait until you hear about Nero singing his own love songs in the circus." Veturius snickered, "He has a thin, reedy voice, and he's a *horrible* poet—"

Sergius kicked Veturius in the ankle. Veturius shut up.

"Look," Agricola interrupted, "I'd like to stay and talk, but I should go and report to Crispus. He has a terrible temper that I don't want to incur."

"What about us?" Sergius asked.

"Wait here," Titus replied. "The governor's likely to send for you soon." He waved and began to walk away. "Cheer up. There's not much happening now, but come spring we'll have the chance to slay a few Britons, guaranteed."

"Mad," Veturius moaned, as Agricola and Titus disappeared. "They're all war happy and mad."

"And you have a loose tongue."

Veturius shrugged, "Titus is all right."

"Maybe, maybe not. Want to bet your life on it?"

The summons came after an hour's wait.

His father's words rang in his ears as Sergius entered the commander in chief's office in the praetorium. "Gaius Suetonius Paulinus is tough, relentless, and as cold as they come. Cross him, and you might as well say good-bye to any hope of a career. You'll receive more sympathy from the Britons than from him."

His father had been legate of the Twenty-second Legion, the *Primagenia,* until a German barbarian had broken past the guard, shattered his thigh, and sent him home a crippled amputee, facing years of recuperation. He knew about dealing with governors.

"Look Suetonius in the eye," Appius Sergius Rufus had advised, "and don't back down."

Suetonius Paulinus stood behind a table littered with maps and letters. Lamplight warmed the otherwise utilitarian office.

Emperors journey with pomp and luxury, but high military commanders travel unencumbered. Sometimes, anyway, Sergius corrected himself. The great Julius Caesar had kept a mosaic in his tent to remind him of home. But Suetonius apparently maintained the professional soldier's abhorrence of the frivolous.

Sergius crossed the room, halted opposite the table, and saluted.

"Tribunus legionis Marcus Sergius Lysias reporting, sir."

After a long moment, Suetonius raised his head and looked up.

Tough, relentless, and cold. Suetonius appeared the part. His hair had receded until only a fringe of iron adhered to his temples and the back of his head. His eyes weren't brown as Sergius anticipated but gray as the northern ocean, set beneath firm brows in a face carved from marble. A few furrows in his forehead and at the corners of his eyes gave the only hints of middle age. Suetonius's lean frame yielded a few inches to Sergius.

"A tribune," Suetonius said, his voice as hard as his eyes. The words sounded like an epithet.

"Sir."

"I suppose you think you're a soldier."

"No, sir."

"No?" The gray ocean flashed. "Then what are you doing here?"

Sergius tried to keep his voice level, "I'm here to learn how to become a soldier, sir."

Suetonius's gaze burned into him. Sergius wanted to tear his own eyes away from the intensity of Suetonius's scrutiny, but he didn't.

The governor grunted. He glanced at a piece of papyrus. "You are twenty-one years old," he continued in the same crisp, dry voice, "and were triumvir capitalis of the city of Aquileia."

"Yes, sir."

"Tribune of a legion is considerably different from arresting criminals."

"Yes, sir."

"You think being stationed in Britannia is an excuse for an easy life."

"No, sir."

"No, it's not!" Suetonius snapped. The marble skin of his face suffused.

Sergius, who had relaxed slightly, stiffened.

Suetonius continued, "I have campaigns to conduct. I have no time for highbred puppies playing at being men."

Sergius cleared his throat. "I have to start somewhere, sir," he said. "Even Julius Caesar began his career as a tribune."

The color faded from Suetonius's face. "So he did," he replied in a quieter tone. "Why aren't you in an auxiliary regiment, then? You would at least have some field experience behind you."

He's testing me, Sergius thought. *He knows my rank.* Knightly class, equestrian young men joined the auxiliary regiments as junior tribunes of infantry or cavalry. Senatorial aspirants such as Sergius began at higher positions.

"My father wished me posted to a legion, sir."

"Your father?"

"Appius Sergius Rufus, sir."

"I know the name. An unfortunate incident." Suetonius stirred the papyrus with a stubby forefinger.

"My father fought the Germans, sir."

"And so the son will fight the Britons?" The corners of Suetonius Paulinus's lips twitched. "We shall find out, Lysias. You at least have the physique to be a soldier, unlike some of the girls I see who can barely lift a sword." The hint of a smile vanished. "You will join The Fourteenth Legion, the *Gemina,* under Gellius Marcianus. Since your commander is here, you'll be temporarily attached to headquarters staff."

Sergius saluted. "Sir. Uh—"

"What?"

"Shouldn't I see what life is like with the legion first, sir?"

"You're an officer, Lysias, not an enlisted man. I don't care if you can dig a trench or not."

"Yes, sir."

"You'll be experiencing field service soon enough. Don't be impatient."

"No, sir." Sergius faced the door.

Suetonius's voice followed him, "I'll be watching you, Lysias."

Outside, Sergius spotted Gaius Veturius pacing a narrow circle.

Veturius gripped Sergius's elbow. "Well? What is he like?"

"Remember what my father told me?"

"Yes."

"He's worse."

Veturius's jaw dropped. He cast a startled glance at the door.

"Good luck." Sergius slapped Veturius's shoulder, then angled across the compound, toward the legates' quarters. If he was assigned to the *Gemina*, he should introduce himself to his new commander.

Before being transferred to Britannia, the *Gemina* had been stationed on the Rhine. Service on the frontier, facing the trackless forests of Germania, seasoned troops quickly. The men of the *Gemina* were battle-hardened veterans: men like his father.

Gellius Marcianus, in contrast to Suetonius Paulinus, greeted Sergius warmly—possibly because, since he looked to be about thirty, he wasn't as far removed from his own days as tribune.

"Glad to have you, Lysias," Marcianus rumbled, in a surprisingly deep bass.

Sergius returned the legate's greeting. "I'm glad to be here, sir."

"Are you?" Marcianus chuckled. "Done any soldiering?"

"Not yet, sir."

Marcianus wiped a strand of brown hair back from his forehead. "We've had a profitable two years campaigning, which you've arrived in time to miss. But no matter. You've the winter to become acclimatized." Marcianus's languid gaze sharpened. "If you intend to, that is."

Sergius nodded, "I do."

"I think the women of Londinium saw more of your predecessor than I did."

"Indeed, sir."

"Suetonius wasn't impressed with him," Marcianus said. "And neither was I. His file in army headquarters bulges with demerits. But it's up to you: Britannia's pleasures aren't as bountiful as other places, but they exist; otherwise, you can learn a lot. And the best place to learn soldiering is from the centurions. They're the true professionals, not your fellow tribunes."

"Yes, sir."

"You've found your quarters, I assume?"

"I have."

"Report to the acting chief of headquarters staff. We've only a partial contingent clattering about the countryside at present, so the princeps praetori is in Londinium with most of the staff. Find his second, the cornicularius. He'll detail you an aide and an orderly and explain your duties." Marcianus paused for breath. "If you've no questions, that's all."

Sergius inclined his head. "None, sir." He saluted and went in search of the adjutant.

Ailidh jogged along a tree-lined trackway just outside Camulodunum's limits, a pack of dogs strung out behind her. She ran at a steady pace, a pace she could maintain for hours if necessary. Egomas hadn't complained when she informed him of her intention to exercise the dogs. Healthy dogs fetched more money.

And running the dogs acted as a tonic, a healing draft for body and soul. She needed a draft.

Her heart had skipped a beat at the sight of Lovernios. She hadn't expected him to be effusive, but she'd thought there'd be some show of emotion. Instead, he'd been so cold! Something had changed about him. He'd always been intense, but the intensity had deepened, as if a new purpose had gripped his passions. A lake had deepened into an ocean.

Of course, the relationship between them could never be the way it had once been, but . . .

The trackway rose up a hill, and Ailidh slowed her pace to conserve her breath.

She thought she'd moved beyond pain, that the years had dulled her anguish and scarred the wound in her heart.

Did she still hope—just a little—that Lovernios might have changed? If he could not accept her new religion, could he at least concede that it mattered to *her?*

She crested the hill and sped down.

He hadn't even needed to ask her if she still followed her new path. He had seen it in her eyes, just as she had seen his response in his. He thought of her as a traitor. To him, to accept the Way meant to become Roman at heart, to yield to the conqueror.

Lovernios was not a man to change. He'd spent his life learning the Druid way. He believed it, every word.

And he would not—would never—accept the Way.

Lovernios or the Way: she'd made her choice, and that choice couldn't be unmade.

Dogs brushed against her shins. The touch of fur made her tremble. Dogs were simple, uncomplicated creatures.

Fellow humans weren't.

Each senior officer was entitled to an aide—beneficiarius. The cornicularis assigned Sergius a long-serving aide named Quintus, who had outlasted several tribunes. Quintus seemed only too happy to initiate Sergius into legionary life.

Hours later, his head swimming from an interminable briefing, Sergius called it quits. "I don't think I'm capable of absorbing any more today."

Quintus heartened, "Don't worry, sir. It seems confusing now, but it will all fall into place before you know it."

"I'll take your word for that."

At the bathhouse he found Veturius lounging in the tepidarium.

"How's the governor's favorite?" Veturius grinned, setting down a strigil with which he'd been scraping himself.

"I can see the day's been too much for you," Sergius replied, lowering himself into the water. "You're losing your mind."

"Far from it."

"I expected you to be a quivering mass of anxieties after your interview with Suetonius." Sergius closed his eyes, and allowed the warmth to soak into him. He worked his shoulders and neck to relax tense muscles. "Why the facile expression?"

Veturius sounded smug. "Because I was posted to the *Hispana*. While you're mucking around the frontier with the *Gemina*, I shall be in the nice, quiet north, far removed from any hostilities."

"You'll still have the requisite administrative chores."

"I can handle those, now that I know I won't be under constant threat of premature demise."

Sergius grabbed Veturius's shoulders.

"What—?" Veturius exclaimed.

"I wouldn't be so certain." With a quick motion, Sergius plunged his unsuspecting friend under the water.

FIVE

Procurator Decianus Catus, chief financial officer of the province of Britannia, paced back and forth over the brightly colored mosaic that graced the floor of the private office in his Camulodunum villa. His short steps tapped a staccato rhythm over a bacchanalia, treading on the faces and bodies of lovers, revelers, and satyrs alike. He glanced between the two men who stood nervously a pace apart from each other: quaestor Alypius Juba, his senior financial advisor, and Sextus Fuscus, centurion of his personal guard.

The journey from Londinium to Camulodunum had left Catus in a sour mood. Riding a horse inevitably upset his digestion. And horses were such malodorous beasts.

He slapped a hand against his thigh. "We must find a way to increase tribute."

"Is that wise, sir?" Fuscus cautioned. The career soldier's pinched face mirrored his disposition. "The Iceni are growing restless."

"So what?" Catus waved off the protest. "If anything, we're too lenient with them. King Prasutagus is a feeble old fool. He'll be lucky to live through the winter. Who will that leave to rule the Iceni? His widow and a pair of teenage daughters," he sniggered, "unless the Iceni find somebody more suitable."

"But to increase tribute—"

Catus stalked around the office. "Think of it in the same manner as having the enlisted men pay money to avoid fatigues. Which would you rather do: give up a few sestercii or clean out the latrines?"

"I take your point." Fuscus rubbed his stubbly chin.

"Good."

Trust a military officer to have no grasp of finances. But one thing centurions always understood, Catus knew, was the concept of bribery. And he could read Fuscus's mind as if it was his own. The centurion thought Catus made too much of the issue of taxes.

But why shouldn't Catus be more acquisitive than the average procurator? When the leaders in Rome gloried in profit, why shouldn't the provincials, who had to work harder for smaller gains? Why should his nest be unfeathered? Even the Stoic philosopher Seneca, Nero's pet advisor, knew how to turn a profit when he wasn't churning out reams of sentimental verse.

Catus knew he would never reach Seneca's level of influence. Nor did he want to. Closeness to the emperor could all too easily prove detrimental to one's health. But wealth—the benefits told a different tale.

He'd reached as far as his social rank allowed. The procuratorship of Britannia was a dead end. He might as well be marooned in the North African desert selling mules. No further promotions awaited him. And, as everyone knew, a man had to make three fortunes: one to live on, one for bribes, and one for retirement.

Consider this villa. Although the financial offices were situated in Londinium, Catus maintained this villa for the times when he desired a more refined atmosphere. Londinium, though larger, proved nothing but a rude excuse of a town, not a proper colonia like Camulodunum, where one could imagine being in Rome. But villas cost money, as did the mosaic from the studio of Aletius in Neapolis, the wall frescoes by Pedanius of Heraclea, and his collection of silver statuettes. Catus surrounded himself with objects of beauty. Anyone could buy imitation artwork, but good taste—and Catus prided himself on his taste—meant the purchase of items of legitimate artistic value.

And women! By Venus, women were expensive!

Add in the sums he paid his ex-wife Acilia to keep her fat carcass out of his way . . .

Catus's sandals slapped the polished marble. "Can't you two cretins think of anything?"

Outside the room waited his secretary to draft orders, messengers to distribute them, ten beneficiarii and troops under Fuscus to enforce them, and exactores and publicani to collect the money.

Juba cleared his throat. "We've raised the land and property taxes, increased the head tax, imposed death duties and inheritance taxes, and had the merchants purchase selling licenses for Camulodunum and Londinium." He paused. "There's always the portoria—"

Fuscus interjected, "If we raise the port tax higher, we'll drive away shipping."

Catus clenched his fists. "We want something to tax the Britons, fools, not our own people."

"What about the annona?" Juba warbled.

Catus stared at the dwarfish quaestor. With his high-pitched voice and grotesquely enlarged head that wobbled from side to side on a scrawny neck, Juba looked anything but a financial expert. In Italia, normally such a child would have been exposed at birth and left as carrion. How Juba had survived was anybody's guess—but Catus had found Juba's deviousness matched his own, and the quaestor's command of financial acquisition was second to none.

"What about the grain tax?" Catus demanded clarification. "We already tax those tribes that grow grain."

"Exactly. But what about those that don't?"

"Those that don't?" Fuscus exclaimed. "That's absurd! How can we tax people for what they don't have?"

Catus stopped his pacing, each foot pressing down upon a half-naked woman. He smiled, "It's really not fair to tax some tribes for grain and not others, is it, Juba?"

"Not fair at all, sir."

"The procurator should treat all tribes equally."

Fuscus complained, "I still don't see—"

Catus snapped, "Put your mind to work, Fuscus! Listen: If we levy a grain tax, paid in grain, on those tribes that don't grow grain, what are they going to do? Think, man!"

"Buy it somewhere."

Catus snapped his fingers. "Buy it from *us*, of course. And we will be considerate enough to buy it back—at a lower cost."

Juba appended, "The grain doesn't even have to leave the granaries. All that needs to change hands is money."

"Excellent," Catus purred. "Juba, you're a genius."

"Such a tax would affect the Iceni more than other tribes," Juba continued, "because their main source of revenue is selling horses, not grain."

"Even better. Prasutagus has more money than he knows what to do with. Have my secretary draft the order: the usual language."

"Excellency." Juba bowed and departed.

Fuscus's palm grated over his jawline. "The tribes won't like it."

Catus sneered. The tribes never did. When a noble of the Trinovantes called him—to his face—rapacious, he accepted it as a compliment before stripping the noble of his lands and having him flogged.

"So you've told me," Catus growled. "They don't have to like it. All they have to do is pay." His eyes narrowed. "Your men can handle the complaints, can't they?"

"I suppose so."

"They'd better—unless you want to be transferred to an active duty legion. Maybe you'd get on better with the Silures or the Ordovices."

Fuscus shuddered. He dropped his gaze to the mosaic, where a voluptuous nude gazed back in marble invitation. "Not necessary, sir."

Catus crossed the room and perched on a cushioned couch angled so that he could look out over the interior courtyard. A slave tended to what the autumn had left of the garden.

"Good. It would be a pity to lose you, Fuscus. Have your troops prepared for whatever measures need to be taken."

Fuscus nodded, "As you command, sir."

Catus reached for a drinking horn of choice wine from the slopes of Mount Vesuvius and sipped. "And Fuscus, I will require a woman for tonight."

"I'll see that a slave is readied, sir."

Catus straightened, "Not a slave! And not an expensive whore either: all paint and no passion. Get me a Briton. Tonight, I need fire."

Fuscus's pinched face tightened even further. Ramrod straight, he marched from the room.

"Fire," Catus murmured to himself. By all the gods, the Britons must be good for something!

First he'd visit his private balneum for a bath and then linger for a massage by the balneator. When the attendant's supple fingers had finished with him, he'd be ready—for whomever Fuscus found.

"Does the governor have a wife?" Sergius asked Agricola.

The four senatorial tribunes shared a meal in the officers' mess. Junior tribunes scurried with flagons of wine, serving their seniors.

"Say what you like, Britannia produces good oysters." With a sigh of satisfaction, Agricola popped a Rutupiae oyster into his mouth, chewed, and swallowed. "Wife and three children. Why do you ask?"

"Just curious."

Titus added, "Plain faced, flat chested, and skinny. With pimples."

"Not that bad," Agricola countered.

Titus shrugged and reached for his goblet. "I wouldn't look twice."

"You seem to have noticed enough as it is," Agricola commented. He directed himself to Sergius. "Her name's Livy. She's never strayed from Londinium to my knowledge."

"Why's that?" Veturius asked.

"I'd guess because Londinium receives more commerce than Camulodunum. There's more social life." He gestured. "Retired soldiers aren't the most sophisticated people, and a colonia isn't high society."

Veturius accidentally splashed water into his wine. "More bad luck."

Agricola gnawed a chicken leg. "You'll meet her sometime. The governor will probably invite us to dinner at his Londinium villa."

Veturius perked, "Really?"

"Don't get excited," Titus cautioned. "The only reason is because so few people of senatorial rank reside in the province other than the legates and an occasional visitor."

Sergius clarified, "We're guests of necessity, not choice."

"Right. He needs us to make up numbers."

They ate in silence for a few minutes, then Sergius asked, "Why are we in Camulodunum, then?"

Agricola answered, "Suetonius has several capital cases to try. His approval is required before some poor wretch is sentenced to death or the mines. He checks in on the temple from time to time, supervises the city authorities—that kind of thing."

"Oh." Sergius plucked a date from a bowl.

"Mind you, his heart's not in it. He'd much rather be in the field."

"Not I," Titus expressed. "Not in winter, anyway."

"I suppose a fortress lacks all amenities," Veturius suggested.

Titus chuckled. "Not all. Just the important ones."

"A fortress makes you appreciate the city more," Agricola added.

"That's the way it goes," Titus continued, "up and down the country, back and forth and back again. It's a pain, but there it is." He raised up on an elbow. "Orderly—more wine, and some dessert!"

"God bless you," the old woman thanked, touching Ailidh's arm with a withered claw.

Ailidh gave her a quick kiss on the cheek. "And you."

She slung her now empty basket over her arm, pulled her birrus tight to her throat, and stepped into the dark street. Behind her, lamplight from the woman's house was extinguished as the door closed.

A few crusts of bread and a flask of beer—it was little enough, though Egomas would begrudge the loss. But Mavelle had virtually nothing, being widowed years past, and now her only son had died in a rockfall at the quarry while cutting stone for the Temple of Claudius.

Mavelle lived in a decaying shack at the edge of town that made even Egomas's poorly furnished rented house seem palatial.

Ailidh hurried along the street.

"Towns are unnatural," Lovernios had told her once. "Life was better when the people lived as families."

As she passed row after row of identical houses, Ailidh thought perhaps her cousin was right. People shouldn't live clustered together like sheep or rabbits. They should spread out over their lands and holdings; that was the proper way.

Figures passed her in the night. She kept one hand close to the haft of her dagger.

Her course took her through the center of town, past the cluster of official buildings where the elite of Camulodunum lived.

She slowed her steps briefly by the houses reserved for army officers, then continued on.

Cara tugged against her chain and whined. The big dog's ears pricked forward, and every muscle of her lean body quivered. Sergius had to throw his weight backward to hold her in check.

"What's the matter, girl?" Sergius stared down a cobbled street into the night. He spoke to his companion, "Can you see anything, Gaius?"

"I see a city lying down for sleep," Veturius answered, "closing its eyes, wearied from too much work, even the pleasures of the night beyond its stilted grasp—"

"Hush, fool! Cara senses something."

"Probably a rat. All I see is a couple of drunks and an ugly whore," Veturius yawned. "Let's go back to bed. I don't know why I let you talk me into going for a walk at this time of night."

"You need the exercise."

Cara whined louder.

"Something's bothering her," Sergius interpreted.

"She needs more wine. Like me," Veturius suggested.

"Come along." Sergius allowed Cara to pull him down the street. Veturius exhaled noisily but nonetheless followed a pace behind.

The moon swam behind pasty clouds, teasing with hints of illumination but refusing to break clear. Camulodunum wasn't as dead as Veturius pretended. From the various buildings they passed came the sounds of laughter, love, argument, clinking goblets, and wheezing snores.

Cara pulled him left, then right, then left again.

"Does that beast really know where she's going?" Veturius asked skeptically.

"More so than you, I expect."

Cara barked. Another dog yapped a reply from the distance.

Something was definitely amiss. In the days since he'd purchased her, Cara had been a perfect model of obedience. Sergius rested a hand on the wolfhound's head. "Quiet, girl."

"What's that?" Veturius asked.

"I don't—," and then he heard it. From a street entrance ahead came familiar sounds: the clank of armor and the booted footsteps of soldiers. "Troops," Sergius identified.

"An odd time for maneuvers."

"Agreed." Sergius concentrated on the sounds. "If they'd been drinking, they'd be making more noise."

"Where are they?" Veturius whispered in Sergius's ear. "I can't see a thing."

"There." Sergius indicated a narrow alley, its entrance nearly invisible in the dark.

A grunt. The smack of flesh on flesh. The scraping noises of a scuffle. The clatter of metal hitting stone. The quickly stifled cry of a woman.

"Nighttime fun," Veturius hissed.

"I don't think so."

A male voice cried, "Grab the dagger—aagh! By Mars, look what the slut—"

"Easy!" a second man enjoined. "The procurator doesn't like damaged goods."

A yell of pain escaped, then a woman's voice hurled, "I'll give him damaged goods!"

"Ailidh!" Sergius gasped. Cara barked and bounded ahead. Sergius bolted for the alley, his gladius instantly out of its scabbard and into his right hand.

He rounded the corner into the alley, and came face-to-face with a soldier. The man recoiled and froze as Sergius's sword point touched his chest, resting on the steel plates of his lorica.

Cara hunkered low, hackles raised, a low growl rumbling in her throat.

A moonbeam broke through the clouds and washed the alley with silver. Sergius looked past the soldier. A burly legionary held Ailidh immobile. Blood dripped down from parallel gouges in his cheek. Another private leaned against a building, clutching a bloody cloth to his upper arm.

Sergius snarled, "Let her go."

The lead soldier, an optio of infantry who ranked just below a centurion, took a step backward. He withdrew his own sword.

"Procurator's orders," he pronounced. "Let us pass."

"What are you doing with her?"

"Tribune," the officer grated, "Procurator Catus ordered us to bring him a Briton woman."

"Is the procurator so poor that you must drag an innocent woman from the streets?"

"That's not for me to say, sir."

"Well, I say this woman is not for him. Let her go."

"I am obeying orders, sir," the optio insisted stiffly.

Sergius raised his sword and dropped into a fighting stance. "Would you rather face the procurator or my gladius?"

The optio glanced at his men, then back at Sergius and the crouching Cara, as if weighing the odds.

A sword slithered from its scabbard beside Sergius. Veturius took up position beside him.

"Well?" Veturius challenged. "Does the procurator's guard wish to take on the legion? How long has it been since we killed anyone, Sergius? My sword thirsts for the taste of blood."

The optio ran his sword into its scabbard. "Release her," he ordered his men.

Ailidh yanked free. She stooped to pick up her dagger from the street, and then a second object. Sergius glimpsed a lethal-looking bronze hairpin with a shaft at least a handbreadth long. Ailidh shoved past the optio, and moved to Sergius's free side.

"Did they hurt you?" he asked.

Her face rigid, she replied through her anger, "Not as much as I hurt them." She stabbed the bloody pin into her hair but maintained a tight grip on the dagger.

"Let's go," Sergius said.

"Will you explain to the procurator, sir?" the optio asked.

Sergius paused, then nodded, "I would be delighted." To Veturius, he commanded, "Take Ailidh back to her house, Gaius. Leave Cara there to guard. I'll be along once I've spoken to Catus."

"Sergius—" Ailidh began.

He touched her cheek, then he gestured with his gladius to the optio, "Lead."

Decianus Catus, bathed, fragranced, and clad in his softest tunic, the one reserved for nighttime company, took a final glance around his dormitoria. The walls of the bedroom shone with brightly painted frescoes. Nudes cavorted on the beach with men and animals. An elegantly carved lectus bore a mattress, cushions, and sheets. A flagon of wine and goblets rested on a low table.

Perfect.

At a knock on the door he smiled and opened it. "Welcome, my dear—"

He halted at the stolid face of the optio. He tried to peer past him. "You? Where's my woman?"

"I was bringing you a woman, sir, but was prevented—"

"*Prevented?* What in Hades!"

"As we returned, sir. A tribune and his companion confronted us and wouldn't allow us—"

"Where's the miscreant now?"

Sergius brushed past the optio. "Right here."

Decianus Catus's blotchy cheeks turned pink, red, and finally purple. "This is inexcusable!" he shouted. "Who do you think you are to interfere with my men in the performance of their duty?"

"Kidnapping is their duty?" Sergius's nose wrinkled at the perfume wafting from Catus.

"Anything I give them is their duty!"

Sergius had intended to address the procurator in a reasonable manner. Honor required a senator's son to show deference to equestrians of higher civil office than himself, even one whose short tunic bulged over a paunch to reveal a pair of ridiculously knobby knees. But at the sight of Catus's lust- and wine-reddened cheeks, Sergius's control deserted him.

He clenched his fists. "Even rape?"

Catus's jaw muscles bulged. "What my men do is none of your business! My actions need not be explained to a stripling!"

"They do to me."

Catus drew breath and appeared to make an effort to pull himself together. "What's your interest in this woman?"

"Do I need an interest? Isn't the sight of Roman soldiers assaulting a woman interest enough?"

"Look, Tribune . . . "

"Sergius Lysias."

"This is all a misunderstanding." Catus smiled. "The woman is my mistress. Sometimes she becomes a little . . . ah . . . recalcitrant if she's had too much to dri— Aagh!"

Sergius lunged at the procurator. As Catus scuttled back, the lectus caught him behind the legs, and he fell onto it.

"Liar!"

"Tribune!" The optio grasped Sergius's hands and pulled him away.

Sergius stared down at Catus. "The woman is a friend of mine. She would have nothing to do with your sort."

Catus coughed and rubbed his neck. "Your commander will hear of this."

"Good. I hope you have a wonderful explanation for him." Sergius spun on his heel and stalked out.

The optio licked his lips. "Do you want me to procure another woman, sir?"

Catus struggled to his feet. "No! Get out of my sight!"

His hand trembled as he reached for the flagon of wine and slopped it into a goblet. "I should have him crucified!" he muttered. "Senator's son or not."

But law in Britannia worked the same as everywhere else—you couldn't crucify a citizen. Jupiter! Catus abhorred that the young whelp's purple stripe ensured immunity from his retaliation!

Catus gulped down the expensive vintage, not caring about the drops that splashed onto his tunic.

By the time he reached Ailidh's house, Sergius's anger had diffused from boiling fury to a dull, smoldering rage—and a twinge of anxiety.

He shouldn't have lost his temper. It wasn't proper. His father wouldn't have acted that way. Catus was the procurator for heaven's sake! He ranked as the second highest official in Britannia, below only the governor.

Veturius lounged against the doorpost, Cara lying at his feet. The wolfhound sprang up as Sergius approached.

"How is Ailidh?" Sergius asked.

"About as angry as you, I imagine," Veturius replied. "You're white."

"Nothing compared to what I was. Go on home, Gaius. I'll catch you later."

As Veturius's footsteps faded, Sergius knocked on the wood, tried the door, and found it unlocked. He pushed it open. An unfamiliar woman appeared from the depths of the house: a Briton.

Sergius blinked. "I was looking for Ailidh."

"She's asleep."

"So quickly?"

"I gave her a draught to help." The woman smiled, but the smile didn't reach her eyes.

"If she wakes, tell her I came by, would you? My name is Sergius."

"Vale, Tribune."

Sergius had sufficient insight to know that he could never sleep in his current state of nervous excitement, so he walked, listening to the city revels die down. Finally, tiredness blunted the edge of his anger.

Cara seemed indefatigable, keeping a constant pace by his side.

He made his way back to his quarters only to find lamps burning, Veturius and Agricola playing a game of tali, and Titus snoring beside the brazier.

"You're later than we expected," Veturius commented, rattling the knucklebones in his hand and casting them on the table. "Blast! Another vulture." He gathered the four aces and prepared for a second throw.

Sergius shed his cloak and weapons, crossed to a couch, and flopped down. Cara dropped in a heap and rested her muzzle on her paws. "I forgot to ask: Didn't Ailidh want Cara?"

"She said to bring her home," Veturius replied. "She had another dog in the house."

"Is it true?" Agricola inquired. "You went to rebuke the procurator?"

"I tried to strangle him. That man's a complete ass."

"Yes," Agricola agreed. "But he *is* the procurator."

"And that gives him the right to trample over innocent citizens?"

"Your friend isn't a citizen," Agricola corrected quietly. He continued before Sergius could protest, "But in principle you're correct. Catus is the type to give all politicians a bad name. You can smell him a mile away, like an uncovered sewer."

"Why does the governor allow it?" Veturius questioned.

"You'd have to ask him. I suppose Suetonius has other things on his mind. The procurator's actions don't concern him."

"Even if Catus's actions affect the attitude of the population?" Sergius posed.

Agricola shrugged. "Catus doesn't answer to Suetonius anyway. Only Nero."

"That alone speaks volumes."

Agricola studied his fingernails. "Britannia isn't quite what you expected, is it?"

Sergius shook his head, "No."

"You came here dreaming of adventure, of planting the banner of civilization in a new province. You didn't expect it to have the same dirty and sordid side as Rome. I thought the same way when I arrived."

"I didn't expect Catus's type, no."

"There are bad apples everywhere. You can't let them discourage you, because despite them," Agricola said, "we do bring civilization. Except on the frontiers, the Empire is at peace. We have time for music, literature, and the arts. Rome's glory is not a fiction. In a place like Britannia, there are bound to be growing pains. Like it or not, people sometimes get trampled underfoot."

Sergius brought his fist down on the couch. "That doesn't mean I have to stand by and allow it to happen."

"Of course not. But it does mean you need to exercise discretion. Catus can be a powerful enemy. It won't help your friend any if you're knifed in the back on a dark night."

Sergius's head shot up.

"You hadn't thought of that, had you?" Agricola said. "From what I've heard of him, Catus isn't above underhanded tactics when they suit him." He rose to his feet. "Watch your step, friend."

He gestured negatively with his hand to Veturius, who held out the tali. "Keep them," he insisted. "I've won enough for the night."

Agricola paused by the door. "What did Catus say to you?"

"That he'd report my actions to my commander."

Agricola nodded slowly. "You might be all right. But don't cross Catus again." He planted his foot in Titus's side. "Up you—find your own bed."

Titus blinked and rose groggily to his feet. "What time is it?"

"Too late." Agricola steered him through the door.

Veturius yawned. "Now that you're back in one piece," he directed to Sergius, "I'm going to bed, too."

"Thanks for your help tonight," Sergius responded gratefully.

"Anytime. Think I could face your mother if anything happened to you? Besides," Veturius laid a hand on Sergius's shoulder as he passed by, "if you were knifed, they'd be trying to foist Claudia off on me."

He tossed the tali onto the table. Each side landed differently. Veturius twisted his face in disgust. "Now I throw a 'Venus!'"

SIX

"Excuse me, sir." The voice of his beneficiarius Quintus interrupted Sergius's train of thought. Not that he was thinking all that clearly to begin with. The events of the night had conspired to limit his sleep, and this morning his head felt as dense as the fog that had drifted in overnight and blanketed Camulodunum in a mantle of gray.

How Ailidh felt, he could only surmise.

Legate Marcianus had detailed him a temporary office and plenty of administrative work. Sergius had been trying, with Quintus's help, to understand the inner functioning of a legion; in particular, a senior tribune's duties. He'd begun with the discharge and benefit arrangements of retiring veterans, since, with the year drawing to a close, a number of *Gemina*'s legionaries were reaching the end of their twenty-year enlistment. Lucky men to have survived the multiple hazards of military life for such a period of time.

He wanted to see Ailidh, and he toyed with the idea of visiting her. But he couldn't very well leave his office, not with the threat of disciplinary action hanging over his head.

Disciplinary action. Just the sound of the words caused cramps to knot his stomach.

He rubbed his temples and wondered, for the thousandth time, what spirit had motivated him to speak so intemperately to the procurator. His father could have rebuked Catus with impunity, but not Sergius.

The procurator's actions were beneath contempt, but did that excuse his lack of charity? Where did one draw the line between justifiable indignation and sinful anger? Didn't God hate unjust officials who abused their position?

"Sir?" Quintus repeated.

Sergius looked toward the slender, slightly stooped aide. Quintus wore a fixed, neutral expression, one that Sergius suspected the aide had cultivated for many years.

"Yes, Quintus?"

"A message from Legate Marcianus, sir. Your presence is required."

Sergius's heart plummeted. So soon? He'd expected to be summoned but hoped against hope that Catus wouldn't carry out his threat. Instead, the procurator had wasted little time. He must have sent a message via the morning courier.

Sergius hauled himself to his feet. "Very well. In his office?"

"No, sir. The governor's office."

Sergius puffed out his cheeks. Gellius Marcianus and Suetonius Paulinus together. It didn't sound promising.

"Thank you, Quintus. Stay here and work on these audits. Double-check my figures."

"Yes, sir."

Sergius arranged his armor and cloak as he entered the fog and aimed himself toward the praetorium. Although Camulodunum no longer functioned as a legionary fortress, the basic outlines remained the same; so, even though he could see only a few feet ahead, he knew which way to go without becoming disoriented.

The short distance between the tribunes' houses and the praetorium gave him time to think—and to worry—on the way.

Sergius identified himself to the sentry positioned outside Suetonius's office. The man leaned through the door, announced him, and then held the door open for him.

Sergius entered and saluted. "Tribune Lysias reporting as ordered, sirs."

Suetonius and Marcianus stood side by side behind a table. Suetonius, with his lean build, made the corpulent Marcianus seem even fatter by comparison. A pile of dispatches lay on the table. Discharge orders? Punishment slips?

The commander in chief's cold gray eyes flickered up, but he said nothing. Gellius Marcianus spoke instead, his round mouth tight beneath his overhanging cheeks. "I've received a complaint about you, Lysias, from Procurator Catus." He held up a crisp papyrus between his index and middle fingers—tentatively, as if he had grasped something unclean.

"I thought you might, sir."

"Is it true?"

"What does he say, sir?"

Marcianus consulted the closely spaced writing. "That you interfered with his men in the performance of their duty, that you insulted him and threatened him with physical harm, and that you created a disturbance in his household."

"That is true, sir."

Marcianus blinked as if he'd expected a denial. His eyes almost disappeared into the folds of his face. He slapped the papyrus onto the pile of documents. "By the gods, man, you've only just arrived! Why'd you even bother getting off ship?"

Sergius asked, "Does the procurator give the reasons for his complaint?"

"He does not."

"May I explain, sir?"

Marcianus gestured, "If you *have* an explanation."

"Procurator Catus's men were abducting a local woman for his personal pleasure. The urban cohort was not in evidence, so I secured her release, and at the insistence of Catus's soldiers, reported to him personally. I was outspoken, sir."

"Very outspoken, it seems."

"I hadn't intended to speak so, sir, but in the heat of the moment—"

"What was your concern in all of this?" Marcianus demanded.

Sergius groped for a phrase. "The woman was known to me, sir."

The legate remained impassive but for a narrowing of his eyes. "You didn't wish to share your bed partner, is that what you're telling me?"

"No, sir!" Sergius gasped. "She's not my partner. Just a friend. She's the dog-seller's daughter, sir."

"Dog-seller's daughter?" Marcianus repeated blankly.

"I bought a dog, sir."

"Explain yourself."

Sergius complied, "In the market . . . the dog-seller accused a Greek visitor of theft. . . . I purchased the animal."

When he finished, Marcianus questioned, "Expecting to have time for idle pursuits, Lysias?"

Sergius shook his head. "No, sir. But a dog may protect a man's back if he lacks other companions."

Marcianus cocked his head to one side. "Do tell. What about the woman?"

"I returned her to her home, sir."

Marcianus glanced at Suetonius, who maintained a studied disinterest.

"Am I to understand that this fuss was over a *Briton* woman?" the legate asked, the scorn in his voice undisguised.

"Yes, sir."

"Ye gods," Marcianus sighed. "Do the words *discipline* and *self-control* mean anything to you?"

Sergius recalled that one of the fruits of the Spirit is self-control. He answered, "They do, sir."

"Not as much as they ought." Marcianus rubbed his fleshy palms together, then folded them and raised them to his chin.

Sergius's fingertips and toes tingled with anxiety as he waited for the legate's verdict. Suetonius had apparently delegated the decision to *Gemina*'s commander.

After what seemed an eternity, Marcianus said, "I accept your explanation, Lysias—" he extended a finger, "but I don't condone your conduct. The emperor's delegates deserve respect, no matter if their social standing is inferior to your own. A tribune should learn how to conduct himself in the presence of all officials. It's known as gravitas."

Sergius swallowed. "I know, sir, but—"

"But what?"

"Are we to allow wrongdoing to go unnoticed, sir?"

"Of course not. Part of the army's task is the preservation of law and order."

"Then I respectfully submit, sir, that I was correct in the performance of my duty."

Suetonius spoke for the first time. "The procurator is not a commoner or a slave, Tribune. He is the appointed official of the emperor. His business is none of yours."

"It is my understanding, sir, that nobody is above the law."

Suetonius spoke through clenched jaws. "His business is none of yours. *Is that clear?*"

"Yes, sir," Sergius mumbled.

"If you see evidence of misdoing in high office, report it to your legate or to myself. We will handle it. Not you. Not your dog."

"Understood, sir."

"There will be no repetition of such an incident."

"No, sir."

Suetonius gestured. Marcianus said, "Dismissed. Await my decision outside."

Sergius saluted. "Thank you, sir."

When the tribune had departed, Suetonius queried, "How do you intend to discipline him?"

Marcianus rested his hands on the table. "I believe his story. I wouldn't put anything past Catus—he's a cesspool of desire wearing an official toga."

"Agreed. I suggested to the emperor that Catus wasn't the man for Britannia, but nothing came of it. I suspect my report was filed somewhere it wouldn't be noticed. What about Lysias?"

Marcianus replied, "As far as I'm concerned, Lysias is guilty only of a breach of etiquette."

"A serious breach."

"Jupiter knows I've wanted to insult Catus myself."

"But you haven't."

"Not yet. And haven't we all experienced youthful exuberance, especially where a woman is concerned?"

Suetonius grunted. "It may have been premature to have assigned him to headquarters staff."

"What can we do, short of sending him home again? His father undoubtedly has senatorial or army connections."

"That's not a consideration," Suetonius stated. "I don't owe his father anything."

"Still, it never hurts to have amicable relationships with those in influential positions. His father is a praetor, after all."

"Sycophancy?" Suetonius spat.

"Common sense." Marcianus waved a hand. "Lysias will mature. And perhaps the experience will do him good."

"I hope so. For his sake."

Marcianus said thoughtfully, "The boy is right, you know."

"Yes. But I haven't the time to play social or political games with the procurator." Suetonius slid a papyrus over to the legate. It bore an

Imperial seal. "This arrived by courier. Orders from the emperor. He confirms my plans. I am commanded to break the power of the Druidae."

Egomas shoved a chunk of bread into his mouth, and followed it with a draught of beer.

Ailidh watched him eat, her own meal lying untouched in front of her.

"Perhaps you should have gone with the soldiers," Egomas said, chewing. "The procurator could be a powerful friend."

Ailidh's fist smacked the table. The tableware rattled. "You'd see me raped by that bloodsucker?"

"Well—"

"I'd take my own life before letting that animal have it."

Egomas swallowed. "It was only a thought."

"You two-faced hypocrite! Roman-hating Egomas complains if I see Sergius, yet when the dogs of soldiers want to take me like a whore to their devil of a master, it's a good idea!"

Egomas sat bolt upright. "Me, two-faced? You're the one that rushed headlong into the arms of their new religion! You dare to call yourself Iceni!"

"I am Iceni!" Ailidh glared.

Egomas sighed. He reached for his beer. "Calm down, Daughter."

"Calm yourself."

"You were right to resist the procurator," Egomas conceded. He leaned back and wiped froth off his stubble. Suddenly he seemed old, as if life had abruptly caught up to him. "The truth, Daughter, is that I don't know how to deal with the Romans."

Ailidh arched her eyebrows. "You take the Romans as customers, not as friends. You cheat them."

"They cheat us," Egomas retorted. "Why shouldn't I return the favor?"

"When they arrived in our land, you welcomed them. I hear no tales of Egomas the warrior."

"I never welcomed them. I tolerated them."

"You've made your home among them."

"I've made my *business* among them," Egomas corrected. "Not my home."

"So?"

Egomas belched. He grimaced and rubbed his belly. "I hate them, yes. I hate their Temple of Claudius. I despise their arrogance, the way they treat us."

"And yet?" Ailidh prompted.

"Are we worse off than before?"

Ailidh folded her hands. "There was trade in dogs, wasn't there?"

"Some. Not as much. And when our tribes were in conflict, who had time to buy hunting dogs? We're more prosperous here than ever."

"You'd sell your soul for gold," Ailidh said.

"If there is right and wrong, who knows?" Egomas countered.

"What if it came down to a choice," Ailidh asked, "between our people and the Romans? Whom would you choose?"

Egomas quaffed beer and reached for more bread.

Ailidh waited, but the dog-seller didn't answer.

After his dressing-down by Marcianus, Sergius returned to his office and attempted to concentrate on the financial figures that Quintus thrust in front of him.

The dressing-down could have been worse. At least that's all it had been—he hadn't been dismissed from the army. To become anybody—a person of stature, like his father—he had to distinguish himself in the military. There was no second option.

He'd had the same worries when he'd first joined the Way. His parent's reaction of polite dismay had been typical of the responses he'd received. So far, his embracing of the Way hadn't led to social or professional repercussions.

Yet.

He didn't make a habit of telling people of his adherence to the new faith, although he made no secret of it if asked. For the most part, those whom he told reacted as Agricola had done: with a shrug of the shoulders.

Sergius shook his head. The Way wasn't the problem; his reaction to Procurator Catus was.

Sergius's knuckles clenched his stylus. He *would* learn gravitas. He refused to be dismissed from the army and forced to make his living as a merchant, a writer, or a tutor, or—God forbid—an actor.

After lunch, he attended a general staff meeting. He left with the implications of that meeting whirling in his head. Despite his successes, Suetonius's ambitions hadn't been tamed. Work lay ahead of the army in Britannia.

By the time Sergius tore himself away from his official duties to walk to the town center, late afternoon had thinned the fog to a gauze.

In the marketplace, the dog-seller's stall was closed. Wooden shutters barred the door and windows.

Sergius spoke to a cosmetician in the adjoining booth. "Have you seen Egomas the dog-seller?"

"No," the woman replied. "Normally he and his daughter are here all day long, but today they never came."

Had something happened? The thought speared through Sergius's mind as he dashed along the narrow streets toward Egomas's rented house. Had an enraged Catus taken revenge on the household of Egomas?

He counted dwellings and hoped he chose correctly. The house appeared unchanged. Sergius pounded on the door, drawing stares from passersby.

Ailidh opened it and halted in the doorway. "Sergius? What's wrong?"

"Thank God you're all right!" He reached for her but didn't complete the motion. Something about her posture dissuaded him. "When I saw the stall closed, I wondered if Catus . . ."

"Oh," she stiffened. "Egomas has an upset stomach, so we didn't open. He doesn't trust me to manage the stall by myself." Her expression serious, she added, "Besides, we'll be leaving Camulodunum soon anyway."

"Leaving? So soon?"

"Winter's coming. Nobody buys dogs in winter. You've been our only recent customer. So we're returning home, to our place outside the tribal center. It not far, only a few miles."

"But—"

"In the spring, we'll return to Camulodunum."

"I'm glad in a way," Sergius consented.

She frowned, "Glad that we're leaving?"

"Glad you'll be away from that lecher Catus," he clarified. "I'm leaving, as well. Suetonius has ordered me to Viroconium, where the *Gemina* is stationed."

"You?"

"Not *just* me. Marcianus is taking fresh troops to join the legion." At her inquiring glance he said, "I don't know the specifics."

Ailidh consoled, "It's only for the winter, I suppose."

"A long winter." After an uncomfortable pause, he suggested, "We can write."

"Possibly."

Sergius added, "Couriers will be coming to Camulodunum regularly. For a few extra sestercii, one would deliver a personal letter to the countryside and bring back a reply. I'll worry about you."

"What for? I'll be among my people. It's only the Romans I have cause to fear."

The sudden surge of emotion in her voice startled him. Sergius took a step back. "Ailidh—"

"If only you weren't Roman, Sergius."

He spread his hands. "You can't punish me for what that swine Catus did. We're not all like him. I know what happened last night was upsetting—"

"Upsetting?" Her eyes dilated. She stabbed a finger to his chest. "Is that what you call it? In case you hadn't noticed, Sergius Lysias, I'm not one of your Roman women! *We* don't appreciate being taken against our will to satisfy a man's pleasure!"

Her chest heaved. "The Romans bring civilization," she mocked. "You certainly don't bring morality! You know nothing about standards!"

"I do!" Sergius flared, "And I wasn't thrilled about having Marcianus chew my head off because I told Catus exactly what I thought of him!" He took a deep breath. "Look, Ailidh, I'm Roman. You're Briton. We can't help that, any more than we can alter the fact that I'm a man and you're a woman."

She calmed. "I know, Sergius, but . . . right now, I'm confused. I don't know what to do. I like being with you, but . . . I feel as if I'm betraying my people. Are there good Romans? I don't know. Besides, there's—"

She broke off.

"There's what?"

She shook her head.

"Egomas?"

"No. Don't ask me, Sergius."

"What happened to being one in Christ?"

"It doesn't seem practical at the moment."

"But—"

"Don't push me, Sergius. Not now. Not ever."

She turned and entered the house. The door banged shut behind her, leaving Sergius staring at the knotted wooden planks.

"What's the matter?" Veturius asked that evening, when he entered Sergius's living quarters on the pretext of looking for a missing gaming piece. "You look like I felt on ship. Does the course of love run roughly?"

Sergius tightened his fingers around the ivory stylus with which he'd been figuring accounts on a wax tablet. He reversed the stylus, and with the opposite end, broad and flat, erased the figures.

He waved a hand to the scribe who sat taking his dictation. "Leave me."

When the scribe had disappeared, he replied, "Run roughly? I don't think it runs at all."

Veturius leaned against the edge of the table. "Tell me."

Sergius rubbed his eyes. "Last night really upset Ailidh. She doesn't want anything to do with Romans—including me."

"It's hard to blame her," Veturius reasoned.

"You'd think I was the villain."

"That bad?"

"Maybe worse. I don't understand her."

"She's a woman. You're not supposed to."

"A lot of help that is." Sergius pulled a rueful face. "I thought you were my friend."

"After the way Catus's men treated her, we must appear as a pretty poor lot."

"Yes, well . . ."

"Well what? The Britons haven't had centuries—or decades, even—to become used to our ways like the Greeks or Syrians or Illyrians."

"Are you suggesting Ailidh should smile and let Catus have his way with her?"

Veturius shrugged, "That's how it goes."

"It shouldn't have to," Sergius declared.

"Claudius's ghost, this 'Way' of yours has given you some strange ideas! I'm saying that you can't expect life to run smoothly all the time. There are bound to be bumps in the road."

"I've heard enough philosophizing from Agricola," Sergius scowled. "It's a good thing Cerialis is taking you to join your legion. I can't abide listening to the two of you anymore."

"There's no need to be insulting." Veturius jumped up. "If that's the way you feel, I'll take myself in search of finer pleasures. And something to drink."

He hesitated at the door. "It's too bad, though. She's very good-looking."

Sergius picked up his stylus and returned to his figures.

"These things happen," Veturius continued. "But at least there's hope. If there's one pretty woman in Britannia, there's bound to be more."

Veturius remained with his hand on the door. "Bath tonight? It will help take your mind off your troubles."

"I don't—"

"We won't have a chance on the march."

"All right," Sergius accepted. Perhaps a lingering soak would help. He knew it certainly wouldn't hurt. "I'll meet you at the bathhouse in an hour. I should be finished by then."

"Great."

"Send the scribe back in, would you?"

SEVEN

The succeeding days whizzed by in a blur of activity. The army could move quickly in an emergency; otherwise, transfers from the capital to the legionary forts and fortresses scattered throughout Britannia were performed in an unhurried, orderly manner. Troop dispositions, accounts, weapons and armor, supply invoices, horses, and every last item had to be meticulously registered and documented.

Roman order was one of the defining qualities of their civilization, Sergius thought, one of the factors that distinguished them from the barbarians. But it made for hard work.

The magnitude of his tasks helped distract Sergius's mind from fretting about Ailidh, except at night. Then, his thoughts roamed far and wide, to the detriment of sleep.

He told himself not to worry, that she'd come around, and even, in a Veturian moment, that she was only one girl among many. But he couldn't bring himself to believe the hollow words.

Working late into the evenings prohibited him from attending Paullus's meetings. But one day, in the hopes of receiving solace, he visited Genialis, the silversmith.

Genialis spread his empty hands. "I'm sorry, Tribune, but Paullus is no longer here."

"Is he staying somewhere else?"

"Gone to Londinium, he said."

"I hadn't heard—"

"He announced it at a meeting."

That was that. Sergius couldn't saddle horse and ride to Londinium for the apostle's advice.

Twice he called at Egomas's house, only to have the neighbor woman tell him, with a patience that sounded strained, that Ailidh couldn't be disturbed.

To come so close and yet be turned back at the door made his heart burn even more fiercely. So he did what he could: he prayed. But if there was an answer, he didn't hear it, and he ended his prayer times as unenlightened as when he started.

But if God didn't seem to move, the army did.

Legate Petilius Cerialis departed Camulodunum first, taking his staff, a wing of cavalry, and a cohort of auxiliary troops to rejoin the Ninth Legion at its two forts, one west of Iceni lands and the other farther north, not far from Lindum, closer to the Brigantes and the Parisi.

On the day of departure, Sergius and Veturius stood in the shelter of a doorway to avoid a chill rain that sleeted in fits from banks of sullen gray clouds to run down slick cobblestones into the drains. Smells of wet horse and wet wool mingled as the troops assembled into marching order.

"Aaa-choo!" Veturius sneezed. He wiped his nose on his cloak. "Aesculapius! Did I sacrifice to him? And Carna? Oh gods, if I forgot them, and die of illness—"

"You'll be fine," Sergius reassured.

"And Febris!" Veturius touched his brow. "Am I hot? Great gods, if I have a fever . . ."

Sergius felt his friend's forehead. "Cool. You're fine. You'll be well in no time."

"I hope so. I don't want to be wiping my nose all winter long."

Sergius gripped Veturius's forearm. "Take care of yourself, Gaius."

"And you," Veturius returned the gesture, then peered into the rain, "wherever on this forsaken island luck dumps you."

"I'll pray that God keeps you safe."

"Thanks. Every one helps."

"There is only one. Some day I'll get you to realize that."

"Until then," Veturius said, "there's safety in numbers."

"You'll be stationed closer to Camulodunum than I will," Sergius began. "Ailidh lives somewhere near the tribal center—"

"If I get a chance, I'll check on her for you."

Sergius grinned. "Just look, mind. Or you'll have me as well as the Britons on your tail."

Veturius grinned back. "Trust me." He abandoned the protection of the doorway and swung himself into his saddle. "I expect I'll have a quieter winter than you. You'll be too busy wondering if the Deceangli will launch a surprise attack to worry about Ailidh."

"No chance of that, Gaius."

Veturius wheeled his horse to take up his position in the cavalcade. "See you in the spring, my friend!"

"In the spring, Gaius!"

"Aaaa-*choo!*"

Sergius remained in the doorway until the line of troops clattered into the rain, away from the barracks and toward Camulodunum's north gate. Then he returned to the relative warmth of his office, and by the light of a pair of lamps resumed work.

Not long after, Agricola departed to join the *Augusta* in Isca, Titus went to the *Valeria* in Glevum, and the military presence in Camulodunum seemed scant. And with Paullus gone to Londinium, and Ailidh not speaking to him, the city seemed to have lost all its life. Only Cara remained to give Sergius company.

He plunged deeper into work.

One afternoon, Quintus announced, "A visitor to see you, sir."

Sergius caught the note of query in his beneficiarius's voice. His aide's eyes glimmered with puzzlement.

"Who is it?"

"A Greek, sir. An 'Aristarchus.'"

"Send him in."

The aide retreated to the door and ushered in the tall figure of Paullus's traveling companion.

"Greetings," Sergius said, standing to welcome the Greek. "I hadn't thought to see you again."

"Why not?" Aristarchus replied.

"I'd heard that Paullus had left for Londinium."

"Paullus and Lucanus. I've remained here a little longer. You haven't been to any meetings."

Sergius shook his head. "I've been too busy." He gestured, "May I offer you a drink?"

"Please." Aristarchus settled himself on a stool. He withdrew a scroll from the sleeve of his robe and laid it on the table.

Sergius called for his orderly to bring flagons of water and wine, and goblets. The man returned promptly.

Sergius diluted his wine—even Veturius on his most dissolute days had more character than to drink his wine undiluted; he noticed that Aristarchus drank his weaker yet.

"Is Paullus well?" Sergius inquired.

"Yes. For some reason, he felt an urgency to proclaim the gospel in Londinium."

"Why was that?"

Aristarchus set his goblet down. "We've been in Camulodunum for several weeks. Paullus gets these urges on occasion. The rest of us have found it useless to argue with him."

"I expect that Paullus's mind, once set, is hard to budge."

"To put it mildly. So far, he hasn't expressed a desire to visit the more remote parts of Britannia, although he did receive an invitation from Queen Cartimandua."

"The Brigantes are a client kingdom," Sergius commented. "I believe they're generally pro-Roman."

"Probably more so than the Iceni," Aristarchus added.

"Has Paullus preached to them?"

"No. King Prasutagus is old and sick, or he might have welcomed us. But his wife, Queen Boudicca, would have nothing to do with us— another delegation of Roman bandits, she called us. We were fortunate to escape with skins intact."

Sergius furrowed his brow. "A strange attitude for a client kingdom, surely?"

Aristarchus gave a lift of his shoulders. "I wouldn't know. If the Spirit wills us to visit Cartimandua, we'll go. But otherwise, Londinium calls." Aristarchus indicated the scroll. "He asked me to bring you this."

"Paullus did?" Sergius reached for the papyrus.

"Lucanus stayed up late to write it before he left."

Sergius opened the roll, the black ink clean and fresh, and read. "Paul, an apostle called to faithfulness, with Lucanus and Aristarchus, to our friend Sergius Lysias, grace and peace." He looked to the Greek. "I don't understand."

Aristarchus said, "Paullus thought it might help you."

Sergius traced a finger along the lines of script. "Why did he feel it necessary to write to me? I'm a soldier, not an influential person."

Aristarchus's expression was unreadable by Sergius. "Paullus insisted you have it."

"I'm grateful," Sergius said, "even if confused."

"Undoubtedly all will become plain," the Greek replied. He rose. "I must go."

"I'll read the remainder later," Sergius promised. He rolled up the papyrus. "Thank you for bringing it."

"It's the least I could do. You were kind enough to extract me from an awkward situation."

Sergius indicated the roll. "I'll take good care of it."

"God be with you," Aristarchus blessed.

"And with you."

With a rustle of robes, the tall Greek departed.

Sergius handled the papyrus. Paullus usually wrote his letters to churches, like the church in Rome—Sergius had heard that letter read out loud—to Philippi and Colossae, Thessalonica and Ephesus. Why would he bother with him?

He opened the scroll again and studied Paullus's message in Lucanus' neat letters.

> I write to encourage your faith—stand fast! Rather, I want us to be encouraged by one another's faith—I by yours and you by mine. Think of the spiritual gifts you have received and stir them up within you. I call to your remembrance that true faith results in the manifestation of the Spirit—in love, joy, peace, patience, kindness, goodness, fidelity, gentleness, and self-control. These gifts will strengthen your spirit; against such things there is no law.
>
> For the time will come when, as the Scripture says, "The Lord expected justice, but saw bloodshed; righteousness, but heard a cry."
>
> Since the Spirit is the source of your life, let the Spirit also direct its course.

Scrawled across the bottom in large, shaky letters that contrasted sharply with Lucanus's flawless script was the signature, "Paullus."

Justice and bloodshed? Righteousness and cries? The Spirit directing the course of his life?

It sounded good, but . . . Sergius shook his head in wonderment. What help was it? At the moment he could hardly make sense of the conflicting messages he had received. Paullus only added to his confusion.

Cara whined at the door.

"Do you need to go out?" Sergius asked her, setting down a scroll that he read by lamplight. He attached the dog's chain to her collar.

Outside, the wind blew damp and chill along dark streets: a clean wind, yet hinting at further rain before the night was over. Sergius pulled his cloak tight.

Soldiers on guard duty outside the principia and praetorium talked in low tones. He caught the tail end of a joke about Agrippina—"She said, 'No, I'd rather swim!'"—that had made the rounds in Aquileia months ago. Men laughed. Faint thwacks and scrapes indicated counters being moved across a game board.

Sentries weren't supposed to play games on duty, but in a place like Camulodunum, far removed from combat zones, centurions frequently turned blind eyes to such minor infractions. Better the men play games than turn to drink, or sleep, or—worse yet—desert their posts for women.

He walked away from the principia, allowing Cara to lead him.

He glimpsed a movement in the night. He tensed, hand seeking the hilt of his gladius.

"Sergius!" A cloaked woman emerged from shadows to stand in a puddle of light.

"Ailidh?" he gasped. "What are you—"

"I was watching your house."

"Why didn't you knock?"

"I didn't know if you were here or if you'd left."

"I thought Cara needed to relieve herself. But maybe she sensed you." He touched her arm. "You shouldn't be out alone."

"Egomas forbade me to see you, but I had to. I couldn't let us part without saying good-bye. I was wrong to shut you out."

"You were hurt."

"I still am. And angry. But I shouldn't have included you in my anger."

Sergius pointed toward his quarters. "Do you want to come in? I don't have much to offer you. Everything portable is packed."

"No. I can't be out long. Walk me home."

"Gladly."

They began to walk, slowly, along the street. Cara's toenails clicked on the cobbles.

"Brina told me you stopped by," Ailidh said. "Egomas didn't want me to know."

Sergius snorted.

"When do you leave?"

"In the morning." Sergius reached for her hand and squeezed. Her fingers were warm and soft in his.

"I wish it was Catus that was leaving." Ailidh shivered. They crossed another street, and Ailidh confessed, "I'm afraid, Sergius."

"Afraid? Of what? Catus?"

"Not him. I don't know what. It's just that . . . Camulodunum doesn't feel right. It looks peaceful enough, on the surface, but underneath . . . "

"It seems all right to me."

"You haven't been here long. The ways of the Celtae are strong, Sergius. A people can't change overnight. Camulodunum looks Roman, but the people in the lands aren't."

"I don't follow you."

Ailidh gestured with her free hand into the night. "Imagine you're Trinovante, living in the tribal center. You look out of your hut and not two miles away you see Camulodunum. Look at it with our eyes, Sergius. What do you see?" Her gaze challenged him.

He groped for words, for insight. "A city?" he guessed, saying the only thing that came to mind.

Her head bobbed. "A city. A shining white city that disfigures the hills and mocks the green of the forests. An alien concept. Ways and people that are different."

Sergius thought of Italia, where cities were the norm. The Empire was filled with cities: Athens, Corinth, Jerusalem, and many more. Filled too, with different peoples and foreign ideas, with multiple gods and innumerable philosophies.

He said as much.

Ailidh sighed. "You really don't understand."

"How can I? I look at Camulodunum and see a new city. I see the future. But to you . . . it's something else entirely."

"Some of our leaders are half Roman already. But the others aren't."

"Do you want to leave?" Sergius asked.

Her face clouded.

"Must you stay with Egomas?"

For a long moment, she didn't speak.

"What's wrong, Ailidh?"

In a low voice, she explained, "I have no relations. A single woman has no place. Where could I go?"

The words slipped out of their own accord, "With me."

"With you?" she gasped, and Sergius thought he'd gone too far.

Then she laughed and put a finger to his lips before he could answer. "Your heart outraces your common sense. Besides, the Trinovantes and the Iceni are my people. I can't leave them, Sergius. Don't ask me to."

"I'm sorry," he muttered, feeling the heat burn in his cheeks. "Here I am, running my mouth like Veturius."

"Besides, you haven't even told me your household name," Ailidh chuckled.

Sergius blinked. "I never use it. I forget I have one. It's Marcus."

"Give it time, Marcus Sergius Lysias. And if God wills . . . "

She let the sentence hang.

He gently swung her face around to him.

Her eyes twinkled like twin stars. Her hair fell in moonlit folds onto her shoulders. Her full lips were slightly parted. He caressed the back of her head, then slid his hand onto her back and urged her forward.

For a long moment, she rested against him, and he felt the beating of her heart echoing the sudden pounding of his own. With his lips, he searched for hers. Just when they seemed ready to touch, she pushed him gently away.

"No," she said.

"Why not?" he asked, again conscious of something that came between them, of a resistance that he couldn't place.

"Fight your battles, Marcus, as I shall fight mine. The winter will pass." She pressed something into his palm. "An apology for rudeness."

Sergius hadn't noticed until now that they stood outside Egomas's house.

Ailidh bent to ruffle Cara's head. "Take care of him," she told her.

Ailidh slipped away. Her lips framed a single word, *cara*. The light from the house illuminated her figure briefly, then she stepped inside and closed the door.

Sergius held up the item she had given him, trying to identify it in the moonlight.

It gleamed golden, though not gold but bronze, with red enamel inlay for eyes, tongue, and ears. He pinned the brooch, a dog's head, onto his cloak.

"I'll be back, Cara," he whispered. "I promise."

Ailidh stood next to Egomas as the Roman troops left the city, following the main street away from the garrison. Rank on rank they passed, infantry cohorts, cavalry, auxiliaries, supply train. Both legionaries and pack animals bore heavy burdens.

"Not a moment too soon," the dog-seller said. "Good riddance."

Ailidh studied the ranks of mounted officers. She waved, and one of the men raised a hand in salute and followed it with a smile. He pointed to an ornament on his cloak.

"I don't know what you see in him," Egomas snorted. "All fine robes and wind."

Ailidh ignored the comment.

"Besides," the dog-seller continued, "he'll probably be leaving Britannia before you know it. Back to some wealthy girl in Rome, no doubt."

Ailidh watched the troops march around a street corner. "I thought you were beginning to like Sergius."

"He could be worse, as Romans go." Egomas agreed grudgingly. He turned his back on the procession. "Even if it hasn't crossed his thick mind to wonder why a woman of your age isn't married."

Ailidh pressed her lips together.

"By all that's holy, girl," Egomas exclaimed, "you could have had your choice of any man! Young warriors of the Iceni or Trinovantes would have fought to wed Cathair's daughter!"

He breathed heavily, hands balled. "And now look at you—heading past your prime, and your chances of finding a husband as slim as those accursed foreigners ever leaving our land!"

"Uncle—"

"You've thrown your life away once already, and now you'd do it again for some iron-plated soldier boy?"

"What does it matter to you?" Ailidh snapped. "You've done nothing but fling my life into my face every chance you get."

"Because I hate to see it go for nothing!" Egomas yelled.

Ailidh opened her mouth and closed it again. Quietly, she said, "It won't."

Egomas calmed. "Perhaps Lovernios would change his mind—"

"I have no interest in my cousin. Nor he for me."

Egomas humphed. "You're a woman."

"How perceptive of you."

Egomas's bushy brows pulled together. "Women don't know what they want."

"They need a man to tell them, I suppose."

Egomas nodded, "Exactly."

Ailidh turned away. "Good. I'll write Sergius and ask him."

Sergius's heart warmed as he saw Ailidh's slender, shapely figure standing alongside Egomas. The thickset dog-seller glared, the movement transforming his splayed-out nose into a regular hog snout, but Ailidh's smile as she waved was worth a thousand of the old man's fierce looks.

He waved back and tried to fix her face in his memory: her reddish hair that seemed almost golden when the light caught it properly, her sparkling green eyes and fair complexion, her narrow, turned-up nose dotted with freckles. She looked so different from the dumpy, spotted girls he'd known in Rome.

Veturius would tell him that he was being overly romantic, that Roman girls were just fine, thank you, and that he should listen to his friend Veturius who had *far* more experience.

"If they're so nice, why do you want to go to Syria?" he'd retort, and Veturius would make a fatuous comment about variety.

The bystanders hid Ailidh from view.

And then, at the entrance of an alley up ahead, he spotted a robed figure with upraised hand. The Druid Lovernios? Sergius squinted. The figure mouthed words, and an upraised right hand swept to encompass the Roman ranks. Distance rendered the words inaudible, and Sergius couldn't understand the Briton tongue well enough anyway. But the Druid certainly wasn't blessing the troops. More likely he was calling down curses from some hideous Celtae divinity.

A tremble of apprehension churned in Sergius's stomach.

The Druid courted danger to show himself in daylight. If the urban cohort encountered him, they'd make short work of him, Celtae gods or no.

And then the cavalcade drew level with the alley. It wasn't Lovernios at all but a heavyset woman waving a farewell to a son or husband in the auxiliary, perhaps.

Sergius sighed in relief and chided himself for his anxiety.

The cavalcade wound through the streets, narrowed to squeeze through the city's western gate, and passed through the low mounds—all that remained of the defenses of the one-time legionary fortress.

The history of Roman progress in Britannia was like a pebble thrown into a pool. The Roman rock had landed in the southeast. From there, the Occupation rippled out. Soldiers built, used, and then abandoned forts in favor of new installations constructed as the armies penetrated deeper into Britannia.

Augusta the Second had bludgeoned a path into the southwest, confronting the Domnunii. *Valeria the Twentieth* had fought westward from Camulodunum all the way to Glevum in Dobunni and Silure land. Sergius's own *Gemina the Fourteenth* had aimed northwest from Mancetter to Letocetum and now to Viroconium in the heart of the Cornovii. *Hispana the Ninth* secured the north against the Coritani, the Brigantes, and the Iceni.

The troops entered open country and assumed routine marching order, the same order a full legion would take. Auxiliaries led, followed by legionaries. The cavalry guarded the wings, and the baggage train brought up the rear. There weren't many legionaries, no more than a cohort's worth of replacements to replenish ranks thinned by retirement and battle loss.

Either Suetonius or Marcianus ordered a standard marching pace of twenty miles per day, which translated into nine or ten days until they reached Viroconium. There was no need to push the heavily laden legionaries. First they'd make Verulamium and then pick up the main road heading northwest to the frontier.

Sergius swayed easily in the saddle, enjoying the slow pace, glad he didn't have to carry a battle kit. All he bore was his armor, sword, wineskin, rations for the day, and roll on his saddle, which contained the letter from Paullus and his few books. Cara ran alongside, never straying far. But despite the dog's presence, Sergius felt alone, missing Veturius's empty-headed chatter and Agricola's philosophizing.

He'd even have settled for Titus's bloodthirsty ramblings.

And Ailidh would soon leave Camulodunum for her tribal home. Once away from the Romanizing influence of the city, among her people, would she still remember this single Roman soldier?

Love, patience, fidelity, self-control.

He repeated the words to himself and raised his hand to touch the dog's-head brooch. Suetonius and Marcianus wore their battle honors proudly; the centurions jangled with phalerae and armillae.

But he wouldn't trade the dog's head for them.

Cara.

From the safety of a thicket, Lovernios watched the Roman troops leave Camulodunum. His attention focused on a young man who rode stiffly erect.

This young man puzzled him. He hated the man for who he was, although he had done no wrong. . . .

It wasn't right to hate so. The way of the Druid taught forgiveness. Lovernios was a judge. He knew how to separate his emotions from his duties. He knew better than to let passion sway his rationality.

Was it because of Ailidh? Was it because this man had caught Ailidh's affection in a manner that Lovernios hadn't?

Or was it because this man shared Ailidh's belief in the new religion? What kind of a religion was it that could snatch a young woman of Ailidh's intelligence from the traditions of her people?

Lovernios fingered his short beard.

Why did this young man puzzle him?

Why did it seem that in some strange fashion, akin to his dream, that this man's destiny and his own were intertwined?

Lovernios turned aside from the spectacle of Roman military might. He strode briskly down a forest path.

His time among the Trinovantes completed, he had business next with the Iceni, his own people.

In the back of his mind, an idea tingled—an idea that filled him with loathing. Still, the idea might save his people. Lovernios thrust aside a spasm of revulsion. He could set aside his emotions. For the good of his people, he'd have to.

He paused beside an oak and laid his hand on the rough bark. He stood for a long moment with his eyes closed.

Then he walked on.

PART TWO

Winter, 802–803 A.U.C.
(A.D. 59–60)

EIGHT

Snow blanketed the hills—a dry, flaky powder that muffled the clop of the cavalry horses' hooves on the stone-hard ground. The exhalations of men and horses mingled; white plumes hung motionless in the air before dissipating. Snow had fallen intermittently through the early part of the winter, but the small accumulations had melted in a day or so or were washed away by the frequent rains. But this mid-December snowfall, protected from melting by cold days and even colder cloudless nights, promised to remain.

Today, it was no disgrace to wear bracae. Even the centurions and officers had overcome their reservations regarding the feminine habit and donned knee-length leather trousers and wool socks. Ordinary men stuffed their boots with wool or fur whenever they ventured outside the barracks.

Hands froze to exposed metal, and Cara's paw pads cracked and bled. To the wolfhound's evident disgust, Sergius had confined her in the marginally warmer stables to heal.

Sergius shaded his eyes against snow's glare and followed the dips and contours of the horizon. Nothing. No sign of human life. Not even thin columns of smoke to show where a few families of Britons huddled for warmth in their conical huts. The clear breeze brought no scent of fire, only the sweaty smell of his men and horses.

His ears detected only the breathing of men and horses, the clink of armor and jingle of bronze horse-trappings, and the wind gusting over the hills. And on a day so crisp and clear, sound carried well.

Surely the few troopers of his patrol weren't the only living creatures in a wasteland of snow and ice.

He knew otherwise.

From out of this desolation had roared a Briton raiding party, sword and spear blades hungry for Roman blood. Maybe they lurked over the next snowy ridge.

"Do you see anything?" Sergius asked the troop commander.

The decurio shook his head, his hands wedged under his thighs to warm them against his mount. "Nothing, sir. If any Britons are about, they're invisible."

Sergius took a last look around.

To the southwest, the river Deva glistened gray and somber, as a snake undulating along the valleys. *Gemina's* fortress lay hidden behind a fold in the wrinkled countryside. Some twenty miles south, a detachment of the *Valeria* occupied a secondary fort. Legions normally camped separately because otherwise rivalries developed between men of different legions—rivalries that occasionally erupted into conflict.

Sergius beckoned to the troop commander, "Let's go a little farther."

The decurio waved to the troop of cavalry, "Forward."

Sergius led the column. The troopers followed single file. As he rode, he thought of what the winter had brought so far.

Legio XIV *Gemina* had spent little time at Viroconium. Barely a month after Sergius arrived, the entire legion excepting a cohort left to maintain the fortress had marched west to Deva. There, in the territory of the Deceangli, advance parties of surveyors and engineers had laid out the plan for a new fortress.

Inactivity made men restless, and winter, when campaigning ground to a halt, was the most inactive season of all. But at Deva, for a few weeks, activity became the norm. While Sergius and the officers supervised, the soldiers worked. Legionaries were more than mere fighting men—they built roads, constructed walls, and now, became carpenters.

Deva's new fortress hummed with life and resounded with sound: the thump of ramparts being raised from earth gouged from defensive ditches; the crack and scrape of wood being split and trimmed; nails being hammered into buildings and timber palisades. The fortress boasted the principia and praetorium first, then barracks replaced the legionaries' leather tents.

Before the fall rains changed to snow, *Gemina* completed the new fortress: defenses, headquarters buildings, houses for the tribunes and centurions, barracks, stables, workshops, storehouses, and bathhouse.

The speed at which it happened filled Sergius with amazement. The coordinated efforts of five thousand legionaries brought order out of confusion. In the army, every man knew his place and his task.

When construction finished and the true inactivity of winter began, Sergius had requested and received permission to take out patrols of cavalry. Indeed, Gellius Marcianus seemed pleased when Sergius had presented the idea.

"You would rather ride in the cold than sit in your house working—or gambling or reading?"

Sergius nodded, "Yes, sir, I would."

"The centurions will grumble about a tribune performing field duties."

"Undoubtedly, sir."

"And the junior tribunes will complain about a senior man usurping a place with the auxiliary."

"That too, sir."

Marcianus had thumbed his lip. "I'll speak to the cavalry prefect. If he doesn't object, then permission is granted."

"Thank you, sir."

Sextus Didius Pertinax, prefect of the First Thracian Cavalry, had raised no objections. A handsome native of Cannae, Pertinax himself had been an equestrian rank tribune only a few years past. Sergius had felt an immediate affinity for the open-faced, quiet-voiced prefect.

"Bring the men back safely, Lysias," Pertinax had said. "That's all I ask."

Now, Sergius reined his horse and raised his hand. The troop paused on a knoll.

"They're out here somewhere," he remarked to the troop commander. "They have to be."

"Hiding, no doubt. Biding their time."

The previous day, a swarm of Britons had emerged from the forest and attacked a working party of tree cutters. Three legionaries and twice as many Britons had died before a sortie responding to the shouts of battle dispersed the raiders. One of *Gemina*'s junior tribunes, cut by a sword in the arm, lay feverish in the fortress hospital. Sergius had visited the hospital earlier and overheard the medical officer discussing amputation with his assistant. He hadn't lingered.

Pertinax's response had been to send out numerous patrols to scour the countryside for the raiders.

The Britons wouldn't dare attack the fortress itself. They knew better than to assault a fortified position. But then, experienced soldiers claimed, Britons didn't usually attack at all in winter.

Sergius wondered what the Britons hoped to achieve. Small raids would present only temporary inconveniences. He could only assume that desperation because of the planned Roman assault in the spring drove the Britons to unusual action.

The spring assault—it had to be.

Two weeks earlier, the governor had arrived at the newly completed fortress. At a staff meeting, Suetonius had briefed the senior officers: Marcianus, Pertinax, *Gemina*'s Chief Centurion Helvius Adventus, the camp prefect, Sergius, and the junior tribunes.

"I expect you're wondering about the move to Deva," Suetonius began. "We'll punish the Deceangli and the Ordovices further, yes. But our main purpose is to destroy the Druidae and their sanctuary on Mona."

A murmur ran through the room. Sergius noticed the surprised expressions. Marcianus alone seemed unfazed, but he'd undoubtedly been included in Suetonius's deliberations long before.

"Destroy the Druidae?" someone asked.

"Completely and permanently," Suetonius replied. "For too long they've fomented discontent, provided a haven for malcontents, organized opposition to Rome, and threatened the borders of the province. That opposition is to be eradicated."

The iron-hard tone of his voice left no room for argument.

"Mona is an island, sir," a tribune offered.

Suetonius glared. "Of course it is. We'll need boats."

"The *Classis Britannica,* sir?" The question came from Helvius Adventus, the chief centurion.

Suetonius shook his head. "No. We won't request the fleet from Gesoriacum. Spring weather's too unpredictable. A storm could disrupt the offensive," his gaze seemed to linger on Sergius, "as Julius Caesar discovered."

Not once, but twice, Caesar's fleet had been heavily damaged by storms. To bring the entire *Classis Britannicus* merely to cross a narrow strait seemed a risky undertaking.

Suetonius folded his arms across his chest. "The Menai Strait is barely a fifth of a mile wide. We'll use flat-bottomed boats for the infantry. The cavalry can ford or swim."

"Where will the boats come from, sir?" Adventus asked.

Sergius shook his head at the recollection of the meeting. The Menai crossing presented the army with a problem. It was unlikely they'd be able to commandeer enough boats from the Britons to accommodate nearly ten thousand soldiers. That left Suetonius with two options: either to build boats at Deva and float them the seventy miles to traverse a strait that one could shoot an arrow across; alternatively to camp and build boats across from Mona itself, risking attack from the Druidae stronghold.

Suetonius's third option had startled him when Suetonius mentioned it. But in retrospect, it was simplicity itself.

A smile had flitted across the commander's thin lips. "We'll appropriate whatever craft we can find. The rest will be assembled on the spot from prepared lumber. This winter, the men will become boatbuilders."

Ready-made, disassembled boats! Sergius marveled at the governor's innovation.

In the vicinity of the Deva fortress, trees could be felled and boat parts prepared in safety. Carting the sections from Deva to the shore opposite Mona would present no problems for the pack animals—one item that Britain offered in plenty was horses. With a day or two to assemble the boats, the invasion fleet would be ready.

Could this Briton raiding mean they learned Suetonius's plan?

Sergius wasn't aware he'd spoken out loud until the troop commander answered, "I don't see how, sir."

"Neither do I." The Britons couldn't have divined Suetonius's plans in detail. But from the army's operations over the previous two seasons, they must have surmised that Mona would be the next target.

The patrol resumed its course along the edge of a forest. Wary eyes peered into the dark trees. The patrol wound along the course of the river. Sergius tried to imagine what Mona looked like: probably dark, gloomy, and forested. The sacred island of the Druidae seemed so remote from civilized Camulodunum. And thinking of the one Druid he had met, Lovernios, sent a chill down his spine. No matter what Ailidh said, the Druid gave him the shivers.

He could also imagine the misgivings the other tribunes, and the legionaries, harbored. Fighting barbarians was acceptable—but to take on their gods?

A crackling in the snow startled him. His horse reared as he spun around. His stiff fingers tore free from his reins, and he was airborne. The ground jolted him, graying his vision and snapping his neck.

He blinked to restore his sight.

He scrambled to his hands and knees in time to see a hare, breaking out of concealment, bound away in panic.

He climbed to his feet and brushed snow off his breastplate and kilt.

"Are you all right, sir?" The decurio held out Sergius's reins.

Sergius rubbed his neck. "I'll be stiff tomorrow." He remounted. "The hare caught me by surprise."

The troop commander's expression appeared solemn.

"What's the matter?" Sergius asked. "It was only a rabbit."

The decurio shook his head. "A bad augury, sir. The hare is sacred to the Druidae."

The troopers eyed the coppice as if a band of Druidae lurked behind the sheltering trunks.

The hare had vanished. "Too bad I missed it," Sergius said. "It would have made a good lunch."

Several cavalrymen chuckled, but the laughter sounded forced.

"Look!" a man cried.

A black shape plummeted from the sky. It disappeared beyond a ridge. A cut-short scream pierced the day. In a moment the black shape rose again; the limp form of the hare dangled from an eagle's talons.

"There," Sergius pointed. "The Roman eagle devours the Briton hare. What better augury could you ask for? Come on, let's find where the raiders are lurking."

The cavalrymen grinned. Sergius caught murmurs of agreement. A favorable augury indeed!

"Onward!" the decurio shouted, and the horses' trappings jingled as the troop resumed its patrol.

The troop, chilled and empty-handed, returned to the fortress as dusk draped long shadows over the sullen landscape. Wind and blown snow had obliterated whatever traces yesterday's raiders had left.

"It's as if they emerged from nowhere and returned to the same place," Sergius reported to Marcianus and Pertinax.

"No one else found traces either," the legate said. "Try again in the morning."

Sergius left the legate's office in search of a bath and a meal.

As he made his way to the bathhouse, a quartet of men scurried to intercept him. Sergius glanced around but saw no avenue of escape. The legion's official seers—augurs and haruspices—had him surrounded.

Sergius scowled. The cavalrymen had wasted no time spreading the tale of the eagle and hare.

No legion ventured into the field without its corps of diviners, its priests, and its sacred chickens. He should have expected this reception.

"Is it true, Tribune?" an augur asked. "Did you see an auspica oblativa?"

An unrequested portent was the most potent kind.

Sergius shrugged. "I saw an eagle hunting its meal. What you choose to make of that is up to you."

"A hare. It was a hare?"

"From what I glimpsed, yes."

The soothsayers nodded and whispered. Then they pelted him with more questions. Was it truly a hare and not a rabbit? Definitely an eagle made the kill and not a hawk? Had the eagle cried as it made its kill? How did the hare hang from the talons? Had he seen any other birds? Which direction did the eagle fly?

Sergius answered as quickly and concisely as he could. He wanted nothing more than to brush off the augurs and their imaginings. But the legionaries—superstitious to a man—wouldn't understand if he refused to answer the seers' questions. Morale should be maintained. Happy, eager soldiers made the best fighters—not men afraid of invoking the anger of the gods.

Finally, his patience frayed. "Enough, already!" he resigned, weary of the interrogation. "I'm cold. Save it for tomorrow." He broke free and escaped to the bathhouse, leaving the augurs chattering among themselves. He had no doubts that the next day the entire legion would know the story.

Prasutagus of the Iceni lay on his bed in his palace in Venta Icenorum, dreaming. Lately, it seemed his only activity. But his thoughts flowed over themselves and tangled around each other so much that he could never tell if he was awake or asleep; thinking coherently, or lost in realms of fantasy.

He'd been remembering the time when he became king of the Iceni, assuming the highest position in the tribe; the time when the Iceni had become a client kingdom of Rome.

In return for allegiance to Rome and the payment of tribute, they'd been allowed to retain their freedom: their laws, their land, their society. The agreement allowed him to become king—subservient, yes, but king nonetheless.

But the cost . . . oh, the cost . . .

The rounded coolness of metal touched his lips. Prasutagus parted them, and the sharp, warming taste of wine flowed into his mouth. He swallowed, and the wine warmed its way to his stomach. He opened his eyes.

A gray form, outlines indistinct but recognizable, emerged from the mists.

"Boudicca."

He tried to raise a hand, but it wouldn't move. He hadn't eaten for days, and his strength had fled.

The end was near. He could feel his life flowing away as wine from a spilled beaker, soaking into the ground. But spilled wine was wasted, whereas his life had run its course. Let others die with regret, he had only one complaint—that he died like an old man.

Oh gods, for one last raid against the Catuvellauni . . .

He lacked strength, but strangely, he realized with a start, his pain had vanished. For once, without the haze of pain, his mind seemed clearer than it had for weeks. Still, it remained attached to his body by the slenderest thread of spider's silk.

"More?" Boudicca asked. Her voice seeped through a roaring in his ears.

"Thank you, no." His breath gurgled in his chest. A cough would clear his lungs, but he lacked even the power for that simple act. "What news?" he whispered.

The bed indented as she sat next to him. "You're always thinking of your kingdom. Rest your mind."

"I must know. I've spent my life for the Iceni."

"Catus raised taxes. He's sent his servants to seize land from those whose debts remain unpaid."

"He's a fool."

"The nobles meet at night in houses and groves to plot rebellion."

"Rebellion?" Prasutagus struggled to rise. The weight of Boudicca's hand resting lightly on his chest restrained him. "They must not!"

"It's all talk. They're too afraid."

He gasped, "Who leads them?"

"Airell among the older; Weylyn for the young men."

Prasutagus waited until his breathing slowed. "They mustn't fight. It's suicide. The Romans are too strong."

"Don't worry." She stroked his forehead.

"No one can defeat them."

"We fought before."

"When Ostorius Scapula tried to disarm us," he said. "We lost."

"More than ten years ago."

He forced his dry lips to move. Boudicca remained in the same position, but somehow she seemed farther away, as if the handbreadth that separated them had curiously lengthened. The roaring in his ears crescendoed. "We were a powerful tribe. But in a single battle the Romans destroyed all who resisted."

She held the goblet to his lips again. "You gained the kingship."

He dipped his tongue into the liquid. "At a price."

His vision darkened. A weight descended upon his chest, and he couldn't push it away. The roaring became a waterfall of sound drowning out all else. He felt himself slipping and tried to touch Boudicca's hair one last time.

The thread snapped.

"Don't fight," he tried to say but didn't know whether his lips framed sound or not.

As if from a great distance, he felt Boudicca kiss his forehead. Then her voice bade, "Farewell, my warrior."

Boudicca left Prasutagus's chamber and leaned against the portico of the house. The midwinter sun gave light but little warmth.

She should have felt grief, but she didn't. Her tears had been shed slowly, at intervals over the long autumn and winter. Now, they were spent.

She'd prepared for this day; its coming lacked power to upset her. Instead, she felt relief. Death finally released Prasutagus from the ignominy of his lingering illness. He'd gone to the otherworld, to live again in health and strength. It was a time to celebrate.

She looked across the expanse of open ground in the center of the village. Two girls raced horses across the brittle yellow grass, riding bareback. Between the houses they rode, around traditional circular huts and the more substantial Roman-type dwellings of the wealthier nobles. Fair red hair and dark cloaks streamed as they urged the horses to gallop.

Two years separated Aife from her younger sister Cinnia, yet they were so alike they could have been twins.

Prasutagus had always desired a son, but when fate denied him, he delighted in his daughters. He had never spoken of his disappointment, though Boudicca knew it existed. Every man wanted a son. Prasutagus was no exception.

And she had tried. She had followed every instruction the Druí physicians issued. She had prayed to Andraste and Epona, to Maedb, and most of all to Bride, for fertility, but after two daughters, her womb had not born again.

She had urged Prasutagus to take another wife—a servant woman, even—but he'd refused.

"Two wives are enough for any man," he'd said.

"One is dead."

"And the daughters of Boudicca are sufficient for me."

The girls leaned the horses into a corner and disappeared from sight.

They were her daughters, yes, but there was much of Prasutagus in them: in hair darker than her own, in carriage, and in facial features. Aife, in particular, inherited her father's carefree expression.

Boudicca sighed. One of Prasutagus's last requests had been that she find a husband for Aife. At fourteen, Aife had reached the age for marriage.

Boudicca rubbed her cheek and flicked away a drop of moisture from the corner of her eye. Aife's marriage would have to be arranged come spring.

Aife had expressed no preferences; she tantalized many, encouraged none—unlike Boudicca.

Boudicca had made it abundantly clear that she wouldn't marry just anyone. Her parents had shrugged their shoulders at their headstrong daughter. She'd remained unmarried until she met a man who would accept her on her terms. She'd waited until a handsome noble named Prasutagus, whose cocky demeanor concealed an inflexible will, challenged her to a horse race and won. He won, but he refused to gloat; he won, but he accepted her as an equal.

The girls reappeared. Cinnia looked toward her, and Boudicca beckoned.

Prasutagus had left the decision to her. She would have to choose carefully so that the royal line of Prasutagus would continue. One of her daughters would bear the son she herself had never conceived.

She shook her head. Prasutagus deserved a hero's death, not a lingering wasting away that stripped the flesh from his bones and left bags of skin hanging where once firm muscles had rippled. But the will that had enabled him to carve a truce with the Romans, to resist when the cause was great, and then to rebuild his shattered tribe had not permitted him to die easily. He had lived, and while he lived, he ruled.

The Romans wanted peace; the Iceni, freedom. And so Prasutagus had accommodated the Romans but never loved them.

He deserved a hero's life, but instead he chose the path of devotion to his people.

Prasutagus experienced neither a hero's life nor a hero's death. But he would have a hero's burial. She vowed it.

The girls cantered over, reined their horses, and swung lithely to the ground.

"Yes, Mother?" Aife asked.

"Aife, Cinnia," Boudicca's voice broke over a lump in her throat, "Your father has died."

Lovernios sat close to his fire in his small hut beside the river. He sat unmoving, eyes focused on the dancing flames. He held his golden staff of office, turning it over and over in his hands.

A branch crackled and flung a shower of sparks into the air. They flickered, fell to the ground, and died.

Almost at the same moment, he heard a cry—faint because of distance—coming from the direction of Venta Icenorum.

The flames dropped.

Lovernios blew out his breath.

It had begun.

What he had seen in his dream, what the gutuatros had viewed in his trance, was coming to pass.

Lovernios stood, straightening his cloak.

He chanted:

> "I have been a salmon in a stream,
> I have been a deer on a mountain.
> I have been a rod of gold."

He kicked dirt over the remnants of the fire.

> "I have been a horse ranging the meadows.
> I have been a fox.
> For I have been dead, and I have been alive."

He faced the entrance of his hut. "For I am Lovernios."

He knew he should be happy, anticipating the feast and the games. He should decide to rejoice, as when he'd forced himself to glory in his father Kirwin's passing.

He should be happy, glad that Prasutagus enjoyed a new, better life.

But instead, a great sadness weighed upon him.

Did pride make him fight against what seemed inevitable? Or did hope? Could he—he, Lovernios—dare hope to change the minds of the gods? Did it lie in him to contest fate and win?

Could he accomplish what Caratacus, what Togodumnus, and what Kirwin had failed to do? What Prasutagus—for all his nobility, his courage and honor—had never attempted?

He must. For justice was with him.

If the Iceni were to live again, he must succeed.

The winter wind brushed his cheeks. Lovernios made his way across the frozen landscape to where, he knew, the people of the Iceni celebrated the rebirth of Prasutagus into the otherworld.

NINE

The clear note of a tuba pierced the afternoon air, easily audible over the clamor of the fortress. With well over five thousand men plus horses packed into a fifty-acre enclosure, noise was unavoidable.

Shouted commands followed, coming from the direction of the main gate.

Sergius laid down a report. Three steps carried him to the door of his quarters. Cara jumped to her paws, her tail wagging.

Sergius held the door open. "Come, Cara."

With the wolfhound trotting at his heels, Sergius headed toward the commotion to see whose arrival the tubicen had announced with his playing. Mostly, the tuba sounded the watches for the guard and working parties, and the advance and retreat in battle. But working parties usually exited and entered through the secondary gates, and no battle raged.

"News, do you think?" A junior tribune, Septimus Justus, fell into step beside him, boyish face alight with hopefulness.

"Why, are you expecting something?"

"I have a girl back home in Syracuse."

"One that's waiting for you?"

Justus's head bobbed. "I hope so, sir."

They made it as far as the hospital, where the unlucky junior tribune still lay, three weeks after the skirmish, his recovery from his wounds and amputation still in doubt, when the creaking of the gates of the porta praetoria indicated the arriving party had entered the fortress. Sergius glimpsed a guard on the watchtower wave to someone below.

The two men stepped aside as a cavalry troop clattered along the via praetoria and halted outside the principia. Their patchwork uniforms showed they weren't regular cavalry, which stayed reserved for battle readiness, but a unit of lower-paid and lesser-trained cohors equitatae. The lead rider, a courier, led a second horse laden with bags. The courier dismounted while his escort wheeled their mounts and cantered toward the stables.

Sergius's heart raced: a courier! He'd be bringing the usual dispatches from Londinium and Camulodunum and Rome but also letters. Dare he hope?

Beside him, Justus quivered with anticipation.

A pair of clerks emerged from the principia to help the courier take his bags inside. The corniculais himself appeared in the opening, keeping a sharp eye on his staff.

Sergius longed to rush over and rip the bags open. But he'd have to wait until the dispatches were sorted and distributed. His turn would come—in order, as always. Suetonius and Marcianus received priority.

But the courier turned, spotted Sergius, and gave him a broad wink.

"Plenty of letters today, sir," he called.

Sergius walked across, conscious of Justus's envious gaze following him. He forced himself to appear calm and unhurried. He'd written to Veturius and his parents, though he hardly expected a reply so soon from Aquileia. He'd also penned a few lines to Ailidh. Sergius had made certain several denarii found their way into the courier's pocket to assure that letter's safe delivery.

"Any problems?" Sergius asked.

"No, sir. Quiet ride." The courier patted a saddlebag. "There's a special one here."

He paused, expectantly.

Sergius groped for a denarius and passed it to the courier. The man secreted the coin in a pouch attached to his belt. He opened the saddlebag, extracted a folded papyrus, and held it out.

Sergius took it. "Thank you."

"Thank *you*, sir," the courier saluted.

"There may be a reply."

"I'll be sure to check with you before I leave, sir. But I'm hoping for a few days rest."

The courier ambled into the principia.

Sergius walked around the angle of the building and leaned his back against the wall. Cara gazed up at him.

"Do you know who this is from?" Sergius asked her. He held the papyrus to his nose, but all he smelled was the leather of the courier's bag.

He broke the scrap of red sealing wax on the papyrus, unfolded it, and smoothed out the creases.

The ink flowed across the page: clean strokes in a flowing feminine hand. Sergius had never thought to ask Ailidh if she could write. The average Briton, he'd learned, was illiterate and relied on oral communications and prodigious feats of memory. Perhaps Egomas had encouraged his niece to learn the art of reading and writing so he'd have a literate assistant to help deal with Roman customers.

Of course, if Sergius *had* asked, Ailidh would probably have taken the question as another display of Roman superiority and arrogance.

The papyrus was dog-eared and wrinkled. Smudges showed where a previous letter had been scrubbed off. Egomas the dog-seller wouldn't be one to waste papyrus, not when it cost good money to buy fresh sheets.

> From Ailidh, daughter of Cathair the warrior, to M.
> Sergius Lysias, tribunus laticlavius, Legio XIV *Gemina*,
> greetings.

No mention of Egomas the dog-seller, Sergius noted with a wry smile.

> Sergius, my friend in Christus;
> The winter passes as a cloud before the sun, and I
> long for spring when I may see you again. But spring
> begins the wars, when no man is safe. I pray God each
> day for your health and protection.
> Veturius came to pay respects in your name. I fear
> he offended Egomas—no hard matter, but I thought
> Egomas would beat him.

Sergius grinned. Trust Veturius to put his well-meaning foot in his mouth. He wondered what his friend had said to offend the dog-seller.

> But Veturius left as he came, no dog for him. Does
> Cara guard you well? Give her a kiss from me.
> Lovernios predicts trouble in the spring. I know it
> not right to believe the prophecies of one who follows
> the old gods, but in this I think he is correct. The Iceni
> grow restless, and the Trinovantes grumble as well.
> Catus levies harsher taxes, and we groan. Justice has
> become a stranger in our land.
> I long to talk to you face-to-face. May God be with
> you.

Sergius held the papyrus to his chest. Cara brushed against him.

"From your mistress," Sergius explained. "But I'm not kissing you."

Later, Quintus brought him the letters that a clerk deposited in his office. Bundles of wax tablets held military communications. Those, he stacked to one side to be read and answered later.

Another papyrus roll contained a letter from Veturius.

> From G. Veturius Longinus to his friend M. Sergius Lysias.
>
> Greetings from the north where I shiver and pen letters with fingers grown white from cold. Truly Britannia is an accursed country! I loathe the rain and the snow.
>
> Ailidh sends her greetings, Egomas his curses. While I salute your choice of beauty, I cannot but consider that the presence of the dog-seller outweighs the charms of his daughter. You will not agree. But while you recompensed him the cost of a dog which he had not even lost, he would not repay me the cost of a kilt that his dogs devoured while it was yet upon my person.
>
> For three days, I could not sit.
>
> Speaking of cost, my friend, it grows expensive keeping oneself entertained in these parts. Can my friend—who surely would not begrudge the cost of a kilt damaged while performing him a favor—spare a few denarii to keep one who wishes him well from the pangs of despair?
>
> See, I ask but little.
>
> The vultures lurk at my door, while Venus keeps her arms far from me.

Sergius grimaced. Veturius's luck at tali would never change. Neither would his way with women.

> I grow so eager for home, that I could almost brave the abominable Claudia to see the streets of Rome again.
>
> See how desperate I am. Have pity upon me, my friend.

Sergius fingered his coin pouch. He had made it a point not to finance Veturius's gambling debts. But a kilt . . . he could imagine Egomas setting a dog after Veturius and his friend turning tail to flee.

News of Ailidh was worth it. He could send Veturius the cost of a kilt.

> I know you too well to think that you will fail me. I
> will send you word if I hear further from Ailidh. May
> Maia and Aurora bring us dawn and spring.
> Veturius.

The third letter originated in Aquileia, from his parents, although from the tone of it, his father had done the writing.

> My dear Marcus;
> I hear from a friend still in the army that your com-
> manders are pleased with your performance to date.

Sergius frowned, then his face cleared. Marcianus—and Suetonius also, perhaps—would send reports to army headquarters in Rome reporting the performance of the tribunes. Marcianus had apparently not seen fit to include the incident with Catus—thank God for that. His father's friend could be an officer, or maybe no more than a clerk with access to the reports.

> I confess that I was worried that your religious incli-
> nations would interfere with your military duties; I will
> be delighted to see my worries proved groundless.

His parents didn't understand his change of heart. The Way? What was that? A minor Jewish sect of no particular distinction. Better that the son of a legate worship Jupiter or Mars or Apollo.

> I would see you rise higher in the cursus honorum
> than the gods willed for me. Follow the honorable
> course, Son, and bring respect to the family name. Re-
> member the words of Seneca: "It is a rough road that
> leads to the heights of greatness."

Sergius sighed. It wasn't hard to see Appius's regret and the ashes of his own dreams in those words. Young men who aspired to high positions prepared through a series of mixed civil and military appointments to take their place in society. As legate, his father had been reaching the culmination. Ahead should have been appointment to proconsul of a province, a senior army command, or even a consulship. But fate in the form of a Germanic barbarian had slammed the door of advancement in his father's face.

> All who remain here are well. Your sister Julia,
> brother Manius, and mother Lydia send their greetings.
> Your mother cautions you to dress warmly, eat well,
> exercise, and avoid the temptation to pleasure, which
> has distracted many men from their course. I am sure
> that in this sound judgment will prevail.
> Above all, Son, study. Through exercise of the mind
> comes many virtues.
> We look for your safe return to Italia.

No mention of money. Veturius's parents would undoubtedly send their son a gift. Well, no matter: he would make it on his own and prove to his father that following the Way did not make him any less a Roman.

Also no mention of Claudia. Hopefully, in his absence she'd find someone else to snare with her cloying attention.

He rolled the papyri carefully and inserted them into their covers. Later, when he had time, he'd write replies.

Early the following morning, when shivering legionaries on fatigue duty hurried to stoke fires in braziers to new life and others heated water to warm wine, Sergius trudged to the stables to attend to his horse. He passed a departing work detail, twenty men under the command of a tesserarius, carrying weapons as well as tools. He watched them go, then entered the stables.

He inspected his horse and fondled her muzzle while she ate a bag of grain. When she finished, he issued instructions to the grooms. Some twenty minutes later, he led her toward the rear gate, the porta decumana, to assign her to the attendants managing the forage area.

He'd almost reached the gate when he heard shouts from the direction the work detail had taken.

Or did he?

The shouts were so faint as to be ethereal, blunted by distance and absorbed by snow-covered trees. The men around him didn't appear to have noticed.

Then his eyes met those of a cavalry decurio, and he knew that he hadn't been mistaken.

"Gather your men!" he yelled.

Sergius swung himself onto his horse's bare back. Several Thracian auxiliary cavalrymen, rough men wearing leather jerkins and coarse cloaks, loitered nearby also tending to their animals.

"With me!" Sergius shouted. Without waiting for a reply, he kneed his horse forward.

"Tribune!" Someone thrust an oval cavalry shield and a lance at him. He leaned over to grab them even as horses clopped into line behind him.

"Open the gate!"

Two guards leaned their weight into the portals and swung the gate open. Sergius raced through the opening. The horses pounded across the packed snow. Hooves flung clods of snow and ice into the air. Sergius realized belatedly that he wasn't wearing a helmet or greaves—he hadn't planned on riding. At least his chest was protected by his lorica. His cloak billowed behind.

Over the racing horses' and his own rushed breath the sounds of battle grew louder.

Half a mile from the fortress, the troop thundered through a screen of trees and burst into a snow-covered meadow.

Sergius took in the situation in a split second.

The work detail confronted half again as many Briton foot soldiers. The men of the detail had dropped their tools and managed to form a ragged formation. Several bodies, both legionaries and barbarians, lay stretched upon the ground. A wave of screaming Briton attackers exploded against the ranked legionaries.

At the sound of the horses' hooves, the Romans raised a cheer. The Britons wavered, then with a savage yell swung to face the new threat.

Sergius lowered his lance.

The cavalry plowed into the Briton flank.

Howling, blue-painted warriors surrounded him. He struggled against a sea of contorted faces, streaming hair, and muscular arms swinging long, heavy swords.

A blow that nearly knocked Sergius from his horse rattled against his shield.

A barbarian loomed before him, sword arcing for the kill.

Sergius could see nothing but the man's face twisted in fury, his teeth bared and a foam on his lips.

He crouched, braced his lance against his side.

The shock as his lance met the barbarian's naked chest shuddered through Sergius's body. The man's eyes widened as the lance tore through flesh and gristle to emerge out his back. He fell to the side. His weight snapped the lance shaft. Sergius threw the useless stump away.

His horse stumbled over the fallen Briton.

Sergius snatched for his gladius—shorter than a cavalry sword, but it would have to do. He parried a blow with his shield and swung in return. His blade crunched against bone. When he raised it, the blade shone crimson.

He heard a scream, and then a weight hit him from the side. His horse staggered, and he fell, the ground rushing up to meet him in a breathtaking flurry of powder.

He rolled as he hit, somehow maintaining his grip on his gladius. A shadow blotted out the sun, and he thrust the blade upward. The weight grunted and crashed limply on top of him.

Sergius braced himself against the frozen ground and shoved the corpse aside.

He jerked his sword free and staggered to his feet, readying himself for the onslaught of the next Briton.

But there wasn't one. There wasn't a Briton near him.

The survivors, a tangled mass of painted, savagely dressed warriors, pelted for the security of the forest.

The cheering Romans hurled invectives after the fleeing Britons.

Sergius lowered his sword arm. He gasped for breath. His hair dripped sweat into his eyes.

"Halt!" he called. "Don't follow them. Regroup!"

He counted five legionaries down to a dozen Britons.

The man he'd stabbed lay on his back. Despite the cold, he wore only trousers and a cape fastened about his neck.

Sergius took a step toward him.

The young man, not even Sergius's age, showed the beginnings of a beard, only fuzz on his cheeks. He appeared the age when he had to prove himself.

The bile rose into Sergius's throat. His vision grayed. The ground swayed. Congratulating hands reached out to steady him, and then he lost his stomach contents over the ice and snow and blood-stained earth.

"A delegation from the Iceni to see you, Procurator," Centurion Sextus Fuscus announced, stepping into Decianus Catus's office in Londinium.

Catus glanced up from a financial statement that rested on an imported lemon-wood table. A trio of braziers warded off the cold, and the office glowed with lamplight. A woolen tapete rested on his lap to keep drafts off his legs.

Catus raised his eyebrows. His guard commander could have sent a trooper to announce the Iceni arrival but hadn't.

"So?"

"There are two of them, named Airell and Weylyn."

Catus flexed his left leg to ease a cramp and straightened it again. "Are they of more importance than the average Briton?"

"My spies tell me they're in Boudicca's confidence. I think it would be worth your while to hear what they have to say, sir."

Catus shrugged, "Send them in, if you must. And fetch Juba. He might as well be present."

Catus sat slightly more erect as the two Britons entered, but he wasn't about to rise to greet them. He wrinkled his nose. No matter what anybody said, Britons smelled different. He'd have to have fragrance brought in after they'd departed.

Both Britons wore heavy torques, armbands, rings, and swords beneath their cloaks. Catus noticed without bringing attention to the fact that Fuscus had posted soldiers at strategic positions in the room and had angled himself between the Britons and Catus. It wasn't likely that the Britons would attempt hostilities, but Fuscus was prudent. Catus paid him well to keep him alive.

Alypius Juba arrived and stood in a discrete corner.

The older of the two Britons greeted, "My name is Airell, Procurator. This is Weylyn. Thank you for granting us an audience."

The Briton spoke politely, despite his vile pronunciation, but Catus didn't engage in pleasantries with subject peoples. "Get on with it. What do you want?"

The Britons exchanged glances.

Airell said, "We bring a message from Queen Boudicca."

"She calls herself queen, does she?"

"She *is* queen!" Weylyn burst.

"Mind how you address me, boy," Catus snapped. "What message?"

Weylyn flushed. Airell continued, "King Prasutagus named the Emperor Nero as coheir with his daughters. You are the emperor's representative, Procurator. Queen Boudicca respectfully asks that you honor that will."

Catus scratched his thigh. "Respectfully? Not likely. Besides, the decision isn't mine to make. The emperor has Prasutagus's will in his hands. He will undoubtedly send word as to his wishes in the matter."

"But you can influence him with a recommendation—"

"Is that all?" Catus interrupted.

Airell halted in midsentence.

"Well?"

"She craves your patience with the loans."

"Is she going to pay?"

"She asks for patience, that's all."

"She's had patience. You've all benefited from my patience."

Weylyn raised his voice, "How can we pay when you keep raising taxes? Grain tax, temple tax, horse tax—"

"Silence!" Catus shouted. "It's your duty to pay, not complain."

Airell added, "We've paid for years. There are only so many horses, so many dogs—"

Weylyn interrupted, "The temple tax alone drains us. Why should we pay for *your* gods?"

"You pay because you're conquered," Catus smirked. "And because you waste my time with your endless complaining." He leaned forward. "Tell this so-called queen of yours that the taxes will not be lowered and that when I hear from Rome about this will of Prasutagus I will inform her personally."

Weylyn's hand dropped to his sword hilt.

Six drawn gladii from the guards answered him.

Airell rested his hand on Weylyn's and pushed the younger man's hand away from the hilt.

"We will not pay more," Airell grated. "We cannot."

"Are you refusing me?" Catus replied. "Tell Boudicca that taxes are hereby increased by 5 percent."

He gestured to Fuscus. "Get them out of here."

"Troops!" the commander barked.

"It's you who will pay!" Weylyn shouted over his shoulder as the guards hustled the Britons from the room.

Catus slumped back. "Jupiter, spare me from such as those."

Fuscus cleared his throat. "Maybe they're telling the truth. Maybe they can't pay more."

Catus scowled. "Whose side are you on? They're still wearing gold, aren't they?"

"Gold isn't inexhaustible."

"There's more where that came from. Prasutagus has been trading horses for years—selling them to us! The Iceni have gold, all right. They feign difficulties, that's all." He gestured, "One of you get me a drink."

Juba handed him a goblet.

"Have you ever heard anything so ridiculous?" Catus snorted. "Send a letter to Nero on their behalf. I ask you!" He drank. "The emperor probably made up his mind what he was going to do when the will was first filed years ago. And I can guess what his answer will be."

Fuscus puffed out his cheeks. "The Iceni worry me."

Catus enjoyed his warm wine. "They're a lot of conquered savages. What can they do?"

"Ten years ago they were disarmed. They're not now."

"We have legions," Catus said, "and a governor who likes to fight." His gaze swept from Fuscus to Juba. "Besides," he said, "why should you two worry? You get a sizable cut of the revenues." He laughed. "The Iceni don't know where the gold goes."

The Romans stripped the dead Britons of their valuables, removing gold and silver brooches, bronze ornaments, and woolen scarves. When a cavalryman found a sword or a cloak he liked better than his own, he took it. The remaining weapons would be taken to the fortress, inspected by the custos armorum, and if satisfactory, distributed among the auxiliary units. If not, the iron and bronze could be melted down as scrap and be reused.

Waste not, want not. If the quartermaster at Rutupiae proved dilatory in sending weapons, the legions obtained them elsewhere.

Sergius observed the activity in a sort of dazed detachment, leaning against his horse's flanks for support. His mind felt dissociated from his body. His shoulder ached from where he'd hit the ground, and a bruise on his thigh indicated a blow he didn't remember receiving. His mouth tasted of vomit. While his mind noted these things, it seemed to consider his injuries of no consequence. Perhaps they belonged to another man.

His legs refused to move, and a dull chill had settled inside him. The sweat had dried to a clamminess on his skin.

Battle shock, a voice inside his mind whispered.

"Secure the perimeter!" a new voice barked. A centurion jogged up with reinforcements from the fortress. Pickets scattered and assumed position around the clearing.

Sergius doubted the Britons would attack again, but there was no harm in being safe.

"With your permission, sir?" the centurion added, as an afterthought.

Sergius nodded.

The centurion pursed his lips as snow flurries flung fresh flakes earthward. His gaze flicked to the gray clouds.

"Best not pursue them in this."

"Yes," Sergius agreed.

The centurion moved away. "You, men—gather the bodies!"

Sergius watched the centurion detailing troops.

"Pardon, sir?" A new voice interrupted Sergius's thoughts.

Sergius shook himself. "Yes?"

The tesserarius in charge of the working party held out a ring. Sergius stared at it.

"From one of the barbarians you killed, sir." The tesserarius indicated the man who'd taken Sergius's lance. The other—the boy—hadn't worn any jewelry. "I thought you'd better have it before one of this lot grabbed it."

"I can't," Sergius refused.

"It's yours, sir."

"You have it."

The tesserarius hesitated, then closed his fingers over the ring. "Thank you, sir." He looked over the battlefield. "They had us hard-pressed until you arrived. We'd have beaten them, but we'd have lost more good men doing it."

Abruptly, the tesserarius turned away to rejoin the depleted work detail.

The legionaries hoisted the bodies of their fallen comrades, closed ranks, and marched toward the fortress.

Sergius adjusted his scarf around his neck. He draped the cloak from a dead Briton over his horse as a makeshift saddle, swung himself up, and at a slow canter joined the flank of cavalry that ringed the work detail.

At the fortress, he stopped at his quarters to shed his uniform and wash the blood from his arms and face. A legionary on camp duties took his uniform away to be cleaned. Then he made his way to the praetorium.

"Tribune Lysias reporting, sir." Sergius entered the commander in chief's office. Four men were present: Suetonius, Legate Gellius Marcianus, Chief Centurion Helvius Adventus, and Cavalry Prefect Didius Pertinax.

Sergius searched Marcianus's brown eyes and fleshy face for a clue to the mood of the Fourteenth Legion's commander. He knew it would be useless to hope for a hint from Suetonius; his face was as immovable as a marble statue's.

Marcianus's expression seemed open. If storm clouds brewed behind the droopy brows, Sergius couldn't detect them. Once again, Marcianus spoke first, while Suetonius remained a silent observer.

"You are not in duty uniform, Tribune," Marcianus stated without preamble.

Sergius cleared his throat, which ached, raw and dry. He must have yelled during the fight, although he couldn't recall doing so. He glanced at his belted tunic, and his spare cloak pinned over his shoulder.

"No sir. My uniform is being cleaned. There was a lot of blood on it."

Blood and dirt. Sergius didn't envy the legionary who'd been given the task of polishing his lorica, washing his cloak, and scrubbing stains off his leather belt and apron.

He continued, "I thought it better to report like this than to wait."

Marcianus directed, "You will give an account of this morning's action."

"I was tending my horse when I heard sounds of conflict from a working party, sir. I gathered a troop of horsed auxiliaries and went in relief."

"The way I heard it, you dashed off without waiting to see if anybody was following."

Sergius flushed. "I assumed they would, sir."

"You *assumed*." Marcianus placed a heavy emphasis on the word. "Never assume anything, Tribune. Waiting to ensure that you were accompanied would have taken little time. Reactions are commendable, preparation even more so."

"Yes, sir," Sergius accepted. "I took it for granted that the men would follow me."

"The *Gemina* and its auxiliary units are well-trained and disciplined," Marcianus said with a nod of his head toward Pertinax, "including the cavalry. Not all legions are the same."

"I'll remember that, sir."

"Carry on."

"When we arrived, the working party was hard-pressed. We attacked the enemy's flank. After a brief skirmish they were routed and fled into the woods."

"You didn't pursue." A statement, not a question.

"No, sir."

"Why not?"

Because I was too busy throwing up to be able to, Sergius thought. Instead, he said, "I didn't consider it advisable, sir. The horses would have been at a disadvantage in the woods. The Britons could have regrouped and ambushed us. And it was starting to snow again."

Marcianus nodded. "Very prudent. Never waste men on foolhardy ventures, Lysias. Know when to press and when to be content."

Chief Centurion Adventus, a burly, grizzled veteran, said, "Tesserarius Saufeius told me you killed three Britons."

"I . . . ," Sergius shook his head. "It happened so fast—"

"No need for false modesty," Marcianus snapped.

Adventus continued, "Saufeius also said that when the cavalry burst onto the scene the Britons never knew what hit them."

Marcianus pulled himself erect. "Tribune Lysias, you were rash, impetuous, and entered battle unprepared."

The words hit Sergius like a slap on the cheek. His voice was a whisper, "Yes, sir."

"Nevertheless, you acted with commendable promptness when presented with an urgent situation; you showed courage and resourcefulness and exercised good field judgment by attacking the enemy's flank and by not offering pursuit into dangerous territory. I think it safe to say that many men owe their lives to your prompt and efficient action."

A warm glow suffused him.

"In sum, your efforts were commendable and honorable."

Prefect Pertinax slapped him on the shoulder. "Well done, Tribune."

Sergius said, "The honor belongs to the cavalry."

Pertinax started to reply, but Suetonius's voice broke across the cavalry commander's compliments like a dash of cold water.

"Legionaries and cavalrymen are paid to fight, Tribune. Commanders command."

Sergius faced the commander in chief. "I understand, sir. There are many fighting men but only a few commanders."

"Every man is trained for a specific task," Suetonius said. "Remember yours."

"You're dismissed," Marcianus concluded, with a gesture that encompassed Pertinax and Adventus as well.

With a final pat on the shoulder, Pertinax hurried away, but Adventus matched his pace to Sergius's.

"You're pale," he observed, as they exited the praetorium.

"I feel strange."

"First time you've killed a man?" the chief centurion asked.

Sergius nodded.

"You'll get over it. The first time is always the hardest. They're only barbarians, remember. They wouldn't have had second thoughts about killing you, believe me." Adventus tapped his chest.

Sergius saw again the screaming horde of half-naked men and shuddered. "I didn't imagine they were like that."

"Battle's not a pretty sight."

"I thought I'd be afraid. But I wasn't."

"When a fight comes at you so quickly, you don't have time to feel afraid. It's only when you've time to wait for it that fear gnaws at you."

Sergius studied the rank of six phalerae that Adventus wore on his chest. The silver-plated bronze discs bore relief images of deities. Thick armillae dangled from Adventus's wrists—honors from some other conflict. The chief centurion had seen years of service and survived many tours of duty. He spoke with the voice of experience.

"When you're in battle, your body races," Adventus continued. "There's no time for first thoughts, let alone second ones. After the battle's done is when there's time for reflection. The energy fades. It's natural. But you did well. Fight by my side anytime."

Sergius mustered a smile. God alone knew how many battles the chief centurion had weathered. Coming from a man of Adventus's experience, the compliment was high indeed.

"I'm honored," Sergius expressed. "But the commander didn't seem pleased."

"He's like that," Adventus replied. "Don't take it to heart. If you'd shown cowardice, *then* you'd have heard about it."

Later, in the quiet of his quarters, Sergius wondered who the unknown Briton had been—the owner of the ring the tesserarius had tried to give him.

Did it really matter?

Weren't they all the same?

Maybe Adventus was right.

Maybe the Britons were barbarians.

Maybe killing them did become easier. His father had never seemed to have a problem with it—not that he'd expressed, at any rate.

But whenever Sergius revisited the battlefield in his mind, the nausea returned.

Something didn't feel right.

He removed the belt from his tunic and stripped to his underwear. He extinguished the lamp and lay down on the unadorned lectus the military provided.

Fatigue washed over him. Fatigue, and a sense of vague unease, or dissatisfaction, that he couldn't define.

He closed his eyes.

But when he did so, he looked into the eyes of the dead young man. And yet, they weren't the man's eyes that he saw.

They were Ailidh's.

Boudicca received Airell and Weylyn's report in stony silence when they returned from Londinium after a six-day absence from Venta Icenorum. Lamplight flickered, creating a circle of light around her, while leaving the edges of the room in darkness. Her hands rested on her thighs while she listened.

"We pled your case," Airell informed. "Catus threw us out."

"I wanted him to feel my sword," Weylyn said hostilely.

"Your impetuosity almost saw us killed," Airell retorted. "Those guards were itching for an excuse to fight."

"It would have been worth it to have taken him with us."

Airell paused, then said to Boudicca, "With respect, Queen, Prasutagus was wrong. I was his friend, and it cuts me to speak so. But the Romans have deceived us."

Weylyn blurted, "We *tried* their way. But they don't respect us."

Airell added, "I was there, Queen, in the beginning. 'Make peace,' the Romans said, 'and we will be your friends.' We kept our lands and some of our freedoms, but now Catus guts our wealth, and Nero—mark my words—he won't respect the king's will."

"Better for us to have retained our own way of life," Weylyn said, "than to acknowledge such animals as masters."

"We grow crops for them," Airell said. "They take the choicest of our animals. They tax us both when we're alive and when we're dead. That is the legacy Prasutagus has left us."

"Preferable to have died fighting," Weylyn interjected.

Boudicca nodded. "There is truth in what you say. And we have only ourselves to blame. We should have flung the Romans into the sea the moment their sandals trod on our soil."

"Prasutagus—" Weylyn started and bit his lip.

"No!" Boudicca flared. "Prasutagus continued the policy that the people decided before he became king. We Iceni are isolated," she said tightly, "separated from both our enemies and our friends. The Romans didn't wish to fight us: they left us alone, and we left them alone. It seemed a good agreement. After all, they broke the power of the Catuvellauni, which we were unable to do. We may look back now and wish we had taken another path, but we can't change what has happened."

Weylyn's face twisted. "The Romans are nothing! They're no braver than we are! Their numbers are less than ours—"

"Enough!" Boudicca exclaimed. "Winter is no time for war."

"What are we to do?" Airell demanded. "Sit in our huts and acquiesce like frightened children to Catus's demands?"

Boudicca shook her head. "What we do requires careful thought." She made a dismissive gesture. "We'll see how Nero replies. He may prove more reasonable than his procurator."

"Do you believe that?" Airell asked. "Where do the Roman lies originate but with the emperor?"

"Leave me now."

"But, Queen—" Weylyn began.

Airell touched the younger man's elbow. "There will be more time for talk. Let's go."

When the nobles had departed, a man stepped from the shadows of the queen's chambers. "Airell is correct."

Boudicca didn't turn. "So you have said before, Druí."

Lovernios came into the circle of lamplight. "The Romans will never be satisfied."

"That too, I know." Boudicca sprang to her feet and paced. "What would you have me do, Druí? I despise the Romans as much as you do. I curse the day they visited our shores. I detest the wombs that bore them and the breasts that nursed them. But I have more than myself to think of. The Iceni look to me as their rí. And I . . . I have daughters to consider, the children of Prasutagus."

Lovernios spoke softly. "Whereas I think of all the Celtae, both in Albu and Ériu."

Boudicca paused. "I spoke in haste, Druí."

"There is no offense." Lovernios folded his hands. "But we shall never be safe so long as a single Roman sandal treads our soil."

"You ask much."

Lovernios touched the corner of his eye with his index finger. "My eyes have seen." He moved it back. "My ears have told me the words of the gutuatri."

Boudicca stroked the cool blade of her longsword. "Why do you hate the Romans so, Druí? Is it solely because of your dream?"

Lovernios slid his arms into his sleeves and folded them across his chest. After a moment he replied, "Roman ways also took from me one who was . . . dear to me."

Boudicca exhaled loudly.

Lovernios said, "You are correct. Winter is no time, but spring will come."

"What will spring bring?"

Lovernios turned so his face was in shadow. "Life or death. Rebirth or the grave."

Boudicca returned to her seat. She pulled her long hair so that it hung over her shoulder. "Have the gods deserted us, Druí?"

"The gods are there."

"If we perform the sacrifices as we have for generations, why does ill fortune dog our steps?"

Lovernios's voice was low. "Perhaps there's need of a special sacrifice."

Boudicca's chest tightened. "Strange words to come from you, Lovernios."

"No one respects life more than I. But there comes a time when hard choices must be made. It is better for one man to suffer than all."

"Is there one such?"

The Druí's face was expressionless. "There may be. But there can be no mistake. The one must be worthy." The darkness cloaked him as he moved to the door.

Alone, Boudicca laid her sword across her lap. The sword was a duplicate of the one that rested with Prasutagus in his grave. They'd commissioned the twin swords many years ago from a weaponsmith of legendary skill. She turned it so that lamplight reflected off the silver metal and the carvings of wolves and bears engraved along the blade.

She raised the gleaming length to her lips.

And she felt, for the first time, what Prasutagus must have felt many times—the loneliness of one who ruled, of one who could solicit advice and opinions but on whose shoulders alone rested the decision.

And she stayed, until the lamps burned low and the flames diminished into glowing embers.

TEN

Day after day, the patrols continued. Keen-eyed soldiers straggled in companies over the barren winter landscape. Despite the best efforts of men who wanted to locate the Britons, if only to return to the warmth of the fortress, the Britons' camp proved elusive. For all the traces the searchers found, it could have become invisible or subsided into the interior of the hills. Whispers said that the gods of the Celtae protected it. Counter rumors reiterated the auspices of Sergius's sighting of the hare and eagle.

But if their camp was invisible, the Britons weren't. The raids intensified.

A cavalry patrol on a training exercise was ambushed in a defile and cut to shreds. Despite precautions, Briton raiders attacked another work detail, to be repulsed with casualties on both sides. A detachment of recruits found themselves overwhelmed while on a routine march.

Suetonius's irritation with the Briton tactics manifested itself in a short temper. Even the normally placid Marcianus lost his composure over insignificant incidents. Pertinax wore a grim expression as his cavalry patrols returned empty-handed.

A letter from Titus informed Sergius that the division of the *Valeria* had been the target of raids also, and its commander sounded as harried as Marcianus.

Titus wrote:

> Falco has been chewing his nails to the quick in frustration. We think the raiders have a camp to our northeast, but we haven't been able to locate it. Meanwhile, if there's a man here who doesn't have either a snotty nose, a cough, or frostbite, I haven't met him.
>
> If the Britons were smart, they'd let their weather do their fighting for them.

Sergius wondered briefly how Veturius's health was holding up. He thanked God that he himself had so far escaped illness.

Finally, a courier and his escort vanished on a clear day, almost within sight of the fortress. Only his horse was found, lame, wandering in the snow.

Suetonius's patrician face became a mask of frozen anger.

"Find the Britons!" he demanded of the patrol leaders. "By Mars, find them if you have to turn over every rock between here and Caledonia!"

Sergius thought of Titus's letter as his patrol trotted out of the fortress.

A camp to the *Valeria*'s northeast—that would place the raiders to the southwest of the *Gemina*. Could it be the same group of Britons harassing both legions? A party of Deceangli hiding in the hills?

The idea made sense.

He took his patrol on long sweeps to the southwest, scouring the mountains, venturing as far afield as he dared without risking a night in the open.

But to his dismay, it wasn't his patrol that finally located the camp a week later, but another.

The cavalrymen, panting but flushed with excitement, rode into the fortress to the cheers of their comrades. "We found them!"

The decurio dismounted and hurried to the praetorium where the command staff assembled to hear his report.

"They were careless and left a trail, sir," the decurio announced. "They're in a valley about fifteen miles to the southwest."

Sergius clenched his fist. He'd been right!

"Show me." Suetonius slid a map across the table. Large gaps indicated mountain areas the army hadn't yet charted.

The decurio stabbed a finger into one of those areas. "Here, sir."

Sergius leaned closer to look. Within range of the *Valeria*'s base, also.

"How many?" Suetonius asked.

"From tracks we estimate a minimum of a hundred warriors with horses, sir."

"Very good, decurio. Prefect Pertinax will see that you and your men are suitably rewarded for your diligence. Dismissed." When the decurio had left, the governor opened, "Recommendations?"

"Attack at once," Marcianus replied promptly, surprising Sergius with his vehemence. "If we leave them alone, they'll only continue to harass us, and if they spotted the patrol, they might move their camp."

"A hundred warriors pose no real threat," Chief Centurion Adventus countered. "Now that we know their location, we can be on our guard—"

"The cavalry can restrain them—" Pertinax began.

"We could coordinate with the *Valeria*," a junior tribune offered.

Suetonius listened to the senior officers' arguments, then said, "Thank you. Your recommendations will be considered." The staff meeting continued for a few more minutes before Suetonius dismissed the officers.

"Wait, Lysias," Suetonius commanded. Then he drew Gellius Marcianus aside and spoke to him quietly before leaving. Sergius waited.

Marcianus turned to him. "You spoke little, Lysias."

"It seemed there was little to add, sir."

"If you wish to be an officer, you must speak out. Venture your opinions. Else, how will we know whether your thoughts are sensible or not? What is your assessment? What action should be taken?"

"I agree that if we leave the Britons alone, they'll continue to harass us. We'd render ourselves vulnerable on our flanks or rear."

"We should strike first?"

"Definitely."

Marcianus nodded. "It's required prolonged searching to discover their camp. If they escape now, we'll have to start all over again." He pursed his lips. "The scouts estimate the Britons have a minimum of a hundred warriors camped fifteen miles away from us. How would you approach them?"

Sergius folded his hands and thought for a moment. "I'd take two centuries of legionaries, plus two troops of cavalry."

"Two hundred and twenty-four men to face one hundred?"

"The scouts could be wrong, sir. I'd want to take enough men to be certain I had a comfortable edge but not so many as to make winter travel over unfamiliar territory dangerous."

"Sound thinking. No auxiliaries?"

"Besides the cavalry?" Sergius hesitated. In general, auxiliary troops bore the brunt of fighting, leaving the more highly trained legionaries as backup. Better to lose auxiliaries from other lands than Romans. Some auxiliaries were more comfortable in harsh climates than Romans, but—

"No, sir," he answered. "Not for a raid where every man counts. We'd have to strike hard and fast if we hoped to return before nightfall. Otherwise we'd need a supply train to provide for an overnight camp."

"I'd do that anyway," Marcianus said, "in case the weather changed abruptly. A blizzard could do more harm than the enemy. Pack animals won't slow a column down much. Besides, there aren't roads to the Britons' camp, and a strike force would either have to fight late in the day and risk fatigue or camp overnight."

Marcianus paused. "You'll leave in the morning."

Sergius gaped. The room closed in upon him. Sudden heat caused him to break out into a sweat. "Me, sir?"

"You'll take a century from the sixth cohort and one from the ninth."

"But—"

"But what, Tribune?" Marcianus barked. "You said you wanted to learn the art of command. Here's your chance."

"I . . . uh . . . th-thank you, sir."

Marcianus continued as if Sergius hadn't interrupted. "Ofonius Nepos, senior centurion of the sixth cohort, will be your chief officer. The sixth are all good men. Junius Bassus, third centurion of the ninth cohort, will be your other officer. His men are recruits. A taste of action will be valuable for them. You seem to know the cavalry: choose two troops. Pertinax will honor your request."

"Yes, sir."

"Not many tribunes receive this opportunity," Marcianus emphasized. "Make good use of it."

"I will, sir."

Sergius's head whirled as he crossed to his quarters. He'd been given field command! Although tribunes technically ranked immediately below the legate in the chain of command, in reality it was the senior centurions who commanded the cohorts. The battle-hardened centurions didn't often take kindly to novices like tribunes assuming field command.

He straightened. His father would be proud.

"Quintus!" he shouted as he entered his office.

"Sir?" his beneficiarius responded, emerging from his own chamber.

"Send me a clerk. There are orders to write. We march in the morning."

Morning came soon, and Sergius's command crawled over the wind-swept hills. Sergius had heard it said that this was the harshest winter in recent memory, and he believed it.

The wind possessed a mind of its own, sending icy tendrils to poke through gaps in cloaks and tunics, slip between chinks in armor, and wriggle like a worm past the most tightly wrapped scarf. The sun refused to show its face through a mass of dull, low-hanging clouds that coughed snowflakes. Some senior Roman officers belonged to the cult of Mithras, Sol Invictus—the Unconquered Sun. Today, it seemed the sun had been badly beaten, stripped of light and warmth, and dismissed by the clouds without a fight.

No matter how many extra tunics or socks were worn or how much fur stuffed into boots, it wasn't enough. Hands froze, faces tingled, ears became numb appendages.

Sergius pulled his scarf tighter.

Veturius's jokes about Syria didn't seem so funny. True, the desert could be cold at night, but at least it didn't snow, and one could look forward to a warm day ahead.

His command marched in order. The century of the sixth cohort led the train, in the place normally occupied by auxiliary troops, followed by their pack animals. Then came the officers, with the century from the ninth cohort next followed by their animals. The cavalry guarded the flanks and the rear. Scouts and pickets ranged ahead, choosing the easiest path for the troops to take and steering clear of sites where there could be a potential ambush.

Sergius wondered if it would be better to walk, using body heat to keep warm, or to ride, sitting on warm horseflesh? As commander, Sergius rode. The two centurions, who—if truth be told—probably preferred to walk with their men, were mounted alongside him.

On a good road, at a rapid march, fifteen miles would take a little over three hours. Even at a normal pace, it could be done in under four. But as Marcianus had remarked, there weren't any roads. Even if a track existed, made by Britons or wild animals, it lay invisible, buried under snow.

His force had to pick its way across uneven terrain, over hills that deceivingly appeared low and easy, across partially frozen streams that crackled beneath a veneer of ice, and over hidden rocks that skidded underfoot. Slipping and sliding, the swearing legionaries stumbled across the torturous landscape.

They had to remain constantly alert for hazards, both natural and man-made.

"They're watching us," Nepos commented.

The bull-necked chief centurion of the sixth cohort sat rigidly erect, his small, dark eyes flickering ceaselessly over the wilderness.

"Count on it," the slighter, older Bassus replied before Sergius could. The ninth cohort's third centurion had grown gray, lean, and leather tough in the army. He was reputed to have the quickest vitis in the legion and a tongue that could lash a recruit into quivering submission.

"I haven't seen them," Sergius said, suddenly uneasy. On all sides, the horizon blended into the unforgiving sky. He couldn't tell if a ridge lay ahead or if it was only low clouds.

"Neither have I," Nepos replied. "But that means nothing. I can feel them."

"If they know we're coming, that means they'll be ready for us."

Bassus gave a dry laugh. "Exactly."

Sergius swayed with his mount. Command had seemed an exciting prospect at first: fall upon the unsuspecting Britons, win a quick victory, and return to the fortress in triumph.

But if the Britons were waiting . . .

Suddenly it wasn't a game. He wasn't playing boyish mock battles with Veturius on the hillsides of Aquileia, outflanking his friend by a quick scuttle through the city drains to fall on him with wooden sword from the rear. His decisions meant life or death. He had to think like a Briton to outfox them but fight like a Roman to defeat them.

One hill after another.

Cold wind.

And always he wondered how a Briton would think.

The column took almost ten hours to cover thirteen miles.

When the scouts reported that the Briton camp lay a scant two miles distant, Sergius called a halt at a site selected by two surveyors as suitable for a camp. He'd sent the surveyors ahead, with instructions to find a site defensible and hidden as far as possible from the Britons' prying eyes. If the Roman presence had already been noted, the precaution might be useless, but giving the Britons any advantage seemed senseless.

The level site the surveyors chose lay near a stream. The location sat in a slight hollow but well clear of trees and underbrush. At night, the forest could provide concealment for intruders, but the intervening distance to the camp would allow the guard to sound an alarm before potential attackers could cross the open space.

Sergius studied the location. He sensed that Nepos and Bassus were waiting for him to speak. "We can't cut a ditch or build a rampart," he began.

Nepos stamped a foot. "Ground's too hard."

"But we can still make a fence." Each legionary carried two seven-foot long, pointed palisade stakes. Flattened at midshaft, the stakes could be bound together with thongs. The palisade was designed, however, to keep animals out, not determined adversaries.

Sergius looked to the two centurions. "Do you think the Britons will attack?"

Nepos shook his head, "They'll wait for us."

Bassus nodded agreement.

"Then we'll be content with the palisade," Sergius decided. "Make camp!"

The surveyors had lined out a one-acre space for the camp, in the typical T-shaped formation, and marked tent locations. They'd allocated one site on the riverbank for drawing water and, downstream, another for the horses. Latrines, rubbish pits, and cooking hearth spots were also marked.

The legionaries scrambled into action. Each contubernium of eight men was allocated a ten-by-ten-foot leather tent, or papilio. Soldiers placed these above and to the sides of the T.

Sergius had a tent to himself situated at the cross point of the T where the praetorium in a larger camp would normally be. The centurions likewise had individual tents. The standards of the two centuries and the vexillum of the cavalry were planted where the principium would have stood, to flutter in the breeze.

The centurions and their optios barked orders. Men cleared the ground and erected the tents. Others dug the pits for the latrines and rubbish, while yet others constructed the palisade. At the base of the T, called the annex, handlers and grooms gathered the mules and horses. Also, a special ablutionary tent was raised where small cauldrons of hot water would be heated to wash away the grime and the aches of the march.

Sergius had debated about the use of fires and the extra weight of the cauldrons. He didn't want to advertise the Roman presence and burden the pack animals unnecessarily, but in the cold, the men deserved a hot meal and hot water. Content men would fight better on the morrow.

Each contubernium cooked its own meal. An orderly brought Sergius his meal of baked wheat biscuits—buccellata—wine, and olives. To emphasize the swiftness of their strike, Sergius had ordered that only three day's rations be carried. If the mission lasted any longer, the strike force would have to hunt or forage for food.

A small brazier fended off the worst of the cold in his tent. The men, six to a papilio with two taking turn on guard duty, relied on the accumulation of body heat for their warmth.

When darkness crept as a thief over the countryside, Sergius removed his lorica and pulled his thick woolen cloak over his twin tunics, glad for the extra warmth.

Outside his tent, horses snorted and sentries stamped their feet. Hoods pulled up against the night, legionaries patrolled the perimeter of the camp. Sixteen men at a time from each century took a turn on watch, peering into the gloom, trying to determine which areas of darkness were shadow and which could be Britons trying to sneak into the camp. Sergius doubted anyone would fall asleep on guard duty tonight.

His thin mattress rested on the ground. In campaign season, soldiers created three-sided couches out of earth and stone. But in winter, even that small measure of comfort wasn't possible. The cold seeped up from the frozen earth.

Sergius tried to sleep. But despite his efforts, his nerves tingled, his thoughts chased speculations over the coming morning, and the cold hard rock of fear lodged in his stomach.

Battle again? So soon after the last time?

He rolled onto his back and clasped his hands on his stomach, trying to will the churning to cease.

Chief Centurion Adventus was correct. Waiting *was* harder than the trauma of battle.

He didn't fear death. But he did hope for spring and another sight of Ailidh. Before that, though, he'd have to fight men who, if not of her tribe, were cousin Britons. Did she see them as different? The Briton tribes, after all, didn't coexist peacefully. Or, in her eyes was the world divided into two peoples: Celtae and Roman? Roman eyes saw Romans on one hand, barbarians on the other.

He had no answer.

Half asleep he reached out a hand, but he touched cold hard ground where a shaggy body normally rested: Cara. He should have brought Cara.

ELEVEN

Even before the sun breasted the horizon, the marching camp stirred. The legionaries dismantled the temporary facility as efficiently as they'd erected it the day before. Each papilio was rolled into a long sausage shape and tied onto a mule. The palisade came down, the officers' and ablutionary tents collapsed, and mess kits, tools, rations—everything not needed for battle—found storage space in the baggage train. If the camp had been more permanent, Sergius might have left the train behind under guard. But he didn't want the Britons to attack a minimally defensible location like this makeshift camp and destroy his supplies.

Such an elementary oversight would not only cripple the expedition's chances for survival but also gain him Suetonius's instant ire and a dishonorable discharge.

An orderly fastened the hooks and buckles of Sergius's lorica. Quintus normally performed the task, even though personal attention wasn't strictly a beneficiarius's duty. But Sergius had left his aide, despite protests, at the fortress. The disappointment in the beneficiarius's eyes had clawed at him, but Quintus was nearing retirement age, and Sergius couldn't in good conscience allow him to face a hazardous winter excursion. Of course, he couldn't tell Quintus that—it would demean the man's courage—so he'd made an excuse.

Sergius adjusted his cloak, made certain his sword and scabbard swung easily on his left side from his baldric, and fastened the ornamented belt.

He caressed the sturdy, dark-with-age leather. Scars and nicks crisscrossed the broad band. The orderly had done his best to polish the worn decorative bronze plates until they shone. The belt had belonged to his father. Appius had worn it during his last action in Germania. Sergius thumbed the blade of his pugio; the dagger, also, had been his father's. But the gladius, handcrafted and honed until the balance satisfied him, belonged to him alone.

He straightened his scarf, making sure it covered areas where the lorica might chafe. In his tent, an orderly fitted his helmet with its tall plume onto his head and lowered the cheek pieces.

Lastly, Sergius clipped the dog's head brooch to his cloak.

He found the two centurions waiting outside.

"Will you address the men?" Ofonios Nepos asked.

"Yes." Sergius strode to the top of a low mound, giving him a few more inches of height to view the assembled troops.

What should he say? The question had vexed him through the night. Something stirring, naturally, to boost the soldiers' morale, but what?

He wished for a book of prebattle speeches. Why hadn't some great general—Julius Caesar perhaps; or Cornelius Scipio, victor over Hannibal; or Scipio Africanus, conqueror of Carthage; or Aulus Plautius, even—thought to write one?

"Men of the *Gemina*," his voice, louder than he anticipated, pierced the cold, crisp morning air, "I cannot promise you glory."

Nepos and Bassus stiffened on either side of him. Sergius could imagine the centurions' consternation. No glory? What was the untested tribune saying?

"What I can promise you is a morning of fighting, blood, and death. But if we fight our hardest, give our best for the cause of Rome, then glory will indeed be ours."

Not bad words, but they didn't ring. They lacked life.

Suddenly the words he sought came to him. The analogy he needed lay right at hand. He pointed. "Beyond that forest, the Briton hare quivers in his den. He trembles, knowing the Roman eagle circles overhead. He knows that when the eagle swoops upon him, he dies."

Sergius bent his fingers into claws, and raised his arms.

"Men of the *Gemina*! We are the eagle. Let us fall upon the hare, seize him in our talons, and bear him aloft: our prize of victory!"

The legionaries cheered. For a moment the well of sound washed over Sergius, and the blood pounded through his veins like the tramp of a thousand feet. Was this what the emperor felt when he led his victorious armies in triumph between the pines of the Appian Way into Rome?

The sun broke through a cleft in the clouds.

"See! The sun himself shows his face to view the Britons' defeat!" Sergius yelled. "Signifers—raise the standards! March!"

The two signifers, lion skins draped over their armor, hoisted the signa.

The two centuries formed lines for the march, the red shields of the sixth cohort contrasting with the blue of the ninth.

"Will you ride, Tribune?" Centurion Bassus asked.

"No. I march with the men."

Bassus made no reply, but Sergius sensed he had replied correctly.

The iron hobnails of his caligae gripped the ground. Snow creaked underfoot.

As before, the cavalry ranged the flanks. Scouts and a skirmish line of pickets preceded the column to flush out waiting Britons.

But if Britons waited, they made themselves undetectable. The Romans could have had the land to themselves for all the signs of life they saw. The scouts flushed a pair of deer and some rabbits, but that was all.

"Have they fled?" Sergius wondered out loud.

"Not likely," Nepos replied. "They're out here, all right."

The chief scout reined his horse to a halt beside the officers.

"Well?" Sergius demanded.

"Down there, sir," the scout pointed. "Clear traces of a large number of men."

Sergius eyed the terrain ahead.

"Down there" belonged to a narrow valley between two densely wooded hills. The bare trees stood tall and menacing, grim sentinels guarding . . . what?

Unsuspecting Britons resting in the security of their camp?

An abandoned camp—the Britons off on a raid?

Sergius narrowed his eyes. Why a valley? Normally, the Britons constructed hill forts, crowning the crest of a suitable hill with ditches and ramparts. Perhaps they faced the same difficulties as the Romans: winter was no time for constructing forts. Or perhaps . . .

Sergius chewed a knuckle. "A perfect place for an ambush."

Nepos nodded. "Precisely what the Britons want. For us to charge ahead into a trap."

"That's what happened to Manilius Valens and the *Augusta* a few years back," Bassus added. "Mauled before they knew what was happening."

The valley appeared as desolate as the surrounding wilderness. But from somewhere, Sergius knew for sure, hostile eyes watched them.

Sergius glanced into the sky, then back to the white hills that appeared so different in winter than in summer green.

"We outflank them," he decided at last. "We enter their trap but send the cavalry to circle around the hills and attack from the rear."

"What about a way of escape?" Nepos asked.

Sergius frowned.

"Cornered men will fight to the death," the centurion continued. "Leave a way of escape for the Britons, and they'll flee. Fleeing men can be cut down."

"Very well," Sergius agreed. "Where's the senior decurio?"

Preparation and planning was what distinguished the Roman army from barbarian opponents. Victory with the least expenditure of men and material was the object—not personal venture and not risky, low-probability action.

If he failed in his mission and lived to tell about it, he'd have Suetonius to face.

Please God, he prayed, *help me make the right decisions.*

When the cavalry commander arrived, Sergius ordered, "Take the cavalry and the baggage animals back as if you're leaving the field to the infantry. Then circle the cavalry around the hill to the left, and fall upon the Britons' flank and rear. Three notes upon the tuba will indicate that we've engaged."

The decurio saluted, "Yes, sir." He wheeled and shouted orders to his command.

Sergius watched until the horses disappeared in a fold in the terrain. "Let the Britons wonder," he said. "Scutum and pilum."

Each legionary swung his scutum, a rectangular, curved shield, from his marching shoulder strap and held it in his left hand to protect his body. In the right, he gripped a javelin.

"Forward."

Cautiously, scanning each tree and bush, the legionaries advanced.

Sergius remained in the rear, obeying Suetonius's directive to be a commander, first and foremost.

The valley narrowed. Gnarled oaks, leafless gaunt skeletons, hemmed them in on either side. In the shadows, Sergius imagined Druid priests flitting between the trunks, casting dire curses on the Roman troops—nonsense, of course.

But at any moment, he expected a savage yell, and the explosion of a hundred Briton warriors.

They moved deeper into the valley, and still, no sign warned of Britons.

Could the scouts have been mistaken? Could they have chosen the wrong valley or confused the tracks of a herd of deer for those of men and horses?

Deeper.

His fingers cramped around the hilt of his gladius.

Where were the Britons?

He sniffed and initially smelled only the tang of trees and fallen leaves.

But then the scent of wood smoke teased his nostrils, mingled with the aroma of roasted meat.

The Britons were here.

Somewhere.

And then he saw the huts, crude, circular dwellings of branches and thatch.

A cooking fire smoldered in a rock hearth.

The place appeared deserted: no men, no dogs, no horses—nothing.

"Where are they?" he whispered.

The legionaries paused, as uncertain as he, looking around with quick, nervous glances.

"They were here," Nepos stated, stirring the ashes with his foot, "not long ago."

The call of a bird sounded, a strange, eerie note that wavered and faded.

The woods were still.

And then the silence splintered with a hundred shrieks and the Britons were upon them.

From the huts, from the trees, from the very air itself it seemed, poured a legion of Briton warriors.

Some wore cloaks and trousers and shirts, others animal skins, a few ran naked but for blue streaks of woad daubed on their chests or faces. They wielded swords, axes, clubs, and stones.

A few troopers had time to throw their javelins, and several Britons screamed and fell as the iron points pierced them.

The remainder of the legionaries dropped their javelins, pulled their short swords free from their scabbards on their right hips, and braced, shoulder to shoulder.

"Tubicen!" Sergius shouted.

Three notes from the tuba echoed down the valley.

The leading Britons hurled themselves upon the Romans. Blows from heavy longswords rained down upon Roman shields. One Briton's swing beat down a legionary's shield and dropped him to his knees. A second blow finished him. His comrades closed ranks and the Briton went down to a thrust from a gladius.

Sword blows thudded off the plywood shields and clanked off bronze bindings.

The Britons fell, by ones and twos, but the sheer fury of their attack took Sergius's breath away. Step-by-step the legionaries yielded ground.

A Briton vaulted a fallen legionary and swung at Sergius. The sword curved in a great arc. Sergius met it with his scutum, and while the Briton's arm was still raised, lunged. His sword sank between the man's ribs. The Briton's face contorted, and he fell.

Gaps appeared in the Roman ranks.

They had the weight of numbers, and yet the Britons forced them backward.

Where was the cavalry?

A thought chilled him.

Had the cavalry been ambushed? Had the Britons anticipated the maneuver?

What if the cavalry wasn't coming?

Beside him, Nepos hacked down a bearskin-clad Briton. Nepos's experienced men held their own, but the untried legionaries of the ninth century wavered. Bassus yelled encouragement to his green troops.

From all sides, Britons poured at them, hacking, slashing, cutting.

The legionary in front of Sergius screamed and went down, a sword point protruding from between his shoulder blades. Looming in his place was a giant of a man, well over six feet tall, his burnished muscles bulging. He wore trousers and a wolfskin fastened over his shoulders by a bronze brooch. A thick gold torque gleamed around his neck. Blue streaks of woad flashed on his cheeks and his breast. Long russet hair streamed to his upper back.

Sergius's glance encompassed the man's appearance in an instant. With a savage yell the warrior flung himself forward. Sergius braced himself.

The man's heavy sword smashed against his shield. Sergius reeled, stunned by the man's strength. He counterattacked, but the Briton was ready, parried the blow, and jumped out of range. Warily, the Briton circled Sergius, looking for an opening. Sergius followed his every move.

The Briton had a sword's length and reach and strength. Sergius had a shield and armor and training.

The Briton crouched, feinted, and swung.

The blow shivered Sergius's shield.

Again, the Briton backed off before Sergius's thrust reached him.

Around them the battle raged. The Romans held, but barely. Sergius couldn't tell which side was winning. But the standards still stood tall; as long as the signifers held the standards aloft, the battle wasn't lost.

The cavalry still hadn't come, and the world narrowed to a bare circle of snow-packed ground containing himself and the giant Briton.

The Briton's sword cleaved air.

Sergius ducked beneath the shining blade. The plume of his helmet fell to the ground.

This time Sergius's sword drew blood.

The Briton glanced at a red streak across his upper arm. His lips parted in a toothed smile.

"Come, Roman," he invited in heavily accented Latin.

Sergius shook his head. "You come to me."

The Briton grinned and launched himself.

Sergius's shield split under the fury of the Briton's attack. Sergius swung it. The metal boss caught the Briton in the chest. Sergius followed with a jab that scraped the Briton's ribs, and a swing that smashed the Briton's sword to the ground.

The tip of his gladius touched the Briton's throat.

"Yield," he said.

The Briton stared him in the eye. "You're afraid to kill me."

Sergius hesitated. "Surrender, and your life will be spared."

"To be a slave of Rome? Never!"

The Briton's boot caught him in the groin.

Sergius cried and staggered.

The Briton stooped and grabbed for his sword, reversed it, and jabbed.

The butt caught Sergius on the rim of his helmet. He wobbled back, stunned, his vision suddenly dark. Another blow from the Briton dashed his splintered shield to the ground. He waved his gladius in a protecting arc.

The Briton's laugh met his ears.

A thought of Ailidh flashed through Sergius's mind, followed by an instant of regret.

At any moment he expected the fatal blow.

He heard, rather than saw, the Briton's sword cut air.

He jerked backward. His foot caught something soft and yielding—a body—and he fell.

He hit the ground with both shoulders.

The shock rattled his teeth and jarred his gladius from his hand. But his vision cleared, and he realized that his own blood streaming from his forehead had been obscuring his sight. He wiped his cloak across his face.

"Die, Roman swine."

The Briton stood above him, sword held in both hands, point down. He stabbed for Sergius's chest.

Sergius rolled, and the point glanced off his lorica.

The Briton cursed.

Sergius hooked the man's legs with his own and pulled.

The Briton toppled.

Sergius jumped on him, gripped the man's sword arm, and forced the deadly blade back and down.

The Briton was built like a bear. The muscles in his neck and chest tensed. He heaved and flung Sergius away.

Sergius lashed out with his foot. He connected with the Briton's wrist. The longsword dropped to the ground.

But the Briton's hands clamped around his neck and squeezed. Sergius choked.

His vision grayed. He fought for breath. He strained, but the giant Briton was too strong.

His hand bumped something. His fingers closed over the hilt of his pugio.

The blood roared in his ears.

He scrabbled his father's dagger from its scabbard and thrust and twisted.

The Briton gasped.

The giant hands shook in a convulsive spasm, and then the pressure on his neck released.

Sergius pushed harder, and the limp Briton rolled off him, the dagger buried to its hilt. Sergius pulled the blade free.

He wobbled to his feet.

Bodies littered the ground, some moving, others still in death.

The fight seemed to have halted, as if some mysterious force had frozen the combatants in place. Sergius realized with a start that he was at the focus of their attention.

He thrust a fist into the air. "Eagles!" he yelled with all the breath he could muster.

As he stood over the body of the warrior, a cry of dismay went up from the Britons, only to be drowned by a cheer from the legionaries.

The Britons wilted, as if the heart had been stripped from them by the death of their leader. The legionaries seized the advantage, and pressed ahead. Ranks closed; they cut a swath through the Britons.

And then, as the Britons broke and turned to flee, the welcome thunder of hooves beat down the defile. The cavalry swept into the valley and rode down the Britons that remained on their feet. Horsemen pursued the few fugitives that threw their weapons aside and sprinted for the trees.

In moments the battlefield was still, save for the cheers of the victors and the moans of the wounded.

Nepos, sword dripping red, strode across to him. "Well fought, lad. I thought he had you."

Sergius raised a hand to his neck and ran his fingers over swollen tissues that burned like fire. If he hadn't bruised already, he would. His voice emerged as a hoarse croak. "He almost did."

The centurion stirred the body with his boot. "A noble by the looks of him. Maybe a prince." He bent over and yanked the gold torque from the man's neck. "This belongs to you."

Sergius's gaze fixed on the glittering ornament, and for a moment he recalled a ring being wrenched from a boy's hand.

"You earned it." Nepos urged, "Take it."

Sergius's fingers closed around the smooth gold. "It hasn't been awarded."

Nepos laughed. "Awarded? Marcianus won't deny you. Not when he hears how you fought." The older man surveyed the field of battle. "A victory indeed."

Sergius picked up his helmet.

Nepos cast a grim look at the sheared-off plume.

An optio and a legionary assessed the wounded Britons, dispatching those too wounded to survive and making prisoners of the remainder. The prisoners would stand no chance of release, but as slaves in Rome they'd live a little longer, perhaps to provide entertainment in the circus.

Sergius found his gladius and sheathed it. "How many did we lose?"

Nepos called for the optio.

"Twenty-five of ours dead," the officer reported, "sixty-one Britons and fifteen prisoners. We have twelve seriously wounded. The rest are minor injuries."

"Send a man to bring the medical officer," Sergius instructed Nepos. "The cavalry can transport the wounded to camp."

While he waited for the medical officer, he watched the legionaries sort through the debris. Troops searched the huts, removed what little valuables they found, and then torched the dwellings. Eager tongues of flame licked up the dry wood. Smoke billowed into the air, a signal to any watching Britons that the Romans had proved victorious.

The medical team arrived on the field, a medicus ordinarius assisted by two dressers with medical supplies.

"Let me see your wound, sir," the medicus said.

"It's nothing," Sergius replied. "There are others more injured than I."

"With respect, Tribune, I'll be the judge of that. A man's head is worth more than his legs." He pointed to a tree stump and requested, "Sit here, please."

Sergius complied and allowed the medicus to probe the scalp wound and feel the bruises.

"You need stitches."

"It's really not necessary—*ouch!*"

The medicus rinsed the laceration with turpentine from a flask, then readied his needles and sutures. "This will only take a minute."

The medicus handed him a stick. "Bite on this."

Sergius's teeth ground into the splintery wood as the needle and suture pierced his scalp.

The medicus worked quickly but without haste, obviously used to performing the procedure.

"Done," the medicus said at last. "Let your hair grow, and no one will see the scar." He beckoned, "Capsarius! Put some salve and a bandage on the tribune's head. Quickly now!"

Sergius sat impatiently as the dresser bandaged his scalp, then directed the man away.

He coughed: from the smoke, the raw air, his bruised throat. Then he turned away from the carnage.

"Sound the withdrawal," he instructed the tubicen. "We're returning to main camp."

The clear notes of a tuba from the fortress's ramparts welcomed the strike force's return late the following day. The heavy wooden gates creaked open.

The signifers led the procession, holding the centuries' standards high, followed by the victorious legionaries marching in close ranks. Guards with weapons drawn herded the Briton captives. The three mounted officers—Nepos and Bassus slightly in advance of Sergius—preceded the cavalry.

Cheering troops lined the via praetoria. A victory for part of the legion was a victory for all. Legio XIV *Gemina* had added to her laurels.

The column halted in the parade ground before the principia. Sergius dismounted and saluted Legate Marcianus, who stood at the entrance of the headquarters.

"Tribune Lysias reporting the success of the expedition, sir. The Briton camp was found and destroyed."

Marcianus raised his voice to address the whole company. "The *Gemina* takes pride in the actions of all her soldiers. Your actions reflect not only on the legion but on Rome herself and the emperor. Centurions, see that the men are rewarded for their valor."

Marcianus gestured, "The signifers may replace the standards."

The standard-bearers carried the centuries' ensigns into the principia. Sergius and the centurions followed them into the great, wood-framed cross hall. Their boots echoed in the cavernous enclosure. The standard-bearers marched to the sacellum, parted the carved screens that enclosed the fireproof stone shrine, and replaced the standards. Ranked around the walls of the shrine glittered the standards of each century and cohort and, most important of all, the golden eagle of the legion and the image of the emperor.

"Come with me," Marcianus called to Sergius, Nepos, and Bassus. He led the way to the praetorium. "The commander in chief wishes to hear your reports firsthand."

The warm glow of victory faded. Sergius wondered what kind of a mood Suetonius was in. As usual, he couldn't tell from the governor's expression.

"Proceed, Tribune," Marcianus instructed.

Sergius picked a spot on the far wall and fixed his eyes on it as he spoke. He detailed the raid as concisely as possible. When he came to the part about his fight with the Briton leader, he could sense the commander's displeasure.

"I was in the proper location to exercise command when the Briton broke through the ranks and confronted me," he explained. "I wasn't seeking personal glory. I had no choice but to fight."

"I saw it," Nepos supported. "The Briton made straight for Tribune Lysias. He was looking for our commander. I was too distant to intervene."

"As was I," Bassus added.

Suetonius nodded, a curt movement.

Sergius continued, "After I slew the Briton, the fight turned. We took the advantage, and then the cavalry arrived and routed the survivors."

Sergius laid the gold torque on the table. "This I took from the Briton."

Marcianus picked it up. "A fine piece. Describe the Briton."

Sergius complied. "A big man, over six feet, taller than most of the Deceangli. His hair was lighter. He wore a wolfskin and woad."

Marcianus exchanged a meaningful glance with Suetonius. "Culhwch: prince of the Deceangli." His gaze returned to Sergius. "Their most renowned warrior." He lowered the torque.

Centurion Bassus contributed, "He was a warrior indeed. I've never witnessed a fiercer fight."

"Continue, Tribune," Suetonius encouraged.

Sergius completed his report with the list of casualties sustained on both sides. "The Briton force was annihilated, sir."

"It's never good to lose men," Marcianus concluded, "but all in all, I think the losses were acceptable."

The legate gestured to the two centurions. "You may leave."

When they'd gone, he asked, "Your opinion of the centurions?"

Reporting on the centurions was a tribune's function, but Sergius hadn't become comfortable with the duty. He answered, "They are both capable men who performed their duties superlatively."

"Who suggested the cavalry attack from the rear?" Suetonius interjected.

"I did," Sergius replied. "Centurion Nepos considered the prospect of ambush likely. I'd thought to send cavalry around both flanks, but he recommended that we leave a way of retreat for the Britons."

"You took his advice?" Suetonius asked.

"Yes, sir."

"An able commander uses his men wisely," Suetonius said. "He listens to advice from those whose experience exceeds his own."

Marcianus asked, "How did the troops perform?"

"The sixth century fought well. The recruits of the ninth appeared nervous, but they held their ground. I have no complaints."

"Why the cavalry's late arrival?"

"The decurio explained that dense forest slowed the flanking maneuver. Otherwise the cavalry would have arrived sooner."

"You should have delayed your approach," Suetonius judged.

"But if the cavalry had arrived first, the surprise would have vanished, sir," Sergius qualified. "Without knowing the Britons' precise location, some uncertainty was unavoidable."

"The best you can do," Suetonius said, "is to plan for the contingencies you can envisage. Otherwise, you have to be flexible and adapt your tactics to the needs of the moment. That is what made Julius Caesar great."

"Yes, sir."

Marcianus raised the torque. "You have my personal congratulations on an assignment performed well. You may wear this torque as a symbol of your honor in your first major action." He held out the gold ornament.

Sergius's hand trembled as he took it. "Thank you, sir." He adjusted it around his neck. Before returning to the fortress, he'd wondered how to wear it if Marcianus allowed—around his neck, as the Celtae, or fastened to the breast of his uniform as the centurions wore their phalerae. He'd decided to wear it as the Celtae did, although he wasn't sure why. Perhaps it gave him a sense of identity with Ailidh.

"I will most certainly include a favorable account in my next report to Rome," Marcianus assured.

"Thank you," Sergius repeated. His father would undoubtedly learn of his success through Marcianus's report.

"Dismissed."

Sergius saluted the legate and then the governor. The unaccustomed weight of the torque felt heavy on his neck as he exited the praetorium.

Later, after the *Gemina's* senior medicus had reexamined and redressed his laceration, he visited the bathhouse. When he'd allowed the different pools to soothe the aches and pains, scraped the dirt from his skin with a strigil, and received a massage with healing unguents, Sergius returned to his quarters.

He picked at the meal an orderly brought and drank sparingly of wine. Three days of field rations and posca should have left him famished, but instead, his appetite seemed to have deserted him.

He'd have more work to perform in the morning: battle meant administrative duties as well as fighting. An official report to be written, burials to be conducted, the soldiers' financial affairs to be closed, weapons and armor to be returned to supply, reports sent to headquarters in Londinium and Rome, and hardest of all, letters mailed to families and loved ones—all were his responsibility, even though they bore Marcianus's name.

Quintus could do the actual writing, but Sergius would add a personal comment and his signature. The standard wording sounded cold and heartless.

> L. Gellius Marcianus, *legatus legionis*, Legio XIV
> *Gemina* regrets to inform you that G. Seius Quadratus
> died in battle 23 December 802 A.U.C. and was buried
> with appropriate honors. Personal possessions and

moneys may be collected by applying to army headquarters. . . .

Twenty-five of them.

Sergius laid the torque on a table. For the first time he studied it in
detail. He turned it over in his hands, allowing the lamplight to play
over the sparkling gold, running his fingers over the silky smooth, unblemished metal.

A triplet of gold strands twined around each other, culminating in engraved rings at either end. The relief decorations were perfect; Sergius
could see no flaw in the intricate designs. Stylized, curiously disjointed
wolves snarled across the gap between the two rings. One was a he-wolf,
the other, a she-wolf with child.

Roman taste favored symmetrical, geometrical design; only a Briton
would craft a free-flowing pattern such as the torque.

And only a man of wealth and rank, a noble, would wear such a fine
ornament.

What kind of a man had Culhwch, prince of the Deceangli, really been? A man who hated Romans, certainly, but didn't all of the
Deceangli?

Brave, certainly: he faced the Romans in winter. And intelligent: he
conducted a harrying campaign to wear them down, rather than risking
a full-scale battle.

He differed in appearance from the majority of the shorter, darker Deceangli. Culhwch had more of the Gaulish appearance, as did Ailidh.
Perhaps his mother had come from one of the other tribes, obtained
through an arranged marriage to the ruler of the Deceangli.

But Sergius had beaten him in single combat. He'd faced the best the
Britons had to offer and laid him on the ground.

He picked up the torque.

What did Paullus mean that Sergius wasn't a soldier? Didn't this
torque prove it?

TWELVE

"Annaeus Seneca is here, Caesar," announced a centurion of the Praetorian Guard.

"He may enter," came the instantly recognizable voice of the emperor.

The sentry stood aside, and Seneca entered Nero's audience chamber. He glanced around, as he always did, to note who else had Nero's ear. Afranius Burrus stood with his back to a window, the worried look that had become normal engraved upon the praetorian prefect's brow.

The emperor slouched on a cushioned cathedra, the chair's back fixed at a comfortable angle. A silver bowl heaped high with raisins was placed on a low table within easy reach. The fragrance of balsam wafted from an incense burner.

"What is it now?" Nero yawned. "Burrus has already been boring us."

In contrast to the soldier, the emperor appeared anything but worried—but then, he rarely did. Life was a game to Nero, not a matter for serious consideration. His penchant for lack of deliberation was a trait that could be both advantageous and dangerous.

As Seneca crossed the mosaic floor, the emperor helped himself to a handful of raisins.

"News from Britannia, Caesar," Seneca reported. "Prasutagus has died."

Nero popped the raisins into his mouth and spoke with it full, "So Prasutagus has died. Are we to lament his passing?"

Seneca tightened his lips. He shot a glance at Burrus and received a minute shrug in return.

He persisted, "There's the question of succession, Caesar."

Nero chewed and swallowed. His dark eyes glared at Seneca.

The advisor informed, "In his will, Prasutagus left one half of his kingdom to you."

Nero's head snapped forward. "Who gets the other half?"

"His two daughters."

"How very generous," Nero sneered.

"That's probably what Prasutagus thought," Burrus reasoned, entering the conversation for the first time.

"Who does he think I am," Nero roared, "that I need the generosity of a barbarian? Does the emperor of the world require charity?"

"There is legal precedent," Seneca said, deciding not to respond directly to the outburst, "that has nothing to do with generosity. It's common practice for a wealthy individual to leave a share of his estate to another to ensure that his will is executed in accordance with his wishes. In this case, part of the Icenian territory would become Imperial estate, and you'd receive a portion of the royal treasure."

"Only a portion," Nero complained.

"Yes, unlike the will of Attalus III of Pergamum who left his entire kingdom to Rome—"

"Spare me the history lesson!" Nero slashed his hand through the air. "This Prasutagus assumes—or should I say, 'assumed'—much." He snickered at his joke.

"At the moment," Seneca continued, "Prasutagus's widow, Boudicca, rules the kingdom."

"A woman," Nero leered.

Seneca closed his eyes and opened them again. "What I'm asking, Caesar, is whether you desire that the Iceni remain a client kingdom or they're to become integrated into the province."

"I knew you'd come to the point sooner or later." Nero leaned back and nibbled a raisin between his front teeth. "What's your advice?"

Seneca looked to Burrus, and the praetorian prefect took up the cue.

"Of the three client kingdoms in Britannia, the Brigantes form a buffer against the hostile Caledonian tribes to the north. In the south, Cogidubnus of the Regni and Atrebates rules his kingdom because he's settled, and it's easier to leave him in place until he dies."

"The Iceni?" Nero demanded.

Burrus said, "They serve no useful purpose. They were bought off by the divine Claudius because the location of their territory made it easier than fighting them. That hasn't changed."

Seneca added, "Procurator Catus says that the Iceni are troublemakers, and Boudicca the worst of all. If she remains in power, we can expect only difficulties."

"What does the governor say?"

"Suetonius expresses no opinion on the matter."

"The whole situation seems troublesome," Nero grumbled. "Three client kingdoms in an area the size of Britannia? Ridiculous."

"In Pontus and the Alps," Seneca reminded, "we abolished the client kingdoms when they'd outgrown their usefulness."

Nero reached for the raisins and turned the movement into a dismissive gesture. "The decision is simple. We will recognize neither this Boudicca nor Prasutagus's daughters as his heirs. We declare the line of Prasutagus extinct. The kingdom of the Iceni is officially part of the province."

"But—" Burrus began.

"A wise decision," Seneca overrode his fellow councillor. "It shall be done." He beckoned to Burrus.

Nero stopped the men at the door. "And tell Catus that the wealth of the Iceni is mine. Not half. All of it."

"Yes, Caesar."

As soon as the door closed, Burrus took Seneca's elbow and steered him into an empty courtyard. A marble bench ringed a fountain. This location served as a convenient meeting place. Seneca knew from times when he had tried to overhear a conversation that the splashing waters concealed speech admirably.

"What did you mean by forcing the emperor's decision?" Burrus demanded. "We agreed—"

"Abolishing the client kingdoms is the logical next step in making Britannia a proper Imperial province. The policy has succeeded elsewhere."

"I'm worried," Burrus confessed. "You remember what happened eleven years ago when Ostorius Scapula tried to disarm the Iceni."

"He defeated them without much difficulty, as I recall, using only a wing of dismounted cavalry. One battle."

"The point is," Burrus stressed, "that his terror tactics—which is what his disarmament policy amounted to—provoked rebellion. It would have been simpler to have let the Iceni keep their weapons. They presented no particular threat at the time. My concern is that if they rebelled then over a relatively insignificant matter what will they do now if their queen is deposed?"

"Do you think we should leave her in power? According to Catus, Boudicca's a formidable woman."

"Man, woman, what matter? I'm saying that we're risking rebellion. Yes, leave her in authority. Leave the Iceni their status. Eventually, they'll become Romanized enough that their entry into the province will occur as a matter of course."

Seneca spread his hands. "You're overestimating the Iceni military capability, Burrus, my friend. Besides, the Iceni have been quiet for a decade. They can see Camulodunum. They know the benefits civilization brings."

"And I think you *under*estimate them," Burrus retorted. "Which is the greatest danger? You're not a soldier. But I can tell you from experience which presents the more hazardous course."

"Suetonius is as good a general as Scapula," Seneca said. "Maybe better. If the Iceni are disinclined to accept their change in status, I'm sure he can persuade them."

"Are you willing to risk your money on that?"

Seneca stood. "If I didn't know you better, I'd be insulted."

Burrus also rose. "The Iceni are a powerful tribe. What would you think if the whole province was lost?"

Seneca laughed. "Lose Britannia? You've been in your cups too much, Burrus."

He walked away from the fountain. "Besides, the debts have already been recalled."

"But not fully paid."

Seneca halted. "No. Not paid."

"Culhwch has been slain."

Boudicca, reclining on a lectus, looked over at Lovernios. Despite a pair of glowing braziers, the house at Venta Icenorum seemed cold. Roman-style villas weren't designed for the winter. Boudicca preferred a conical house, warm and cozy. Since the death of Prasutagus, the house seemed empty; her husband's presence had filled it for so long. . . .

"Is it so?"

"Slain by a Roman war party," Lovernios replied. He stood with his hands in his sleeves, staring moodily at the glowing coals.

"A warrior of warriors," Boudicca said wistfully. Culhwch might have made a suitable husband for Aife. An alliance of the Deceangli and the Iceni would have made the Romans tremble.

Still, there would be other suitors.

"He died well, in single combat against a Roman officer, so it is said."

Boudicca didn't reply. Faintly, from the adjoining room came voices: her daughters being instructed by a Druí scholar. She wondered if conversations such as the one she was having with Lovernios occurred between her parents and a Druí advisor while she was a young girl learning her lessons.

"One by one we perish," Lovernios continued. "The Romans whittle us down."

"Do you regret the path you have chosen?" Boudicca asked quietly.

Lovernios's gaze flicked toward her. "Can the wolf change his way, or the dove hers?" He looked back at the brazier.

Boudicca nodded. To her had fallen the mantle of Prasutagus. The gods let her carry the sword as he had done.

The door to the adjoining room opened. Cinnia entered followed by Aife.

"Mother, do you want to hear the poem Aodhan has taught me?" Cinnia asked.

Boudicca beckoned her youngest daughter to sit beside her. Aife leaned on the arm of the lectus. "I'm sure you know it as well as he," Boudicca encouraged.

Cinnia tossed back her hair. She smiled at Lovernios, who had swung around to watch.

> "I shall not see a world that shall be dear to me.
> Summer without flowers,
> Kine will be without milk,
> Women without modesty,
> Men without valour . . . ."

Boudicca stroked her daughter's hair while she listened. Cinnia drew to a close.

"Not a happy tale, the Morrighan's prophecy," Boudicca said when Cinnia had finished. She sought out Lovernios's gaze.

The Druí's lips twitched. "Let me tell a better," he said.

> "I am the son of poetry,
> Poetry, son of Reflection,
> Reflection, son of Meditation,
> Meditation, son of Lore,
> Lore, son of Study,
> Study, son of Knowledge,
> Knowledge, son of Intelligence,
> Intelligence, son of Comprehension,
> Comprehension, son of Wisdom,
> Wisdom, son of the three gods."

Cinnia's forehead puckered. "It's too long."

"Practice," Boudicca said.

The two girls left, Cinnia's lips moving as she repeated the words to herself.

"Thank you," Boudicca said to Lovernios. "Aodhan has too gloomy a mind to teach young girls."

With a pair of tongs, the Druí poked the brazier to life. "If the Romans have their way, there will be none to teach the children about our past. The legacy of our ancestors will perish; the stories of our people will vanish as morning mist. Without learning we will be as a cow that has no memory of yesterday and no thought for tomorrow."

A knot tightened in Boudicca's stomach. "Then we must not allow the Romans to have their way."

"No," Lovernios echoed, as flames sprang into the air. "We must not."

Following the excitement of the successful action, time at the fortress at Deva settled into winter monotony. One day seemed much like another. The soldiers drilled daily, both in the drill hall and on the parade ground, practicing sword techniques and javelin throws. They fought against wooden stakes to represent the enemy or against each other with dummy weapons. The drill instructor's steely eyes sought out the slack or lazy and assigned extra marches, in addition to the weekly nineteen-mile march, to the unfit.

The more vigorous soldiers arranged boxing events, wrestling matches, and footraces. The less active bribed centurions to release them from participation. Wagers were placed when the officers weren't looking, and more than a few coins changed hands; although with the mandatory payroll deductions for clothing, bedding, food, and boots, and the contribution to the soldiers' savings bank, the legionaries didn't have much money to waste. The librarii depositorum wasn't amenable to bribery; besides, one never knew when it might be necessary to have cash on hand to convince a centurion to look the other way. So most of the money remained in the iron-bound box beneath the shrine of the standards.

As tempers grew short, minor infractions became commonplace: insubordination, fist fights, failure to obey orders promptly. The centurions doled out punishment. An erring legionary found himself on fatigues, digging latrines, dressing wild game, cleaning the barracks, or polishing the centurion's uniform and boots.

During one gloomy week, the rounds party discovered a sentry asleep on watch, and regulations mandated Sergius, as senior tribune, to attend the man's court-martial.

Each day, the watchword was written on waxed wooden tablets, or tesserae, which were passed through the centuries, countersigned, and returned to a duty tribune. Troopers from the legionary cavalry made rounds, and inspected the pickets and guards, and received a separate tessera from the man in charge at each post. At daybreak, they reported to the tribune and handed in the tesserae.

Normally, it was purely routine. But this time the rounds party lacked a tessera and reported a guard asleep. The duty tribune, Septimus Justus, summoned the centurion in charge who paraded his men for Justus to question.

Occasionally it happened that a man had crept behind a building or bush to relieve himself, or investigated a noise in the night without alerting his partner, but hadn't actually deserted his post. Simple cases like those resulted in punishment by the centurions. But this time the sentry had clearly been asleep on duty, as witnessed by the rounds party.

Justus, as regulations required, reported his findings to Chief Centurion Adventus and to Sergius.

"Court-martial him," Adventus announced the proper course of action curtly.

"But he's been a good man until now," Justus protested.

"Doesn't matter," Adventus said. "Regulations."

"There's nothing else we can do," Sergius agreed. "Sleeping on watch is a major offense."

He, Marcianus, Adventus, and Camp Prefect Sabinus conducted the inquiry under the supervision of Suetonius.

Sergius closed his eyes as the guilty man stammered and stuttered a lame apology but couldn't deny his guilt. When the time came for Sergius to announce his verdict, he declared "guilty" along with the rest.

Suetonius pronounced judgment: "The fustuarium."

The legionary paled. "Please, sir, not that! Anything but that! I'll—"

"Silence!" Suetonius thundered. "You endangered not only your life but those of your comrades. Take him away."

Guards escorted the unfortunate man out of camp. The officers watched as the men of his own century set on him with cudgels and stones. The man crumpled under a hail of blows, which didn't stop until he ceased to move.

"A just punishment," Adventus remarked, as the body was hauled away.

There was only one other fustuarium meted out that winter, to a soldier convicted of theft. He, miraculously, survived to be dishonorably discharged and slunk away to make what he could of himself in civilian life.

Sergius didn't envy him. Death might have been preferable to dishonor. Roman society was not forgiving in matters of honor.

Sergius himself was in and out of camp, occasionally escorting the governor to one of the forts or smaller towns. But, as Suetonius seemed more inclined to winter in the field than at Londinium, Sergius found himself mostly in.

Sergius wondered if the governor had marital problems that disinclined him to winter with his family.

The boat building continued at a steady pace. Free from the fear of a surprise attack, work crews felled trees. The carpenters trimmed them and prepared planks for the joiners. Under the watchful eye of a centurion who'd seen service in the navy, the raw materials for the crude, flat-bottomed boats accumulated.

Sergius's forehead healed with only a minimal scar. More seriously, the wounded tribune from the first Briton attack, after languishing in the hospital for weeks after his amputation, still succumbed to fever. He was buried in a cemetery outside the fortress.

Sergius took part in the training and the sports. He avoided the tali and other gambling games except on a friendly basis. From time to time he wondered how Veturius and Agricola fared. He hadn't received another letter from Veturius; he could imagine his friend writing desperate letters home begging for money.

A letter from Agricola read more like a philosophical treatise than a conveyance of news. Agricola wrote:

> I still cannot make heads or tails of your liking for
> this new Way. For starters—and Titus agrees with me
> in this—nothing good has ever come out of Judea. This
> fact alone should give you pause.
>
> When the offer of high position comes, as it must,
> will it be offered to a member of the Way? Tolerant as
> we Romans are, I would be leery of anything that could
> affect my chances for promotion. I won't argue that this
> Christus had some good ideas, but he was, after all, a
> troublemaker. And as for being seen alive following
> crucifixion—such things don't happen, as every soldier
> worth his salt knows.

Agricola's letter gave Sergius food for thought. He hadn't considered the idea that the Way could hinder his promotion.

Sergius reread Caesar's *Gallic Wars* and Vergilius's *Georgics,* a present from his mother included in a packet of underclothes. But it seemed that everything he read gave him heartache. The *Georgics* made him long for Italy, especially when the snow melted and rain soaked the ground for days on end.

> But neither flowering groves
> Of Media's realm, nor Ganges proud,
> Nor Lydian fountains flowing thick with gold,

> Can match their glories with Italia.
> Hail, O Saturn's land,
> Mother of all good fruits and harvests fair,
> Mother of men!

Sergius could have added, "Nor Britannia's oaken forests shrouded with the hoar of frozen dreams." He wrote down the phrase on a scrap of papyrus.

And Seneca's *Agamemnon*, sent to him by his sister, made him long for Ailidh.

> Too dire my grief to wait time's healing hand.
> My very soul is scorched with flaming pains;
> I feel the goads of fear and jealous rage,
> The throbbing pulse of hate, the pangs of love.

Well, perhaps not the pulse of hate. But whenever he clasped the dog's head brooch to his cloak, his heart fled to a dog-seller's booth in Camulodunum. He told himself that it was stupid to fret over somebody he barely knew—who might, for all he could tell, already have a love among her people. Such self-recrimination didn't alleviate his yearning.

In his more contemplative moments he read Paullus's letter, over and over again, and tried to make the words part of him.

Was he showing the manifestations of the faith that Paullus emphasized? Did he exude the love, joy, peace, patience, kindness, goodness, fidelity, gentleness, and self-control?

The army didn't prize such virtues—fidelity and self-control excepted.

Some days Sergius paced the ramparts, hoping to glimpse a courier, and whenever one arrived, he hurried to meet him. But though he received plenty of official documents, no letter came from Ailidh.

Once he requested a day's leave, which Marcianus good-humoredly granted, and went hunting. He took Cara, a pair of legionaries, and Septimus Justus. The fresh-faced youth seemed slightly in awe of Sergius and hadn't yet decided whether to take his position of tribune seriously or to join the other young men in pouring the wine in the officers' mess and being helpful in a doggy sort of way.

Cara proved her worth on the hunt. Septimus bagged a brace of rabbits with a sling, but Sergius waited for bigger game, which he got when Cara flushed a wild boar. He dismounted to face the animal with a javelin. When his foot slipped on a slick rock and he dropped his weapon, he had a vision of himself impaled on a pair of wicked tusks.

But Cara worried the boar's flanks and deflected its charge long enough for Septimus to pitch him another javelin.

Sergius gathered his breath while the legionaries dressed the carcass. Legio XX *Valeria's* emblem was the running boar. Sergius had wondered at the choice of such an unusual symbol. Now he knew. The boar's ferocity and speed had surprised him.

Fast and fierce—a good symbol for a legion.

Thank God for Cara.

The wolfhound trotted contentedly beside him as the satisfied hunting party returned to the fortress.

And the winter continued its weary progress.

Two days after the boar hunt, Quintus poked his head through the door to Sergius's office. "The governor wants to see you, sir."

Sergius pushed a writing tablet aside. "See that these names are copied and sent to the head office in Rome, Quintus."

"Yes, sir," the beneficiarius replied. He studied the list. "Retirees. Think they'll retire to Camulodunum, sir?"

"Not if they have any sense," Sergius replied. "Although I suppose if you like your towns small, with plenty of land available, or want to start a business, it's not so bad."

Quintus chuckled.

Sergius hurried to the praetorium.

Suetonius paced a tight circle, his steps short and sharp. Color highlighted his carved cheekbones.

"Pack your gear, Tribune," the governor said without preamble, as Sergius entered his office.

Sergius stopped dead in his tracks. "Sir? Have I offended?"

"In the morning I leave for Londinium," Suetonius continued. "Your presence will be required on the headquarters staff."

Sergius swallowed. "Yes, sir."

"Reassign your current duties to one of the other tribunes. We ride early."

Sergius saluted. "Thank you, sir."

Londinium!

The commander in chief's family, of course, lived in a fine city villa. But Londinium was close to Camulodunum, and Ailidh.

Sergius hurried to obey. In the corridor he almost bumped into Gellius Marcianus. He rushed a salute and continued on his way.

"Is it wise," Marcianus asked, "to give the boy so much authority?"

Suetonius opened a hand. "No more so than to give him command of a maniple and send him out against the Britons."

"I suppose not."

"Besides, how many choices do I have? Agricola shows definite promise, and I sent orders two weeks ago for him to prepare for us in Londinium. Cerialis tells me that Veturius performs his administrative duties competently, but without any real enthusiasm. I haven't decided about Titus—he'll either go far or nowhere."

"Point taken," Marcianus said.

Suetonius sighed. "Before they arrived, I was convinced that Rome purposed to saddle me with flippant dandies whose only aim in life was to pour a glass of wine without spilling it."

Marcianus shook his head. "To think that the future of Rome lies in hands like those."

"One can hope that youth grow up or die." Suetonius paced across the room. "You'll remain here for the winter, Gellius. I must deny you the pleasures of Londinium. The Deceangli aren't completely pacified, and I can't have the spring offensive threatened."

Marcianus shrugged. "My wife won't object. I'm getting too old for young men's pleasures. The boats will be completed and the troops prepared for the spring campaign."

"I don't dare leave the preparations in inexperienced hands. With the destruction of the Druidae, resistance in Britannia will crumble. Nothing must go wrong."

"Rest assured, it won't."

"Hold the fort, Gellius." A narrow smile creased Suetonius's thin lips.

The squadron left at daybreak: a wing of cavalry with baggage animals, couriers, clerks, beneficiarii, and other headquarters functionaries. Suetonius rode a fine horse, the equal of Sergius's animal, and one that garnered envious looks from the cavalry prefect.

Sergius took Cara; he didn't want to leave the dog behind in strange hands. The wolfhound seemed content to lope along at the sedate pace set by the baggage animals. She cast wistful looks at the forest but never strayed far afield.

"An excellent animal," the governor remarked, breaking a silence that had lasted for miles.

"She saved my life on the hunt, sir," Sergius confirmed, unsure whether Suetonius approved of his acquisition.

"Guarding your back?"

"My front, sir."

The direct route from Deva to Londinium bypassed Viroconium, but Suetonius turned aside to pay a surprise inspection on the fortress. From Viroconium, the route followed a chain of forts and fortlets—Uxacona, Pennocrucium, Letocetum, Manduessedum, Venonis, Tripontium, and Verulamium, to name some—most located an easy day's infantry march apart.

The temperature moderated as the squadron headed south, although the weather never became pleasant. Sergius took ill and spent three days wiping his nose, sneezing, and shivering in his saddle.

Suetonius seemed unfazed by the harshness of the climate. Sergius noticed that the commander never demanded from the troops what he wouldn't brave himself. One day, when a storm swept down from the north and flung shattered snowflakes and half-frozen raindrops past men and animals, Suetonius called a halt and helped erect the tents himself, sharing a humble papilio instead of his own larger tent.

The next day the snow had completely disappeared.

When after nearly two weeks the outskirts of Londinium emerged from low-lying clouds, the weather had changed to a clinging drizzle that penetrated cloaks and left men chilled and wet beneath masses of sodden wool.

The small cemeteries that lined the approaches to the city stood stark and somber in the gloom. Ground-hugging mist muted the hues of Londinium's red tile roofs. The timber and plaster buildings dripped with rain as if they wept.

Perhaps it was but a trick of weather and mood, but to Sergius Londinium seemed profoundly unhappy, although he couldn't put a finger on exactly what gave him that impression.

Londinium should have been a happy town. After all, only recently had the military and financial government of Britannia been transferred to Londinium from Camulodunum. Camulodunum remained the capital, and the Temple of Claudius ensured its prominent religious stature, but Londinium had rapidly overtaken its sister city as the center of the province. Trade flowed up the river to Londinium's docks and then migrated out across an expanding network of roads. Camulodunum, seated outside the main roads, seemed destined for eclipse.

Londinium, in the heart of secure territory on the north bank of the Tamesis, required no legionary fortress, only a garrison fort. The small temple couldn't rival Camulodunum's Temple of Claudius, and that spared the city's inhabitants a sizable tax burden. But the governor's villa, the procurator's house, army headquarters, and the financial offices formed a substantial urban center.

The road led past Procurator Decianus Catus's house. Lamplight flickered through cracks in the shutters.

Did servants reside there? Or was the procurator in residence?

Sergius hoped for the former.

The cavalry escort clattered off to the barracks and stables at the fort.

Suetonius's personal guard dismounted with him at the governor's villa. A servant pointed Sergius toward the row of tribune's houses, and directed Quintus to quarters in the same building.

Cara's sudden barks alerted Sergius to the opening of the house door next to his. A familiar figure appeared in the opening and called, "Welcome to Londinium, winter paradise of Britannia!"

Sergius crossed to clap the other man on the shoulder. "Julius!"

Agricola's keen eyes examined him. "You've won honors."

Sergius touched the torque. "The first step on the path to glory."

"I'm envious. Back on HQ staff now?"

Sergius nodded, "Officially."

Agricola's expression brightened, "Good." He stepped back and beckoned, "I'm keeping you outside in the rain. Come in and tell me all about the northwest and your battle with Culhwch."

"You know of that?"

"News travels. You're a hero—minor, of course," Agricola laughed.

THIRTEEN

Y ou don't know how glad I am to have help," Agricola expressed the following morning as he and Sergius made their way to their offices in the principia. "But mark my words, you'll find work in headquarters considerably different from the legionary offices. You only had a taste before. Now you won't have Marcianus as a buffer. Suetonius expects work to be done right the first time." He rubbed his side. "It still hurts from the last time he ripped a strip off me."

"I don't expect it to be easy," Sergius replied.

"It's hard to believe that so great a war hero as yourself would need assistance," Agricola teased, "but if you find yourself desperate for advice, just ask."

"Is it true you were returned to Londinium because your presence in Isca threw the Dumnonii into such great panic that it was feared the *Augusta* might actually have to fight?" Sergius retorted.

"Nothing could panic that bloodthirsty lot," Agricola chuckled, "let alone my gentle demeanor."

In daylight, with a clear sky, Londinium didn't seem so bad. The red roof tiles shone slick with yesterday's rain. The governor's quarters and official buildings overlooked a prospect of the river where the masts of sailing ships berthed for the winter huddled together. The long bridge stretched southward to the smaller settlement on the far bank, which blended into woods and fields.

If he ignored the shabbiness of much of the city's remainder, then maybe he could survive until spring.

The hopes Sergius had entertained of a quick reunion with Ailidh were dashed almost immediately. Agricola's prediction of work proved correct. Overseeing the deployment of some fifty thousand legionaries and auxiliaries scattered in a network of fortresses, forts, and camps proved vastly more taxing than the affairs of a single legion.

Every day brought couriers from yet another far-flung fort whose location Sergius had to determine from the large-scale provincial map. His head swam with the magnitude of details. Deaths, retirements, reassignments, promotions, transfers, disciplinary actions, and other personnel matters formed only part of the work. Supplies, weapon shipments and fabrication, grain stores, road construction (suspended for the winter), and everything from lead mining to tile works came under the governor's scrutiny.

As if military matters weren't enough, judicial affairs consumed additional time. As the highest authority in the province, Suetonius administered justice in both civil and military cases, particularly capital crimes. That aspect, at least, was familiar to Sergius from his experience on Aquileia's capital crimes police.

In consequence of these functions, headquarters swarmed with staff: commentarienses, adiutors, cornicularii, and stratores. Beneficiarii oversaw the security of supply routes; speculatores had custody of prisoners. Sergius found it hard to move without tripping over a functionary.

And of course, a watchful eye needed to be kept on the fractious Britons, both the recalcitrant tribes that gnawed on the fringes of the province and the supposed allies like the Iceni and Brigantes whom no one completely trusted.

Despite appearances, not every matter came to Sergius's attention. As the liaison to the Fourteenth Legion, his concern focused on matters relating to the *Gemina*. Similarly, Agricola's concern centered around Second *Augusta*. Veturius and Titus remained in the field but sent reports from time to time about the *Valeria* and *Hispana*.

Sergius wondered why they weren't at headquarters.

"Perhaps they're not ready for it," Agricola speculated without a hint of smugness, as if it was merely a matter of course.

As Agricola had foretold months previously, on one occasion they dined as guests at the praetorium—to make up numbers for dinner with a trio of visiting dignitaries. Contrary to Titus's remarks, Suetonius's wife Livy, though plain, wasn't spotty and proved to be a charming hostess. Her sparkling personality contrasted with her husband's dour gravitas. The governor's children remained out of sight. The excellent food tasted far better, Sergius thought, than anything Veturius was getting in the north.

By dint of hard work and diligence, Sergius managed not to incur Suetonius's anger and even received compliments on the quality of his work.

Sergius and Agricola spent many evenings together, discussing matters of mutual interest in the bathhouse or over friendly games. While various junior tribunes came and went and pursued women and lascivious entertainment—no small feat in a small provincial town—Sergius and Agricola discussed philosophy.

Agricola was a serious student. "My father thinks I study too much," he said once.

"Do you agree?"

"Of course. But I do it anyway."

"My father had no time for philosophy. He said it was the last thing he needed when facing a forest full of Germans."

"The stylus might be mightier than the gladius," Agricola concurred, "but sometimes the gladius comes in very handy."

On a day in late February, as they passed the Temple of Jupiter—far smaller than Camulodunum's grandiose Temple of Claudius—Agricola asked, "Is it true that members of the Way refuse to worship the Imperial cult?"

The unexpected question from the areligious Agricola caught Sergius by surprise. "It's true," he confirmed. "We don't consider it compatible with the worship of God."

"Why not? The Imperial cult binds the Empire together in a common philosophy and purpose."

"Our founder Christus said 'render to Caesar that which is Caesar's, and to God that which is God's.'"

"Meaning what?" Agricola frowned.

"Meaning that we should respect government, obey its laws, strive for the common good, pay taxes even, but not give it things it doesn't deserve. We may respect and honor Caesar but not worship him."

"Sometimes it's easier to worship than respect," Agricola said wryly.

"Seditious today, are you?" Sergius chuckled. "Only God is worthy of worship."

"But if the emperor is a god?"

"Do you really believe that Claudius was divine?" Sergius scoffed. "Or that Nero will be?"

Agricola assumed a pensive expression. "No. If I recall, both Tiberius and Claudius denied any claims to deity."

"Exactly. The Senate decreed they should become gods. What kind of gods are ones we create ourselves?"

"I'll accept that point," Agricola related. "But worshiping past emperors promotes loyalty to the Empire."

"Does it?" Sergius asked. "What was it you called the Temple of Claudius—'a blatant bastion of alien rule'?"

"Whose priests use every pretext to drain the country dry," Agricola finished. "I was being facetious. Not every temple is as oppressive."

"So tell me how gods who suck the wealth from a country build loyalty, too. The doctrine is a lie."

"But the official pantheon," Agricola protested. "Jupiter, Juno, Minerva? How can you deny them their place?"

"How many gods can there be?" Sergius asked. "Whenever the Empire incorporates a new province or people, their gods are added to Roman ones. It seems there are as many gods as there are people. Did you know that in Athens there's an altar to the 'Unknown God,' just in case they forgot one?"

"Cautious people, those Greeks."

"One of our members, Paullus, saw it."

Sergius became abruptly conscious of the fact that he hadn't made an effort to seek out the apostle. He wasn't sure why not; perhaps he didn't want to hear Paullus making cryptic comments about his military career.

"In fact," Sergius continued, "Paullus is here in Londinium. Maybe you'd like to come and hear him speak sometime."

Agricola held up a hand, "No thanks."

"He's a very learned man. He debated philosophy with the Athenians."

Agricola's expression grew wary. "I'll think about it."

They passed Jupiter's temple and the tiny Mithraeium.

"Don't you claim that Christus was divine?" Agricola asked.

"Yes, God with us."

"So what's the difference between him and the emperors?"

"Did Claudius rise from the dead?" Sergius countered.

"Of course not. Neither did Julius Caesar, or Augustus, or Tiberius, or—Hades forbid—Gaius Caligula. I know where you're going and I don't believe it. Spare me your ridiculous legends."

"One of our centurions, Publius Maximus, was in charge of Christus's crucifixion. Afterward, hundreds of people saw Christus alive and talked to him. Some of those people are still living."

"Have you met one?"

Sergius nodded, "In Corinth. A man named Cleopas."

"A lunatic."

"A wine merchant. Very astute."

"Myths for the plebeians."

"Sergius Paulus, the governor of Cyprus, became a believer a few years ago. So—I hear—is Aulus Plautius's wife."

Agricola shook his head, "It's too much for me. Good hard philosophy is enough for my tastes."

"Hard philosophy?" Sergius questioned. "Is that like solid sand?"

Agricola wagged a finger. "We'll make a philosopher out of you yet."

Later, Sergius put his reservations aside and made an effort to discover where Paullus was staying. In a city of forty thousand people, he doubted it would be easy.

And it wasn't.

It took a week of patiently questioning people he met in the forum, local officials, anyone he thought might know, before he discovered where Paullus was teaching. One evening, he finished work early, broke away from Agricola, who politely declined to come, and made his way to the house of Caecilius Constantius, a potter.

Caecilius owned a two-story, timber-framed building on a street a few blocks removed from the forum.

A servant led Sergius through the closed downstairs shop, where local crude pottery, sold at not too exorbitant prices, rested next to shelves of expensive red-toned Samian ware imported from factories in Gaul. Bowls, beakers, amphorae, jars, flasks, and cups nestled together in comfortable profusion.

Caecilius prospered well enough to have solid cement floors and plaster walls but not enough to afford mosaics or a better building closer to the fashionable forum. The potter's private rooms consisted of a series of low-ceilinged rooms above his shop.

"The soldier returns!" a familiar voice greeted, as the servant ushered Sergius into an upper room.

The tall figure of Aristarchus, stooped to avoid low beams, made his way through a knot of a dozen people—some Roman and several Britons.

Sergius greeted the Greek. "Suetonius has seen fit to transfer me to Londinium for the winter."

"We're glad to see you. Come, take a seat."

Sergius sat on a low bench.

"You're alone?" Aristarchus reclined beside him.

"Yes. Why?"

"Your young woman, Ailidh," Aristarchus replied. "I thought she might be with you."

Sergius shook his head. "I haven't seen her for months. In fact, I'm not even sure exactly where she lives other than outside Camulodunum. I'd hoped to be able to take a trip to find out but haven't been able to get away."

Sergius glanced aside. "The Briton locals aren't exactly eager to volunteer information to the army."

Aristarchus pursed his curved lips. "I'm sure there must be someone who knows where Egomas the dog-seller's house is. I'll try to find out for you."

"Thank you," Sergius replied with sincerity.

Aristarchus stood. He raised his voice to garner the attention of the worshipers. "Let's sing a hymn while we wait for Paullus." His voice boomed confidently through the room:

> "Endeavoring to keep the unity of the Spirit
> in the bond of peace.
> There is one body,
> and one Spirit,
> even as you are called
> in one hope of your calling;
> One Lord,
> one faith,
> one baptism,
> One God and father of all,
> who is above all,

and through all,
and in all."

Sergius, unfamiliar with the tune, sang it the best he could.

When the hymn had finished, Paullus entered, leaning on Lucanus's arm for support.

Once again, Sergius wondered how so frail-appearing a man could boast such an indomitable spirit. Paullus's eyes peered through the lamplit room, fastened for a moment on Sergius, and then moved on.

"I will talk to you tonight about fighting," the apostle began. "Perhaps you've had enough of war and conflict. For the most part, the Empire lies at peace. But outside our borders live tribes and peoples to whom war is a way of life.

"As followers of Christus, our struggle isn't against human foes but against the authorities and potentates of this dark age."

It's as well Agricola didn't come, Sergius thought. *He'd take Paullus's words as applying to government; the emperor himself, perhaps.*

"We fight the forces of evil in heavenly places. To do that, every one must find his strength in the mighty power of the Lord," the apostle proclaimed. His arm extended, index finger pointing at Sergius. "Tribune, what do you do before battle?"

Sergius, caught by surprise and conscious that all eyes had turned on him, stammered, "Prepare for the fight. Put on my armor."

"Would you fight without your armor?"

"Not if I could avoid it."

"What do you wear?"

"A lorica, a helmet, belt, shoes, gladius, shield—"

Paullus's upraised hand halted his recitation.

"The armor of God," Paullus said, "will enable you to stand your ground against the forces of evil." He mimicked buckling a belt. "Fasten on the belt of truth that binds all together. As your lorica, your breastplate, wear integrity to protect your heart and vitals. Let the caligae on your feet be the gospel of peace, to give you firm footing."

Paullus paused for breath.

"Take up the great scutum, the shield of faith, to quench the burning arrows of the evil one. Accept salvation as your helmet. Your gladius is the sword the Spirit gives you, the word of God."

Sergius listened intently, trying to commit Paullus's words to memory. Some of the apostle's teachings he found hard; try as he might, he couldn't relate to Jewish history and law. But this was soldier talk. This he could understand.

"Constantly ask God's help in prayer, and pray always in the Spirit," Paullus concluded.

The apostle sat. Lucanus took his place, brought out bread and wine, and led the assembly in the simple ceremony that Christus had commanded.

Aristarchus dismissed them with a hymn.

> "Now unto the King eternal,
> immortal,
> invisible,
> the only wise God,
> be honor and glory for ever and ever.
> Amen."

With the taste of wine on his tongue, Sergius joined in singing the familiar tune.

As the congregation filed out, Paullus beckoned to him. Sergius moved next to the apostle.

"You wear no armor tonight," Paullus observed, fingering Sergius's heavy winter cloak. Beneath it, he wore only his belted tunic, and, as usual, his sword.

"I wasn't expecting a fight," Sergius replied.

"The enemy strikes when least expected."

Sergius smiled. The comment sounded like one Suetonius would make.

"War is the same wherever it's fought," Sergius stated.

The apostle shook his head. "War against men will eventually end. War against evil has eternal consequences."

Paullus made to turn aside, but halted. "Seek your friend," he said abruptly.

"Excuse me?" Sergius blurted.

"The girl. Seek her." Paullus's watery, clouded eyes shone with reflected lamplight. "Gird yourself and find her."

"Why are you telling me this? Is she in danger?"

Paullus shook his head, "I cannot say. All I know is that you must seek her."

Sergius rose. "I'll go now."

Paullus laid a hand on Sergius's arm, the strength in his fingers more than Sergius expected.

"There's no need to act in haste. Prepare first."

Aristarchus spoke from the shadows. "Wait until I find where the girl's home is located."

Paullus beckoned, "Lucanus, my friend, help me. I would pray before I rest."

The physician crossed the room quickly. He gave Sergius a quick smile.

Again, Paullus's old eyes sought Sergius's. "Pray too, my young friend, that you stand firm in the testing days ahead."

Buoyed on his physician's arm, Paullus shuffled from the room.

"Does he always speak in riddles?" Sergius asked Aristarchus.

"Frequently," the Greek replied. "But a wiser man than Paullus doesn't live."

Sergius took his time walking to his house. Was Ailidh in danger? The thought gave him chills. If so, what kind of danger? When Procurator Decianus Catus was here at the financial offices in Londinium, did he pose a threat to her? Sergius had taken great care to avoid crossing the procurator's path. Surely he'd have no cause to harm Ailidh—he probably didn't even know who she was. All he knew was that Sergius had robbed him of a night's pleasure.

Was she threatened from Camulodunum? Again, by whom?

He didn't know the town or the people well enough to hazard a guess.

The country of the Trinovantes lay at peace. They allied with their northern neighbors, the Iceni. The Catuvellauni, since their defeat at Rome's hands, left the Trinovantes alone.

Sergius slapped his thigh. Why had he delayed visiting Ailidh? Surely, if he'd made a greater effort, he could have wangled a few days leave—goodness knew, junior tribunes managed it; they didn't care about making a good impression on the governor. But no, Sergius had spent evenings working late, attending official dinners, and putting work ahead of his own desires.

Just what duty called him to do.

And now . . . what if it was too late?

It couldn't be. Surely God wouldn't have sent him a message through Paullus if it was too late.

He shook his head. He couldn't traipse across the countryside in a wild quest, asking everyone he met where Egomas's dwelling might be.

Sergius prayed Aristarchus fulfilled his promise quickly.

Another thought crossed his mind. The courier who'd delivered his letters must know where Egomas dwelt. So did Veturius. Why hadn't he ever queried his friend?

He quickened his footsteps.

In the morning, he'd seek out the courier.

FOURTEEN

Dry leaves, the brown and withered relics of summer, crackled and rustled as Sergius cantered along the track that led away from Camulodunum toward the Trinovantes's tribal center. His horse's hooves trampled last year's greenery into the dirt and mud. Romans built their gravel and stone roads to where they wanted to go; if the Britons preferred to live at the ends of dirt tracks, the choice belonged to them.

Behind him rode a pair of cavalrymen from a cohors equitate that Sergius had appropriated to accompany him from Londinium. The men didn't disguise their dismay at riding into the bleak midwinter countryside, but they kept their comments to themselves. Sergius intercepted numerous dark looks exchanged between them but pretended not to notice.

He'd debated about the size of the escort he should take. This close to Camulodunum, among the half-Romanized Trinovantes, he might not need one at all. But he'd decided upon a pair of troopers as enough to dissuade any malcontent Britons from harassing him.

His horse sidestepped holes and the worst of the ruts the Britons' wagons and chariots had gouged into the turf. Cara trotted alongside, tail erect, ceaselessly alert, stopping only now and then to chew mud balls from her paws.

Aristarchus had made good on his promise. The pottery seller knew a bronzesmith from Camulodunum who in turn counted Egomas the dog-seller among his acquaintances. Aristarchus's efforts had preempted Sergius's barely initiated inquiries about the wayward courier.

At his first chance, when he judged the moment opportune, Sergius had requested several days leave.

His initial day's ride brought him to Camulodunum, where he had stayed at the garrison. That evening, the sight of the Trinovantes's tribal town two miles distant brought a quickening of his breath. Now, on a cold, clear morning when the air nipped at his nostrils and the tips of his ears, he headed for the center.

Smoke from cooking fires heralded the town's presence. They called this a *town*? No Roman would misuse the word. Camulodunum and Londinium were towns, not this.

He turned aside down a fork in the road, skirting the tribal center just before he reached the earth rampart that guarded the clump of huts the Trinovantes called their capital. As many of the tribe's nobles as cared to lived here; the remainder and the commonfolk resided in huts on their own land.

The terrain undulated in gentle hills, similar to the area around Deva, and lay cloaked in a forest of gaunt, leafless trees. The track meandered, never taking a straight course when a more sinuous venture presented itself. At times, Sergius had to duck away from the grasping fingers of overhanging branches.

The track wound out of sight of the town until only the clop of the horses' hooves disturbed the profound stillness; no other travelers intruded on the day.

Sergius ignored the multitude of sidetracks that branched off the main road and continued for another mile until the track parted the forest and opened out into a cleared area several acres in extent.

A six-foot tall palisade of crudely pointed, roughly hewn stakes enclosed Egomas's homestead. Twin gateposts upheld cross beams and a lattice designed more for decoration than defense. The gate was closed, but the conical, thatched roof of a circular hut peeked over the top of the palisade. Smoke drifted into the still air.

As Sergius reined to a halt, a chorus of dogs erupted into frantic barking. Cara pressed her nose to a gap in the palisade and whined, her tail thrashing back and forth.

A male voice shouted in the Briton tongue. Sergius had picked up enough to make out the words.

"Quiet, dogs! Who's out there? Go away!"

The dogs barked unabated.

"Quiet!"

A light wickerwork gate covered with animal skins stood open at the hut's entrance. A stocky figure appeared in the square doorway. He brandished a stick.

"Go away, I said!" He squinted toward the front gate.

Sergius waved.

A scowl appeared on Egomas's face. "You," he gibed, switching to Latin. "I thought we'd seen the last of you."

He came halfway to the gate before stopping to swing his staff at the dogs. "Quiet!" The stick connected with an animal. The dog yelped; the remainder cowered.

When the barking had subsided, Egomas growled, "What do you want?"

Sergius gestured to the gate. "May I come in?"

"Why?"

"To visit Ailidh."

Egomas cast a furtive glance toward the hut. "She's not here."

"Where is she, then?"

"Gone. To visit her father's people in Venta Icenorum."

Sergius peered at the dog-seller. Then he looked past Egomas at the hut. He cupped his hands around his mouth. "Ailidh!" he called. "It's Sergius! Are you home?"

"Silence!" Egomas snapped. "You'll start the dogs off again." He brandished the staff.

Sergius ignored him. "Ailidh!"

"Go away!" Egomas demanded.

A woman's figure appeared behind the dog-seller. "Sergius?"

Egomas flushed. "Back in the hut, girl!"

Ailidh came slowly out. Egomas extended an arm. She skirted him. "Don't be silly. Where's your hospitality?"

Egomas stabbed the butt of the staff into the ground and planted his feet.

Ailidh raised the bar and swung the gate open.

Sergius dismounted.

Ailidh halted in the opening. "Did you lose your way?"

Sergius blinked. "Ailidh? What's the matter?"

She looked to the ground, then back up. "When you didn't answer my letter—"

"But I did!" Sergius protested. "I wrote three times."

"I never received them. I thought your interest had waned."

"Waned?" Sergius clenched his fists. "That wretched courier! I paid him good money! Wait 'til I get my hands on him. I hope his horse throws him into the biggest pile of dung—"

Ailidh bent to fondle Cara.

"Cara! Have you missed me?" She checked the dog's eyes and ears and patted Cara's haunches and belly. She looked up at Sergius. "You've taken good care of her."

"She's taken good care of me," he replied. "She saved my life on a hunt."

Ailidh beckoned, "Come in."

Sergius pivoted toward the two cavalrymen, who quickly wiped smirks from their faces. Their expressions proclaimed they'd sooner be anywhere else than in a Briton's hut.

What could he do with them?

The Trinovantes's territory seemed peaceful enough. And one of the horses had developed a limp, enough to slow it to a walk. It would take considerably longer for the men to return to Camulodunum than it had to come this far.

"Return to Camulodunum," Sergius gave leave. "You may have liberty, but wait for my return this evening."

The senior man grinned, "Yes, sir. Thank you." He saluted, and the two men wheeled their mounts and rode off down the track.

Ailidh took Sergius's horse's halter and led the animal inside the palisade to where two other horses browsed on mounds of hay. She swatted its rump, and it trotted to join the others.

"Welcome to my home," Ailidh invited.

"He's not staying," Egomas stated. "Say your piece and be gone, Roman."

Ailidh held Sergius's arm. "Ignore my uncle. Sometimes his speech doesn't match the tenor of his mind."

Still holding Sergius's arm, she directed him toward the doorway of the hut.

"I'm not having a Roman inside my house," Egomas said.

"You take their money inside," Ailidh retorted.

"I'll thrash you—" Egomas began.

He bit the words off at a glare from Sergius. Sergius held the dog-seller's eyes until the older man lowered his gaze.

Egomas muttered under his breath, hoisted his staff, and stumped around to the back of the hut.

Sergius waited until the dog-seller had vanished from sight, then said, "He hasn't changed. Still as friendly as ever."

"He'll never change," Ailidh sighed. "But this is a surprise, to see you here."

Sergius remembered Paullus's words. "Are you all right?" he asked.

"I'm fine."

"Are you in any danger?"

Her eyebrows rose. "Danger? No. Why?"

"I saw Paullus in Londinium," Sergius explained. "He said I should visit you, which I would have done in any case."

"Did he say I was in danger?"

"Not in so many words, no. But he made it sound as if something was wrong."

"Not wrong, exactly," she admitted, "but . . . ." She tugged his arm. "Inside."

Sergius ducked beneath the doorway. The heavy thatch cut off daylight. A lamp burned on a low table, a fire crackled on a pair of iron firedogs, and a small caldron hung by a chain from a tripod near the flames. The hut's interior was warm and smoky. It smelled like the tribal town, only concentrated. Sergius removed his heavy traveling cloak and scarf.

Ailidh straightened from stoking the fire. Her expression darkened. "Where did you get that?"

"Get what?"

"The torque."

Sergius fingered the golden loop. "From a Deceangli whose war party was attacking us."

She came close and touched the torque. "I was right to be worried about you." She took her hand away and traced the scar on his forehead. "This was close." She turned away. "You wear the torque as my people, not as a trophy on your armor."

"It seemed the right thing to do."

Her eyes cast amber glints from the firelight.

"I sought to honor you," Sergius said. "The man was a noble."

She lowered her eyelids and indicated an animal skin laid on the earth. "Sit with me."

He sat close.

She folded her hands in her lap. "Lovernios has visited."

Sergius's heart missed a beat.

"He warns me that great disaster will fall upon the Britons. He says it's because we've neglected the old gods. They're punishing us by sending the Romans."

She bit her lip. Sergius waited for her to speak, then he prompted, "What do you think?"

"I thought that I would never consider the old gods again. But . . . oh Sergius, when I'm constantly being urged, and shunned because I don't join in the rites . . . there goes the daughter of Cathair, she's an outcast, she's rejected the gods. I can read it in people's eyes, Sergius."

Sergius squeezed her hand.

She gulped. "There's a part of me that wants to go back. Some days I just want to belong . . . to stop being different. . . ."

Sergius held her quivering hand in both of his. "I know, Ailidh."

"Does it bother you, too?" Her eyes searched his.

He nodded. "When I don't observe the festivals or worship the Imperial cult—I'm disloyal to the Empire, Agricola thinks, although he doesn't say it. But we've been taken away from the old, false gods. We can't turn back."

"No." She sighed. "Just having you here, having someone I can talk to who understands, is a comfort. I've wanted to go to Londinium to see Paullus. But who would care for the dogs?" She jumped to her feet. "Enough of this. I'm being remiss. Will you have a drink?"

"Please."

Ailidh decanted a dark liquid from a small barrel into a pottery beaker.

Sergius sipped. He coughed. "What is this?"

"Beer. We don't have mead," Ailidh apologized, "and Egomas won't buy good wine, just thin and vinegary acetum. He saves for the future he imagines he will have."

Sergius studied the interior of the hut. A partly woven garment hung on a loom. A clay oven and a low table bearing small effigies completed the domestic arrangements. "Is it just you and he?"

"Merna, his wife, died two years ago. His son was killed fighting the Catuvellauni."

"You Britons fight much among yourselves."

"It is how it has always been. Always will be, I suppose. We're an independent people."

Egomas's harsh voice bellowed from outside the door. "Girl! Your dogs need tending."

"I'm coming." Ailidh cast a rueful glance at Sergius. "When they need tending, they're my dogs; for sale, they're his."

Sergius followed her into daylight.

Egomas leaned on his staff some paces away. His gaze avoided Sergius. Sergius moved to stand by the dog-seller and watched as Ailidh hoisted a pair of buckets and fetched stream water for the dogs.

"You're fortunate to have such a helper," he said.

Egomas grunted. "She works well enough, I suppose—when she's not being distracted."

"Do you know, when I was in Londinium, I met several people who knew of Egomas the dog-seller?"

"We go to Londinium in the spring." Egomas remained curt, but Sergius thought he detected a flicker of satisfaction in the dog-seller's voice.

"I'm sure you'll sell many dogs."

"What would you know of it, Roman?"

Sergius seated himself on a bundle of hay. Cara trotted over and flopped down beside him.

Ailidh selected a wolfhound bitch and guided the dog through her paces, making her sit and stay, retrieve, and walk by her side. The dog obeyed, seeming to enjoy the praise Ailidh dispensed.

Sergius's eyes, however, were not for the dog but for Ailidh. He couldn't tear them away from her graceful figure: now standing, now stooping, but always supple. Her reddish hair fanned out over her shoulders.

Once, she caught him staring. Her smile teased him, and then she turned away.

"Beautiful," he thought aloud.

"The dogs are that," Egomas agreed.

Sergius chuckled.

Egomas hoisted his staff and started off on other business. "You should be going, Roman."

But Sergius stayed as Ailidh selected another dog, male this time, and went through the same routine.

The afternoon fled past, with Ailidh occasionally calling out to him.

A snowflake splattered on his arm, and then another, and with a start he realized that the sky boiled with sullen, roiling gray clouds, and the temperature had plummeted.

"You've overstayed your welcome," Egomas berated. "A pity that you'll have to ride in the snow."

Ailidh gasped. "He can't go out in this!"

"It's not so bad," Sergius understated.

"It will be," she replied. "You could easily lose your way in the forest."

As if to emphasize her words, the snow intensified, blowing in streaky gusts. The dogs fled for shelter.

"Come inside," Ailidh instructed.

Egomas scowled but withheld comment.

They'd barely entered the hut when the wind burst over the thatched roof, and driving snow blotted out the light. Ailidh closed the wicker gate and arranged skins and robes to cut off drafts.

"I don't know which is worse," Sergius commented, as he stripped off his armor and warmed himself by the fire, "snow or rain."

"Stay in Rome," Egomas urged, "and enjoy the sun."

Lovernios paid scant attention to the clouds that descended from the winter sky as he rode south from Venta Icenorum. He would have blessed Lugh for a sunny day, but if truth be told, this day of wind and threatened snow served him better. The Roman cravens wouldn't venture from their forts on a day like this. With the soldiers huddled by their braziers, he needn't fear encountering a patrol or a courier.

Perhaps it was rash to venture afield with snowfall in the offing. But the news that he'd received had presented him with an opportunity he couldn't refuse. First, he'd learned from one of Boudicca's spies that a Roman officer, the conqueror of Culhwch, had been assigned to Londinium. This news was not terribly significant. The information that the officer had inquired the location of a dog-seller's hut near Camulo-dunum, however, was interesting. Lovernios had sensed a possibility in the making and instructed a trustworthy man to monitor the officer's movements. Yesterday, an exhausted warrior had brought word that the officer had ridden for Camulodunum.

Lovernios had saddled his horse and departed Venta Icenorum at night. Night riding proved tediously slow, but he had forty miles to cover. Come daylight, he'd been able to travel faster.

Lugh grant that he'd arrive in time.

And when the officer arrived at the Trinovantes's tribal center, then what? The Roman officer had ridden into a land where every pair of eyes belonged to a spy. Lovernios would have no problem following his movements.

Lovernios squelched a spasm of unease. He must do what had to be done, distasteful or not.

He bent low over his horse as snowflakes sped past his ears.

By the time dusk, a dimming of the already dim sky, arrived, the storm showed no signs of abating. Wind whistled and moaned around the hut. Thick mantles of snow festooned the trees. From time to time the sharp crack of breaking wood indicated a branch yielding to the weight.

Sergius parted the heavy woolen blanket that helped insulate the hut's door and peered into the gloom.

"You'll have to stay the night," Ailidh announced over his shoulder.

Sergius spoke to Egomas, "I'm sorry to impose."

"Can't be helped," the dog-seller grumbled. "But I expect you to pay for your lodging."

"Uncle!" Ailidh exclaimed.

"I wouldn't wish to be a burden," Sergius excused. "Egomas may have a few sestercii to recompense him for his hospitality."

Ailidh wrapped herself in a densely woven robe. "I'm going to check on the animals."

Sergius picked up his cloak. "I'll help you."

He followed Ailidh into the storm.

The wolfhounds, apparently impervious to cold and snow, curled against the lee side of the hut, noses buried under tails. The horses, necks bowed in resignation, accepted the weather with calm stoicism. Sergius collected an armload of firewood and carried it inside.

Cara followed him through the doorway gate.

"Not the dog," Egomas growled from his seat by the fire.

"She always sleeps beside me," Sergius insisted.

"A spoiled dog is useless," the dog-seller retorted.

"But a cared-for one is loyal," Sergius countered.

"It's bad enough my house will smell of a Roman, without stinking of wet dog as well."

After attending to the animals' needs, Ailidh fetched bowls and ladled from the cauldron. The humans ate a stew of meat and grain with a few dried vegetables. Sergius wolfed the meal as if it had been one of Veturius's Aunt Drusilla's famed banquets.

At the completion of the meal, Ailidh sorted through a pile of clothes. She selected several trousers and blouses in need of repair and began to stitch and mend them.

Sergius stretched out on his side.

"Tell me of Rome," Ailidh requested.

"A big, smelly city," Egomas sneered.

"It is big—a million people—and can be smelly," Sergius agreed.

"So it's not perfect," the dog-seller delighted in the affirmation.

"Hardly. But Rome is called the Mother of Men."

He turned to Ailidh and launched into a description of the magnificent buildings, the temples and statues and triumphal arches; the circus maximus; the forum; the crowds of well-dressed wealthy people; the life of the city; and the theaters and entertainments.

Egomas interrupted once. "If your cities are so fine, why do you want our poor hovels?"

"Because . . . ," Sergius groped, "to bring civilization . . ."

"We have our own."

Ailidh rescued him. "Sergius doesn't create Roman policy, Uncle."

Egomas muttered something that Sergius didn't catch.

Sergius told her of the rulers: the great Julius Caesar who defeated Marc Anthony and laid the foundations for the Empire; Octavius, the first augustus, who reformed the tottering Republic and fashioned the Empire; dour, suspicious Tiberius, who executed people every day of the year; mad Caligula, who tried to invade Britannia but collected seashells on the coast of Gaul; the fool Claudius, whose foolishness concealed the mind of a shrewd ruler; and Nero, becoming emperor at sixteen after his mother Agrippina murdered her husband Claudius with poisoned mushrooms.

"I heard," Sergius relayed, "that at a banquet someone remarked that mushrooms were the food of the gods. Nero agreed. He said, 'My father Claudius became a god by eating mushrooms.'"

"Very good!" Egomas chuckled. "Would that more of you ate mushrooms."

Ailidh frowned as she stitched. "Your rulers sound very unpleasant."

Sergius thought immediately of Titus and his father Vespasian who hid from Agrippina's wrath. "It doesn't pay to rise too high," he agreed. "Tell me of your people."

"All right." Ailidh regaled him with stories of the warriors of the Celtae: Cassivelaunus, enemy of the Trinovantes; Cunobelinus of the Catuvellauni, whose sons Togodumnus and Caratacus opposed Claudius's invasion; Caratacus himself, bitter opponent of Rome who now lived as a free man in Rome; Prasutagus, king of the powerful Iceni; and Vercingetorix of the Gauls.

Every story had two sides, and Sergius realized that for the first time he was hearing a side of the invasion that he'd never learned in school.

"What of your family?" Ailidh asked.

"My father, Appius Sergius Rufus," Sergius explained, "was a legionary commander until being wounded on the Rhine. Now he's a judge. My mother Lydia is a very cultivated woman. She's always sending me books to read. She's not happy I'm in Britannia."

"Why?"

"She worries about my safety among the . . . uh . . . foreign peoples."

"Barbarians," Ailidh said, eyes on her sewing.

Sergius hurried on. "But she accepts it because, to obtain a decent position in society, I have to fulfill military as well as civil positions." He paused. "My mother's an excellent judge of character. I think you'd get along."

"Me? A savage Briton with a patrician woman of Rome?"

"You don't seem so savage to me."

Ailidh blushed. She asked, "Siblings?"

"My sister Julia is very much like you."

"Really? In what way?"

"High-spirited. My brother Manius, now, he's very shy. He looks up to me. I wonder sometimes how he's going to turn out."

"This is so interesting that I'm going to bed," Egomas announced curtly. "See to the fire, girl."

The dog-seller crossed the hut and flung himself onto a pile of blankets. Within minutes, snores emanated from his recumbent form.

Sergius stared into the crackling fire. "I'd like to take you away from here," he wished, after long moments had passed.

Ailidh gave a soft laugh. "This is my life, my home."

Sergius spread his hands. "You deserve better."

Her laugh was deeper. She stood and pirouetted. "In Rome? Dressed in finery, wearing jewels and perfume?"

"Yes!"

"Oh, Sergius! Don't you see? I'm happy here. I enjoy living in the country, with my dogs, among my people—"

"With him?" Sergius jerked his head toward the sleeping Egomas.

"Shhh! I don't need baubles or a fancy house."

"But still—"

"And the city . . . Even Camulodunum is too large. When I'm there, I long to return here. I shudder to think of Rome with all its people."

"Oh." Sergius looked down at the packed earth floor. "So you're perfectly happy and content."

"There is one thing that would make me even happier," she informed, very softly.

He didn't look up. "What?"

Her fingers touched his chin, raising his head. Her eyes glowed in the firelight. Her lips were inches from his.

Egomas coughed, loudly. Sergius looked across the hut but couldn't tell whether Egomas was awake or asleep.

Ailidh giggled. She raised Sergius's hand and pressed his fingers to her lips.

She rose. "You can sleep over there." She directed him to a pile of bedding a discrete distance from hers.

"Good night, Ailidh," Sergius murmured. He lay down in his tunic and pulled a woolen blanket to his neck.

"Good night, Sergius, Cara," Ailidh whispered so softly that Sergius doubted Egomas could have heard, even had he been awake and listening.

Sergius awoke.

He blinked, trying to pull his senses together.

The hut had cooled, and his cheeks tingled, but he remained warm under his blanket. A dull radiance glowed from the banked fire. The whistle of the wind had vanished.

What had awoke him?

Ailidh's breathing came soft and regular from some distance. Egomas's snores—

There weren't any.

Beside him, Cara whined: a low, urgent whine that trembled in the back of her throat.

"Easy, girl," Sergius said quietly and reached out to smooth the sharp bristles of the wolfhound's hackles.

And then he heard them: voices. Two men spoke in low tones outside the hut. He strained to hear and to translate the Briton words. He'd become better, but hardly fluent.

"I'm an old man! I harm no one." That was Egomas's wheedle.

"Come, Egomas. Where is your heart?"

Sergius frowned. The voice sounded familiar. He should know it, but he couldn't place it.

"My heart's not at fault. It's my limbs that ache with winter cold."

"Where was the sword of Egomas when the Roman invader arrived?" the voice mocked. "It's not every man who's given a second chance."

A long pause, during which Sergius racked his brains. Who was the second man?

And another thought occurred to him: what of the dogs? They raised no outcry. Only Cara, quivering beneath his hand, seemed disturbed.

The second man spoke: "A Roman stays with you."

He made the remark a statement, not a question. *Have I been observed?* Sergius wondered. *Did someone follow me from Camulodunum?* The thought tingled down his spine. Perhaps he shouldn't have dismissed his escort so casually.

The Trinovantes were surely used to the sight of Romans coming and going. Why would anyone follow him from Camulodunum here?

"He's a friend of the girl's," Egomas defended, "not mine."

"I know who he is. He's the conqueror of Culhwch."

"*Him?*"

"He follows the same Way that enslaved Ailidh. He's a dangerous man, Egomas, and he's in your house."

"What am I supposed to do?" Egomas sounded both pleading and scornful. "Put a knife between his ribs?"

"It would show your loyalty."

"And am I, an old man, able to carry his carcass to bury in the woods?"

"Perhaps not. But if he were to return to Camulodunum by a certain path, and others were waiting . . ." The sentence trailed away. "It could be done decently, with honor to the gods."

After a pause, Egomas consented, "That I can do. But I would need to ride with him."

"No great matter, surely."

"But if he fails to return to Londinium? He has men waiting in Camulodunum. What if they come looking?"

A laugh. "A Roman who ventures alone through the midwinter forests and disappears? They'll shake their heads at his foolishness."

So will I, Sergius thought. *I should have retained the escort, paid a brief visit and departed. The guards could have sat outside for a while. It wouldn't have hurt them.*

Egomas asked, "But why?"

The voice hardened. "Need you ask, Egomas? When the night is dark and the gods turn their backs on us? A Roman of rank and power will be an acceptable sacrifice."

"Sacrifice?" the dog-seller echoed.

Sergius could almost see the old man shake.

"Squeamish, Egomas? This is no time, unless you wish to be . . ." The threat trailed off, unspoken.

Egomas's voice was a hoarse whisper that barely penetrated the sod. "I will do as you say."

The voices faded as the men moved away, and Sergius could no longer distinguish the words.

For a few minutes, silence reigned. The wicker gate creaked, and the heavy blanket covering the door parted. Sergius closed his eyes.

He thought he sensed a presence stand over him for a moment.

Footsteps crossed to Egomas's bed. Sergius heard a grunt.

He lay awake, trying to make sense of the conversation. Egomas disliked him—no great surprise—but apparently he bore him no deadly ill will. But who was the second man who desired his death? Who wanted him as a sacrifice?

He remembered the grotesque god his father had brought home from Germania and trembled at the thought of being offered in a hideous ceremony.

He took a deep breath to steady his nerves. But the smell of Egomas's hut—reeking of sweat, wood smoke, and animal hides—only reminded him that here *he* was the stranger. Britannia might belong to Rome, but not this hut.

And not the men who whispered in the night.

Ailidh was right; the Britons were different.

He thought—not that it had any relevance to the situation—what it must have taken for her to express friendship toward him. Surely she must have been anxious—afraid even, of what his reaction as a member of the conquering army might have been. She probably felt afraid to befriend him, and afraid of offending him.

He exhaled slowly and forced his mind into a different channel.

How was he to counter the threat that awaited him in the morning?

FIFTEEN

He couldn't breathe.

Fingers covered his mouth, pushed into his cheek, stretched the skin around his eyes.

A hushed voice from far away called, "Sergius!"

He twisted. Another hand forced his shoulder down. Despite his best intentions, he'd fallen asleep, and now—Christus, have mercy, he prayed—it must be morning, and they'd come for him.

Death. Death had stolen up on him, and—

A half-formed cry died in his throat at a whisper in his ear, "Quiet. It's me."

His consciousness floundered to awareness.

Ailidh? Sergius mouthed.

Her hands moved away.

He sat up. She stood next to him, a slender form leaning over, silhouetted by the faint firelight.

Still speaking in a hushed voice, she urged, "Hurry. You must leave while Egomas is still asleep."

He replied equally quietly, "Egomas was talking with another man outside the hut last night."

"I heard them."

"I thought you were asleep."

"Cara's whines woke me. Rise quickly."

He pushed the blankets aside and straightened his tunic.

"Outside," Ailidh whispered and disappeared into the gloom.

Sergius tiptoed across the hut, testing each foot before he set it down so as not to trip over anything in the dark. Even so, he almost blundered into the loom. Egomas grunted and snored from his bed, a shapeless mound of gray. It seemed impossible to tell which end was his head and which his feet.

The wicker gate stood ajar. Sergius parted the blanket and stepped into pallid dawn.

Wet, slushy snow dripped from the hut's roof and squelched to the ground from overburdened trees. The sun peeked through the forest, casting elongated shadows and lightening the eastern sky to a pale yellow. The smells of wet thatch, grass, and animals assailed the morning.

Ailidh stood by his horse, its bridle and saddle already buckled in position. Cara wagged her tail.

"Hurry. Into your armor."

She held his lorica for him. Careful not to make the metal plates clash, he thrust his arms and head through the openings. She fastened the hooks. He tightened his belt and baldric and arranged his light cloak and the heavier traveling sagum.

"I was planning to rise early and creep away," he explained. "But you obviously rise earlier than I do."

Ailidh smiled. "You were still snoring."

"Besides," Sergius added, "I wouldn't know which way to travel to avoid an ambush."

Ailidh pointed. "If you continue on into the forest, you'll come to a place where the track divides. Take the left-hand path. The right rejoins the road to Camulodunum, where they'll be waiting. The left is longer, but it's rarely used."

"How do you know which path they'll choose?"

"Egomas won't ride farther than necessary. And he'll think, what is more natural than you returning by the same way you came?"

Sergius rested his hands on her shoulders. "Come with me."

She shook her head and looked away. Once more Sergius received the impression of a secret that she wasn't ready to share.

She assured, "I'm in no danger."

"Egomas will be angry if he finds out you helped me."

She shrugged. "I've dealt with his temper before. Go now, before he wakes."

Sergius led his horse to the gate in the palisade. Cara loped along.

"I don't want to leave you."

"You must." Ailidh lifted the bar and opened the gate just wide enough to allow the horse to pass through.

"I'll write," Ailidh promised, "and find a way to get it to you. If it's safe for you to return, I'll let you know."

Sergius paused. He knew Ailidh spoke rightly, but how could he desert her to Egomas's wrath?

As if sensing his thoughts, she said, "*Please*, Marcus. Go. I can't protect you from . . . from those who seek to harm you."

"Who is it that seeks that?"

She bit her lip. "A fox."

He frowned, then he squeezed her close, feeling the softness of her body against him and her breath on his neck. She pushed him gently toward his horse.

He vaulted onto the animal. "Promise me you'll let me know if you're in trouble. I'll come."

She nodded. "Ride quickly."

The gate swung to. Ailidh dropped the bar into place.

"God be with you," Sergius said.

"And with you."

Sergius urged his horse into a canter. Cara followed alongside. Before the track disappeared into the woods, Sergius turned to look back. Ailidh stood by the entrance to the hut. She waved. Sergius returned the gesture. Then the trees cut off sight of girl and hut.

Cara whined.

"I'm worried too," Sergius confessed.

Ducking to avoid low-hanging branches, Sergius rode as quickly as he dared.

At any moment, he expected armed men to jump out of the forest. Cara should give him warning, but still he kept one hand close to his sword hilt at all times. Birds fled squawking from trees, and once a deer startled him by bounding across the track ahead of him.

He'd thought a ride in Trinovantes's territory would be safe. But the nape of his neck prickled.

He reached the division in the track. He paused to look down the innocent-appearing path, rimmed with fresh, undisturbed snow. He saw no sign of either men or animals.

Alert for danger, he turned left, as Ailidh had advised.

The track narrowed until it became a mere rut, barely wide enough for a horse. He plastered himself to the horse's neck as branches thrust at him.

Only when he'd put several miles behind him and the hut—and possible danger—did he finally realize whose voice had been conversing with Egomas in the dead of night.

"A fox," Ailidh had said.

The second man was Lovernios, the Druid.

Ailidh waited as long as she dared, then she stirred the fire until it quickened to life. She added more branches. As the flames flickered higher, Egomas mumbled and rolled over.

He snorted, sniffed, and finally heaved himself up. He squinted against the firelight. "Is it morning, girl?"

"It is."

He stood, stretched, and yawned. "Your friend sleeps late." He reached for his staff and prodded Sergius's bedding. "Rise, Roman."

He blinked, bent over, and yanked the blankets away. "He's gone!"

Ailidh still knelt by the fire. "He rode early for Camulodunum."

"By the gods!" Egomas bolted for the door. He halted in the opening, surveying the trampled snow outside.

Then he spun around. "This is your doing!"

"What is?"

"Helping him get away."

"Get away?" Ailidh asked innocently. "From whom?"

"I—," Egomas stopped short. "Don't cross me, girl." He raised the staff and took a step toward her.

Ailidh kept the fire between herself and the dog-seller. "I'm not a small child or a dog to be beaten at your whim! Touch me, and you'll pay for every blow."

"Bah!" Egomas threw the staff away. He collapsed to a sitting position on the floor. "Romans, Druí, willful women! Die, Egomas, and be done with all of them."

Ailidh circled the fire and rested a hand on his shaking shoulder. "You wanted Sergius gone," she reminded.

Egomas shrugged her hand away. "Leave me alone. You don't know what you've cost me."

Ailidh picked up the small cauldron of leftover stew and carried it to the fire. She attached it to its chain hanging from the tripod. "I do," she countered softly. "But it's no more than I've cost myself."

The sun stood high overhead when a man's voice called from the gate. "Egomas! Are you home?"

The dog-seller trembled, hunched beside the fire. "Answer him," he directed to Ailidh. "I can't."

Ailidh hesitated, then rose and went to the entrance. A robed, cowled figure stood outside the palisade. "The gate is unbarred, Cousin," she called.

The man pushed the gate open and entered. Long strides carried him over to Ailidh. "Is Egomas at home?"

Ailidh nodded, "He is. Be welcome."

Lovernios paused. "You seem nervous, Cousin."

"Tired, that's all."

The dark eyes assessed her. Then the Druí stooped and entered the hut.

Egomas raised haggard eyes. He waved Ailidh away. "You stay outside."

"Let her enter," Lovernios countermanded.

Ailidh leaned against the doorpost.

"He didn't arrive," Lovernios reported to Egomas. "I saw tracks of only one horse outside the palisade. You failed me, Egomas."

The dog-seller paled. "It wasn't my fault!" He pointed to Ailidh. "It was her doing! I woke, and the Roman was gone already."

Lovernios turned. "Is this true, Cousin?"

"Is what true?"

"Did you speed the Roman on his way?"

"Yes. Sergius rose early. I helped him mount and ride." She glanced at Egomas. "We were quiet so as not to disturb you."

The Druí's expression didn't change. "You knew I sought the Roman," he said flatly.

"How could I possibly know that?"

"Didn't you, Cousin?"

Ailidh straightened. "Yes."

Lovernios sighed. "Did you hear us talking?"

"I heard you and Egomas, yes. So did Sergius. If you wish to plot at night, Cousin, you should speak more quietly."

"Why did you help him escape?" Lovernios asked.

"Because he's not yours to sacrifice."

"So now the Druí will take me!" Egomas wailed from his position on the floor. "Have I treated you so harshly that this is the way you repay me?"

Ailidh met Lovernios's gaze. She held her hands out to him. "Take me, instead of him, if you will."

The Druí shook his head slowly. "You have no cause to fear me, Cousin. I wouldn't see the color of your unwilling blood."

He turned his back to the fire, where he stood, his face in shadow. "Only one who loves her people can be a fitting recompense for the evils that have befallen us."

"I do love my people!" Ailidh flared.

"And yet you betray them. You follow an alien god and love an alien man. You consort with those who enslave us, those who grind us into the dirt as if we were beasts."

"I follow the true God, and Sergius . . . Sergius is worth more than any of our tribe!"

"You don't understand." Lovernios pushed back his cowl and folded his hands within the sleeves of his robe. "I have seen the auguries with my own eyes. A year of destruction faces us. How are we to turn the favor of the gods toward us without a fitting sacrifice?"

"It is you who don't understand. Sergius and I . . . we have become members of a family. He is my brother in Christus. His life doesn't belong to you."

"What is one man compared to the lives of all Britons?"

"You exaggerate."

"I don't." Lovernios showed her an empty palm. "Believe me, Cousin. This is what the future holds for us. Nothing. Emptiness. Ruin."

"Listen to him!" Egomas pleaded. "What is one Roman life?"

Ailidh proclaimed, "Life is a precious gift from God."

"Life is both cheap *and* precious," Lovernios elaborated. "It is the greatest gift we can offer."

"Life, yes. Death, no."

"They are the same."

"Once, Lovernios, you told me you abhorred the sacrifice of any man."

"That was in another time, Cousin."

"You can't have Sergius," Ailidh pronounced. "You may have my body if you will—"

"And your spirit?"

"Never that."

"What is body without spirit?" Lovernios asked. "Is a corpse a fitting vow?" He stroked his beard. "Tell me, Cousin: Would you give your life for your god?"

"Yes. But I wouldn't take another's."

Lovernios held out a hand. "Wine, Egomas."

The dog-seller scrambled to his feet and scurried to fill a beaker. He passed it to the Druí. With measured movements, Lovernios upended it. The wine flowed out and soaked into the dirt. "This is the blood of the people, poured out like cheap wine on the altar of Roman ambition." He cast the beaker aside.

"The one I worship spilled out his blood. And God accepted that sacrifice and raised him from the dead."

"One man cannot die for all."

"Yet you would take Sergius."

"We must do what we can. Perhaps not all the gods will be placated, but if it is enough to avert wrath from us . . ."

Ailidh closed her eyes. When she opened them, Lovernios hadn't moved. "Believe me when I tell you that I love our people. But I cannot serve them the way you do."

"Once—"

"Is past!"

"Then their doom will be yours." Lovernios pronounced the words in a grave tone.

Ailidh asked quietly, "Do you threaten your own kin?"

"No. I speak what must be." Lovernios shrugged his cowl over his head. "Think well, Cousin. It's not too late. Don't let the hope of false love lead you astray."

"I have thought. My love is not false, and my answer is unchanged."

"So be it." Lovernios paused at the door. "The winter will be long, and I have much to do. I cannot tell if we will meet again."

"Then I will pray for you, Cousin."

His face was hidden behind the cowl. "And I for you. We will see whose god is most open to our entreaties."

"What of me?" Egomas quivered. "Have pity on an old man, Druí."

Lovernios paused. "Live with your dogs."

The Druí departed.

Egomas struggled to close the wicker gate. "Why don't you listen to him, girl? We shall all suffer, and it will be your fault!"

Ailidh turned to follow Lovernios's steps, pushing past Egomas through the gate. "I'm going to tend to the dogs."

"Haven't you done enough to disgrace our family?"

Tears stung her eyes as she stepped outside. There was no sign of Lovernios in the compound.

Sergius retrieved his escort in Camulodunum. He thought the two men seemed surprised to see him. Surprised, and perhaps disappointed that he'd returned sooner than they'd hoped, cutting short their leave.

He toyed with the idea of collecting a detachment of troops and returning to the hut, but to what avail? Ailidh wouldn't come with him willingly, and he couldn't very well scour the countryside for Lovernios. The Druid seemed to possess the ability to come and go as he pleased. If he didn't desire to be found, Sergius doubted that a legion of troops could ferret him out.

So he collared the escort and rode hard for Londinium, slowing only to prevent the animals from succumbing to exhaustion.

By the time he reached the garrison and dismissed his escort, fatigue wore at him, and worry chewed at his vitals.

He left his horse at the stables in a groom's care. As he crossed to the tribune's houses, a familiar figure came the other way.

"The wanderer and his dog return," Agricola waved.

"Hello, Julius."

"How's the lover?"

Sergius shook his head. "Puzzled."

"It is ever so," Agricola replied. "It's best not to take women seriously."

Sergius continued toward his house. Agricola fell into step beside him.

Sergius queried, "How did you know where I was going?"

"Obvious," Agricola replied. "Why else would you go rushing off without telling me where?"

"You're right, as usual."

Sergius opened the door and beckoned Agricola inside. Sergius stripped off his cloak. He tossed his sword onto a chair, and his armor followed it. He subsided onto a second chair. Cara flopped at his feet and fell asleep.

Agricola fetched a pair of beakers, filled them, and handed one to Sergius.

Sergius sipped. "Thanks."

"So tell me," Agricola prompted. "What happened?"

Sergius related the events of the previous night.

Agricola rubbed his chin. "The Druid wanted you for a sacrifice?"

"That was his intention, yes."

"Why you in particular?"

Sergius shook his head. "I have no idea. He seems to think I have qualities of nobility."

Agricola guffawed. "Easier, I'd think, to ambush a courier on a lonely road."

"Or a drunk."

"You're lucky to have escaped."

"You don't need to tell me." Sergius set his beaker down on the floor. "So what do I do?" he asked.

"Do?" Agricola echoed. He ran a hand through his light brown hair. "The Druidae are a weird bunch, which is why previous emperors suppressed their ghastly religion. My advice is to forget the girl and keep as far away from the Britons as possible."

"I can't forget Ailidh," Sergius said.

"And as for the Druidae," Agricola continued, "come spring, there won't be enough of them left to fill a hut, let alone conjure their devils."

"Spring is a long way off," Sergius replied. An emptiness inside him already seemed to spread as far into the future as he cared to imagine. If Ailidh wouldn't leave her people . . .

"*Since the Spirit is the source of your life, let the Spirit also direct its course.*"

What else could he do?

Reliance on another, even the Spirit of God, didn't come easily.

"*I will be with you always,*" Christus had said.

Christus had not said that life would be easy, its pitfalls removed, or its course visible for years ahead—but he would be there.

And if he'd be with Sergius, he'd be with Ailidh, too.

Spring still seemed far away.

PART THREE

Spring, 803 A.U.C.
(A.D. 60)

SIXTEEN

Decianus Catus replaced a murrhine vase on its display table and extended a manicured hand to the travel-stained courier who entered his office.

"What is it now? More dreary messages from Isca or Noviomagus? Give them to Quaestor Juba."

The courier shook his head. "Dispatches from Rome, sir, to be delivered to you personally."

Catus snapped his fingers. The courier pressed a canister into his palm.

"You may leave."

The courier saluted, turned, and exited.

"From Rome indeed. Probably more amendments to the tax code." Catus slid out the papyrus. "Thousands of words to tell me how to tax beans."

At the sight of the Imperial seal, he paused. Then he broke the seal and read.

And he smiled. "Fuscus, Juba!"

He heard the guard outside the door relay the summons. While he waited, he read the dispatch a second time, and a third.

The centurion entered, followed closely by the dwarfish quaestor.

"Yes, Procurator?" Fuscus asked.

Catus held up the papyrus. "The emperor Nero has resolved the matter of Prasutagus's will. Prepare an escort, Centurion. I'm going to deliver this message personally to Queen Boudicca."

"In Camulodunum?"

"No. In Venta Icenorum itself. In the palace of the Iceni."

"May I, sir?" Fuscus indicated the papyrus.

Catus tossed it over.

Fuscus scanned the lines of print, then pursed his lips. "She won't like this." He handed the dispatch to Juba.

"Not at all," Catus smirked.

"Is it wise to confront her, sir?" Fuscus continued. "I mean, with her warriors—"

"Two hundred men, Fuscus," Catus announced. "That should be a sufficient escort. Boudicca won't have more than a handful of able-bodied warriors available at this time of year. They'll be planting, or tending their herds, or whatever savages do." He rubbed his palms together. "I can't wait to see her face when she reads this."

Juba warbled, "I'd rather not travel, sir." He indicated a heavily bandaged foot. "My gout—"

"A plague on your gout!" Catus thundered. "You're my financial advisor. I'll need you to value the Iceni possessions."

Juba bowed his head. "Of course, sir."

Catus gestured curtly to Fuscus. "Make the arrangements. The sooner that harpy is put in her place, the better."

He turned on his heel to face the newly arrived vase but halted. He glared at dark splotches of mud marring the shine of the mosaic floor where the courier had stood.

"And send a servant to clean up this mess."

Sergius hurried to his place in the ranks of men assembled on the spring soft grass outside the Deva fortress. The entire *Gemina* plus auxiliaries, far more men than the parade ground inside the fortress could accommodate, stood shoulder to shoulder.

He squeezed between Agricola and Chief Centurion Adventus just in time.

"Hail the commander!" a centurion shouted. He stabbed a finger at a waiting musician. The legionary raised the curved horn of a bucina to his lips and blew. The clear notes floated over the assembled soldiers. The bucinator played his instrument on only two occasions: for executions and to announce the commander in chief's presence.

Today, he played the *classicum* fanfare.

Sergius watched as Suetonius Paulinus strode through the main gate of the Deva fortress. The commander wore his scarlet cloak of office. An honor guard of hand-picked men accompanied him. Suetonius stopped at a dais erected on the level ground outside the ditch and rampart and climbed the steps.

The deeper notes of the cornu and the tuba joined in a final burst of sound.

A junior haruspex followed Suetonius, a lamb cradled in his arms. He walked slowly, whether exercising caution to avoid stumbling or from nervousness at performing his task in front of more than five thousand men, Sergius could only guess.

The headquarters staff themselves had arrived at Deva from Londinium only two weeks ago. After long months of relative inactivity at headquarters, broken only when Suetonius made an excursion to one of the towns, Sergius itched for action. Even though the action took him further from Ailidh again.

She'd sent a brief message informing him of her well-being, to which he'd penned a longer reply. To his dismay, though, she urged him to remain in Londinium.

> Lovernios travels the countryside to Venta Icenorum, and even, so I hear, the country of the Brigantes. The residents of Camulodunum are disinclined to venture far, so great the unrest grows. Do not risk your safety on my account.

Sergius was tempted to risk travel anyway but eventually bowed to prudence. He sent a note to Veturius, suggesting the *Hispana* be alert for the presence of the Druid, but in a response two weeks later, Veturius replied that no reports of a Druid had been received, and he wasn't getting involved in anything to do with native religion, thank you very much, and did Sergius have a few denarii he could spare?

> I met a girl, the daughter of the camp prefect who had come to visit her father, but having depleted my last denarius the previous day, I had nothing with which to entertain her. Another opportunity spoiled! Must the Fates always outwit Venus?

Sergius grimaced, reading the word *depleted* to mean "lost." Typical Veturius: both bad timing and poor technique plagued his friend. He'd written back to offer condolences—but not money.

Suetonius seemed either oblivious to or unconcerned with the hints and murmurs of dissatisfaction among the Britons. When Sergius had attempted to raise the subject of unjust taxation, the governor had brushed the complaints aside. "Procurator's business," he said, and Sergius let the conversation drop.

Now, Suetonius Paulinus stood stiffly erect, off on one side of the dais which supported a carved stone altar, newly dedicated to Minerva. Behind it waited the senior haruspex, arms folded across his chest.

On the ground closest to the dais, Sergius bumped elbows with the other senior officers, all wearing full-dress uniforms, cloaks, and brushed helmet plumes. Behind the senior officers ranged the centurions in order of seniority and then, shifting anxiously from foot to foot, the legionaries and auxiliaries, each eager to hear the haruspices' predictions.

"What do you think?" Agricola whispered to Sergius.

"Favorable, of course. They wouldn't dare predict otherwise. Look at Suetonius's face."

The commander's expression was set. He was obviously not in the mood for either games or bad news.

"He's in a *good* mood," Agricola joked.

Sergius snorted. "If the haruspices prognosticate unfavorably, I wouldn't be surprised if Suetonius ordered *their* entrails to be examined."

Suetonius, he knew, wanted the right kind of news, because at the morning staff meeting, Suetonius had detailed his plan for the invasion of Mona.

The governor's calloused fingers had jumped from point to point on his large map as he spoke. "*Hispana* will remain at its bases in the northeast to guard the Iceni border. Cerialis is concerned about the mood of the Iceni. The presence of a full legion will act as a deterrent and prevent the spread of any unrest to the Brigantes.

"*Gemina* will march along the coastal route to Mona. The division of the *Valeria* will follow the river route down the Conwy Valley and root out lingering resistance. Two cohorts of the *Augusta*—all that can be spared from watching the Dumnonii—have already been detached from Isca. They will collect auxiliaries from Glevum and take a southern route to Mona."

He pointed to the tiny island off the northwestern edge of the province, at the coastline facing the Druidae sanctuary. "We will combine forces here, at Segontium."

Sergius studied the dispositions. Except for a few small forts manned by auxiliaries, signal towers, and the nominal garrisons in the major towns, all the fighting strength of the legions lay on the frontier.

Agricola's voice returned him to the ceremony. "No mistakes so far."

The junior haruspex mounted the steps successfully. He laid the lamb on the altar and stepped back.

The senior priest spread his arms. His robe rustled in a slight breeze. The blade of a knife shone in his outstretched hand.

"To Jupiter, Juno, and Minerva we give glory! To Minerva, wisest of the gods, we plead for wisdom. Let her wisdom be as bright as steel, as unsullied as a young lamb!"

A legionary at the base of the dais blew a brief fanfare on a lituus.

The senior haruspex stooped. His junior bared the lamb's throat. The knife flashed a single time. The lamb slumped without a cry, jugular veins and windpipe severed. Blood flowed over the altar.

A murmur went up from the troops at the cleanness of the cut; for the lamb to have cried out would have been a bad omen. Sergius had seen it happen before.

Even Suetonius seemed to relax.

With another motion, the priest slashed open the lamb's belly. He removed the entrails, running them through his hands. Then he leaned over the carcass to inspect the liver.

Finally, he straightened, and again spread his hands, this time red with blood. "The animal is clean!" he announced. "*Exta bona!* The auspices are favorable."

The troops cheered. With the haruspices' blessings, the campaign season could open.

For five days now, in preparation for the culminating day of this March's Quinquatria, the opening of campaign season, the augurs had been tracking the flights of geese and eagles, peering at cloud formations, studying the winds, and scrutinizing the frantic pecking of the legion's sacred chickens. They pronounced their auguries with growing confidence.

Although more highly respected than the haruspices, it was the latter that most influenced the troops. Bird flight was erratic, the interpretation of cloud formations esoteric, and skeptics asserted that hungry chickens *would* scrabble more vigorously. But a lamb sacrificed and studied in plain sight, now one could believe that.

Similar ceremonies were occurring all over the Empire, wherever Rome stationed her troops. At *Hispana*'s bases, at *Augusta*'s Isca fortress and *Valeria*'s Glevum camp, legates Cerialis, Crispus, and Falco performed the same rites that Suetonius did here. Twenty miles south, the division of *Valeria* sacrificed, to assure their safe participation in the spring offensive. And in Rome herself, Emperor Nero, as *pontifex maximus*, blessed the Praetorian Guard.

Over the days of the Quinquatria, many legionaries had offered their own vows to the deities most important to them. Centurions dedicated small altars, and the soldiers pledged whatever they felt appropriate to the magnitude of their request. Many soldiers offered to appease the spirit of the land of Britannia. Sergius kept a close eye on Cara in case an overzealous devotee of Hecate desired a dog for a sacrifice.

The Quinquatria made Sergius uneasy. Festivals and sacrifices filled the Roman calendar; men picked and chose the gods they wished to honor and the festivals they wanted to observe. With so many deities available, nobody paid much attention to who sacrificed and when. So Sergius avoided participating in the festivals without arousing attention.

So what if he followed an obscure religion? Rome was tolerant. Nobody minded.

But the Quinquatria was different. In the army everyone had to participate.

Sergius had been worrying for days about his first Quinquatria since joining the army. How should he respond?

The junior haruspex removed the carcass of the lamb.

Agricola nudged Sergius. "You were right."

"My father told me a story once," Sergius revealed, "about when he was commanding his legion. He was preparing to attack the Germans when he realized that the barbarian position was too strong. He ran the risk of being outflanked. To make matters worse, the weather was changing rapidly."

"What did he do?"

"He couldn't withdraw because the troops were eager for battle, and retreat would have demoralized them. So he called for the haruspex to offer a sacrifice and told him in no uncertain terms that he wanted an unfavorable omen to delay battle."

"And?"

"The priest complied, the men were satisfied with the delay, and a week later they defeated the Germans."

"Ah, the intricacies of the military mind. Not to mention the gullibility of the masses," Agricola mused. "At least your father had more intelligence than Varus."

The reference caught Sergius off guard. It took a moment for it to register.

The story of Quinctilius Varus and his lost legions had become a legend familiar to every military man. Fifty years before, Varus and three legions—the Seventeenth, Eighteenth, and Nineteenth—were trapped in the Germanic forests and annihilated by Arminius of the Cherusci and his allies. Three legions disappeared, their eagles hung in barbarian forest shrines, the subject of derision by the gloating Germans. Years later, an expedition commanded by Germanicus retrieved the standards and buried the bones of the lost legions.

Honor was reclaimed, but the legions never could be.

Agricola speculated, "Did Suetonius really prompt the priest, I wonder?"

Sergius shrugged. "I don't pay any attention to those forms of worship."

"You were the subject of an auspica oblativa yourself," Agricola reminded.

"Eagles hunt hares all the time. I just happened to witness a successful catch, that was all."

"Tell that to your men."

Soldiers carried a series of stone altars and arranged them in front of the dais. Animal attendants led out five fine, unblemished bulls, one each to be sacrificed to Jupiter, Apollo, Mars, Neptune, and Hercules; four cows for Juno, Minerva, Victory, and Diana; and one male ox for all the past emperors and for the welfare of Nero and his family. Sergius couldn't suppress a smile. For all his desire to ensure the placation of the gods and the contentment of the troops, Suetonius wasn't about to sacrifice individually to the likes of Tiberius, Caligula, or Nero.

Trailed by the haruspices and augurs, Suetonius dedicated all the new altars except that to Jupiter, which had already been consecrated on January 3. Then he stood back and allowed the priest, from the Temple of Claudius in Camulodunum, to take charge.

To the music of lyres and flutes, assistants presented the first animal. With his toga draped over his head to guard against any sound or sight of ill omen, the priest recited a prayer.

"To Jupiter, greatest of the gods, this altar is dedicated. You are worthy to receive a sacrifice of a strong, healthy bull for success in the coming campaign. At the bidding of the governor and the commanders of the army, I do it; may it be rightly done. To this end, in offering this bull to you, I humbly beg that you will be gracious and merciful to us. Will you deign to receive this bull that I offer you, to this end?"

He sprinkled the head of the bull with wine and sacred cake.

A waiting slaughterer swung a two-edged ax. The blade cracked against the bull's skull. The animal crumpled. Before it could revive, the slaughterer plunged a knife into its throat. Another assistant held a bowl to collect the blood.

When it was full, the assistant handed the bowl to the priest, who poured the blood over the altar.

"Receive this sacrifice, great Jupiter, and grant our petition!"

Assistants hurried to skin and cut up the bull. The entrails would be roasted on the altar fire and fed to the important participants, then the bones and fat burned as an offering to the gods. At the end of the day, the meat would be cooked as a feast for the troops.

The priest moved to the next animal. One by one, with appropriate ceremony and prayers, accompanied by the shrill notes of an aulos to drown out unwanted noise, the animals were slaughtered. Blood soaked into the ground.

As each animal died, the soldiers shouted to the god.

"Great is Jupiter Maximus!"

"Great is Mars, god of war!"

"Hail Diana!"

Agricola hissed in his ear, "Shout!"

Sergius glanced to see Suetonius staring at him, unsmiling, eyebrows slightly raised.

Sergius looked away. "I can't," he told Agricola.

He wiped his sweaty palms on his kilt.

The last animal fell. The shouts crescendoed, tumbling over each other into a deafening waterfall of sound.

Surrounded by five thousand men, Sergius felt alone.

"Great is Jupiter! Great is Jupiter!"

Sergius trembled. He wondered if any Britons—Lovernios even—heard the massed shouts from their haunts in the hills.

Finally, the shouts died away.

"Suetonius must be worried," Agricola commented.

"Why?"

"To make such a big sacrifice. I suppose marching against the Druidae has him concerned."

"Do you blame him?"

A cornu sounded from the direction of the fortress. Led by the cornicen, his large circular instrument resting on his wolfskin-covered shoulder, a file of standard-bearers processed from the fortress. Bearskins enveloped their uniforms, mouths arranged so that teeth flashed above the men's foreheads. Two aquilifers carried the eagles of the *Gemina* and the *Valeria*. Sun shone off gold and silver. Garlands of laurel and early spring flowers decorated the standards. Battle honors hung beneath the thunderbolts clasped in the eagles' talons. The running boar of the *Valeria* fluttered in gold on a scarlet flag. On the *Gemina*'s standard, the Capricorn sign of its founder Augustus surmounted Mars.

Behind the aquilifers came the imaginifer, bearing the image of the emperor Nero, then the signifers, carrying the standards of the cohorts and the centuries. The square vexilla of the cavalry and the auxiliaries fluttered from staffs carried by each wing's vexillarius. Gold on scarlet like *Valeria*'s emblem, the vexilla soared proudly.

The troop halted before the dais.

Sergius's chest was suddenly tight. The moment was coming. He'd tried to reassure Ailidh, but could he reassure himself?

Suetonius met the aquilifers. He anointed each eagle with oil from a gold vial.

"I dedicate these standards to the glory of the empire and the emperor! May no one ever disgrace them!"

"To the Empire!" soldiers shouted. The legionaries drew their swords. Above the assembled legions flashed a silver forest of steel, raised in salute.

A priest kindled a small fire on a tripod beside the altar of Jupiter. Suetonius took a pinch of incense from an engraved bowl and dropped it into the flames. "To the emperor, Nero Claudius Drusus Germanicus, and those who preceded him in his divine office."

One by one, the senior officers followed the commander's lead, offering a pinch of incense to the emperor.

Sergius hung back.

"Aren't you going to offer?" Agricola asked.

"No."

"Idiot! You have to."

Sergius looked his friend in the eyes. His mouth was dry. "I've told you I won't."

"You're crazy," Agricola shook his head and moved forward to take his turn.

The officers, seeing Sergius's hesitation, gave him a wide berth.

The words of Paullus came to him: *"I write to encourage your faith—stand fast."*

Had the apostle known he would need those words?

"I want us to be encouraged by one another's faith." He could be encouraged by Paullus's faith, yes. Paullus was a great man who spoke his message regardless of the hostility that message aroused. But could Paullus be encouraged by his meager faith? How?

When the officers finished offering, the legionaries streamed past to take their turns at the main altar and at others around the ground.

The sweet scent of incense filled the air.

Agricola returned. "Go up there, fool!" he hissed. "Be religious some other time."

"No."

"Commit suicide, then." Agricola moved away.

Sergius watched him go. He tasted copper and realized he'd bitten his lip.

Maybe offering wouldn't be such a big deal if it ensured his continued success in the army. Paullus had never actually said he shouldn't—

He glanced at his feet.

Just pick them up, take a few steps forward. What is a little incense? Nothing, really. It doesn't matter as long as you don't mean it—

Sergius started. A man stood at his shoulder. He hadn't seen him arrive. The man carried the shield of the third cohort of the *Gemina*.

"I follow the Way, also," the man said. "I cannot offer."

Sergius beckoned him forward. "Stand beside me."

"There are many of them, but few of us," the man commented.

"I'm glad for your companionship." Sergius's sense of isolation vanished.

Together, he and the unfamiliar legionary watched until the last soldier had offered his sacrifice.

When the ranks reformed, the man slipped away. Sergius realized he'd never asked his unknown ally for his name.

The bucina sounded again.

The governor had again surmounted the dais.

"Men of Rome," Suetonius said in a voice that carried across the field. "The season for rest has ended; the season for war has arrived. We have striven the past two years to turn Britannia into a secure province. This year we will complete that task. You have heard the omens. They are favorable. No Briton can stand before us. We *shall* succeed."

He waited for cheers to die down.

"If each man does his part, we shall add to the glories carried by the eagles. Complete your vows. Tomorrow, we march!"

He turned away. Preceded by the standards and his honor guard, carried on a wave of shouts, Suetonius descended, and reentered the fortress.

The legions dispersed.

Someone touched Sergius's shoulder.

"Tribune, in my office," said Gellius Marcianus in a voice like ice.

Sergius's feet felt leaden as he trailed after the legate.

When they reached the privacy of Marcianus's office, the legate pivoted.

Marcianus's normally jovial expression had vanished. His fleshy features firmed into a serious, parade-ground hardness.

"Explain your dishonor of the emperor, Tribune," he demanded.

"I meant no disrespect, sir," Sergius replied, trying to keep his voice level despite a lump in his throat.

"You refused to offer sacrifice. What did you intend if not insult?"

Footsteps entered the room behind him. Without looking, Sergius knew that Suetonius stood there. Sergius explained, "I am a follower of the Way, sir. We worship only one God."

Marcianus drummed his fingers on a table. "The Way?"

"I follow Christus—"

The drumming stopped. "Oh, yes. A king other than Caesar."

"A spiritual king, sir."

"Who demands your loyalty?"

"The loyalty of my heart—yes, sir."

Suetonius spoke. "A man of divided loyalties is of no use to me."

Sergius turned to face the governor. "Sir, when I enlisted, I swore the sacramentum. I am a loyal Roman! I am as loyal to Caesar as any man here! As loyal as you, sir."

"Enough! I'm well aware of the oath of loyalty." Suetonius's eyes blazed.

Sergius broke off, amazed at his own audacity. His breath froze in his chest. What would his father say if he returned home in disgrace—or worse, in chains?

Was this what Paullus had meant when he asked what Sergius had given up?

But his army career? . . .

Sergius said, "I will honor, respect, and obey the emperor, sir. But I cannot worship him."

Marcianus said, "The question is not of worship, Tribune, but of loyalty. I don't care what god you worship—although I'd hope that an officer would worship a greater deity than some minor Jewish god whose prophet was crucified. Mithras, for example, is worthy of a soldier. But to refuse to offer incense to the emperor is to deny his authority."

"I don't deny his authority, sir. I will stand before the troops and declare my loyalty."

"That is what the offering does."

"An offering denotes worship, sir."

"Tribune," Suetonius's voice quivered with suppressed emotion, "how you regard the spirits of the former emperors is of no concern to me. Neither do I care whether you accept or deny their divinity, or that of any other god. Deny Jupiter or Mars if you must. Follow your 'Way.' Worship your dog or your horse if it gives you some spiritual benefit! But your action this morning disgraced both Emperor Nero and the legions."

"I meant no affront, sir."

"Whether you meant it or not doesn't matter. You say you are loyal. Offer incense to the emperor, and I will believe you."

Sergius spoke quietly but firmly. "I cannot, sir. My actions on the battlefield declare my loyalty."

Marcianus threw up his hands. "You'd sacrifice your career for this Way of yours? That's what it will come to, Lysias. The men will not follow an officer who refuses to honor the emperor. The army won't tolerate him."

"I have said that I will honor the emperor, sir. But I won't offer to him."

Marcianus rested a palm on his shoulder. "You're young, Lysias. You have a career ahead of you. There are many religions; don't let some foolish belief threaten your entire life. A pinch of incense is no large matter. Believe what you will, but go through the motions. No one but you need know that you don't worship." Marcianus gave a short laugh. "If truth be told, most of us don't think the emperors are divine. But we show our devotion to the state by our actions."

"Sir, I appreciate your concern. But I can't. I will show it in any other way than that."

Marcianus's hand fell away.

Suetonius tried, "Determination is an honorable attitude. Stubbornness in the face of reason is not."

"Are outward actions meaningful if the heart doesn't follow them, sir? Is it honorable to deny my God by worshiping, or pretending to worship, another? Is a man to be trusted if he says one thing and does another?"

"Lysias—" Marcianus began.

"Sir, I value my honor, and the honor of the God I worship. I cannot offer to the emperor."

Marcianus gritted his teeth. "Your refusal will go in my report to Rome."

Sergius bowed his head. "So be it, sir. I will accept whatever punishment you decide."

"Dismissed."

His hands and feet numb and cold, Sergius left Marcianus's office.

When the tribune had departed, Marcianus admitted, "In a way I admire him."

Suetonius swung on the legate. "That's no excuse for failure to honor the emperor."

"Of course not. But a man who refuses to deny what he believes—"

"Is either arrogant, stupid, or a fool."

"Or correct," Marcianus said. "Would that all men's hearts and actions were united."

Suetonius rubbed his temple. "Don't tell me you think there's something to this Way."

Marcianus shook his head. "I know next to nothing about it. All I've heard is street gossip."

Suetonius paced around the office before answering. "I know slightly more. The emperor dismissed charges against their chief spokesman, some Paullus from Tarsus, but refused to grant the religion official recognition. It's in an ill-defined status."

"Which leaves us hanging," Marcianus completed. He spread his hands. "I admire Lysias's courage, that's all. His honesty does him credit."

"He could be dismissed from the army for his action."

"Is that what you want me to recommend?" Marcianus asked. "I thought reporting him—"

"No." Suetonius folded his hands behind his back. "Reporting him is sufficient for the time being. Perhaps the case will come to the emperor's attention and encourage him to set a precedent. Lysias shows too much promise to dismiss lightly, and gods know the army needs all the good officers it can get. Give him another chance. He may, if he's lucky, come to see the foolishness of his action."

"Do you think it likely?"

Suetonius shrugged. "Who can tell with youth?" He turned toward the door. "The price of honesty is usually failure. The man who will not bend is broken."

"The world would be better if it were not so."

Suetonius paused. "I'm not a philosopher, Gellius. But I believe you're correct."

He strode through the door.

In his office Chief Centurion Helvius Adventus glared at the six centurions who stood before him, still wearing their dress uniforms. He tapped his vitis against the caligae thongs wrapped around his lower leg.

"The man was there," he gritted. "I saw him with my own eyes, standing beside Tribune Lysias. Do any of you dispute this?"

The centurions, as one man, shook their heads.

Adventus continued, "The man carried the shield of the third cohort. You are the centurions of the third cohort. One of you must know his name."

The senior centurion said, "I, too, saw him by Lysias. But all my men were with me. All offered to the emperor. My optio will confirm this."

Adventus paced before the line. "Do all of you say this?"

"Yes."

"I do."

"All of my men were accounted for."

"And mine."

"Mine also."

Adventus stopped pacing. "So, either one of you lies or is mistaken—"

"Or there was no man," the senior centurion interrupted.

"Don't be a fool!" Adventus snapped. "I saw him. You saw him."

"I said no *man*, sir," the centurion repeated.

Adventus opened his mouth, then the meaning of the centurion's remark registered, and he closed it again.

"That's even more foolish," he dismissed, unable to put conviction in his voice.

"I see no other explanation, sir," the centurion said. "I believe my comrades when they say they don't lie."

"But . . . ," Adventus fought for words. "Not to reverence the emperor?"

"Perhaps as a test . . . ," one of the other centurions added hesitantly.

"Or an omen," another added.

"Or just to observe," suggested a third.

Adventus tightened his grip on his vine stick. "What am I to tell the legate? That this unknown man was a spirit? What if the troops find out? What kind of an augury will they take it to be?"

The senior centurion cleared his throat. "Tell Legate Marcianus that the man was identified and punished severely by his comrades."

"Lie to the legate? What if he demands the offender's name?"

"Tell him that the man offered to the emperor and repented of his folly and that you consider the punishment to be sufficient."

Adventus tapped his stick. "It will have to do." He raised the stick and pointed along the line of officers. "But if one of you has lied to *me*, I will find out. Expect no clemency." He gestured toward the door, and the centurions filed out. "Gods walking as men," he muttered. "Galley bilge!"

SEVENTEEN

The approaching soldiers were spotted hours before the tramp of boots disturbed the tranquillity of Venta Icenorum. A farmer dirtied from spring planting and conversant with shortcuts through the forest brought the news to Boudicca.

"Two hundred soldiers from Londinium," he had panted. "Marched straight across my fields. Trampled my crops!"

He buried his face in his hands. "What am I to do?"

"Plant again," Boudicca replied sharply. Then, ashamed at her outburst, she relented. As queen of the Iceni, she was not so much the ruler of the tribe as its center. She didn't stand at its head but at its heart. The incident with the farmer was but one of a myriad of insults, great and small, offered by the Romans. The man was poor, his fields all he had. She had given the farmer a silver coin imprinted with the horse symbol of the Iceni.

Now, standing outside the portico of her house with her daughters beside her, Boudicca watched as foot soldiers preceded several mounted men through the bank and rampart and into the town.

"It's what you expected, isn't it, Mother?" Aife asked.

Boudicca snugged her criss into place, evening it to allow her sword to swing freely. "Yes."

She'd anticipated Decianus Catus would pay a visit once the weather moderated enough to allow comfortable travel. All winter the procurator had sent threats and extortions delivered by companies of armed messengers. She'd paid what she could. The nobles likewise complied, although Boudicca had no way to judge the extent of their cooperation.

Unlike her Roman counterpart, a Briton rí had no means to compel obedience. Except for slaves and criminals, each man and woman was free—free to cooperate or not. The Romans never seemed to understand.

She rested her hand on Aife's shoulder and squeezed. "Don't worry."

"I'm not afraid," Aife replied.

Cinnia leaned against Boudicca's uncluttered hip. Boudicca's servants filed out of the house to watch, as did the few nobles who remained in Venta Icenorum. The remainder had departed the town to check on fields and animals elsewhere, leaving families behind. Airell, whose son managed his more distant possessions for him, remained, but Weylyn numbered among those absent.

Airell ambled from his house to Boudicca's. "What will you say to Catus?"

Boudicca shrugged, "That depends on what he says to me."

"Then he had best bring good news."

The troops halted in the open area before her house. Two men, Decianus Catus and Sextus Fuscus, dismounted and strode to the portico. A third man with a bandaged foot remained mounted.

"That's Juba, the quaestor," Airell whispered. "His greed matches Catus's."

Procurator Catus's thick lips curved into a mocking smile. The movement set Boudicca's nerves on edge. Romans in general irritated her, Catus more than average. The procurator walked with his head back and chin thrust forward—attempting a haughty dignity, although a spreading paunch bulged his toga and gave a waddle to his walk. His short hair struggled to cover the pink crown of his head.

She stifled a laugh.

This was the best the Romans could send?

The urge to laugh died at the sight of Catus's gloating eyes.

"Greetings, Procurator," she said stiffly in the despised Latin tongue.

Catus put his hands on his hips. "You claim to be queen of the Iceni."

Boudicca nodded. "So I am."

"What kind of a queen neglects to pay her debts?"

"One whose resources are overfaced by rampant extortion."

"A poor example to set for your people," Catus rejoined.

"Ask rather, what kind of a queen would see her people abused and do nothing."

Catus paused as if measuring her words, then clicked his fingers. A man bearing the insignia of a courier pressed a canister into his hand.

Boudicca held her breath as Catus opened it and unrolled a papyrus.

Catus's smirk grew broader. He raised his voice so that all the bystanders could hear.

"This is from the emperor Nero. I'll skip the introduction. He says, quote, 'With the death of Prasutagus, the royal house of the Iceni is declared extinct.'"

Airell's breath hissed.

Boudicca started. Her hands indicated Aife and Cinnia. "Extinct? Cast your eyes, Catus. Prasutagus's daughters stand before you! Or is your vision so blinded by gold that you can't see them?"

"I see well enough. I see two girls of no account." Catus held up the papyrus. "There's more. 'The will of said Prasutagus is declared null and void. The status of the Iceni as client kingdom of Rome is revoked.'"

"You can't do that!" Airell blurted.

"The emperor can."

Boudicca leaned out and snatched the papyrus from Catus's hands.

"I don't lie, woman," Catus sneered.

"Then you're insane, and as stupid as the dolt you call emperor."

The color rose to Catus's face. "Show respect for the emperor!"

"Is it true that he weds boys because he's not man enough for a woman?"

The color faded as quickly as it had risen. Even Fuscus paled.

"By the gods, woman . . . ," Catus spluttered.

"You deserve your lyre-playing girl as your master," Boudicca continued. She tore the papyrus in two, flung the pieces down, and spat on them. "That's what I think of him, of you, and this worthless letter. I am queen of the Iceni, and Prasutagus's daughters *will* inherit."

Airell put a hand flat on Catus's chest and pushed.

The procurator staggered back. He dropped the canister and it rolled away.

"Get out of my town and off my land," Boudicca snarled. "And take your hired sword and your cripple with you."

"This land is Rome's," Catus blustered.

"It belongs to the Iceni. To *all* Iceni. Leave, while you have life to do it with."

Catus looked at Airell. "And you?"

"The nobles will support their queen," Airell declared.

"Did you read the last sentence?" Catus rubbed his chest. "'The nobles of the Iceni, in penalty for debts incurred and taxes in abeyance, forfeit their right to property.'" He stabbed a finger at Airell. "That includes you, old man."

Boudicca's longsword sprang to her hand. "I should gut you where you stand."

Catus flinched, tangled his feet in his toga, and pitched onto his buttocks.

"Arms!" Fuscus barked, and steel rasped from scabbards as the legionaries drew.

Catus picked himself up, swearing. "I have two hundred men. Where are your warriors? All I see are women, children, and old men. Drop your sword, or my men will begin slaying."

"You're brave when you have soldiers behind you," Boudicca sneered. "Would you be so brave on your own?"

Catus ignored the remark and instead swept his arm around the tribal center, past the ring of steel behind him. "Where will the Iceni be without women and children?"

"Pig! You wouldn't dare."

Catus gestured to Fuscus. "If she doesn't drop her sword, kill everyone in Venta Icenorum. Start with the graybeard here."

"Yes, sir." The tip of Fusca's sword touched the center of Airell's léine. The noble didn't budge.

"Decide," Catus demanded. "After the old one, the children die."

Boudicca glared. "I won't forget this, Catus."

"Neither will I. Well? Do you wish this old one's blood to stain your ground?"

Boudicca allowed her sword to clatter to the dirt. "I will never forget, as long as I live."

"You may be sure of that." Catus pointed to two men. "Seize her."

Boudicca writhed as two burly legionaries gripped her arms.

Catus nodded at Fuscus. "Strip this place. Take all the gold and silver you can find."

The centurion lowered his sword and shouted orders. Soldiers plunged into the houses. Several shoved past Boudicca into the royal residence. She struggled, but, despite her height advantage, the soldiers' grips were too strong.

Catus reached to pluck the torque from around her neck. "In payment."

"Swine!"

Catus studied the ornament. "I'll wager that you buried plenty of gold with Prasutagus."

The blood rushed to her head. "If you desecrate my husband's grave—if so much as the toe of your filthy sandal touches it—then by Andraste, I swear that I will hunt you down and give you a death such as no man has ever died. If I have to pursue you from Hades itself, I will do it!"

"Empty threats, woman."

"When the dogs have feasted on your flesh, and your bones moldered, I shall save your skull for a piss pot."

"Mother!"

Boudicca wrenched her neck at Cinnia's cry.

A soldier yanked the brooches from the girl's cloak.

"Leave my daughters alone!" Boudicca yelled.

Catus turned, a gleam in his eyes. He touched Cinnia's cheek, and then, when she recoiled, Aife's. "Pretty girls."

"Keep your foul hands off them!"

Catus's palm cracked off her cheek. "You don't give the orders here, woman."

Boudicca's eyes watered from the force of the blow. She saw through them movement beside her, a clash of steel.

Fuscus's gladius blocked Airell's blow, intended for the procurator.

"For that, you shall die!" Airell shouted. His longsword swung through the air.

Fuscus parried the blow and retreated, drawing Airell from Catus.

Airell pressed forward.

"Don't, Airell," Boudicca called. The noble was too old, his movements slow and inaccurate. But Airell's eyes glittered, and Boudicca knew he'd passed the point of listening.

The centurion ducked as Airell swung again. He closed and he thrust. The noble gasped as the sword ran through his chest. His eyes rolled back.

Fuscus jerked his blade free.

Airell slumped to the tender grass. A crimson stain spread across the front of his léine. Fuscus kicked the corpse, and wiped his sword on Airell's cloak.

"I shall have your heart," Boudicca rasped at Catus. "With my own hands I shall cut it beating from your chest."

"But I shall have something else," Catus said. "Fuscus, bring the girls to me. When I'm done with them, you and Juba can have turns. Then, anyone who wants."

"No!" Boudicca's lunge caught the guards by surprise. She broke free and grabbed for Catus. One of the guards hooked her ankles, and she pitched to her face. Her chin hit the ground, her teeth gouged her lip, and she spat blood.

A knee slammed into the small of her back and forced the air from her lungs. The guards piled on top of her and pinned her arms behind her. They jerked her onto her feet, one of the guards with his hand wrapped in her hair.

"What about her, sir?" Fuscus asked. He fingered his dagger. "Slit her yowling throat?"

Boudicca's teeth clenched as she stared at the smirking Catus. "With my dying breath I would curse you from Hades."

He ordered, "Take her and flog her."

Sergius sat on his lectus, unable to will himself to sleep, yet tired of being awake and of failing to dissipate the anxiety that burned in his stomach. After leaving Marcianus's office, he'd gone straight to his quarters, trembling more than after he'd been in battle.

He'd not eaten an evening meal, and the omission hadn't helped the unabated, raging fire within.

He remembered the words Apollos had spoken to him, three years ago. "You will have to declare yourself someday."

That day in Greece seemed so long ago that it had happened in another time, to another person.

They'd sat on marble steps in the forum in Corinth, outside the government house. Up and down the steps, worn smooth over the years, swept the powerful men of the city, broad purple stripes on their togas proclaiming their status. Below in the forum, the life of the Empire passed in a multitude of languages, garments, and skin colors. Grecian Corinth looked to Sergius like a duplicate Rome.

"Why?" Sergius asked. "Rome is tolerant of all. We force no one to alter their beliefs or deny their gods."

"You have just done that," Apollos replied. "By believing on Christus you have denied that other gods exist. There's no third way."

Sergius stared out over the teeming multitude, at the citizens in their togas, the stola-clad women accompanied by their maids and servants, the tunic-covered freemen and slaves. He could have seen exactly the same sight in Rome.

"Jupiter, Isis, Cybele, and Zeus are at best mere shadows of God," Apollos said. "At worst, they embody all that is corrupt in man."

He laid a hand on Sergius's knee. "The man who believes in all gods can accept everything and everyone except the man who says there is only one way. You have chosen that path, Sergius. You have become that man. There *is* only one way. And you will come in conflict with those who believe otherwise. You've heard what happened to Paullus: the stonings, the beatings, the riots. The Way is not an easy path to walk. But it is the only one that leads to eternal life."

A guard clattered down the steps, hand resting on his sword hilt. "Be off, you two! No loitering!" Sergius and Apollos abandoned their seats in the sun.

Apollos had left Corinth soon after, continuing the peregrinations that carried him from city to city.

Sergius leaned back on his lectus. Apollos had been correct. Neither Suetonius nor Marcianus understood what he had tried to say. To them, he was disrespectful to the emperor, and a man whose loyalties had come under scrutiny and been found wanting.

They would report him to headquarters in Rome!

Such a report might, if he was lucky, be overlooked by a busy clerk, disinterested in the minutia of everyday details. Or it could be seized upon by a conscientious clerk, reported to the army commanders—the emperor Nero himself, perhaps—and Sergius's army career would come crashing down in ruins, leveled like Carthage, plowed into the ground and sprinkled with salt to prevent its regrowth.

What future could a disgraced man expect? He could forget about assuming a seat in the Senate. He might, if fortune favored him, become quaestor of some impoverished provincial backwater. In North Africa, perhaps, he could live out his days in obscurity.

A merchant life? Rome had no lack of lower-class merchants who'd avoid inquiry into a man's background. But eking out an existence on Rome's seamy underside?

He shuddered at the thought.

God, he prayed, *is this what you have for me? Is this what it means to follow the Way—to be cast out of society, flung aside as a broken weapon, as refuse?*

He clenched his fists in the blanket on his lectus.

He *was* loyal. He had no love for Nero, but he supported the Roman way. Despite its flaws, the Empire brought civilization to the world.

Disgrace.

What of his parents? His mother would grieve, but she'd be happy enough to see him home that she'd bury her grief with gratitude for his safety. But his father—

The disgrace would hit his father more violently than the German's club had. His father would recover—a man who refused to die over the loss of a leg wouldn't let the disgrace of his son crush him—but Sergius wouldn't be a full son any longer. He'd be a blot on the family name, best forgotten in the hope that inattention would breed oblivion.

Sergius swung himself to a sitting position.

In canisters stood letters that couriers had delivered across the winter countryside. He opened them, to read their contents again, in the hope of finding solace.

His father had written:

> My dear Marcus,
>   Your first honors! I glow with pride at your achieve-
> ment. Your brother cannot wait to see the fruit of your
> valor. He practices with horse and sword daily, deter-
> mined to be the equal of his elder brother.

Sergius ran a hand over his forehead, across the scar, and through his hair. Not only his parents but also his brother would be dismayed by Sergius's action. Manius had reached the age when heroes dominated his thinking. And his father wouldn't have kept Sergius's honors a secret. He'd have told his friends, his acquaintances—half of Aquileia probably knew.

We have engaged Julia to a young man of Verona, L. Cornelius Atticus, a man of good character, whose father is aedile of the town. She states she will not marry until you are home to participate in the festivities.

I have disheartening news. Claudia's parents have decided she is to be engaged to another, a youth of no distinction whose name would mean nothing to you, but who has the advantage of being close at hand. Your mother and I will seek another for you to wed.

Despite his gloom, he grinned, as broadly as he had the first time he'd read the words. That let Veturius off the hook as well. He'd have to tell his mother of Ailidh. So far, he'd kept his comments very general. Marriage? Disgraced men didn't make good marriage prospects.

Your mother offers the same advice as before. She refuses to believe that Britannia is as decent as you claim and that the natives aren't gnashing their teeth outside your door for your flesh. Manius, however, relishes your descriptions.

May Jupiter and Silvanus guard you.

Sergius rolled the papyrus and restored it to the canister. Did his parents know of the coming spring offensive? He'd thought it best not to worry his mother, so in his letter he'd made no mention of it. Veturius's letter continued where he'd left off before.

Am I a messenger that I should further the course of your endearment while my own languishes? Wild oxen could not drag me back to that accursed dog-seller's hut. Still, if the opportunity presents itself, I will communicate your ardor as I'm sure you wish it done—that is, with propriety and sensibility.

Have you heard the good news about the abominable Claudia? I wonder which stripling was chosen by the gods to bear such misfortune. And you say my prayers are ineffective!

The legion grows restless at the thought of being denied the honor that awaits you at the opening of the season, but I, for one, am glad that conflict awaits you

251

and not me. My blood may be chill, but it is at least my
own.
  I have offered a vow to Silvanus for your safety, as
you yourself neglect the conduct of the gods.
  For all this, would you leave me in need?
  Ah, Venus, I cannot buy your favors with brass
asses, when you desire the silver of denarii. . . .

Sergius grimaced. Veturius's writing trailed off into a tangle of disconnected, indecipherable phrases. His friend had once again been drowning his sorrows with the fruit of the vine.

The third letter he'd kept close at hand since its arrival, wearing the worn scrap of papyrus next to his heart.

  Sergius, my friend in Christus, I rejoice that you rejoined your legion in safety. I would that God had
willed we meet again this winter, but it is not to be.
Lovernios was furious that you had escaped. He urged
me to return to the old ways, but I have kept the faith.
When I waver, I think of you.
  Spring comes, and when you return to Londinium, I
shall be waiting. Give my love to Cara; but the most,
for you.
  Ailidh.

Come morning, the other letters would remain here in the fortress; there was no room to lug personal belongings on campaign. But Ailidh's letter, tucked in a small leather pouch beneath his lorica, would accompany him every step of the way.

Sergius closed his eyes and lay back. Cara snored beside him.

Ailidh kept the faith. So would he.

Sergius waded through a forest of barbarians, rugged, bearded Germans who brandished long, keen-edged swords and brutal battle axes. His sandals slipped on bloody ground. Glowing eyes accused him from mere inches away, and thick lips and tongues screamed an incessant chorus.

Sacrifice to the emperor!
Worship Nero!

His gladius carved gaping holes in their ranks, but the horde seemed endless, as if all the barbarians in the world gathered to contest him.

Sacrifice to the emperor!
Worship Nero!

His sword arm grew tired with the monotony. The barbarians stood like giant oaks, refusing to be hewed down, requiring stroke after stroke after stroke.

Abruptly, they parted. One stood before him, taller than the others, an aura of authority covering him like a cloak. And his face—

Sergius recognized it with a shock.

Suetonius Paulinus.

The barbarian's mouth opened. "Sacrifice to the emperor!" he bellowed.

Sergius willed his arm to move, to raise his gladius. But it wouldn't.

Numb, he stood, as the barbarian pressed his face close, until his lips and teeth pressed against Sergius's eyes and his breath blew hot on Sergius's face.

"Worship Nero!"

Sergius took a deep breath. He forced a single word past invisible fingers that clenched around his throat.

"No."

Massive hands shook his shoulder, fingers grinding painfully into the muscles. "Offer!"

"No! No!"

He thrashed and twisted, trying to escape the hands.

"Sir! Sir!"

His eyes shot open. The forest vanished. The face above him mutated into that of his beneficiarius.

"Quintus?" he squinted.

The aide loosed his grip and stepped back. "It's morning, sir."

With the back of his hand, Sergius wiped a chill sweat from his forehead. "Sorry. Bad dream."

"We're preparing to march, sir."

Sergius swung to a sitting position. "I'd intended to be up earlier." Somehow, he'd slept through the signals of the tuba. "Are we—"

Quintus nodded. "Everything is ready, sir. The orderly brought food for you if you wish." He indicated a plate on a table.

Sergius relaxed. "Quintus, you're invaluable." He hopped off the lectus and reached for a clean tunic. "Help me with my armor, Quintus. I'll eat while I dress."

Sergius exited his quarters into the controlled confusion of an army preparing to march. The air reverberated with the clamor of armed men, the neighing of horses, the tramp of hobnailed boots. Soldiers scurried to find their assigned place in the ranks. Centurions barked orders and berated the sluggish.

Didius Pertinax beckoned to him from in front of the principia. Adventus's and the other centurions' attitude toward him had chilled after the ceremony, but the cavalry commander remained affable. "I thought maybe you weren't coming."

"No fear of that."

Septimus Justus, the fresh-faced tribune who'd joined Sergius's near-disastrous boar hunt, joined them. His eyes shone. "It's true. We're really marching."

"What did you think," Pertinax replied with a wink at Sergius, "that we were going to stay here and whittle wood all year?"

"No, but . . . to be heading into battle!"

Sergius gazed past the young tribune. In his mind's eye he saw Roman soldiers and Deceangli lying dead in the snow. "It isn't that glorious," he murmured.

Justus seemed not to hear. Pertinax did. "Everyone needs a chance for honors, Lysias. You and I have ours, but not everyone has the good fortune to obtain them so quickly."

Sergius gave Justus a small smile. "I'll not stand in your way."

The door of the principia opened. Suetonius Paulinus, arrayed in his dress armor and scarlet cloak, stepped out, followed by legate Marcianus.

As he had at the culmination of the Quinquatria, the bucinator pealed the classicum fanfare.

When the last note had faded, Chief Centurion Adventus stepped forward and saluted. "The legions are ready for your command, sir. One cohort is assigned to garrison the fortress."

Suetonius nodded. He ran his gaze over the tribunes.

"Gentlemen, to war."

Grooms led out the officers' horses. With an agility belying his age, Suetonius swung himself into the saddle. A trooper helped the corpulent Marcianus.

A groom halted in front of Sergius. "Sir."

Sergius patted his horse's sleek neck. The stable staff had taken good care of the animal over the long winter months. He gripped the saddle horns and vaulted up. Pertinax waved and rejoined the cavalry.

Suetonius led his horse down the via praetoria with Marcianus next behind and Sergius as senior tribune ahead of the juniors. Chief Centurion Adventus and his optio brought up the rear.

Outside the fortress, Suetonius halted. The aquilifers brought up the eagles. Suetonius made a signal. The cornicen blew the signal to draw the troops' attention to the standards.

"Advance!" Suetonius shouted. He urged his horse onward.

Sergius and the other officers clattered in his wake.

Once away from the immediate environs of the fortress, the troops assumed standard marching order. Scouts and skirmishers fanned out in front. The auxiliary infantry preceded the legionaries of the *Gemina*. The baggage train followed, long lines of heavily laden mules bearing the prepared boat sections. Sergius grinned. Another reason the seasick prone Veturius should be glad to remain in Lindum—his friend wouldn't appreciate even the short crossing to Mona.

With the right flank protected by the river Deva, the cavalry guarded the left, between the legions and the dark, forested mountains.

Despite his comment to Justus on war's negative aspect, the blood thrummed in Sergius's veins. A crisp breeze carrying the remnants of winter blew from the mountains across a sky of cloud-dotted blue. Sergius inhaled deeply of the sea, mountain, and marsh-scented air.

Even Cara seemed affected. The wolfhound pranced alongside, tail erect.

"The gods couldn't have given us a better day," Justus appreciated.

Sergius tipped back his head to allow the sunlight full play on his face. "It's splendid."

The legions set their pace to that of the baggage train, an easy two miles per hour. At that rate it would take five or six days to reach the straits separating Mona from the mainland.

Such a slow pace would allow the Druidae plenty of time to notice that the legions had begun their advance and to prepare for their imminent arrival. Sergius's skin prickled. He studied the dark blue mountains that clustered inland, hiding the interior from Roman eyes. Were they being watched, even now, by hostile Deceangli? Were the Druidae practicing their horrible rites in an attempt to draw down retribution from their gods onto Roman heads?

Some said the Druidae had no need of watchers in the hills to detect the Roman advance, that their magical arts gave them far-seeing ability.

Sergius had always admired the beauty and grandeur of mountains. Now they gave him pause, and he almost feared to look at them.

Throughout the day, the legions marched along the river, being careful not to venture close to where marsh grass concealed treacherous shifting sands. Alarmed by the approach of so many humans, countless waterfowl flung themselves squawking into the air.

Suetonius scanned the horizon incessantly. Sergius caught himself more than once doing the same.

"Nervous?" Pertinax asked.

"A perfect place for an ambush," Sergius replied, "with quicksand at our backs."

"They won't attack."

"You sound confident."

"The commander bloodied the Deceangli too badly last year, before you arrived. They haven't the ability to launch a major attack—not on this many troops, at any rate. Skirmish, yes. An all-out battle, no. Culhwch was their last hope."

The legions halted for the night where the river broadened, leaving behind the estuary.

To Justus's obvious delight, Sergius sent him ahead with a scouting party to select a location for the first night's camp.

By the time the main body of troops arrived, the surveyors had laid out the ground plan. The camp needed to be more defensible than the makeshift affair Sergius had erected in the winter. For each man who erected a tent, another removed his dolabrum from his belt, and used the instrument—a cutting blade at one end of the haft and a tine at the other—to hack a ditch out of the damp ground and cast the soil into a rampart.

In what seemed a minor miracle of time, a small city of leather tents sprang up on the uninhabited riverbank.

"So much for the first day of campaign season," Pertinax yawned as he relaxed in a hot bath that evening.

From outside the officers' ablutionary tent came the familiar sounds of a camp at rest: centurions assigned duties to the legionaries; men grunted and swore, laughed and complained, prepared the stockade, and cooked the evening meal.

"We made good progress," Sergius replied.

"Is this it?" Justus asked.

"What's 'it'?" Pertinax demanded. "Endless marching? Yes. Day in, day out, march and march again, and somewhere at the end of it waits glory or death."

Sergius rubbed his legs. "Be patient, Justus. We'll reach Mona soon enough."

Decianus Catus smiled contentedly as the cavalcade wound away from Venta Icenorum, heading for Camulodunum.

"A profitable excursion," he gloated, glancing at the wagons loaded with plunder. Not plunder, he told himself. Repayment. Privileges of office.

"I expected more fight," Fuscus replied.

Catus snorted. "If there's one thing in which the Britons excel, it's boasting. But when it comes to fighting, they don't know the meaning of the word." He sniggered. "That's the last we'll hear of the so-called Iceni problem."

Juba said, "Seneca will be pleased at the amount we've recouped."

Catus nodded pensively. "Nero too. He has to appreciate the prompt and efficient manner in which his orders to reduce the Iceni were obeyed."

In fact, Catus thought, there might even be an Imperial commendation for himself. Perhaps Britannia wasn't such a deadend after all.

Maybe he'd be able to look back and see it as a stepping-stone to further advancement.

He looked past Juba's pleased expression to where Fuscus fidgeted on his horse. "What's your problem?"

The centurion shook his head as if to clear it. "I still expected more resistance."

Catus curled his lip. Fuscus was becoming an old woman. The centurion hadn't even touched the girls.

No matter. Catus fingered a pouch of gold and jewels that dangled from his belt and his smile returned. Truly a profitable day.

EIGHTEEN

Boudicca sat bolt upright in her chair, her back rigid, her arms resting on her thighs, her lance laid crosswise over her knees. It was one of the few positions she could maintain for any length of time. If she bent forward or flexed her spine sideways, the raw stripes on her back and legs cracked and bled. Every movement made a muscle cringe somewhere.

The chair had been pieced together from shattered fragments of others and placed in the house's largest room—the one Prasutagus had used for granting audience.

In front of her ranged the nobles of the Iceni, the chiefs of their families. These men and women had won distinction in battle. Their voices spoke for all Iceni, for the thousands and thousands who tilled farms, raised horses, and carried arms.

Three nights had passed since Catus and his troops had arrived at Venta Icenorum. Three nights of mental, physical, and emotional agony gelled her blazing rage into fixity of purpose. Only blood—Roman blood, rivers of it—could quench the fire of her wrath.

She hadn't deigned to satisfy the Romans by crying out as Fuscus's soldiers beat her insensible with rods, but the cries of fear and pain from her daughters had gouged deeper into her heart than the rods into her flesh.

Finally, their lust and greed sated, Catus, Fuscus, and the troops had abandoned Venta Icenorum, leaving behind looted and plundered homes, her daughters barely alive and mute with shock, and herself flung on the ground near Airell's body, unable to move.

Helping hands had carried her into the wreck of her house, where they laid her on skins on the floor. Never, as long as she lived, would she forget her first glimpse of her daughters—Aife cowering against a wall, arms wrapped around her legs, and Cinnia curled into a ball on the floor, her sobs nearly inaudible.

An old woman with healing knowledge tended her and her daughters. "They will live," the woman diagnosed, "but their minds . . . I cannot say."

Despite her pain, Boudicca spent the long night stroking her ravaged daughters' hair, urging them to be strong. She'd prayed to Epona and Andraste to give them strength and to Bride to nurse them as she could not.

And she spoke, certain he could hear her, to Prasutagus.

You are rí now, Boudicca, came a voice in the night—his, hers, she couldn't tell. *You must do what is right by the people. If one way does not succeed, try another.*

Prasutagus was beyond hurt. If she couldn't follow his way, she'd have to carve her own. The Romans had violated Prasutagus's daughters. Whatever course she chose, her husband wouldn't object.

Through the night of pain, she thought she felt his presence near her.

The next day, despite the healing woman's protestations, Boudicca had forced her stiff, swollen muscles to move and limped through the tribal center, talking to the stunned inhabitants—those that the Romans hadn't abducted as slaves. She dispatched messengers to recall the nobles and to spread the word of the Romans' atrocities through the length and breadth of Iceni land.

One by one the nobles filtered into the town; those with possessions and families in Venta Icenorum returned to ravaged homes and shocked families and were joined by those whose property lay elsewhere. All shared the rage of the victimized.

Now, with the nobles assembled, Boudicca sat and listened.

"It's gone far enough!" Weylyn's high-pitched voice rose above the babble. "I say we put an end to the Roman scourge! Do we wait until the grass grows over our graves and the graves of our families and it becomes too late?"

The nobles answered him with a growl of approval.

"Airell paid for his bravery with his life," Weylyn continued. "Must his sacrifice be in vain?"

A burly warrior with a long mustache stepped forward. "Had I been here, Catus would not have escaped so easily. I would have twisted his neck like a chicken's."

"Brave words, Bairrfhionn," Boudicca rasped, "but is there courage and resolve behind them?"

"Yes!"

"Does any man here fear the Romans?"

Bairrfhionn spat. "Fear men who hide behind helmets and breast-plates, who lurk in the protection of walls and ditches? A rough and ready fight would scare the bracae off them!"

"They'd run away and hide," somebody else laughed, "if their armor didn't get in the way! They're afraid we might hurt them."

Mocking laughter rippled through the room.

"They bathe in warm water and wear perfume!"

"And sleep on soft couches with boys for bedfellows!"

"Our women are braver than their men!"

Boudicca listened to the nobles and smiled at the comments, although mirth lay far from her. The jokes and boasts built courage and banished whatever fear might have lingered in the minds of those who remembered the previous Iceni defeat. Some of the warriors still bore scars from that disaster.

Boudicca missed the calm voice of Airell, but perhaps that was as well.

"They're weak," Bairrfhionn added. "They need shade and kneaded bread and fine wine. A little sun, a little hunger or thirst, and they whine for their fancy homes." He thumped his chest with his fist. "But for us, any grass or root is bread, any water is wine, any tree is a house."

The nobles cheered.

Weylyn looked at Boudicca. "Well, Queen? What say you?"

Boudicca gripped the shaft of her lance, swung it to the floor, and leaned her weight on it as a staff. She forced herself to stand, gritting her teeth against the cramps that skewered her calves and thighs.

A man moved to help her, but she waved him away.

"We have purpose. We will make a plan." Pain made her voice harsh. "Let us show the Roman thieves that they are hares and foxes trying to rule over dogs and wolves!"

The swell of emotion that gripped the room overflowed her pain and dulled it to a haze. But only the defeat of the Romans would assuage it completely.

To Sergius the days after leaving Deva assumed a comfortable monotony. The legion and its pack train made slow progress along the riverbank. The few boats they'd commandeered from Britons living near the river bobbed offshore. On the third day the army rounded a point and, instead of the riverfront, marched along beaches bordering the sea.

The wind whipped salt spray from glistening waves that foamed ashore. The gray green, misty mountains pressed ever closer, a constant reminder of the enemy that lay ahead. Outcroppings of naked rock burst from the bracken-covered flanks of the hills.

But the scouts saw not a single Deceangli tribesman. It was as if some supernatural power had denuded the whole country of humans.

"It's creepy," Sergius commented once, as the memory of his pursuit of Culhwch seeped into his mind. "Where are they?"

"Waiting for us," Pertinax replied cheerfully.

The weather remained bearable, with scattered showers, chill morning mist that crept into bones and joints, and clouds that sometimes sank to earth as an overladen ship subsiding into the sea. But no major storms discontented the troops.

On the fourth day a promontory thrust itself out into the waves, and the troops altered course inland. The boats made heavy going around the rocks. Several ventured too close, and the unforgiving coast dashed them to splinters and drowned the crews.

That made the men grumble, and Suetonius had to address the legion.

"Some loss is to be expected," the commander said. "The destruction of a few boats is not a bad omen but a fact of war. Think of the punishment we will inflict on the enemy. Their loss will be your gain."

The troops brightened at the thought of spoil. Druidic gold!

Once across the river Conwy, beaches made for easy travel. In the distance, Mona was a low mound of thickly forested hills, still two days away.

Suetonius indicated open order, and the legions assumed their defensive positions, in case the Druidae or Deceangli launched an attack. They marched three ranks deep, with the baggage protected, able to pivot rapidly to counter any threat.

But still no attack came. The cavalry reported no harrying on the flanks. The Britons seemed content to await the Romans' approach. Perhaps it was as Pertinax said, and the Deceangli had no will left to fight.

Mona drew closer as the straits narrowed, until an archer could shoot across the water onto the druidic stronghold. But the *Gemina* didn't pause, marching a farther eight miles to Segontium, the rendezvous point with the other legions.

That night Suetonius himself inspected the marching camp, assured himself of the depth of the ditch and the height of the rampart, and posted double guards on the camp, the precious boat parts, and the captured vessels drawn up on shore.

The next day, the division of the *Valeria* arrived, footsore from their march down the river valley but bringing additional disassembled boats.

Titus snapped his fingers as he swung down from his horse. "We wanted to be first," he said.

"I hope you didn't lose too much money in wagers," Sergius replied.

"Not much. Besides, we beat Agricola and the cohorts of the *Augusta*. I'll make it up."

"You'd better make something else up too," Sergius commented, wrinkling his nose. "You stink."

Titus frowned, then burst into laughter. "It's good, honest sweat! Point me to the bath tent."

The mountains echoed with the sound of hammering. Under heavy guard, the men of the *Gemina* and *Valeria* worked side by side assembling the boats on the shore.

A day later Agricola arrived with the troops detached from the *Augusta*.

"Late as usual," Titus chided. "Pay up."

Agricola screwed his eyes shut and shook his head. "I can't believe you flat-footed caligatae beat us."

"Fairly." Titus held out his hand.

Agricola rummaged for coins. "I told Legate Crispus we should march faster. 'We'll be there in plenty of time,' he said."

"Remember that when you're a legate. Make the soldiers march quickly."

Seemingly overnight the fleet of transports took shape. Assemblers transformed piles of lumber into flat-bottomed boats.

The evening before the planned attack, Sergius stood on the rampart, looking away from the cluster of tents toward the dark island that lay across the narrow Menai Strait.

Torches flickered through the trees. Was it only wind and waves he heard or chanting and the weird, unfamiliar music of rituals being conducted in a strange tongue?

Agricola materialized beside him. "What do you think they're doing?"

"I keep expecting to hear the cry of a human sacrifice." Sergius crossed his arms on the palisade and leaned on it.

"I'm sure some unfortunate soul is meeting a grisly end. But not on the coast. Somewhere inland, in a grove," Agricola speculated.

A raven cawed from an unseen vantage point.

"This is it," Sergius labeled: "the Druidae's final sanctuary."

"Not quite. There's still Hibernia." Agricola pointed across the sea that flickered in moonlight.

"Too far away, surely."

Agricola made a noncommittal grunt. "With a legion or two we could take it."

Sergius grimaced, "You're not serious!"

"I said *could*, not *would*."

Sergius returned his attention to the eerily wavering lights on Mona's shore. "I think Mona will be sufficient. If we break the Druidae here, they'll never recover."

"If?" Agricola chuckled. "Will. Remember your augury. The eagle grasps the hare." He turned away. "I'm going to bed. We'll need plenty of stamina for tomorrow's killing."

Sergius waved good night.

Agricola disappeared into the darkness.

Sergius remained leaning on the palisade, watching the lights, listening to the camp quieten as men went to sleep, and only the regular pacing and low conversation of the sentries disturbed the night.

He touched his chest where Ailidh's letter rested in its leather pouch. He remembered the night in Egomas's hut. During their conversation, she'd told him in passing about the Druidae.

"They're not all priests," she'd explained, "only some. The Druid represent the highest pinnacle of our culture. They're physicians and astrologers, poets, scholars—"

"Your cousin?" he had interrupted.

"Lovernios is a judge."

"What happened between you?"

He thought she wouldn't answer, but then she said, "The Way came between us. It separated us, as a sword cutting us apart."

"Did you love him?"

She'd responded with a hitch of her shoulders. "I was young. I admired him. My father thought we'd make a suitable match."

"I can relate to that," Sergius replied, breaking the tension. "Only the girl my parents fancied was perfectly abominable."

The remembrance of that night faded. Sergius rubbed an itch on the side of his nose.

The Roman way was best. To imagine otherwise was unthinkable. Roman culture transformed and elevated all others.

And yet . . . what would Ailidh think of him now? When the Romans were committed to destroying the druidic aristocracy, how could she bear affection for him? Granted, she embraced the Way, as did he, and no longer worshiped the old gods of the Celtae, but the Druidae represented the culmination of centuries of Celtae life.

When they were destroyed, when their learning vanished, what would be left?

The common folk, like Ailidh and Egomas, pursuing their ordinary lives in a land without a remembered past.

What would Rome be like if the nobility, the patricians, the emperor, and the artists and poets and architects were suddenly eradicated? If the barbarians flooded the borders and destroyed all the best in the Empire?

He had a vision of the eagle missing the hare to crack its neck against the ground.

He shook it off.

The Empire fall? Silly.

Rome brought civilization; it didn't destroy it. Rome represented all that was greatest and most noble in the world. Rome took the best aspects of other cultures and wove them into the fabric of its own being.

Still, as he stepped off the rampart and made his way through the packed rows of tents toward his, guilt nagged at him.

He paused at the entrance of his tent.

"Forgive me, Ailidh," he whispered as he pushed the flap and entered.

He lit a lamp and set it beside his lectus.

Was it really Ailidh's forgiveness that mattered?

What would Paullus say? What would Christus do in this situation?

Was it right to slaughter the Druidae for their beliefs?

No. Paullus would have gone and preached to them, as he did to everyone he met in Britannia. To Paullus it didn't matter if a person was Roman, Jewish, Greek, or Briton—they all needed to hear of the Way. Faith in Christus leveled the distinctions.

The Roman Army had no such compunctions. The Druidae were enemies of the Roman State; therefore, they had to die. It was as simple as that.

But it wasn't simple at all.

Sergius closed his eyes.

God, he prayed, *help me to do what is right. Help me to understand what you would have me to do. Help me to act as Christus would act.*

Ailidh led the dogs back to the hut after taking them for a late walk. Inside, the fire blazed on a pair of iron firedogs, and Egomas sat beside it, gnawing on a bone.

"You were gone long enough," he grumbled.

"I needed the exercise." Ailidh folded her legs underneath her.

"I'm not coming looking into the woods for you."

Ailidh sat in silence for a moment, then she pressed, "When can we leave?"

"Here?"

She gestured. "People whisper. There's talk of revolt—"

"There's always some young fool looking for glory." Egomas pitched the bone through the doorway; a sudden snarling indicated dogs fighting over it.

"I heard that Catus abused Boudicca."

"Rumors. The man's a fool, but not that big of one."

"Why did he take troops to Venta Icenorum?"

"I don't know. Nor do I care." Egomas picked up another bone and pointed it at her. "And you'd do well to mind your own business."

"The dogs are ready to be taken to market," Ailidh persuaded.

Egomas grunted. "I'll think about it."

Ailidh lay on her pile of bed skins and closed her eyes. Where were the legions? What were they doing? She thought of Sergius and how he'd sat close beside her. She brought to mind the warmth and the scent of him. And she wished he was beside her again.

Egomas might not notice, but the atmosphere had changed. People of the Trinovantes who once went about afraid to speak of Romans now had a new light in their eyes. They walked taller. They boasted of the deeds they would do.

She'd seen women mending scabbards and criss. She'd seen men unearth swords long buried. She had seen youths engaging in mock battles.

And she wanted nothing more than to leave this place of whispers, rumors, and ill-concealed hatred.

She fought down her unease. She was daughter of Cathair, the warrior. The mother she had never known had been a noblewoman of the Trinovantes, skilled in the history of the peoples. And Ailidh herself had fought a hard battle when she accepted the Way.

And Sergius . . .

She squeezed her eyes tight. Why did Romans have to be the way they were? And why did Sergius have to be one of them?

The light from a dozen smoking torches flickered through a grove near Venta Icenorum, illuminating nearby tree trunks while leaving the more distant as stark, shadowy onlookers. Gray veils of fragrant woodsmoke twisted between the trunks.

Boudicca strode along the lane of oaks.

Every step sent a renewed flourish of pain through the scabbed welts that crisscrossed her back. Even her soft linen léine rubbed and chafed. The criss belted around her waist felt as heavy as iron weights.

But the pain served as a stimulus. And with each step she took, her hatred of the Romans burned fiercer.

Boudicca stopped in the circle of torchlight.

Tonight was the sixth night of the moon. She couldn't see the moon, obscured by trees and torches, but she knew it shone over the forest.

Silent, white-robed women peopled the grove, moving spiritlike in the wavering light. As Boudicca approached, the movement ceased. The women stood still as statues.

From the darkness outside the torches, a pair of women led a white bull into the grove and hobbled it. A garland of spring flowers hung around the bull's neck, and its horns had been gilded. The animal snorted and tossed its head, as if sensing the fate that awaited it.

Boudicca put a hand on each side of the animal's muzzle and blew in its nostrils. She ran her fingers along the line of its muzzle and murmured in its ear. The bull stiffened, then relaxed and stood placidly in place.

Boudicca stepped away from the animal. No need for a priestess here. Boudicca herself was high priestess of Andraste. The sacrifice was hers.

A bodhran began a low, pulsing beat.

Six women commenced a keening chant, their voices ethereal, emanating from the night itself, or the stars.

Boudicca swayed to the pulse. She unclasped her cloak and let it fall to the ground. Her léine followed. Naked but for her criss, she allowed her body to fall into the rhythm of the drum and the voices.

The beat quickened.

Three women joined her, bare flesh gleaming in the night.

Boudicca spun. Her hands traced sensuous curves. Her body twisted and flexed.

The scabs split. Fresh blood flowed down her beaten back.

Pain—sharp, ice-cold burning—instead of hindering her dance, sped her movements.

The bodhran pounded through the trees. The women's voices skirled their chant.

The four dancers, sweat dripping from their skin and hair, hurled themselves into a frenzy.

Boudicca's mind fled her body. As if in a dream she watched herself, saw her lithe and muscular form writhe in a dance of light and shadow, her tawny hair spinning a wreath of yellow gold around her.

One woman collapsed, but the others continued, faster and faster, the rhythm of feet matching the bodhran.

And the bodhran beat quicker and quicker, and the voices scaled higher and higher—

Her soles slapped the ground, her heart pumped, her muscles propelled her, upward, upward, toward where torch sparks and stars mingled in a shimmering swirl of exhilaration and exhaustion and ecstasy—

She stretched out her arms. The stars were within her grasp—

A cymbal crash shattered the night into a constellation of ebony fragments.

As the sound faded, Boudicca tumbled into her body. She knelt on the ground, her arms extended to the sky.

Her breath rushed in and out of lungs that burned, her heart thudded in her chest, and her ravaged back flamed in exquisite torture.

The stars ceased their gyrations and settled into place. The torches burned brightly.

Her damp flesh broke into goose bumps in the night air.

She left her léine where it lay but draped her long cloak over her shoulders.

Her legs trembled as she rose.

With her right hand she pulled a bronze dagger from her criss. The torchlight glinted off the sharp blade.

Women surrounded the bull. One held a bronze cauldron. Another hauled on a halter to expose the bull's neck.

"Hear me, Andraste the Unconquerable!" Boudicca cried, head tilted back. "I vow to you! I call upon you as woman to woman!"

With a quick movement of her wrist, she plunged the dagger into the bull's neck over the jugular vein. The animal roared, and blood crimsoned the white hide. The woman with the cauldron held it out to catch the hot stream.

The bull's front legs buckled. With a last loud low, it pitched forward and lay quivering, a heaving mass on the grass.

When the blood ceased to flow, the woman with the cauldron brought it to Boudicca.

She dipped her forefinger into the hot blood and touched it to her lips.

"Andraste! My words are true! I offer you this bull as a symbol of my vow. Grant me victory over the Romans, and their lives and blood will be yours.

"None shall be spared! Their men shall die on the battlefield, their women in their towns and homes, their children on their mothers' breasts!

"The birds shall gorge on their carcasses. And I shall not rest until the plunderers of our land, the ravagers of Prasutagus's honor, and the despoilers of his daughters drink deeply of my retribution!"

She dipped her finger again. "I shall sweep the Roman scourge into the sea!"

She streaked her forehead with blood—"With my mind, I swear it!"

Her chest—"With my heart, I swear it!"

And lastly her abdomen—"With my spirit, I swear it!"

She drew breath. "With my will, I will it! With my being, I pursue it! With my strength, I accomplish it!"

She lifted the cauldron to her lips and drank.

She set the cauldron down again. The women filed past. Each of them marked herself as Boudicca had done, and each repeated the formula.

"The women of the Iceni swear vengeance!" Boudicca cried.

Lovernios peeled himself from the shadow of a tree and stepped into the clearing that stank of smoke and sweat and blood.

Boudicca whirled. Her eyes blazed beneath a wild tangle of hair.

Had he been a Roman, Lovernios had no doubt he would have been instantly put to death. As it was, for a man to enter into the rituals of Andraste . . . only a Druí would dare.

Boudicca rippled with menace, "Do you live in shadows, Druí?"

"I inhabit a world of shadows and light."

"What say you?"

His gaze swept over the women—both naked and partially clothed—over the dead bull, and at the blood that marked Boudicca's body. He said, "Your cause is just."

"It is more than just! And I have offered it to Andraste."

He nodded. "Then if Andraste wills, it will prosper."

"You said there would be life or death come spring. I say there will be both: life for the Iceni; death for the Romans."

"There is a time to forgive and a time for recompense."

"What of your sacrifice? Have you found it?"

Lovernios shook his head. "There was one . . . but he escaped. I still seek."

Boudicca stooped to retrieve her léine. She shrugged off the cloak, pulled on the léine, and adjusted the cloak over it. "No more do we allow the Romans to trample us, to kick us aside like curs, or to sell us into slavery." She raised a fist. "I, Boudicca, queen of the Iceni, swear it."

Lovernios withdrew his gold rod from his belt. He touched her fist with its tip. "The peoples of the Celtae will remember your name."

She turned away. "I care not if my name is remembered, as long as my vengeance is obtained."

"You have many allies. All winter I have traveled the lands of the Iceni, the Trinovantes, the Catuvellauni, and the Coritani, spreading the word of resistance. Sacrifices are being offered. The groves stream with the blood of animals."

"And soon they will stream with the blood of Romans."

Lovernios inclined his head.

Boudicca stalked away from the grove, passed through the ring of torches and disappeared.

Lovernios watched as the bull was butchered, divided, and ported to waiting families. There would be no waste.

The dancing women removed the cauldron.

The torches guttered.

When the women departed, he stood alone in the grove. Only a dark patch on the ground, nearly invisible in the dying torchlight, indicated that a sacrifice had occurred.

Then he followed the path Boudicca had taken, located his horse, waiting outside the forest, and mounted.

He rode west, toward Mona.

Streams of Roman blood.

He hadn't borne arms, would never carry arms. But Roman blood would stain his hands just as surely as if he wielded a sword.

All was coming to pass, just as he had dreamed, just as the gutuatri had foreseen.

The moon shone high in the night sky.

As a youth, learning the Druid way, he'd dreamed of the time when he'd be a judge. He loved the laws of the people. To be able to guide them, to intercede, to see the guilty—those who harmed the tribe—punished, to intervene when conflict threatened, to prevent bloodshed; those had been his dreams. He'd seen himself as part of a great company, of those who held the life of the people in their hands.

And Romans?

A scourge to Gaul, but not at first to Britannia.

But then they'd come.

And his dreams of justice had swirled away, as his father Kirwin's blood had swirled into the river. Safe in Ériu, Lovernios had earned his rank. And he'd administered justice. But never to Romans.

Never until now.

But the Romans would feel the weight of Briton justice. And if they paid for justice with their blood . . .

Lovernios glanced up at the moon's pockmarked face.

So be it.

The truth against the world.

Against the Romans.

NINETEEN

The assault commenced at dawn as the sun crept over the eastern horizon. Slowly, as if Sol Invictus was hesitant to be drawn into the conflict about to commence.

Rain had fallen in the night, a heavy, driving downpour that pounded relentlessly on the tents. But the storm clouds had blown over, and the morning dawned clear, though rain still dripped off leaves and tents and coursed in rivulets through thin sand to the water's edge. Gentle waves kissed the rocky shoreline.

Sergius and Agricola stood apart while Suetonius Paulinus ordered the boats brought forward and the troops assembled.

"If the Britons were hoping for weather to aid them," Agricola commented, studying the few wispy clouds the sky contained, "they'll be disappointed."

"Don't speak too soon," Sergius replied. "You know how unpredictable the weather is here."

He checked his gladius to make sure it slid easily in its scabbard, then peered across the strait at mist-shrouded Mona. The sun lacked the power to burn off the haze draped mosslike over Mona's forests. Breezes stirred the mist but didn't dispel it. The farther shore appeared deserted.

Titus and Justus crunched over the shingly beach.

"Are they hiding?" Justus wondered.

"They were busy enough last night," Sergius replied.

Mist poked long, crooked fingers in their direction, as if beckoning them toward the gray trees. Despite his cloak, Sergius shivered.

"They call it *ceo druidechta*," Agricola said, his gaze fixed across the strait. "The druidic fog."

"They can't really control the weather, can they?" Justus's voice trembled.

"Don't be ridiculous," Titus sneered. "It's morning mist, that's all."

"The Druidae claim another power," Agricola added. "The *fe-fiada*: a cloak of darkness, so they can't be seen."

"Just what we need," Titus massaged his temple. "Invisible Druidae hiding in fog. You're being a great help, Agricola."

Sergius couldn't help but remember Lovernios's seeming ability to appear and disappear from shadow. He glanced at the pale-faced Justus and reassured, "They'll show themselves soon enough."

"That's right," Titus growled. "They're human. They'll be feeling our steel in short order. Magicians or not, I bet their blood is red and flows freely."

The boats drew up in a long line along the shore.

"Commence boarding," bawled a centurion standing next to Suetonius. Other centurions relayed the order along the ranks.

Legionaries filed onto the flat-bottomed transports, one century per boat. On the wings, the cavalry awaited the order to cross.

Agricola jogged Sergius's elbow. "Let's join the cavalry."

"You'd rather swim than float?"

"The water doesn't seem that deep. There should be shallows where it's possible to ride across."

Sergius nodded. "Why don't you three fetch the horses? I need to report."

He sought out Marcianus. The legionary commander waited along with Second *Augusta*'s Porcius Crispus beside the special boat intended to carry Suetonius, his guard, and the senior staff.

"With your permission, sir," Sergius said, "I'd like to join the cavalry."

Marcianus pursed his lips. "It's best you remain with the command staff, Tribune."

"But sir—"

"That's an order."

Sergius saluted. "Yes, sir."

Crispus said, "Bring Agricola with you, Tribune."

When he returned, Agricola and Justus had mounted their horses. Titus held his and Sergius's.

"Marcianus says I'm to remain with the command staff," Sergius informed Agricola.

"You asked?" Agricola replied. "Why?"

"Because I have to be careful not to offend him."

"Oh. Right. Your previous indiscretion."

"Crispus requests your presence as well."

Agricola scowled.

A hoarse bird cawed across the water.

"A raven," Agricola instructed: "Badb Catha, the raven of battle. Her other name is Morrigan, Queen of Demons."

"Shut up," Titus snapped. "What are you, a repository of druidic superstition?"

"You can't serve here without gaining some knowledge," Agricola answered defensively.

"Keep it to yourself." Titus withdrew his gladius and turned the sharp blade over, inspecting the edge with the ball of his thumb. "This is real. Briton fantasies are not. Come, Justus. Let's you and me skewer a few Druidae."

The young tribune's head bobbed.

Titus vaulted onto his horse. He waved to Sergius. "See you on the other side."

"Wait for the signal," Sergius urged.

Titus flashed a grin and rode away.

Sergius led his horse to the command boat. Agricola muttered imprecations. He was careful to stop before coming within hearing range of the legates. Marcianus acknowledged Sergius's presence with a nod, while Crispus seemed oblivious to Agricola's arrival.

Before Sergius led his horse onto the boat, a flicker of movement caught his eye.

To Marcianus he indicated, "There they are, sir."

The legionary commander followed Sergius's finger. On the once deserted shoreline stood a knot of five or six individuals. As the soldiers watched, more emerged from the shadows and mist.

Ghostlike, they created no sound, as if they were phantasms of the forest, wraithlike creatures of mist, insubstantial and vaporous.

"By Jupiter," Marcianus gasped, "they're weird."

A line of figures stretched on the opposing shoreline, illuminated by the rising sun.

"Governor!" Marcianus called.

"Yes?" Suetonius acknowledged from his position in the bow of the boat where he stood with his back to Mona, watching the troops board.

Marcianus indicated the Druidae. "Look."

Suetonius swiveled. Then he studied the array of boats. "Signal the advance."

The tubicen put his instrument to his lips and blew. The tuba's notes echoed off the dark walls of forest.

The boats pushed off from the shore. Cavalry units waded into the chilly water.

As if the tuba's notes provided a signal for them as well, a torch flickered among the Druidae. The flame jumped from one figure to another, racing along the shoreline, until torches blazed from end to end.

The boats reached the middle of the strait.

The sun breached the morning haze; gathering strength as it rose, it burned through the mist. The Druidae solidified.

Sergius gasped.

Hundreds, maybe thousands of white-robed men lined the shoreline, their arms upraised. Interspersed between them, warriors brandished swords and spears. Black-clad women, hair wild about their shoulders, waved torches. As full sunlight reached them, a cry went up from the druidic ranks.

The wave of sound washed across the strait. Faces contorted, the Druidae hurled curses against the Romans. The women screamed their fury.

Sergius understood one word in ten, but it was enough to catch the dreadful import of the druidic invective. Death and Hades weren't enough. The Druidae invoked the most bloodcurdling curses he'd ever heard.

The boats slowed and rocked on the currents.

Transfixed, the legionaries stared at the howling mass of Druidae.

Sergius caught the change in emotion, the sudden fear that gripped the legionaries and awed them into immobility. Fighting mobs of undisciplined warriors was one thing, but to face the Britons' priests—and by extension, their gods—quite another. To simple men, enough was enough.

"Fear begins with the eyes," he murmured.

"What?" Agricola asked.

"Something my father told me. Fear begins with the eyes."

"I'll have to remember that," Agricola replied. He looked to where Suetonius stood, ramrod straight, the druidic curses seeming not to affect him. "What's he waiting for? We're not to be driven off by this rabble, are we?"

Suetonius mounted the prow of the boat and turned his back on Mona. His scarlet cloak blazed. The sun shone on his engraved breastplate; the plume of his helmet stood tall. He had to shout to be heard over the yells and screams of the Druidae.

"Are you afraid of a horde of fanatical women? Are the armies of Rome to be turned back by the threats of an impotent enemy and cast upon the shore in disgrace? You are Romans! Put the charlatans to the sword!"

Suetonius gestured to the oarsmen and pivoted. "Row! Let us be the first ashore!" His outstretched arm pointed arrow-straight across the narrow strip of water.

The men dug their blades into the chop. The boat gained momentum. Some other boats began to move; others hesitated.

A shout came from somewhere on Sergius's left.

"For the eagles!"

A detachment of cavalry thundered through the water, seeking shallows where the horses could wade. Hooves flung sparkling showers of water high into the air. At the head of the cavalry rode Pertinax and Titus.

The hesitation broke.

The boats leaped forward as wild horses themselves.

Legionaries echoed the cry, "For the eagles! To the sword!"

The horses struggled through deep water. Some of the men dismounted to swim beside their mounts.

As the first riders reached the opposite shore, warriors broke away from the Druidae to face them. Swords and lances high, the cavalry swung into action.

The boat grounded in the shallows with a jolt that nearly jarred Sergius from his feet. Other boats beached alongside.

Javelins soared into the air. Some came from the Britons—one thudded into the planks between Sergius and Agricola—and a few legionaries fell, but most came from the Romans.

A Roman point buried itself in the chest of a Druid. The man pitched backward, twitched, and lay still.

"They die!" Agricola yelled. He gripped the quivering shaft of the Briton javelin, jerked it free from the deck, and flung it high over the heads of the legionaries at the Britons.

A second volley of javelins rose into the air, and Britons fell in droves.

The aquilifers, standards aloft, plunged toward the enemy. Led by their centurions, the legionaries poured ashore. The foot soldiers cut into the massed Britons while the cavalry tore into their flanks.

Bodies of Druidae mounted in heaps, slaughtered where they stood, cut down with arms upraised, white robes drenched with blood, their prayers unable to save them from Roman steel. The warriors put up a fierce resistance, but they were too few. Shield to shield, the legionaries presented a bristling front of deadly swords.

The Britons retreated into the trees. The pursuing legionaries spared no one, hacking down both women and men without mercy.

As the shoreline cleared of the living, Suetonius urged his horse ashore, accompanied by his bodyguard and the senior officers. Sergius followed, his horse taking the distance in a few bounds.

Agricola yelled something he didn't catch and raced ahead.

One black-robed Druidess, eyes wide and hair flying, broke past the Roman ranks. Torch waving, she threw herself at the governor. Sergius's sword slipped from its sheath, and he urged his horse forward. A legionary at the same time saw the woman, pivoted, and flung his javelin.

The Druidess's arms flew up, and she pitched face first onto the sand. Her torch guttered beside her, her fingers clenched.

Another Druidess grabbed at Agricola's horse. He kicked out, and the woman reeled back, arms flailing. Her torch touched her hair. It ignited, and she flamed into a human pyre, screaming as she ran until she collapsed in a pile of smoking rags.

And she wasn't alone. The Druidae's fires turned against them, setting both the living and the dead ablaze. Smoke thickened the air, and Sergius' stomach revolted at the stench of burning flesh. He choked down vomit.

Still the Romans pressed ahead, and then they cleared the beach and fought the remnants of the Britons among the trees.

"Put them to the sword," Suetonius had ordered, and the legionaries did. No survivors were allowed.

Sergius followed in the legionaries' wake, keeping pace with the governor, but not joining the fighting.

Did that absolve him from blame—in God's eyes, or Ailidh's?

Roman religion was neat and tidy, a business exchange between men and gods. I'll do this for you if you do that for me. It didn't involve sin, and repentance, and accepting and living a new life ordered according to God's will.

His horse stepped over bodies flung down like empty sacks.

Some of the Druidae, the priests, had tonsured heads, hair shaved from ear to ear. Others didn't: the scholars, astronomers, physicians, and nobles. Each met death.

He caught a glimpse of Titus, riding like a madman, heading for wherever the fray was fiercest. And Agricola, red sword waving, slashed at any standing figure not wearing Roman armor.

"You're not fighting." Gellius Marcianus's voice jolted Sergius from his thoughts. The legate rode alongside him.

"I'm watching the men, sir," Sergius made the excuse, "seeing how the commander directs the battle."

Marcianus nodded. "What would you do?"

Sergius gestured. "Mona is a large island, sir. I'd recall the legions and secure the beachhead. We can scour the island for survivors in an orderly fashion later."

"Whereas . . ."

"If we pursue now, the troops will become separated and disorganized, scattered in the forest."

"Exactly. Our strength is in discipline and order," Marcianus agreed. He indicated Suetonius. "The governor's calling for withdrawal now."

The tubicen sounded the retreat, followed by the cornicen who drew the troops' attention to the location of the standards.

The legionaries farther away took a few minutes to heed the calls, dispatching their final foes. The advance halted, and the centuries reformed on the beach.

Suetonius gestured to Chief Centurion Adventus. "Detail a cohort to make sure this area is clear. Gather the boats and place a guard." To Sergius, "Take a survey party and find a location for camp."

Sergius saluted. "Yes, sir."

He collected a surveyor and two troops of cavalry.

"That way," Sergius ordered, indicating a trackway that commenced at the beachfront and penetrated the forest.

Shields and weapons ready, the horses clattered down the path.

Here and there a body lay sprawled on the ground—a warrior or Druid who had escaped the battle only to collapse and die of wounds.

He thought he saw movement from one body, a young woman whose face reminded him all too clearly of Ailidh, but when he leaned from his saddle to look closer, he saw she was dead, her eyes fixed and staring. What he had taken for movement proved only a trick of light and shadow.

"Over here, sir," a cavalryman called.

Sergius caught the tension in his voice. The man had halted a few feet away. Sergius joined him.

"In the trees, sir." The man pointed into an oak grove.

As Sergius's eyes adjusted to the gloom in the grove, other eyes stared back at him. He dismounted and walked closer, alert for danger.

A row of severed heads.

They were heads of young men for the most part, although one was a woman's. All had short hair and straight noses.

Romans.

Legionaries and couriers probably, lured from their forts or captured when alone and unawares.

Brought to Mona to die.

He gazed at the open eyes of one man, about his age. But for Ailidh, it could have been his severed head decorating the shrine. Had Lovernios been among the crowd massacred on the shore? Somehow, he didn't know why, he doubted it.

"They sacrificed their prisoners." Sergius told as he returned to the waiting troop. "There's nothing we can do now. We can return and give them decent burial later. Let's find a campsite."

The trackway seemed to lead nowhere, meandering through the forest, and then through patches of marsh. But at last Sergius found what he was looking for: a level area beside a small stream, where the ground was raised and dry.

He left the surveyor and one troop of cavalry, while he took the rest back with him to report to Suetonius.

By the time he returned to the shore, order had been restored. The boats lay in neat lines on the beach, with a small camp nearby to house the men assigned to guard them.

"I discovered a suitable location, sir," he proposed, "about four miles inland." He described the site.

"Good." Suetonius called for the chief centurion. "Prepare the legions to march."

"I saw no hostiles," Sergius continued. "But they have executed prisoners."

The commander's brows pulled together. He nodded. "Burial details will be assigned."

"What about the Druidae dead?" Sergius asked. "Should they be removed?"

Suetonius made a chopping motion with his hand. "Let them rot."

"Excuse me, sir." A courier stepped into the command tent the following morning.

The legions had reached the campsite and erected a marching camp the previous night without incident. Tired legionaries had slept well.

Sergius hadn't.

"What is it?" Suetonius halted the morning staff meeting. Sergius swung around to view the courier.

"A message from Legate Cerialis, sir." The courier held out a writing tablet. "It's marked urgent."

Suetonius took the tablet and flipped it open. Sergius noticed the tensing of the commander's face.

"You may leave," Suetonius dismissed. The courier saluted and departed.

Suetonius's gaze flickered over the assembled officers. He handed the tablet to Sergius. "Read this out loud."

Sergius cleared his throat. The tablet had been written in haste. Sloppy strokes cut through the wax surface.

"From Q. Petilius Cerialis, legate, Legio IX *Hispana*, to G. Suetonius Paulinus, governor. Greetings. Word has reached me of insurrection among the Iceni, apparently in response to Procurator Catus's measures in reducing their territory to provincial status. Several small forts and signal stations have been attacked and overrun. While I don't believe that the rebellion is serious or presents more than a minor inconvenience, I have received garbled reports that the Iceni threaten Camulodunum. The city cannot be in any real danger, but prudence compels me to march with half of the *Hispana* to subdue the rebellious elements. I trust that this action meets with your approval. I will notify you directly when the action is completed successfully."

Sergius closed the tablet and laid it on the table.

"Reactions?" Suetonius said.

Marcianus spread his hands. "Iceni dissatisfaction is nothing new, but I'm surprised that it's broken into the open."

"Unless the procurator did something to offend them," Sergius said, then wished he hadn't spoken. All he needed was to reopen another incident for the governor to hold against him.

To his relief, Suetonius merely posed, "Possible."

"I don't see that there's a problem," *Augusta's* Crispus offered. "Cerialis is impetuous, but he knows his job. The Iceni can't stand up to the *Hispana*."

"It may not even be true," Agricola suggested. "Rumors of rebellion could be a ruse to draw us from Mona."

"Too late, then," Titus added.

Valeria's Falco pronounced, "I don't think we need intervene. It's more important that Mona be reduced."

"Precisely," Suetonius agreed. "Eliminating the Druidae is only half of our task. Somewhere on the island are the granaries and storehouses of the Ordovici and Deceangli. I want them found and destroyed."

"The men are unhappy over the lack of plunder," Marcianus noted.

Several officers nodded. Very little of value had been found on the Druidae, Sergius knew, and only a few baubles on the warriors. The legionaries had expected much more.

"Does an army function only on hope of plunder?" Suetonius grumbled.

"No, but it helps," Marcianus said.

Suetonius continued as if he hadn't heard. "I want every grove, everything that looks remotely like a shrine cut down, demolished. Every person—Druid, warrior, farmer; man, woman, child—killed. Mona will be a haven for the rebellious no more."

Sergius cleared his throat. "But sir—"

"Do you object, Tribune?"

"It's an extreme measure, sir—"

Suetonius glared. "The only people on this island are enemies of Rome, Tribune. Is that clear?"

Sergius gulped and nodded.

Suetonius returned his attention to Marcianus, Falco, and Crispus.

"The troops may encounter pockets of resistance, so no units smaller than cohorts are to advance without my express permission. Sweep the island. Tell the men they may keep whatever plunder they find in this accursed place."

His lips thinned. "I can't promise them reward, but they're at liberty to look. Somewhere on Mona the Druidae keep their gold."

Suetonius scanned the officers. "Sack this island."

Day after day cohorts ranged afield. Using the camp as their base, legionaries tramped the length and breadth of Mona, from the fertile hills and plains of the center and east, to the forbidding, rugged west and south, where the sea splintered against the rocky coast.

Oak groves toppled. Giant trees centuries old crashed to the ground in a welter of broken branches and splinters.

Wooden idols were flung into piles and burned, stone ones smashed beyond recognition.

The granaries, likewise, flamed to ashes after the army had removed what it needed. The grain supplies of the Ordovices and Deceangli vanished in great clouds of smoke. During the coming winter, the tribesmen would have to struggle to survive, without recourse to the bounty of past seasons.

Scattered warriors and Druidae perished beneath Roman swords. The legionaries razed entire villages and massacred every inhabitant.

Titus seemed to revel in the carnage. Justus's enthusiasm, however, appeared to wane. Sergius sensed in the young tribune the same reaction that he himself had had to slaughter.

"Do you know what we discovered today?" Agricola asked Sergius once when he'd returned from a foray.

"What's that?"

"Altars with victims still on them. They'd been cut open, and their entrails ripped out. Blood everywhere."

"Human?"

Agricola nodded.

"That's inhuman!"

"Maybe they tell a greater augury," Agricola proposed.

Burial details collected the remains of Roman victims and gave them appropriate funeral rites. But the vaunted riches of the Druidae remained elusive.

"The gold could be anywhere," Titus complained. "Hidden in caves. Buried underground. Thrown in a lake. Perhaps there's a village we've not discovered."

"They can't keep it hidden forever," Agricola replied. "We'll find it."

Day after day the pacification of Mona continued.

Sergius sat in his tent writing, several days later, when a clatter of horses indicated the arrival of a troop of cavalry. Cara barked and nosed at the flap. Sergius didn't stop writing; cavalry coming and going formed a normal part of military operations.

Quintus, standing at the opening of the tent informed, "It's a messenger, sir. Been in action by the look of him."

Sergius grunted a reply.

"He's a tribune," Quintus said: "your friend."

"Veturius?"

"I believe so, sir."

Sergius jumped to his feet, hurried to the opening, and pushed past his beneficiarius.

The troop of cavalry halted, their horses lathered and panting. Their leader dismounted, his movements slow and painful. His cloak and armor bore the stains of a hard journey. A dirty, blood-stained bandage dangled from his left arm. He removed his helmet to show an unshaven and unwashed face.

"Gaius!" Sergius called. He dashed outside.

Veturius tried to smile, but his lips merely twisted. "Might have known you'd be looking fine."

"What happened to you? What brings you here?"

"Help me to Suetonius," Veturius requested.

Sergius extended his arm. Veturius leaned on it. He walked with a limp.

"What happened?" Sergius repeated.

"The Iceni are in revolt," Veturius replied.

"We had a message from Cerialis informing us of unrest. We didn't know whether to believe it."

"Revolt," Veturius repeated. "Queen Boudicca has rallied the Iceni, the Trinovantes, and every other disaffected Briton in the area."

Sergius whistled. "How'd you get hurt?"

"We marched to intercept them." Veturius paused outside the praetorium. For a moment his eyes became cloudy and unfocused.

"What happened?"

Veturius's voice was hoarse. "They cut us to pieces."

TWENTY

Sergius paced back and forth outside the praetorium while Veturius made his report to Suetonius. A crowd of excited and curious legionaries gathered around the cavalrymen. When the numbers swelled, centurions and their optios dispersed the onlookers. After a while, Agricola and Titus jogged across the parade ground, both looking worried and anxious.

"Any news?" Agricola panted.

Sergius hooked his thumbs in his belt and jerked his head in the direction of the praetorium. "Veturius is still in there."

"Is it true?" Titus demanded. "Was the *Hispana* destroyed?"

"Veturius told me that they lost a battle," Sergius said. "That was all."

"Bad enough in itself," Agricola remarked, staring at the praetorium as if willing the flap to open.

"How could we lose a battle to the Britons?" Titus frowned. "Cerialis must be an idiot."

"Before we judge, let's hear what Veturius has to say," Sergius replied.

"My father Vespasian would have made short work of any Britons that opposed him," bragged Titus. "He never lost a battle."

"So you've told us," Sergius commented dryly. "Many times."

"Here he comes!" Agricola exclaimed.

Sergius spun to face the praetorium.

Veturius emerged from the tent. He halted, and cast bleary eyes over the three tribunes.

"I'd hoped there'd be beautiful women waiting for me. But what do I find? Three of the ugliest and hairiest harpies this side of the Rhine—"

"No jokes," Titus interrupted. "Tell us what happened."

"I need a drink."

Sergius gripped Veturius's unbandaged arm. "Come. My tent. You can sit down, drink, and tell us all about it."

Veturius nodded.

Sergius steered him away from the praetorium and the remaining onlookers, who cast envious glances their way. At his tent, he called for Quintus. "Drinks for all. Send for the medicus to come and examine Tribune Veturius's wounds and have someone prepare him a meal. Then have a man erect a spare tent for him. Put it next to this one."

"Yes, sir," the beneficiarius replied.

Veturius shook his head. "I'm only scratched."

"The medicus will decide that," Sergius assured.

Veturius scowled. "You're very bossy."

Sergius winked at Agricola. "You're with the *Gemina* now, Gaius. I'll give the orders."

The tribunes clustered on benches. Sergius left the tent flap open and lit a lamp to augment the daylight.

A legionary on camp duty arrived with a flagon of wine and cups.

Titus took them and poured.

Veturius drank eagerly.

"Now . . . ," Titus prompted.

"All right," Veturius began, taking a final swallow. "I don't know how much you've heard while campaigning, or whether Suetonius has kept you informed on the political situation . . ."

"We know Prasutagus died, and Boudicca assumed leadership of the Iceni," Sergius filled him in.

"Is that customary?" Agricola interrupted.

Veturius shrugged. "Who can tell with the Britons? I don't know how they change rulers. But whether she should have or not, she did. Needless to say, when the emperor decided he'd had enough of the Iceni being a client kingdom and refused to recognize Boudicca—or any Iceni as Prasutagus's heir—the Iceni didn't like it."

Sergius clarified, "They resisted being reduced to provincial status?"

Veturius ran a hand over his forehead. "Decianus Catus is a fool! I hope he burns."

"What did he do?" Titus asked.

"He ransacked Venta Icenorum, dispossessed the Iceni nobles of their lands, and appropriated Prasutagus's household goods."

Sergius whistled. "Just like that?"

Veturius gave a gloomy nod. "His men took whatever they could lay their hands on. Stripped the place. But as if that wasn't enough to anger the Iceni, Catus had Boudicca flogged when she protested."

"Flogged?" Agricola gasped.

"Treated queen and nobles as if they were slaves," Veturius said.

"Which they are," Titus said. "Sounds just to me."

"Try telling them that," Veturius snapped. He gulped more wine and glanced at Sergius. "And then, to top it, he pleasured himself with Boudicca's daughters. When he'd finished with them, he let his troops have them."

Sergius slapped his thigh. "The man's an animal."

"How do you know this?" Titus asked Veturius.

"One of Catus's men, an optio, told me. He disapproved of the actions and protested to Catus, who threatened to flog and discharge him. Since the optio couldn't complain directly to Suetonius, he used a pretext to come to our fort and reported to Cerialis."

"Cerialis intervened?" Titus guessed.

"No. He said he couldn't interfere directly without the governor's approval. He didn't want to get in over his head."

"Good way to lose it," Agricola said.

Veturius continued, "But he sent an emissary to Boudicca, asking for confirmation of the soldier's story."

"And?" Sergius asked.

"The emissary never returned." Veturius puffed out his cheeks. "Have any of you seen Boudicca?"

The three tribunes shook their heads.

"I met her briefly before Prasutagus died, when Cerialis had me make a courtesy call through Iceni territory to Venta Icenorum. She's not a woman to be trifled with. How an old man like Prasutagus ever tamed her is beyond me."

"I thought you liked anything female," Sergius ribbed.

"I may be lovesick, but I'm not suicidal," Veturius replied. "Boudicca's more than I could ever handle." He sketched in the air with his hands. "She's tall, with tawny hair to her hips, a voice like an old crow, and eyes that could light a fire on a rainy day. I was glad to be away from there!"

"Worse than Claudia?"

"Claudia's a rabbit compared to Boudicca." Veturius paused as a legionary entered bearing a plate of food.

He set it on the bench next to Veturius. "Will there be anything else, sir?"

"No. That's all for now."

The soldier departed.

Veturius drew breath. "Then we lost contact with several signal stations, and patrols sent to investigate never returned. By now, Cerialis was thoroughly alarmed. The next thing we knew, Boudicca had rallied the Iceni and the Trinovantes and had attacked and destroyed two forts."

The tent flap parted wider. Quintus appeared in the opening. "The medicus is here, sir."

"Send him in," Sergius beckoned.

The medicus saluted Veturius as he entered. "May I address your wounds, sir?"

"Go ahead. It's not as if I have a choice."

Veturius winced as the medicus unwound the bandage from his upper arm. "Careful! There's still flesh under there."

The medicus laid the dirty strip of cloth aside and cleaned the laceration with astringent. "Deep. A sling-stone wound."

Veturius's eyes watered. "The medicus at our fort used a weapons forceps to get it out."

"He did well. You're lucky the bone wasn't shattered."

Veturius shuddered. "No drilling into my bones, thank you."

"It will heal, in time." The medicus applied salve and rebandaged the arm. "You should rest it."

"There wasn't time before," Veturius replied.

"You're lucky it didn't hit an artery, either," Sergius expressed.

The medicus queried, "Any other injuries?"

"My hip. But it's only bruised." Veturius pulled a face. "I fell off my horse when the stone took me."

"Allow me?" the medicus asked.

Veturius clambered to his feet and lifted his kilt. The medicus palpated the purple area on Veturius's hip and upper thigh.

"As you say, sir, bruised."

"I've been walking on it."

The medicus said, "I'll check your arm again in the morning."

Veturius resumed his seat. "Thank you."

When the medicus had departed, Sergius prompted, "What happened next?"

"We made a reconnaissance in force. Boudicca left no survivors at the forts. She burned and plundered every settlement and way station she passed. That was when Cerialis decided he had to nip the insurrection in the bud."

"His letter made it sound as if the problem wasn't serious," Agricola investigated.

"We didn't think it was," Veturius replied. He flexed his arm against the tight bandage. "Boudicca and a few warriors. Corner them and that would be the end of them."

Agricola asked, "Where was Catus during all this?"

Veturius picked up his plate, but after a couple of bites, he set it down again. "Back in Londinium counting his gold, I expect. He certainly didn't wait around to see the results of his actions."

"Coward!" Titus spat.

"We heard rumors that Boudicca was advancing on Camulodunum, so Cerialis gathered the troops we had on hand—five cohorts and a cavalry wing—and tried to intercept her." He looked down. "We were too late."

Sergius's heart thudded. He leaned forward in fearful fascination.

Veturius said, "A merchant who escaped the city—Jupiter knows how—met us on the way. He told us what had occurred. The town knew the Iceni were coming—a hundred and twenty thousand of them!"

"No!" Agricola exclaimed. "There can't be that many Iceni!"

Veturius shrugged. "That was his estimate." His voice took on a distant tone. "The merchant said weird things happened. The river estuary grew red with blood; people saw houses underwater in the river; groans and cries came from the theater and foreign laughter from the senate house when no one was there; the statue of Victory fell flat on its face as if running away."

Sergius didn't dare to speak. Agricola had paled. Even Titus seemed awed.

"The town officers appealed to Catus for help. He sent them a couple of centuries, poorly armed at that. They arrived at Camulodunum just in time to be slaughtered." Veturius spread his hands. "You know what Camulodunum is like. No ditch. No rampart. And the fools didn't think to build any. They didn't even evacuate the elderly and the women."

"Everyone stayed?" Sergius breathed.

"Like sheep waiting to be slaughtered. Can you imagine, being surrounded by that many barbarians?" Veturius paused. "The colonia's veterans must have fought, because it took the Iceni two days to break in. But they did. They burned everything. The survivors of the garrison barricaded themselves in the temple."

He gave a short, harsh laugh. "But the Divine Claudius couldn't save them. The Iceni fired the temple, too. Those who weren't burned to death were butchered as they ran."

Veturius appeared to force the words out. "The Iceni killed everyone, Romans and Britons alike. They cut their throats, crucified them, and burned the rest."

Sergius could hardly breathe. In a strangled voice, he asked, "Ailidh?"

Veturius turned hollow eyes toward him. "I don't know, Marcus. I'm sorry."

"They killed their own people?" Agricola's eyebrows raised.

"Everyone in the town," Veturius answered. "Everyone they thought was friendly to Romans."

"Your friend lived outside the city, didn't she?" Agricola asked Sergius. "Maybe she's all right."

"Fifteen thousand people they slaughtered," Veturius continued. "When he reached us, the merchant was barely coherent. We thought he was raving. But then other reports reached us: a soldier who escaped from a signal tower because he was digging latrines away from the camp when the Iceni attacked and a courier who hid in treetops by day and crawled at night.

"So we marched south as quickly as we could, toward Caesaromagus, hoping to intercept Boudicca before she turned her sights elsewhere. But somehow . . . she knew we were coming."

He paused to moisten his mouth with wine.

"We were in a valley, marching fast, when suddenly the hills were covered with Iceni, like flies on a corpse. Everywhere we looked, there were Iceni. The ground was black with them. They had us surrounded.

"'Mars help us,' Cerialis said. Only then did we understand the scope of the rebellion. We had a moment to realize our predicament, and then they were on us, howling and screaming."

"Why didn't you take the entire legion?" Titus asked.

"It wouldn't have helped." Veturius shrugged. "Cerialis said speed was vital. He wanted to crush the rebellion before it spread. And we didn't know how many followers Boudicca had. We thought the merchant exaggerated."

"You seemed ready to believe him in other respects," Agricola challenged.

"It wasn't my decision," Veturius retorted with a flash of spirit.

"No. Sorry."

Veturius's eyes took on a faraway look. "We fought. We gave good account of ourselves and cut down thousands of them. But there were too many. We couldn't kill them fast enough. At length, they overwhelmed us.

"I took this stone at some point. I don't remember. Cerialis fought until hope had gone. Then he rallied the remaining cavalry. I found a riderless horse and took it. Somehow we hacked our way through the Iceni and ran for it.

"They pursued us all the way to the fortress before giving up. After we'd got our breath back, we knew we had to get word to Suetonius. I offered to take a few volunteers and attempt to break through the Iceni encirclement."

He broke off. Silence reigned in the tent. Then Titus asked, "How many did we lose?"

"Two thousand legionaries," Veturius replied. "Three or four hundred cavalry. Cerialis and I were the only officers to escape. I saw two other tribunes die." He buried his face in his hands. "They butchered us as if we were animals in the circus."

Far to the south, Poenius Postumus, camp prefect of Legio II *Augusta*, reclined in his quarters in the legionary fortress in Isca and listened to the rain beat down on the timber roof.

It had rained solidly for a week. One day the rain would subside to a drizzle from low-hanging clouds, giving tantalizing hints that the clouds had finally decided to blow over; the next, it sheeted down with renewed vigor, solid walls of water driven by gale-force winds that confined the troops to quarters. Only those assigned to guard duty, or to punishment duties outside, endured the downpour, standing damp and chilled in ankle-deep puddles or slogging through the rivers of mud that comprised the fortress's streets.

Poenius rubbed a knee that ached in the damp and cursed the middle age that afflicted him with such ills.

Besides the obvious benefit of encouraging spring growth, the rain served only one other useful purpose—it kept the perpetually warlike Dumnonii confined to their hovels.

Poenius sighed. Seventeen years earlier, under the legion's greatest commander, the redoubtable Vespasian, *Augusta* had pressed forward during the conquest, defeating the Belgae and the Durotriges.

Bluff, jowly, good-natured Vespasian, always ready to crack a dirty joke!

Forward parties of auxiliaries brought back prisoners and intelligence about the hill forts that frowned dark and menacing on the skyline. Some days there'd be skirmishes with the enemy, other days unimpeded marches, with only the threat of ambush to keep the men alert.

One hill fort after another crumbled to the legion. Advancing under shields, in testudo formation, legionaries stormed the bastions.

Poenius closed his eyes to remember. Back then, seventeen years ago, he'd been a centurion newly promoted, eager to prove himself and show himself worthy of his rank.

The great fort of Mai-dun proved the hardest. One-hundred-foot-high ramparts enclosed an area two-thirds of a mile long and a third wide. Quadruple walls towered on a hill above cornfields. Thousands of Briton spearmen and slingers lined the ramparts—women as well as men, ready to send deadly sleets of projectiles upon the legionaries.

Vespasian decided to attack the weaker eastern entrance, not the maze of passages that guarded the west. He positioned the artillery facing the long, curving ramparts that surmounted the hill as if they'd grown there.

Spring-loaded ballistae raked the ramparts with iron bolts, carved gaping holes in the Britons' ranks, and swept the defenders from their positions.

Under their interlocked shields, the legionaries cut their way from ditch to ditch, rampart to rampart. Stones, rocks, and missiles thundered off the shields as hailstones. Scores of legionaries fell to the

Briton barrage. But the Britons who fought from a distance fell to the pilum; those that closed with the legion, to the gladius.

Poenius exhaled.

It had been a bitter battle.

When the soldiers reached the innermost rampart, they fired the circular huts they found there. As smoke billowed into the air, they stormed the heavy wooden gates set in stone walls.

At the head of his century, Poenius had been among the first to enter.

As the gates fell, a horde of Britons flung themselves against the legionaries who poured through the opening: men, women, even children—screaming, shouting, and slashing with swords, daggers, and farm implements.

Angered by the deaths of their comrades, the legionaries fought back without compunction. His men did as they willed, passed beyond his control; Poenius could only join them in their wrath.

The bodies mounted as the Romans slew and slew. Arms grew heavy, and swords slick with blood. Britons felled by ballista-bolts lay where they had crumpled from the ramparts.

And still the Britons fought.

Poenius could still see a young boy, ten or eleven, wild-eyed and haired, standing beside his mother, wielding a sword claimed from a dead warrior.

They both fell where they stood.

Finally Vespasian, struggling to make his voice heard, halted the slaughter.

"Are we animals," he cried, "that we should kill women and children and old men? The victory is ours! Put up your swords. Cease, I say! Cease!"

And finally, the troops heeded.

The remnants of the Britons were herded together and watched as the victors leveled Mai-dun's defenses. Vespasian himself punished the legionaries who had killed thoughtlessly.

Then the Britons were left to bury their dead, and the legion pushed southwest.

Thirty battles Vespasian won. Twenty forts he subdued.

It took four long, hard years, but the tribes were beaten into submission.

And he, Poenius, an undistinguished son of Rome, won his honors. Those were the days!

Now, under the command of the competent but uninspiring Porcius Crispus, Legio II *Augusta* sat in its fortress at Isca, facing the defeated but unconquered Dumnonii on one side and the restless and unpredictable Durotriges on the other.

With Crispus and the senior tribune, Julius Agricola, joining Suetonius for the assault on Mona, Poenius, as third in line, assumed command.

Command of a legion! But a stationary legion and him grown old in service.

Poenius sighed again.

He rubbed his knee. In one of those battles, he could no longer recall which, a slingshot stone had shattered his kneecap. The skin had healed, the bone mended, but the knee had never been the same.

What was?

Ah, well. He could dream.

Outside, the rain beat down on the timber roof.

In Londinium, Decianus Catus drummed his fingers on the edge of his chair. He crossed his legs and uncrossed them again.

"Idiots!" he snarled. "I send them reinforcements, and still they allow the savages to defeat them."

"Two hundred lightly armed men weren't exactly a guarantee of success," Fuscus understated.

Catus sprang to his feet, startling Juba, who staggered on his bandaged foot. "What of the *Hispana*?"

"No word from Cerialis," Fuscus reported. "We've lost contact with the north."

Catus swore. "Another army incompetent! And as for the pighead of a governor, he should have known the Iceni were threatening revolt. Doesn't the army have an intelligence service?"

"Wh-what are you going to do?" Juba warbled.

"Do? Not sit here in Londinium and wait for them, that's for sure." Catus jerked a finger toward the door. "Gods know I lost enough in

Camulodunum. Fuscus, commandeer every cart and animal team you can lay your hands on. I want everything of value loaded and transported to the docks. Get me a ship—I don't care what you have to promise the captain, but I want a ship for Gaul."

"Sir." Fuscus turned.

"And Fuscus, don't let word get out of the reason for our rapid departure. If anyone asks, tell them I've been recalled."

The centurion nodded and left.

Catus glared at Juba. "What are you still doing here?"

"What about the tabularium, sir?" Juba asked.

Catus paused. The moneys in the financial headquarters belonged to Rome—to the emperor. If the moneys were lost, Nero's displeasure didn't bear thinking about.

He decided, "Get the financial records and treasury ready to go. Put them on a separate ship."

Juba pointed, "My gout—I don't know if I can face a sea voyage."

"Then stay here and let Boudicca tend to your carcass!"

Sergius insisted Veturius finish his meal, then made his friend lie down and rest in his newly erected tent. But instead of returning to his own tent, he paced the perimeter of the camp, listening to the sounds of the day.

The Iceni in rebellion? Thousands dead, Camulodunum burned to the ground, and half the *Hispana* annihilated.

And Ailidh? What of her?

Was she safe, or had she been swept up in the maelstrom of fury that had engulfed the eastern part of the province?

Cara joined him, brushing against his legs as he walked. He ruffled the big dog's ears.

"How is she, Cara? I pray to God she's safe."

He wished he could leap on his horse and dash across the country. But that was impossible. Hundreds of miles, much of it now hostile, separated him from Ailidh. Even if he reached Camulodunum safely, he'd be cut down by the first group of rampaging Britons that spotted him.

And then an idea caused a flicker of hope. Hadn't Ailidh said that she and Egomas would be in Londinium come spring? And Paullus, wasn't he still in Londinium?

"Please, God, let her be in Londinium," he prayed.

He passed by the praetorium, where lamps glowed through the heavy leather. He heard the sound of muffled voices. Suetonius and the legates had remained inside since Veturius had arrived.

Sergius wondered what Suetonius was thinking. He couldn't allow the rebellion to continue. If left unchecked, Boudicca threatened to reduce the entire province to ash.

But how could the Romans bring the Iceni to bay?

He turned away and resumed his aimless wandering. Let Suetonius worry about the rebellion.

He gripped the leather pouch with Ailidh's last letter. A legionary who passed by stared at him; Sergius didn't care whether the man noticed the tears in his eyes.

"We said the Romans couldn't fight," Weylyn swaggered. He not only wore his own longsword and torque but carried a Roman gladius and a cloak wrenched from a dead legionary. "Not even Caratacus won such a battle."

"We caught them unawares," Boudicca cautioned. Weylyn and Bairrfhionn, her most trusted advisors since the death of Airell, accompanied her through the ruins of Caesaromagus. "We lost many good warriors."

"They died with honor," Weylyn replied, his youthful face still flushed from the exhilaration of battle. "And we have many more."

Boudicca nodded. The number of warriors who had rallied around her had astounded her. Perhaps it shouldn't have. She knew the depths of resentment under which the people labored. And Lovernios had done his work well. She stepped over a body, so disfigured by wounds that she couldn't tell its sex.

Following the destruction of the Roman relief force, Canonium and Caesaromagus had fallen without a fight. Unlike Camulodunum, whose spirited resistance Weylyn seemed to have overlooked. Boudicca could still see the gouts of smoke rising into the air from the flaming Temple of Claudius, hear the screams of the dying, and see the Iceni and the Trinovantes exact revenge.

Her heart burned within her to see the recompense extracted from the Romans. She made no attempt to restrain her warriors. Let them do to the Romans what they willed.

But yet . . .

Aife and Cinnia still didn't speak. The girls seemed lost in their own world, withdrawn from those around. Boudicca ached whenever she saw them. She held them to her, brushed their hair, told them in every way she could that she loved them.

How she wished that Prasutagus was with her.

Did the creature Catus have children? If so . . .

She realized Bairrfhionn was talking. "What next?" he asked.

"Londinium."

"And then?"

Boudicca pondered. Two ways lay open from Londinium. Northwest lay Verulamium and the larger force of Roman legions engaged in their conquest. To the east lay Rutupiae, their major supply base. Destroy Rutupiae, and the legions would be crippled.

But what happened would depend on how well she could sway the warriors to her will.

"Londinium first," she urged.

She stooped and picked up a child's toy from the debris that littered the ground. Soon, Catus—all Romans—would be in her hands like this toy. She closed her fist and crushed it.

TWENTY-ONE

Suetonius Paulinus announced his decision to the senior officers the following morning in the praetorium.

Sergius stood beside Veturius, who appeared marginally less haggard after a bath, a meal, and a night's sleep. He'd scraped the stubble from his cheeks and combed his hair. Some color had returned to his complexion. His wound, for all its anger, hadn't caused excessive blood loss. The medicus had applied a fresh bandage—and, by the odor, a foul-smelling ointment. As for bruises, a man didn't die from those.

Sergius himself had slept little. Worry for Ailidh had consumed most of the nighttime hours, and his nerves trembled on edge.

He was surprised to note that dark circles ringed Suetonius's eyes. The governor had never struck him as a man who lost sleep for any reason. But despite what must have been a long night of contemplation, Suetonius moved briskly, and he spoke in his usual decisive manner.

"The problems, as I see them, are two," Suetonius said, leaning with his hands on a table draped with a map of the province. "First, our armies and Boudicca's are on opposite sides of the Britannia. Second, our knowledge of the Britons' forces and disposition is secondhand. Both factors can, and must, be remedied."

"And soon," Marcianus interjected.

Suetonius continued, "Boudicca's actions indicate more than simple displeasure over taxation. Whatever Catus did is done. Based on what we've heard, the Britons won't stop with razing Camulodunum. They won't stop with Londinium. They won't stop until they've rid Britannia of Roman presence."

"Or until we stop them," Titus said.

"*If* we can stop them," Veturius stressed. "There are hundreds of thousands of them—"

"Enough!" Suetonius slapped the table. A flush of anger darkened his cheeks and contrasted with his gray hair. "I won't hear of failure. Life doesn't always hand us easy tasks, but we must make the best of what we're given. It's up to us to stop Boudicca or die trying."

The governor's eyes flashed. To Sergius he seemed every inch the outraged patrician. "We conquered this country before; we can do it again."

"What's your plan, sir?" *Augusta's* Porcius Crispus asked.

Suetonius straightened. "I'm going to take a wing of cavalry and ride for Londinium to assess the situation."

"Risky." Marcianus's fat neck wobbled as he shook his head. "I recommend a move in force."

"Rushing blindly is what brought disaster to Cerialis," Suetonius retorted. "His gallantry outstripped his discretion. We can't afford a repetition."

"What if Londinium has fallen?" *Valeria's* commander Virius Falco—a slight, nervous man—asked. "If our information is outdated—"

"Then we will adjust our tactics accordingly. It's unlikely the Britons will move quickly. They're more interested in pillage than in conducting a logical campaign."

"As I understand their movements," Marcianus countered, rubbing the pink crown of his head, "they—or perhaps I should say, Boudicca—seem to be acting very logically. They eliminated the signal towers and forts and only then turned on Camulodunum. Boudicca anticipated *Hispana's* response and prepared a deadly ambush."

"It won't last," Suetonius assured. "It never does. Recall Caratacus, for example. He succeeded while he stuck to his hit-and-run tactics, but eventually he succumbed to pride and lost a pitched battle." He ran a finger across the crinkled papyrus map. "While I ride for Londinium, Legate Marcianus will march the legions. We need all the troops we can muster."

"But we can't leave the frontier unguarded," Crispus protested. "If we withdraw, other tribes will be tempted to rise. We haven't the manpower to fight on all fronts."

"Agreed. *Hispana* is too badly mauled and is needed to secure the north. We have all the men *Valeria* can spare without being dangerously short. If Glevum is left undefended, the Silures will regard it as weakness. But we can call for reinforcements from *Augusta*." Suetonius turned to Agricola. "See that a dispatch is sent to Isca immediately for *Augusta* to send all available troops. Order them to join with the main force at Letocetum."

"Yes, sir," Agricola said crisply.

"Dispatch messengers to all border forts to send auxiliaries to the same location." Suetonius took a breath. "There's also Queen Cartimandua of the Brigantes to consider."

Falco's breath hissed. "If she allies with Boudicca . . ."

"I think," Suetonius responded slowly, "that she's too suspicious of Boudicca to join her. Two she-cats can never get along. Still, I want a message sent to her."

His eyes roved the assembly and fixed on Sergius. "Lysias, you can attend to that. Tell Cartimandua to keep her sharp little nose to herself. Word it diplomatically—in view of the Brigantes favored status as a client kingdom, and in consideration of past aid received, we request her nonintervention in the current crisis."

"I'll take care of it, sir," Sergius confirmed.

"But leave her in no doubt about our meaning." Suetonius crossed his arms. "That's all." He leaned forward to study the map.

"Sir?" Sergius said as the officers began to disperse.

"Yes?"

"I request permission to accompany you to Londinium, sir."

Suetonius frowned. "This isn't an exercise, Tribune."

"I know that, sir. But you'll need an aide."

"And I, sir," Veturius broke in.

Suetonius's eyebrows rose. "You're in no condition."

"With respect, sir, I am." Veturius's face darkened. "The Britons destroyed my legion. I want another chance at them."

Sergius stared at his friend, mouth agape.

"We're not riding to engage the Iceni," Suetonius reminded, "but to assess the situation."

The sound of a throat being cleared caused the men to look toward the door. Gellius Marcianus had remained behind.

"Yes, Legate?" Suetonius acknowledged.

"While I would have appreciated Tribune Lysias asking my permission first, his suggestion has merit. If anything untoward was to happen to you, it would be valuable to have a man with sound instincts to bring us a reliable report."

"Very well," Suetonius nodded briskly. "We leave within the hour." He turned to Veturius. "I respect your resilience. You may accompany us also. But if your condition worsens, and you can't keep up, then you'll be left at one of the forts. I can't be slowed for any reason."

"Understood, sir," Veturius accepted. "Thank you."

"Be at it then."

The two tribunes followed Marcianus from the praetorium.

"What's with you?" Sergius asked. "Is this the same Veturius who vowed not to shed a drop of his blood?"

"I've already shed it," Veturius replied grimly, touching his bandaged arm. "Now I want the Britons to pay for it."

Agricola hurried over. "What kept you? In trouble again?"

"Not this time," Sergius smirked. "Veturius and I are accompanying the governor to Londinium."

Agricola's eyes widened. "Of all the luck! Why does Fortune smile on you when you don't even believe in her?"

Sergius added, "I have to see if Ailidh is safe."

"Fortune favors you because you're in love," Agricola concluded. "Good luck. Titus won't be happy."

"He should have thought to ask first." Sergius waved a hand, palm out. "But I don't understand why the governor wants to examine the situation in person. We've all seen Londinium; we know what it's like."

"That's his nature." Agricola elucidated. "The desire for accurate knowledge and the urge to see for himself has made him the general he is. Besides, had you forgotten that his family's in Londinium?"

Sergius started. "I had. So that's why—"

"No. The governor won't let personal considerations affect his military judgement. But it will give him extra incentive."

Sergius returned to his quarters with new respect for the governor. He wasn't the only one worried about loved ones.

He called for Quintus and explained the plans. The sudden change caught the beneficiarius by surprise, but Quintus recovered quickly.

"I'll make sure all is taken care of, sir," he guaranteed.

Sergius worked rapidly and was prepared well before the end of an hour. He put the finishing touches on his letter to Cartimandua and sent a courier on his way.

"The rebellion has done one thing," Sergius commented to Quintus. "It's put the routine to one side."

"Some of the men didn't have a long retirement," the aide replied.

It took Sergius a moment to catch Quintus's thought. Some of the legionaries whose twenty-five-year terms had expired had retired to their hometowns—in Gallia, Italia, and Hispana. Others had decided to begin a new life in Britannia, using their pensions to buy homes in the eleven-year-old colonia whose ruins now smoldered in Camulodunum.

"They deserved better," Sergius said.

As soon as he was prepared to leave, with his armor buckled, traveling cloak fastened with the dog's head brooch, his horse waiting, and Cara whining in eagerness, Sergius grabbed a blank papyrus and pen. He wrote:

> Dearest Ailidh,
>
> In a few minutes I ride to Londinium with the governor, to see the havoc Boudicca has wrought. Will I meet you there? Do you still live—or, God forgive me for my doubts—are you in that place he has prepared for us? I wish with all my being that you are yet confined to earth.
>
> Will I survive to reach Londinium, and then endure the battle that must occur? God alone knows. I have entrusted this letter to my beneficiarius, Quintus, in the hope that if I fall, and you still live, you will know that I died with honor and with love for you.
>
> I wish I could deliver these words in person.
> Grace and peace,
> Sergius

He rolled the papyrus, inserted it into a canister, sealed it, and handed it to Quintus.

"If I die, deliver this for me to Ailidh, the daughter of Egomas the dog-seller."

Quintus nodded. "If I can, I will, sir."

Sergius dug in his pouch and extracted a pair of gold coins. "Take these."

Quintus backed away. "That isn't necessary, sir."

Sergius grinned. "A soldier who refuses money? You've served me well, Quintus. Take it."

The beneficiarius's hand closed on the coins. "Thank you, sir. You'll be back from Londinium with a whole skin."

"Really? And how do you know that?"

"You've had auguries, sir. You're lucky."

Sergius clapped him on the shoulder. "See you in Letocetum, then."

Outside, the camp was already in turmoil. The legions scrambled to make a hasty departure. Sergius didn't doubt that Marcianus would have the camp disassembled and the troops on the march well before day's end. For all his seeming slowness, Marcianus could assume instant control of a situation if needed. Sergius plowed through the commotion of yelling centurions and frantically toiling legionaries. He found Veturius waiting on his horse, his wounded arm cradled to his side.

Sergius swung onto his mount. "Are you sure you're up to this?"

Veturius nodded without smiling. "I made the ride here. I can make it back."

The cavalry wing had assembled in the parade ground. There were no pack animals; Suetonius intended the ride to be swift. Each man carried a day's rations and water.

Cavalry prefect Didius Pertinax waved. "Riding with us again?"

"It's a bad habit."

"Glad to have you."

His scarlet cloak arranged in precise folds over his left shoulder, Suetonius cantered up accompanied by six bodyguards.

Pertinax saluted. "We await your command, sir."

Suetonius wheeled his horse to face the via praetoria and the main gate. "We ride."

The wing retraced the trackway to the beach. On Mona's shoreline, mounds of Briton dead moldered. Sergius covered his mouth with his cloak to block the stench of rotting bodies. The horses splashed through the shallows, which helped clear his nose. Once over the strait, the wing picked up the pace and followed the coast until the broad mouth of the river Deva came into view, and then they rode the course of the river itself.

Sergius rode close by Veturius in case his friend needed help. The old, carefree Veturius seemed to have vanished. A grim, unsmiling man who rode in silence replaced him, hard eyes fixed on the path ahead, remaining in his saddle with chill determination. Veturius didn't seem inclined to talk, and Sergius didn't press him.

Cara loped alongside, her rangy legs covering the ground as easily as the horses'.

Despite the danger that lay ahead, Sergius was glad to be free of Mona and its dark groves. He didn't dare ask Suetonius, but what had the legions really accomplished?

Lovernios watched from the hills as the Roman legions crossed the strait in the early afternoon. From a perch on a boulder he muttered curses at the legionaries, the auxiliary cavalry, and most of all at the officers.

When the last animal of the baggage train had disappeared along the coast, he slid from his seat, mounted his horse, and rode to the beach.

He crossed in reverse course where the Romans had, where feet and hooves had torn up the sand, past rows of abandoned boats.

On the far shore he halted and dismounted.

In silence he studied the mounds of decaying bodies, the pitiful, putrefying lumps wrapped in swaths of moldering linen. These had once been people he had known, talked to, laughed and cried with. Even the brisk, sea-salt-laden air failed to remove the reek of death.

His fingernails gouged his palms. Human muscles and sinews had proved impotent against the ruthless cut and thrust of Roman swords.

The Roman invaders had performed their work of destruction with terrifying efficiency—as they did everything to which they set their hands.

Here and there, where decay had not progressed too far, Lovernios recognized a face. One in particular, he knew.

He stooped over the corpse, ignoring the stench that arose. The woman—younger than he, in the blush of youth—had been killed by a javelin-thrust through the body. Her lifeblood stained the front of her robes brown.

He traced the contour of her cheek, his finger a handbreadth above the discolored flesh. Even in death he imagined he could hear her voice.

"Sine," he whispered. "You too. Never more on earth will we hear your voice in song. Sing well for those who now are blessed by your notes."

He straightened, anger a spear of fire in his breast. Had the Romans no respect for any learning other than theirs? What threat did scholars or physicians or bards, like Sine, pose to them?

Sine, who could sing as no one else, who could take a harp or lyre and from it craft such music as could move the gods to joy or tears. Many times in Ériu he'd heard Sine sing the songs of the people. With the firelight shining on her face and hair and white teeth, her throat filled with song, and her long fingers caressing her instrument, he'd imagined himself already in the otherworld.

Now she was there, and this world was the poorer.

He turned away.

No flicker of gold or silver twinkled among the bodies. The Roman murderers had plundered the dead before piling them into heaps as rubbish.

He remounted and rode into the forest, allowing the breeze to dry the tears that coursed down his cheeks.

Everywhere, silence greeted him, as if the birds too had been slain, or refused to sing over the carnage.

Limbless torsos, the trunks of felled oaks, marked the site of a sacred grove. Here too, a few Briton bodies lay unburied. The shrine itself lay in a tangle of upended poles and splintered roof. Charred wooden effigies, severed from their bases, gazed sightlessly from their backs.

Further inland, the wind gusted over ashed villages.

The few people he met walked as if dazed, whether amazed to be alive, horrified at the sights they'd witnessed, or dismayed at the failure of the gods to protect them. They reached out hands to him, but he had nothing—no gift, no word of encouragement—with which to help. A hole had been gouged in his heart, part of his life slashed off. What help could he be to others?

Near dusk he came to Llyn Cerrig Bach, the lake of the little stones. There, standing on the bleak, rocky ground where others had sacrificed before, he removed his torque.

He turned it over in his hands, the gold circle that had belonged to his father Kirwin, and to his father Henbeddestr before him, and to Gwri, and to men of his family for generations. The torque that had been given him when he became ollamh, the highest of his family, the highest a Druí could reach.

He cleared his throat.

"If you listen," he called to the winds, "grant me the lives of my people. Save us from the Roman aggressors. Take this gold as a symbol of my devotion. Grant my request, and I will offer more. I promise you a sacrifice—one to undergo the triple death. This promise that I made in my heart long ago, I make now with my words."

He held the torque high, and with a flick of his wrist sent it spinning over the blue waters.

"Hear me! By the fish in the river, the deer in the forest, the wren in the sky, hear me! By the blue of ocean, yellow of sunshine, red of fire, hear me! By my thought, and by my word, and by my deed, hear me!"

In a golden arc the torque curved above the lake. Then it plunged beneath the surface in a spray of silver droplets.

"Hear me!"

He crossed the ford again at evening.

Why linger on Mona?

He had arrived too late to join his fellow Druid and Druidesses in their futile resistance.

But there was one whose resistance wasn't so futile.

Across the country, Boudicca rose against the Romans.

Heedless of the dark and the uneven ground, Lovernios rode his horse into the night.

Suetonius's party reached Deva by nightfall and stayed the night in the fortress.

The next day, with rested horses, they made good time under clear skies. Following brief halts to rest or exchange horses in the forts at Mediolanum and Pennocrucium, they arrived at Letocetum.

After two days' riding, Veturius's haggard appearance had returned, and fresh blood stained his bandage. But he resisted Sergius's solicitations, simply handing his horse to a groom and staggering off to rest.

"He looks ill," Pertinax commented, as grooms took the lathered horses away to brush, feed, and water them.

"It's only his will keeping him in the saddle," Sergius replied, glancing to see if Suetonius had noticed Veturius's condition. If the commander had, he hadn't spoken of it.

"He's likely to collapse and not get up again."

Sergius followed Veturius's limping progress across the fort. "That's what I'm afraid of."

"Maybe he should remain here."

Sergius shook his head. "I think it would be just as bad. He's determined to revenge himself on the Britons. If he stayed here, it would eat away at him the same."

"It's a shame. Why is he so insistent on coming?"

"He says it's for the honor of his legion."

Pertinax frowned. "He looks to me more like a man who's facing his fears."

Sergius paused. "Perhaps you're right."

Later the senior officers met with the fort prefect during the evening meal.

"We're on constant alert," the prefect said, reclining on his elbow at a low table in his quarters.

"Have you encountered hostiles?" Sergius asked.

"Not directly, no. But I've a barracks full of refugees. Merchants, landowners, local officials—"

"What are you doing with them?" Suetonius interrupted.

"I'm giving sanctuary to those that are citizens, sir. As many of the men as are capable of holding a weapon are receiving basic training."

The prefect spread his hands. "The Britons, the mixed bloods, well, they have to fend for themselves." He shrugged. "I don't have the space for them."

Suetonius said. "I'll need all the troops you can spare."

"Which isn't many, sir. But I'll see that they're prepared to join with the legions." The prefect picked up a hunk of bread. "If the Britons come this way, we can't hold them. But we'll sell ourselves dearly."

"Is it true about Camulodunum?" Pertinax asked.

The prefect nodded glumly. "Wiped off the face of the earth. Hard to believe; I was there only two months ago."

They finished the meal in silence.

Sergius wolfed down the plain fort food. He had to encourage a gray-faced Veturius to eat. "If you're going to make Londinium, you need nourishment," he whispered in his friend's ear.

After Suetonius had finished and departed, Sergius asked the prefect, "Have you heard of Egomas the dog-seller and his daughter Ailidh?"

The prefect furrowed his brow. "I can't say that I have. Unless they're citizens, their names wouldn't likely have come to my attention."

Sergius concealed his disappointment. "How about Paullus of Tarsus, Lucanus, and Aristarchus?"

"Again, no. They aren't here."

"If you do encounter any of them, give them sanctuary, would you?"

"Friends of yours, are they?" The prefect nodded. He made a note of the names. "I'll do what I can. Jupiter knows it's little enough."

The morning brought low clouds and drizzle. Heads bowed, the cavalry pressed onward.

They heard the same story at the forts at Manduessedum and Venonis, and the settlement at Tripontium, now nearly a ghost town. And Sergius received the same reply to his questions.

So far, no signs of revolt had been evident. But as the cavalcade entered the territory of the Catuvellauni, the scene changed. Boudicca's followers either hadn't all remained together in one large mob and fanned out across the countryside, or else disaffected Catuvellauni had seized the opportunity to rise in revolt as well.

They encountered the first wandering refugees, lone individuals and small parties both, trudging along the road. The fortunate pulled small wagons; the less lucky had only the clothes they wore.

Several called out as the cavalry clopped past—one woman held up a baby—but Suetonius refused to stop.

In afternoon, after Tripontium had been left behind, a plume of smoke smudged the sky, and they passed the remains of a Roman-style homestead. Charred timbers smoldered damply in the rain.

Suetonius signaled a halt. He gestured to Sergius. "Take a look."

Sergius dismounted and strode to inspect the ruin. His boots cracked over broken and shattered roofing tiles. Plaster peeled from crumbling walls. At what had been the doorway, he paused and peered inside. A foot protruded from beneath a tumble of beams. He moved to kick away a pile of rags before he realized it was another body, charred beyond recognition.

He turned away from the sickly stench of burned flesh.

The corpse of a middle-aged man lay slumped against the wall of an outbuilding. Sergius tipped back the man's head, then let it fall again. A woman's body lay close by. A red slash on her torso showed where a tribesman, lusts satiated, had finally ended her misery.

Sergius returned to the waiting company. "They're all dead, sir."

Suetonius nodded, as if the words confirmed his suspicions. "Ride on."

As dusk descended on the sodden countryside, the remains of another fire-ravaged villa smoldered near the road.

Again, at a signal from Suetonius, Sergius dismounted to inspect the rubble. He wondered what the commander expected to find. Boudicca's followers seemed to leave only corpses and charred remains in their wake.

He pushed past a tangle of smashed beams. The interior of the house lay open to the air. Furniture had been hacked to splinters, walls smashed, and columns toppled. But where were the bodies?

A shiver crinkled its way along his spine. He gripped the handle of his gladius.

He swung around the remains of a wall and froze.

A woman dangled in the shadows, spectral in the half-gloom.

Sergius recoiled and leaned against the wall.

The woman was dead, mercifully so. She'd been mutilated and impaled.

The room spun. Sergius turned around and vomited. He rested his forehead against burn-marked plaster until his heaving subsided, and a chill sweat mingled with the drizzle on his forehead.

He stumbled away, nearly falling over a male corpse that blocked his way. He didn't dare look to see how the man had been tortured.

"Dead, sir," he muttered to Suetonius. He described the scene.

Suetonius's expression didn't change. "They have a goddess named Andraste to whom such rites are sacred," he said. "Normally they conduct them in sacred groves. Boudicca is her priestess."

As the ride continued, Sergius asked. "Why did you want me to inspect the villas, sir? If you knew what we'd find."

"Because I want you to see the nature of our opponent," Suetonius replied. "I've been campaigning against them for two seasons. This is your first. I want it to be clear in your mind. The Britons are guilty. All of them. There are no innocents."

Suetonius's knuckles were white around his reins. "Boudicca wasn't here to commit these acts personally. Neither did she decide overnight to rebel. The Britons have been plotting their foul deeds, making vows in their sacred groves, and promising their gods the lives of Roman men and women."

He shook a fist in the air. "But it is by their own blood their gods will have their fill. By Mars, I swear it!"

He turned his cold eyes on Sergius. "If you have any sympathy for them, abandon it now."

By nightfall, tired and sodden, the wing reached Lactodurum. Veturius, head lolling, was barely hanging onto his saddle. Sergius helped his friend down and into the way station. When Veturius had changed into dry clothes and collapsed on a mattress, Sergius called for the medicus—surprised and relieved that the tiny station possessed a medical officer.

The man examined Veturius and shook his head. "He's got a fever, and he's near exhaustion. My advice is that he rest for several days."

Veturius shook his head. "I can't rest. I've come too far." He gripped Sergius's hand. "Promise me you won't leave me behind."

"What am I to tell your parents if you die?"

"Promise me!"

Sergius glanced helplessly at the medicus. "I promise."

"Thank you." Veturius relaxed his grip and slumped back.

"Is there anything you can give him?" Sergius asked the medicus.

"I'll mix him something to sleep. But I can't guarantee he'll be ready to ride in the morning."

"That's good enough."

Sergius sought the officers' room. He found the cavalry commander relaxing with his legs stretched out.

"Londinium is still safe as of yesterday," Pertinax told him. "The station prefect told us that Boudicca's forces have been too busy pillaging to make much headway. We're in time."

Sergius breathed a sigh of relief. "Thank God for that."

Verulamium lay only forty miles distant, and Londinium another twenty. If their horses held out, they'd make it on the morrow.

Londinium was safe.

But was Ailidh?

TWENTY-TWO

L ondinium was a city in chaos. Not even the advent of the Furies themselves could have produced a greater tumult than Boudicca's threatened arrival.

To Sergius's eyes, it seemed as if the entire forty thousand inhabitants of Londinium had all taken to the streets at once. Throw in refugees from Caesaromagus and outlying towns and villas, and the scene could hardly have been worse than if barbarian hordes were storming down the Appian Way toward Rome.

Even more disturbing to Sergius than the pandemonium were the gray puffs of smoke that smudged the horizon above the treetops.

Cries of "Make way for the Governor!" went unheeded, and so the cavalry assumed a wedge formation and plowed along the packed streets, crushing aside those who couldn't or wouldn't move apart.

Sergius feared that Cara would be trampled, but the wolfhound was massive enough to force her way through the crowd and agile enough to avoid the horses' hooves.

Suetonius's face set in a grim mask of anger, and Sergius had no doubt why. The population of Londinium milled out of control. Central authority had collapsed.

Suetonius detached a troop of cavalry and Sergius to accompany him. He ordered Pertinax to take the remaining cavalry and Veturius to the fort. Then he said, "To my villa," his voice tight.

Sergius rode alongside the commander through the swarming masses. As best he could tell, the crowds hadn't taken to looting—yet. But eventually someone would break into an unoccupied shop, and then it would spread like wildfire. The inhabitants of Londinium would begin a process of self-destruction that Boudicca's hordes would finish.

The governor's elegant villa stood untouched, a guard at the grounds entrance. Only by a slight relaxation of Suetonius's facial muscles could Sergius detect the governor's relief.

The guard saluted.

"Is all right within?" Suetonius demanded.

"Yes, sir. But your family isn't here, sir."

Suetonius stiffened. "Where are they?"

"At the fort, I believe, sir."

"Very well." The governor beckoned to Sergius. "To the tabularium."

The financial offices, located in the forum, presented a closed front with a pair of guards standing at attention.

"Where's the procurator?" Suetonius inquired.

The senior officer replied, "I don't know, sir. I heard that he was recalled to Rome."

"Who posted you here?"

"Fort Prefect Pollio, sir."

Suetonius glanced at Sergius. "We should have remained with the main body of cavalry, it seems. All the answers are at the fort."

If anything, the crowds seemed denser in the vicinity of the garrison, perhaps hoping for safety in the fort's shadow.

Heavily armed guards patrolled the perimeter and protected the gates. Once inside the fort's timber ramparts, Suetonius dismounted and handed his horse to an attendant. He dismissed the cavalry troop and hurried straight to the prefect's office. Sergius hustled to keep pace.

The prefect, a short, stocky man whose scarred face and lumpy nose bore witness to years of service, sprang to his feet as the two men entered. "Governor! I wasn't expecting—"

Suetonius brushed aside the prefect's attempt at a greeting. "What's going on here? Where's the procurator?"

Prefect Pollio flushed. "Gone, sir."

"Gone? Where?"

"Taken ship to Gaul, I understand, sir, with his staff and his personal guard. Stripped the tabularium to the walls. By the time I found out, it was too late to stop him."

"May Hades swallow him and spit him out!" Suetonius flared. "Catus is supposed to be in charge while I'm on campaign! Who's in command?"

"I am, by default, sir," Pollio said. "But I've too few men to do more than post guards on the more important buildings to discourage looting. The town council is in a panic—more of a hindrance than a help."

Pollio folded his hands. "I had your family brought here. I thought they'd be safer."

Suetonius calmed. "Thank you."

"Do you wish to see them?"

"Later." Suetonius paced around the room. "You said Catus took troops with him?"

"All except the handful under my direct command, sir, and the urban cohort. He sent two centuries to Camulodunum. I expect they're dead."

"How far away are Boudicca's forces?"

"I'd estimate a day, sir. Two at best."

"Where?"

Pollio slid a map onto the table and pointed. "The most reliable reports place her between Caesaromagus and Londinium."

"Has she crossed the river?"

"I've not heard from Vagniacis. Durobrivae reports no sign of unrest. And you came through Verulamium, sir."

"So far, the west country shows scattered incidents but no concerted destruction."

Suetonius pushed the map aside. "There's little time to lose. Assemble the ordo—I'll need to meet with as many members of the town council as are available. Get me exact numbers of the troops in the city. And find me a man who knows the city well. I want to inspect the defenses."

"You'll not find much, sir."

"Do it anyway."

"My optio knows the city as well as anyone, sir. I'll call him."

"Fine." Suetonius turned to Sergius, his eyebrows raised.

"I'll come too, sir, with your permission."

Suetonius headed for the door.

They recovered their horses from the stable and, accompanied by Suetonius's bodyguards and the elderly optio, made the circuit of Londinium. The decision to ride their horses proved wise. It would have been impossible to force their way on foot through the street traffic. Beneath the low hills, the dark waters of the river the Britons called Tamesis flowed as a black snake through the city's belly.

Constant traffic crowded the city's main thoroughfares—refugees arriving, and others fleeing. Boats plied the river. A few put into the quays, but the majority followed the current downstream. With white sails bellied to catch the slightest stray breeze, the ships abandoned the threatened city.

The major concentration of Londinium's buildings stood on the north bank. Only roads and swards kept the forest at bay. Fertile fields bounded the sparsely built-up south bank.

Unlike Camulodunum, Londinium didn't even have the remains of a ditch and rampart, or the Temple of Claudius, as defenses against attack. The only buildings of substance were the garrison, the government offices, the warehouses by the river, and a few villas belonging to more prosperous traders. Otherwise, Londinium was a ramshackle sprawl of half-timbered buildings and sheds.

Suetonius shook his head. "We can't fight here."

"Sir?" Sergius asked.

"Look for yourself." The governor gestured. "There's not a defensible site anywhere. To make a stand here we'd have our backs against the river."

"But the inhabitants—"

"Are part of the problem: forty thousand people who'll hamper troop movements and get in the way. We can't impose order on them and fight a battle as well."

"The garrison—," Sergius began.

Again the governor interrupted. "Too few. The legions won't arrive for another nine or ten days. By the time they get here, Boudicca will have been and gone."

"Can't we delay her?" Sergius asked.

"For what? So that she can slaughter the other legions too? No." The governor wheeled his horse. "Come, let's meet the ordo."

"Where to, sir?"

The council chamber, one of the columned buildings that comprised the forum complex, seethed with the activity of toga-clad men. Gabbled speech echoed off the marble walls. Sergius estimated that most of the ordo's one hundred members were present. Councillors shouted, argued, pushed, and shoved. Rational discussion seemed to have gone by the wayside. Sergius had seen street brawls with more order than the behavior Londinium's councillors showed.

Suetonius's scarlet cloak attracted immediate attention as he entered.

"Governor!" A man in a dirty toga broke away from the gesticulating councillors and scurried across the polished marble floor. Another man followed.

Suetonius muttered to Sergius, "Aemilius Tubero and Curtius Corbulo: the chief executive officers."

Sergius nodded. The chief executive officers administered local justice and presided over the ordo's meetings.

A clutch of other men gathered close. Sergius guessed them to be the remaining senior officials—the aediles, in charge of public works, and the quaestors, responsible for local finance.

"Gods be thanked you're here!" the florid-faced Aemilius huffed. "What do you intend to do, Governor?"

Suetonius's lips tightened. "What does the council think I should do?"

"Why, organize the defense of the city!" Aemilius spluttered.

"What else?" Curtius also voted for the obvious.

Suetonius grimaced. He raised his voice over the babble. "Quiet!"

When the noise subsided, he said, "I have inspected the city and the surroundings. It is my opinion that Londinium cannot be defended."

A moment of dead silence erupted into renewed pandemonium. Sergius pulled some phrases from the tumult.

"You're the governor. Do something!"

"What do you mean, it can't be defended?"

"You son of Hades!"

Suetonius raised his hand for silence. "Boudicca's forces will arrive soon. I don't have the troops to fight her, and Londinium itself is indefensible."

"What do you plan?" Aemilius warbled.

Suetonius answered, "My troops will evacuate the city. I suggest you do likewise."

"That's absurd!" Curtius blurted. "Evacuate the city? Where would we go?"

"Those who can ride may accompany me if they can keep pace with the cavalry. The safest is northwest. I can only guarantee your lives if you move into an area held by the army in strength."

"And what of those who can't ride?" Aemilius protested. "We have women and elderly—"

"South," Suetonius instructed, "to Verica, the kingdom of Cogidubnus."

"The Regnenses?" Curtius spoke the word as a curse.

"Cogidubnus is loyal to Rome. You can shelter in Noviomagus or take ship to Gaul."

Aemilius goggled. "Leave Britannia entirely?" He glanced at his fellow councillors. "Abandon our homes, our shops—"

"Homes and shops are of no use to dead men," Suetonius warned. "But don't take my advice. Stay and seek clemency of Boudicca if you will."

Aemilius paled.

Curtius yelled, "This is outrageous! You're the governor! It's your duty to protect us!"

"No, it's not!" Suetonius shouted back. "Flee and live, or stay and perish. The choice is yours." His scarlet cloak swirled as he strode from the council chamber.

The door slammed shut on a fury of shouts and arguments.

Outside, Sergius asked, "Isn't our duty to the people, sir?"

"No," the governor replied, looking straight ahead. "It's to Rome. We will try to save the province, but to do so means to sacrifice Londinium." His gaze shifted to Sergius. "Pray to whatever god you worship that they heed my advice and flee."

Back at the garrison, Suetonius summoned Prefect Pollio.

"Evacuation of all troops will commence at dawn," he ordered. "Mobilize the troops in Londinium and the surrounding areas."

"The urban cohort?" the prefect asked.

"Yes, the city police as well," Suetonius required. "And I want orders alerting the base at Rutupiae to prepare for action or evacuation."

Sergius asked, "Do you think Boudicca will turn toward Rutupiae, sir?"

"Probably not. Verulamium offers a more tempting target. But it's well to consider all possibilities."

Scribes dashed off copies of Suetonius's proclamation to abandon the city, and messengers posted them on public buildings. Sergius found himself assigned to an office to help coordinate troop movements.

Through the remainder of the day, a steady stream of people presented themselves at the garrison, pleading for help. Elderly, mothers with babies, the pampered wealthy—all received the same answer. The military was unable to assist. Flee while they could.

Toward afternoon, Veturius poked his nose into Sergius's temporary office. "Is the governor serious?" he asked. "We're abandoning Londinium?"

"Very," Sergius confirmed. He shuffled a stack of troop reports.

Veturius sat down. "In that case, you'd better search for Ailidh. I'll finish your work for you."

"But the governor—"

"If you're quick, he'll never know. If he comes asking, I'll tell him you went to round up some wayward member of the urban cohort."

"But it's my responsibility—"

"Look," Veturius rasped, "do you want to find the girl or not?"

Sergius hesitated, then shoved the papers toward Veturius and scrambled to his feet. "Are you up to it?"

Veturius nodded. "I've rested and I don't have anything else to do." He gazed skyward. "Venus, see the sacrifices I make for you?"

"I owe you," Sergius said, clapping Veturius's shoulder.

Veturius winced. "By Hades, you certainly do."

Sergius dashed from the office. The guard at the fort gate looked askance as Sergius exited unaccompanied, but made no verbal protest.

Once outside, Sergius prowled the streets, asking everyone he met if they had seen Egomas or Ailidh. Some people brushed him off, a few cursed, many answered. But the answers were the same.

No.

From the fashionable areas around the forum, he widened his search: through residential districts, increasingly less affluent in character; past factories and workshops; through the warehouse district; until he wandered nameless dirt streets in the city's slums.

And still the answer was no.

If Ailidh and Egomas were in the city, they seemed to have vanished.

He chided himself for abandoning his duties to engage in a futile quest. How could he hope to find one person in a city of forty thousand? Especially a city in upheaval?

Footsore, he returned to the garrison as dusk draped droopy wings over the terrified city and lamps and torches flickered into life.

"Well?" Veturius asked as Sergius entered the room they'd been allotted to share in the crowded garrison.

"No sign of them." Sergius collapsed onto a lectus.

"Maybe they've fled already," Veturius suggested.

"I hope you're right." Sergius's reply came out flat and heavy. But perhaps Veturius was correct. Egomas may have been the first to flee Londinium.

Veturius's fingers dug into his shoulder. "Have faith, Marcus."

Eventually, despite the pressures of work, fatigue claimed him, and Sergius went to bed. But even there the specter of Boudicca haunted him.

He wandered Londinium like a ghost pushing through the packed masses of humanity as if *they* were insubstantial and not he. He searched and searched. Every street, every alley, every dark courtyard and open place.

And then he saw her.

"Ailidh!"

He dashed across the intervening distance toward an auburn-haired woman who moved away from him. He recognized her walk, her build—

"Ailidh!"

She seemed not to hear him.

He ran, as fast as he could, willing his leaden legs into life. But he couldn't catch up. Without seeming to move, she kept a steady distance in front of him. And his cries were swallowed up by the crowd.

She turned a corner and vanished.

He fixed his gaze on the angle of the building, and he forced his way to it.

He rounded the corner.

The square was full of women, all auburn-haired, the same height, wearing the same cloaks.

"Ailidh!"

He grasped the shoulder of the woman nearest him and swung her to face him.

As she turned, her face changed. Her hair became tawny and flowed to her waist. Her eyes became blazing coals that burned into him.

Her harsh voice rasped over him. "I am Boudicca, priestess of Andraste."

He dropped his hand and backed away.

He bumped into another woman.

Her hair hung in tawny strands, and her eyes shone as bright torchlights. She pointed a finger at him. Red blood gleamed on her nails.

"I am Boudicca, priestess of Andraste."

"Ailidh!" he called, to the square full or women. "Where are you?"

And the women swung to face him.

With one voice, they said, "I am Boudicca, priestess of Andraste."

They moved toward him.

He tried to flee, but his feet rooted to the ground.

The tawny-haired women closed on him, chanting, "I am Boudicca, priestess of Andraste!

"Priestess of Andraste!

"Andraste!

"Andraste!

A bloodstained finger touched his cheek—

"Sergius! Wake up."

The priestesses vanished. He stared into Veturius's face, disfigured by the uncertain light of a lamp.

"Gaius!"

"I thought you were having a fit."

"A bad dream."

"Save it for morning, would you? I'm tired." Veturius doused the lamp and reclined on his lectus.

"Sorry."

Sergius dropped his hand to where Cara lay beside him and ruffled her back. He lay awake, staring into the darkness, afraid to close his eyes lest he see tawny-haired women with bloodstained hands. He waited until Veturius's breathing became regular, and finally sleep tugged his eyes closed.

Sergius awoke to shouting, the clatter of metal, and the neighing of horses. He rolled out of bed and struggled into his clothes and armor. Outside the barracks, the garrison roiled with activity. Troops hurried into formation under Prefect Pollio's supervision. The cavalry saddled their horses, and lower ranks readied the baggage train.

To the north, dark masses of cloud glowed with red underbellies. Only the slightest lightening of the eastern sky presaged the coming dawn.

Despite the gloom, Sergius spotted Pertinax. With Cara at his heels, he hurried toward the cavalry prefect.

"Hurry up!" Pertinax shouted at a slow-moving soldier. "Do you think we have all day?"

"What's the excitement?" Sergius asked.

"Hadn't you heard?" Pertinax replied. "Boudicca's forces are approaching the city environs. Suetonius has ordered immediate evacuation."

Sergius started. "So quickly?"

"The rebels must have been making better time than we realized." Pertinax eyed him. "You'd best be making yourself ready."

Sergius nodded. "My horse must be around here somewhere."

"Over there," Pertinax pointed.

Sergius found his horse saddled and ready, with a groom and Veturius in attendance.

"I knew you'd arrive sometime," Veturius said.

"Thanks for waking me."

Veturius shrugged. "I tried. You wouldn't budge. I was going to come and try again."

"How are you?"

"Mending."

Tuba calls sounded across the compound.

"We'd best locate the governor," Veturius advised.

Suetonius and his bodyguard clustered outside the garrison's praetorium. In their midst Suetonius's stately wife sat uncomfortably astride a horse, a heavy cloak covering her stola. Next to her a boy in his early teens grinned at the excitement, and on a third horse a boy and girl under ten gripped each other, their faces pinched and scared.

The governor seemed relaxed until Sergius noticed that the knuckles which gripped his reins were white. His gaze swept over the two tribunes and settled on Pertinax.

"Cavalry is ready, sir," Pertinax said.

"Sound the march," Suetonius ordered. The tubicen blew his instrument.

"Forward."

The gate of the small fort swung open. Preceded by a screen of outriders and surrounded by his bodyguard, Suetonius led the retreat.

Sergius and Veturius wheeled their horses into position behind Suetonius's guard.

The outriders pushed their way through the crowd that surged against the fort's timber walls. Londinium even *smelled* of panic—the city reeked of sweat and unwashed bodies and raw fear.

The horses sensed it. Sergius murmured in his mount's ear to calm the animal as the main body of cavalry and troops followed the leaders into the street.

An elderly man thrust himself close. "Don't leave us! Please!"

Suetonius didn't look in his direction.

A cavalryman pushed the ancient aside.

A woman screamed and cried and held a baby in her arms above her head. She too was shoved out of the way.

Slowly, because of the dense throng, the troop moved away from the city. Others joined the tail of the procession—young men, mostly, who aspired to keep pace with either the cavalry or the infantry. Here and there an older man joined them. And even, Sergius noted, a few women.

Sergius wondered how they thought they'd fare when the cavalry cleared the city and the horses could be given freer rein to move quickly. Could the civilians match the military pace?

The wind blew from the north, carrying with it smoke and the smell of burning. The dawn illuminated dense gray plumes spewing into the air from the forests and fields beyond the Tamesis.

Behind the plumes, Sergius knew, lay ravished homesteads, and the charred and mutilated corpses of their owners.

As they rode, he scanned the faces of the crowd, hoping against hope.

At the western outskirts of the city, Suetonius called a halt. The governor reined his horse next to his wife's.

Sergius was close enough to hear the words.

"The escort will take you south to Noviomagus," Suetonius said. "Take ship to Gaul."

"Come with us," his wife said.

"My duty is here. Would you see me abandon my men and my honor? I would be forced to fall on my sword."

Suetonius reached over to lay a hand on her arm. "Think often of me." He signaled to an officer of the cohors equitate.

"Ride swiftly."

The decurio saluted. "Your family is safe with me, sir."

The cavalrymen formed around the governor's wife and children. They swung away and headed southwest. Not, Sergius noted, toward the town center and the main bridge, but upstream, where they'd cross at a ford and then circle south to pick up the road to Noviomagus.

Suetonius remained still, watching until they disappeared. Then he waved to Pertinax. "Continue."

The cavalry surged into motion.

Cara barked.

"Sergius! Wait."

Sergius had been about to urge his horse on, but Veturius's cry halted him."

"What is it?"

"This man," Veturius indicated one of the refugees, "has seen Ailidh!"

Sergius pivoted. The man gasped for breath, leaning a hand against the flank of Veturius's horse.

"Aristarchus!" Sergius gaped.

The Greek nodded. "I heard . . . the governor was in Londinium. I hoped you might be with him. I tried to catch you, but you'd left the fort."

Sergius glanced at the cavalry wing, moving along the road to the northwest.

"Ailidh. You've seen her?"

"Yes." Aristarchus extended a long finger. "She's still in Londinium!"

Sergius's throat knotted. "Why?"

"Egomas refuses to leave. She stays with him. But if you go to her—"

Sergius wheeled his horse. "Wait here!"

He galloped in pursuit of the main body. He drew alongside Suetonius and matched pace.

"Sir?"

Suetonius swivelled his head. "Yes?"

"Sir!" Sergius blurted. "I request permission to return to the city."

Suetonius stared. After a long moment, he amazed, "Why?"

Sergius gulped. "Because there are those I know—"

"The province could be lost! Londinium must be sacrificed. People will die, yes, but it can't be helped. We must fight Boudicca on our terms, or we face destruction as well. A few lives outweigh many."

Sergius nodded. "I realize that, sir—"

"I need every man, Tribune. I can't spare you to some wild chase."

I love her, Sergius wanted to say, but the words stuck in his throat. He looked down the street which Suetonius's family and their escort had taken. Suetonius, of course, had married a Roman woman. Ailidh was Briton. The governor would never allow him to risk his life to rescue a Briton woman.

"Well?" Suetonius barked.

Sergius found his voice. "I love her."

Suetonius didn't move a muscle.

Sergius continued, "Just five men, sir. We can be in and out before Boudicca's warriors arrive. The risk would be minimal. . . . We'll be quick, I promise."

He broke off, realizing he was babbling.

Suetonius's cold gaze held steady. "What would you do," he said, "if I ordered you to remain in company with us?"

Sergius bit his lip. His thoughts churned, and his gut tightened into a rock-hard knot. Lose Ailidh? To come so far and lose her now?

Each step of the horses' hooves took him farther away.

"I'm waiting," Suetonius said.

Sergius clenched his fists and held back the tears of anger and frustration that threatened to erupt. He looked down, toward the ground, so that the commander wouldn't see his pain.

"I would obey orders, sir," he rasped.

When finally he raised his eyes, Suetonius still hadn't moved. The commander's gaze burned into him.

"Five men," Suetonius relented. "Take no risks. Meet us on the road to Letocetum."

"Y-yes sir!" Sergius gasped.

"I expect you to be there."

"I will, sir."

"Then get moving!" Suetonius barked and moved away.

Sergius gathered his whirling thoughts and galloped toward the waiting Aristarchus. "Decurio!" he shouted to the first troop commander he saw. "Bring four men and follow me!"

Aristarchus and Veturius stood where he had left them.

"Take Cara and join the governor," Sergius told Veturius. To Aristarchus he questioned, "Can you ride?"

The Greek gave a slight nod. "I can stay on."

"Behind me."

Aristarchus climbed up and wrapped his arms around Sergius's waist.

At the head of five cavalrymen, Sergius raced toward Londinium and the flames that licked at the city's borders.

Insanity had seized the remaining inhabitants. Some roamed the streets in confusion, dashing every which way in a frenzy of purposeless activity. Others barricaded themselves in their homes as if wooden bars could keep Boudicca's warriors at bay. Still others fled for the countryside, baskets and bundles of possessions slung over their backs.

The troop's progress slowed to a crawl as the horses and riders strained against a surging tide of humanity. Sergius had never seen such confusion. If yesterday had been bad, today was worse.

Already bodies lay in the streets and doorways.

The weak, or unlucky, had been trampled. The faint of heart succumbed to fear that had precipitated death throes. And probably a few had been killed deliberately.

There would be many more, he knew, before the day ended.

He shouted over his shoulder, "Where is she?"

Aristarchus replied, "Not far from the river: near the warehouses, in the house of a merchant who lives above his stores."

The troop plunged through the city center, skirted the governor's villa with its panoramic view over the Tamesis, and clattered toward the riverfront.

If anything, the confusion in the lower-class areas exceeded that near the forum. The stench of poverty added to the reek of fear.

As they swung around a corner, a knot of youths dashed from a half-timbered building. Flames erupted in their wake. A fire-shrouded figure shrieked in agony before pitching in front of the horses' hooves.

The urge to chase the offenders welled up in him, but Sergius kept his horse headed toward the warehouses. Aristarchus shouted directions to him.

A party of three men reeled across an alley, staggering under the weight of amphorae filled with wine. One loosed his grip, and his amphora fell and shattered. Red wine flowed across the cobbles. The man stopped and screamed at the shattered vessel, as if his profanity would cause it to reassemble itself.

"Almost there," Aristarchus encouraged.

Rows of timber warehouses obstructed sight of the river.

"Left," Aristarchus instructed.

Sergius leaned into the corner and took it at a gallop.

Two-story-framed buildings fronted a narrow street. A clutch of people blocked the alley. The clutch resolved into individuals—Ailidh and Egomas, Lucanus and Paullus.

Sergius reined up and dismounted. "Ailidh!"

She broke from the crowd and ran toward him. "Sergius!"

He caught her up. "I tried to find you. Why are you still here?"

She gave him a hug, then pulled away.

"Because I say so!" Egomas shouted. The dog-seller's face was mottled with anger.

"Are you crazy?" Sergius flared. "Any moment and Boudicca's warriors will be here!"

"So?"

"So you'll be killed."

The dog-seller snorted. "They're my people, Roman. I'm safe enough."

"Not anymore. You're in Londinium, Egomas. That's reason for them to kill you."

"You lie!"

"Listen to me! It will be the same as in Camulodunum. Anyone they find in the city's as good as Roman. As good as dead."

Egomas spat on the ground. "There's no such thing as a Roman who speaks truth."

Sergius gestured to Ailidh. "Tell him."

"I've tried. He won't listen."

Paullus and Lucanus followed the exchange in silence. Sergius turned to the apostle. "Paullus? Are you coming?"

"He is," Lucanus interrupted before the older man could speak.

"My work isn't finished!" Paullus protested.

"Am I surrounded by people who wish to die?" Sergius reached for Ailidh's hand. "There's no time to argue."

Aristarchus slid to the ground. He touched the apostle's shoulder. "We have to leave, Paullus. You won't live through another Lystra. These people won't mistake you for dead."

"Which is better—to live, or die and be with Christus?"

"Live for now," Aristarchus urged. "You can always die later."

Sergius said, "Fine. Egomas?"

"I'm not going anywhere," Egomas reiterated.

"You're a fool, then."

"Better a fool than Roman."

Sergius beckoned the troop commander. "Decurio, mount these men."

The decurio hesitated. "Did the governor authorize us to rescue civilians, sir?"

Lucanus indicated Paullus. "This man is a Roman citizen."

"The responsibility is mine," Sergius persuaded. "Mount them."

The decurio pointed to three of the troopers. "Take them."

The cavalrymen hoisted Aristarchus, Lucanus, and Paullus up behind them.

Sergius tugged Ailidh's hand.

"Let her go!" Egomas roared. He stepped forward. "Girl, I forbid it!"

"Uncle," Ailidh insisted, "come."

"Never!"

"Please."

"Let go of his hand!"

"No." Ailidh stepped with Sergius to his horse and swung lithely up behind him.

"Your last chance, Egomas," Sergius declared. "Come with us."

Somewhere, a woman screamed.

"Sir!" the decurio shouted. "They're here!"

Sergius whirled.

Feet pounded on cobbles as warriors surged into the alley. Swords flashed, screams died in midthroat, and bodies slumped to the stone. The Britons caught sight of the Roman cavalry. With a roar, they sprinted at them.

Sergius glanced over his shoulder. More warriors on foot poured into the alley's other opening.

"We're trapped!" Ailidh cried.

Sergius drew his gladius and leveled it. "Lances! Charge!"

His horse shot forward. The cavalry thundered after him.

The oncoming Britons hesitated, then answered the cavalry with war cries.

Sergius's gladius rang off a Briton's blade as the man fell beneath his horse's hooves. Beside him a cavalryman speared another warrior and then was plucked off his mount by a Briton sword. Then the remaining cavalrymen crushed the Britons to the ground.

Sergius fought his horse to a halt and looked back.

Egomas stood in the alley, facing the oncoming warriors.

"Egomas! Run!" Sergius shouted.

The dog-seller ignored him, opening his arms to the running Britons.

The leading warrior raised his sword.

Egomas' voice, speaking the Briton tongue, reached them down the alley: "I'm one of you! Egomas of the Trinovantes!"

The warrior drew back his arm.

"No!" Ailidh cried.

"Don't look," Sergius said. He pulled her head hard against him.

Bright steel flashed.

Egomas screamed, "I'm one of—"

His head flew from his shoulders, bounced on the cobbles, and rolled.

Ailidh's fingers gouged into Sergius's shoulders. *"Egomas!"*

Then she slid off the horse.

"Ailidh, no!" Sergius called. He waved to the decurio, "Move on."

Briton warriors pounded down the alley.

"Ailidh, what are you doing?"

She bent over a fallen warrior, pried the sword from his hand, and climbed back up behind Sergius. "Guarding your back."

Sergius kneed his horse. They caught up with the troop.

At the end of the alley, he looked right. Smoke drifted down the street and obscured his vision.

"The river's to the left, sir," the decurio said.

Shouts and shrieks wraithed through the smoky gloom that concealed the city center. A building collapsed into a seething pile of fiery rubble.

A dull red glow brightened the skyline. Flames licked the clouds.

"They've fired the city!" the decurio gasped.

Sergius thought. Behind the rubble and the smoke, Londinium's temples and houses burned. Those who escaped the flames faced Boudicca's blood-lust-maddened warriors.

Ailidh's soft breath touched his neck; her body warmed his back. If they were captured . . . . He remembered the mutilated women and shuddered.

He glanced at the decurio who awaited his orders; at Paullus peering with his poor eyes; Lucanus the physician, composed, lips moving in silent prayer; and Aristarchus pale and quiet.

"We can't cut our way through that," he said, indicating the conflagration. "We'll have to chance the river."

"How will we get across?" Ailidh asked.

"Pray that they haven't burned the bridge."

Sergius wheeled his horse away from Londinium's center and toward the river. Breeze from the Tamesis thinned the smoke but didn't disperse it. Reflection from the sky turned the turbid waters to a stream of crimson.

Bodies littered the streets, the quays, and bobbed in the waters. Masts of sunken boats peeked above the swirling current. So much destruction in so short a time!

Renewed shouts alerted him to another band of roving warriors. He glimpsed them before a swirl of smoke blotted them out. The smoke could work both ways, Sergius thought, obscuring them as well as the Britons.

A figure lunged from the dark. Steel sparked off steel as Ailidh wielded her sword and beat the tribesman away. A cavalryman finished the warrior with a lance thrust.

Sergius cantered his horse along the waterfront.

A pillar of smoke rose from the town, reached the still-rising sun, and extinguished it. Shroudlike gloom descended, and the Tamesis became a river of night.

Sergius picked his way along a quayside where rubble and bodies stumbled the horses. "Watch out," he warned. "I don't want to lose anyone to the river."

"There it is," the decurio spied.

Like a pale ghost, the bridge lurched across the river.

"Thank God they haven't burnt it," Ailidh said.

"But we're not safe yet." Sergius strained his eyes at the indistinct far shore, at an irregular shadow.

Ailidh's breath hissed.

The breeze created a transient rent in the smoke.

In the break, the shadow resolved into a force of Briton warriors blocking the bridge.

Sergius's heart plummeted. "There must be three hundred of them," he whispered.

He stared at the cluster of warriors. To come so close and then to find the avenue of escape barred! Boudicca must have anticipated the inhabitants' flight to the south and sent warriors to ford the Tamesis further downstream and cut off the refugees' escape route.

His mind registered Lucanus's voice explaining the situation to Paullus.

Behind him, Londinium's funeral pyre blazed. Before him, Boudicca's warriors waited with thirsty blades.

Ailidh's fingers touched his cheek. Sergius twisted to meet her green eyes.

She said, "Don't worry about me."

His throat spasmed. "We're trapped, Ailidh. They're too many for us. We'd never reach the other side alive." He slumped. "I'm sorry. I failed you."

The tenderness in her eyes brought tears to his own.

"Do whatever I say, Marcus."

"Why? What are—"

Her fingers touched his lips.

She slid from the horse. She stuck the sword through her criss, arranged her cloak to cover her, and pulled the cowl over her head.

"Ailidh!"

She shook her head. "Don't stop me."

"But—"

She faced him. "You saved my life, Marcus. Let me save yours."

She turned away and with measured tread began to walk down the long bridge toward the waiting warriors.

TWENTY-THREE

"All is coming to pass as you said," Weylyn commented, riding his horse next to Boudicca's twin-horse chariot. "The Romans were too stupid to flee."

Boudicca brushed a strand of her tawny hair away from her face. Her chariot crested a low ridge, and she reined back the horses. Below her spread a panorama of destruction, an ugly vista of fire and ash and rubble—for now. But once the Roman scourge was eliminated, the land would reclaim the cities. Trees and grass would grow again, and the people would live as they had always lived. No one need huddle in fear of the conquerors again.

She would bequeath her daughters a land with a hope. The line of Prasutagus would rule over a free people.

She smiled a smile of satisfaction at Weylyn. "Andraste has honored my vows."

Weylyn gestured at the flaming city. "Why don't you claim your share of plunder?"

Boudicca shook her head. "I have my reward, Weylyn. To see the end of the Romans is enough. What need do I have of gold and cloth and wine? Let the warriors feed on the Roman carcass."

"Catus has fled."

Boudicca clenched her fists. "I swore to have the swine. But it is no matter. If I can't have him in this life, I shall await him in the next."

She relaxed her hands and rested them on the edges of her chariot. Aife and Cinnia showed signs of recovery. They were strong girls.

She flicked the reins and rode toward the ruins of Londinium.

Ailidh's sword thumped against her thigh as she strode to the waiting warriors. The scrutiny of hundreds of watching eyes made her breath come quickly to her chest. She forced her breathing to slow and concentrated on the slapping of the sword as a distraction from the pounding of her pulse.

She wanted to run, but that would be suicide.

Her greatest fear was that impetuous warriors would rush to take the Romans. In the heat of battle, her words would be lost. Sergius would die, and Paullus and his companions.

Please, Lord, she prayed, her lips moving silently, *let them hold their peace. If not for me, then for Sergius.*

Perhaps taken aback at the sight of a solitary woman walking unhurriedly across the bridge toward them, or perhaps recognizing her Briton clothing, the warriors made no move to charge. But sword hands never left hilts.

When she came within easy voice range, she held up a hand in greeting, and called, "I am Ailidh, daughter of Cathair of the Iceni, anruth of the sixth level of wisdom."

The closest ranks of warriors stirred. Ailidh caught the nervous looks they cast at each other.

"Anruth?" one asked.

"Who is your chief?" Ailidh called. "Who will speak to me?"

A big, burly warrior elbowed his way through the ranks. A gold torque shone around his neck, golden bands on his upper arms, and rings on his fingers. He wore multicolored trousers but was naked from the waist up. Sweat plastered a mat of hair to his chest. His mustache drooped to his jawline.

He halted in front of her, spread his feet, and planted his hands on his hips. "I am Bairrfhionn. Who are you to come in the company of Romans?"

Ailidh repeated her introduction.

Bairrfhionn sneered. "Cathair? I know no such name."

A grizzled warrior spoke, "I do. Cathair of the Iceni. He died a hero's death in battle."

Bairrfhionn ran an appreciative gaze over Ailidh. "You claim to be his daughter? Why should I believe this?"

Ailidh parted her cloak and drew her sword. "You may believe my word or my sword. Or shall I pronounce the glam dicin upon you? Do you wish a geis, Bairrfhionn?"

The big warrior paled and turned a snicker at the thought of fighting a woman into an apology. "There's no need for a curse, anruth. Sheath your sword. None here shall harm you." He glared at the warriors as if to emphasize his words.

"Good." Ailidh returned the sword to her criss.

Bairrfhionn gestured at the troop of cavalry. Ailidh noted that Sergius and the troops had followed her across the bridge, but remained a discrete distance behind.

"Who are these?"

Ailidh explained, "They are escorting certain learned and holy men from Londinium."

"Roman cavalry escorting Roman priests?" Bairrfhionn spat. "We shall enjoy escorting them to the otherworld."

"Allow them to pass."

The warrior goggled. "Those Roman swineherds?"

"Yes. Without delay."

Bairrfhionn shifted from one foot to the other. "I cannot, anruth."

"I insist, Bairrfhionn."

"The queen has decreed that all Romans in Londinium must perish. I dare not disobey."

"Do you disobey her, or me?"

Bairrfhionn spread his hands. "You place me in an impossible position, daughter of Cathair."

"And how will you decide?"

Bairrfhionn licked his lips. He stroked his long mustache. "With respect, Boudicca is my queen. While you are learned, you are anruth, not ollamh—"

He broke off. The same grizzled warrior who knew of Cathair leaned forward to whisper to him.

Biarrfhionn nodded vigorously. He whirled and shouted, "Where is the Druí?"

Ailidh tensed. She glanced over her shoulder.

Sergius had sat quietly, listening, unable to understand all the words, but following the moods of the exchange by the changing postures of the speakers. When Ailidh drew her sword, his hand had slid to the hilt of his, only to release it when she returned her sword to her belt.

He wondered what she had said that the Briton chieftain showed respect to her.

Now there was no mistaking the anxiety in the glance she cast him.

And he understood the chieftain's shout.

"What's going on, sir?" the decurio whispered.

"I'm not sure. But they're calling for a Druid."

A palpable hostility emanated from the hundreds of warriors. Sergius understood how Veturius must have felt, seeing the hills alive with thousands of savagely dressed and painted warriors screaming for blood.

"Do we fight?" the decurio asked.

Sergius shook his head. "Not if we can avoid it."

"There's no going back, sir."

Londinium blazed brighter and brighter as more fires ignited. Spread by the shifting breeze, flames licked eagerly from one building to its neighbor. No power on earth could halt the conflagration now.

Sergius said, "Give Ailidh a chance."

A voice that took a moment for Sergius to identify as Paullus's inquired, "Have you decided, Tribune Lysias?"

Sergius turned to face the apostle. Paullus sat securely behind a cavalryman, leaning to the side to glimpse Sergius.

"Decided what?" Sergius asked.

"What you must give up."

"This is hardly the time—"

"To be a follower of the cross, a soldier of the Way, requires sacrifice."

Sergius returned his attention to Ailidh.

Paullus continued, "I had to learn the hard way, when God struck me with blindness on the road to Damascus. I rode my horse as an arrogant, prideful man. I picked myself out of the dust a humble one."

"Not now," Sergius hushed.

"A humble and contrite heart is acceptable."

"I'll consider it later."

The ranks of warriors melted aside to make way for a white-robed figure.

Ailidh's breath hissed.

"Who calls for me?" Lovernios asked. "Who desires an ollamh of the seventh degree of wisdom?"

"I call," Bairrfhionn said. He pointed at Ailidh. "The anruth tells me one thing, the queen another. Judge for me, Druí, lest she curse me with a geis."

"Indeed." Lovernios nodded at Ailidh. "Greetings, Cousin."

Ailidh folded her arms across her chest and inclined her head. "Cousin."

Lovernios beckoned and drew her out of earshot of Bairrfhionn and his warriors.

He said, "I'm told there's one here who claims to be anruth."

"And so I am."

"So you *were*," Lovernios corrected. "You are no longer entitled to carry a silver wand."

"I haven't forgotten that which I learned."

"But you departed our ranks."

"I was forced out, because I desired to take up a higher."

"What is higher?" Lovernios asked. "Or what lower? What do you ask of Bairrfhionn? Why do you threaten a noble warrior with a geis?"

Ailidh's gesture included Sergius and the apostles. "I asked him to let these men of peace pass in peace."

Lovernios frowned. "Then I understand his perplexion. The request is indeed difficult."

"But a request I also ask of you." Ailidh paused. "You are a judge, and I trust you will judge fairly."

Lovernios gave a short laugh. "The Romans are guilty. Queen Boudicca has decreed their sentence. Why should I even consider sparing them?"

"Because of justice."

"Is it justice to let these escape, when the queen has ordered their destruction?"

Ailidh pointed to the funeral pyre of Londinium. "How many have perished already? Are a few lives spared so great a request?"

Lovernios drew breath. "The Romans have stripped us of our lands. They enslave our men, rape our women, orphan our children. We labor to build their temples and die in the quarries. They tax us into poverty. How much recompense is sufficient?"

"These men had nothing to do with that. Sergius means us no harm. Is it just to condemn the innocent with the guilty?"

"Do Romans distinguish between us? Aren't all people of the Celtae alike to them? I've seen what they did on Mona, where physicians, priests, and judges were left like dung to rot. Sine—you remember Sine—gods, Ailidh. What they did to her—"

His voice broke. Ailidh glanced away to allow him to regain his composure.

Then she touched his arm. "Lovernios, is there no room for mercy in your justice?"

Lovernios ignored the question. Instead he asked, "The tribune, I know, but who are the others?"

"Paullus, Lucanus, and Aristarchus, leaders of the Way."

Lovernios's face darkened. "They deny our gods and seek to force their beliefs on us. Why should they be spared?"

"They revere the Truth and Word—"

"Not *our* truth or *our* word!"

"*The* Truth and Word. Talk to Paullus, Cousin, if you won't heed me."

"I have no time to waste on vain conversation."

Bairrfhionn strode closer to interrupt. "Enough of talk! Let us slay the Roman sheep!"

The warriors growled.

"Be still!" Lovernios commanded. As if the warriors had abruptly become mute, the muttering ceased.

Lovernios changed to Latin. "It is said that in this Way, one man died to save all. Is this true?"

"Yes," Ailidh whispered, suddenly cold inside.

Lovernios's feverish gaze fixed on Sergius. "Perhaps then I can accommodate your request, Cousin."

The words didn't reach him, but Sergius understood the Druid's look at him. Lovernios had tried to capture him once before.

Sergius slid from his saddle. Under the scrutiny of the Britons, he crossed to Lovernios and Ailidh.

She extended an arm to halt his progress. He lowered it gently.

His gaze locked with that of the Druid.

"Let these others go, and you may have me."

"No!" Ailidh cried. "Sergius, no!"

He turned her to face him. "It's the only way. Otherwise all of us will die."

Lovernios said, "Your Roman is a man of courage and wisdom, Cousin."

"Well, Lovernios?" Sergius asked.

The Druid gave a slight nod. "I will grant you a quick and painless death."

Sergius withdrew his gladius. Slowly, so as not to alarm, he reversed it and handed it hilt first to Lovernios. The Druid's hand closed upon the ivory grip. Without removing his gaze from Sergius, he passed the sword to Bairrfhionn.

Lovernios eased a golden wand from his sleeve. He raised it over his head. "Let these men pass in peace," he commanded loudly. "Let no one harm them."

Sergius turned and walked the few steps back to his handful of men. "See that Paullus is placed on the road to Noviomagus," he instructed the decurio. "The route through Pontes and Calleva is longer but safer. Then take your men and rejoin the governor."

"What am I to say?" the decurio protested. "That I abandoned you? Better to fight and die with honor."

"Tell him that I ordered you. You had no choice."

The decurio nodded reluctantly. "As you say, sir."

"Be on your way."

Sergius stopped the horse carrying Paullus. He wondered how much the old apostle had heard and understood. "God go with you, Paullus."

He expected Paullus to be somber. Instead the apostle gave him a kindly smile and said, "I too was a man of blood. A Hebrew of the Hebrews, who hounded believers to death. But I learned, if I was not to be only another noise in a noisy world, that I must love."

He took a breath. "You are learning that lesson. Surrender to the Spirit of God, and you will yet be a warrior of the Way."

Paullus leaned over to rest his hand on Sergius's head. "God preserve you for posterity here on earth and save your life by a great deliverance."

Paullus peered at Ailidh. "And you, Daughter." He removed his hand from Sergius's head. "Your work in Britannia is no more finished than mine."

Lucanus raised a hand in benediction. Aristarchus reached down to grip Sergius's arm.

The Britons parted to allow the troop to ride away from the bridge and the flaming city.

"Go with them," Sergius pleaded with Ailidh.

"No. I'm safe among my people. They won't harm an anruth."

When the last man had passed, Sergius and Ailidh stood alone before Lovernios.

The Druí beckoned to Bairrfhionn. "Take the tribune under guard to Queen Boudicca. Watch him well, but do him no harm."

Bairrfhionn grinned. "I'll keep his precious Roman skin unblemished."

A warrior gripped Sergius by each arm and dragged him away from Ailidh.

Ailidh fought back tears as she watched the tribesmen haul Sergius away. She'd tried to save him, and she'd failed. Bitterness and frustration welled up within her, a torrent of passion that she couldn't stem.

She rounded on the Druí.

"Why do you hate him so?" she demanded. "You were once a gentle man of peace!"

Lovernios flinched. "I don't hate him."

"Then you must hate me!"

"I could never hate you. But I see more clearly than you what must be done if our people hope to survive."

"A hope based on killing those who mean no harm?"

"His blood is not ours."

"His blood is on your hands."

Lovernios sighed. "I am a judge, not a priest."

"Then you are an unfair judge! I thought better of you!"

"Be grateful I saved the others for you when it was within my power to see them all dead. But the tribune is special." Lovernios reached out to her, but Ailidh backed away.

He said, "One day you will understand."

"Haven't the gods drunk enough of human misery? What has happened to you, Lovernios? You used to think it a noble task to avert suffering."

"Once I was a child, as you are now. But I have seen, Ailidh." His voice trailed away. "I have seen . . ."

He turned to follow the tribesmen. "Go or stay, as you wish."

"I want to see Sergius."

He halted. With his back to her, he counseled, "That would not be wise."

"It is my desire."

"Why torture yourself further? He's as good as dead. Forget him."

"Can I forget the air I breathe or the water I drink? Can I forget the sun or moon?"

Lovernios shook his head. "You have so much to learn, Cousin." He began to walk away. "It is forbidden for you to see him."

"I will see him anyway."

"The guards will be instructed that if you try then you will perish also."

The hordes of tribesmen swallowed him up.

Ailidh bit her lip until the coppery taste of her own blood filled her mouth. Her nails gouged her palms. The emotion rose within her and exploded in a scream like the wailing of the bean sidhe.

The warriors dragged Sergius through Boudicca's horde. Female warriors as well as men stared at him. He expected at any moment to feel the thrust of a dagger between his ribs.

But though many cursed, others spat, and some cuffed him until his head rang, none drew steel against him.

Bairrfhionn swaggered beside him. "What a shame the Druí ordered me not to harm you. I would like to have spitted you, watching you squirm as my sword carved you like a boar."

Sergius kept his face impassive.

"Slowly," Bairrfhionn continued, "so that you would feel every lingering minute."

Sergius looked away from the warrior. While the city across the Tamesis burned, the buildings on this bank remained untouched.

He wondered why, until his captors halted before a small villa. A man stood guard at the door.

Bairrfhionn indicated Sergius. "This is the queen's personal captive, a present from the Druí."

"There's a storeroom. That will do to hold him."

"Inside," Bairrfhionn grunted. He shoved Sergius through the door.

The villa contained half a dozen rooms. Sergius wasn't permitted to see inside any of the others.

The guard opened a door. "In here."

Bairrfhionn planted his fist in Sergius's lower back and flung him into the storeroom. Sergius sprawled face first on a dirt floor.

"Enjoy what remains of your life, Roman." Bairrfhionn turned to the guard. "No need to waste food on him. He won't be alive long enough to need it."

The door slammed shut.

Sergius lay still until the spasm of pain from Bairrfhionn's blow faded. Then he rolled to a sitting position and took stock of his situation.

The room was larger than he expected, about fifteen feet on a side and empty but for a few scraps of sacking. Scrapes and depressions in the dust showed where barrels had once stood. But whatever stores the room once contained had been removed—by either the original owners or Boudicca's looters. A window high on one wall provided ventilation and daylight. But the aperture was far too small to allow egress.

The room smelled of grain and urine and rodents.

Sergius pulled his cloak tight and sat on the packed earth floor. He rested his chin upon his knees.

Ailidh was safe. Paullus and the others had escaped. If it wasn't meant that he too escape, then at least he had that consolation.

But he'd heard Ailidh's cry as the men hauled him away, and the recollection of that cry sent a stab of pain through his heart.

"Oh, God, is this how it's to end?"

His voice bounced off the rafters.

Ailidh caught up to Lovernios later, as the Druí sat on a stone near the water's edge. The sun sank through a haze of red, and bodies drifted downstream to the distant ocean. Wisps of acrid smoke twined across the Tamesis.

She knelt beside the rock and studied his profile, grown haggard over the past months. Gray strands shafted through his russett hair.

"What can I say," she asked, "to make you change your mind?"

Lovernios shook his head. "Nothing."

"You would see me in pain?"

"The whole land writhes. One person's pain is but a drop." He swept his hand over the river. "In those eddies, do you see the fate of our people? Do you see how currents twist the water until a stronger current sweeps them away?"

"Are we to be swept away?"

He raised eyes to her, eyes that seemed hollow and distant. "Boudicca is strong. With her there is hope that the Roman current will be diverted. It happened before, when Caesar came. He strode our shores, but then he left, and we saw the Roman legions no more for a century."

"And in this hope you would sweep away my love?"

"Love." He spoke the word quietly, with regret. "What is love in the hands of war? If the future is dark, where can the light of love be?"

"With us." She touched his hand. "Remember how it was, when we were . . . when we were intended? Whenever you saw a pretty girl, you'd tell me, to make me jealous. And every time I thought you'd found another more pleasing than I. And then, when it could no longer be, I thought you'd find another to mate."

"I was too busy. And now there will never be time." He touched his chest, and for a moment she saw a softening of his handsome features into the Lovernios she had once known.

He said, "Believe me, Ailidh, I hurt too. I hurt for what is happening to us. I cannot change the course of war. But I must do what I can."

"And so you condemn an innocent man."

"No one is innocent." Lovernios's mouth hardened. He gazed at the river. "You have told me this yourself."

"All have sinned, yes. But you are not Sergius's judge—that lies in God's hands."

"Your Sergius walks the same path of self-sacrifice as your Christus. Why do you object?"

"Lovernios!" She gripped the rock.

"I have promised him a quick, painless death, and I will keep my word. He will not suffer." He stared at her white knuckles, as if seeing but not seeing. "I am no gutuatros, no speaker to the gods. But they have spoken to me. There is need of a devoted victim. One whose sacrifice will be acceptable."

Ailidh recalled, "I have told you of the one who sacrificed himself out of love."

Lovernios shook his head. "The sacrifice of your foreign Christus is of no use to us."

"His sacrifice was for all," she emphasized.

"No."

"Then why not take me, if you must have a victim?"

Lovernios tapped a finger on the rock. "You have betrayed our gods."

"I have met the one true God."

"Will the gods accept a traitor? Your Sergius is a man of noble spirit. A sacrifice from among our people must be equally devoted. Yet perhaps . . . " Lovernios's finger stopped.

Ailidh leaned forward. "Yes?"

Lovernios looked into her eyes. "If you were to renounce your worship of this foreign god and return to the gods of our people, then your sacrifice would be acceptable, and your Roman friend could be released."

Ailidh rocked back. She put a hand to her mouth. "I should deny my faith?"

"Which is more to you: this alien faith or the life of the one you love?"

"That's not a fair comparison—"

The Druí's expression set. "Decide, Cousin. If you would save him, that is the exchange you must make. The choice is yours."

Veturius spotted the cloud of dust that heralded the troop's arrival in Durocobrivis. Suetonius's party had made rapid time, only stopping in Verulamium long enough to warn the frightened inhabitants to flee.

He studied the mounted men, then hurried to meet the decurio as the horses halted.

"Where's Lysias?"

The decurio, sweaty and dusty, dismounted. "Dead, sir, if he's lucky."

Veturius gripped his arm. "Dead?"

"Boudicca has him, sir."

Veturius froze. Then he said, "You'd better come tell the commander."

Suetonius listened to the decurio's report in silence.

"I couldn't understand the words, sir, but I believe Tribune Lysias remained behind so that we could escape."

"His life for yours?" Veturius inquired.

"That's what it seemed, sir. It was a Druid who told Boudicca's warriors to let us pass."

Suetonius frowned. "You didn't fight?"

"I wanted to, sir, but the tribune ordered us to decline battle. He ordered me to leave Londinium and rejoin the legions. I followed instructions."

The commander nodded. "There's nothing we can do. Very well, decurio. You acted appropriately. You are dismissed. Report to Prefect Pertinax."

"Yes, sir."

"You may leave, too, Veturius."

Outside the tent, Veturius queried the decurio, "What about the girl? Did you find her?"

"Yes. But she remained behind as well. Actually, sir, I thought she seemed friendly with the Druid."

"Curious," Veturius murmured. He watched the decurio make his way to the cavalry quarters.

"Sergius," he recalled sadly, "I told you one god wasn't enough."

Poenius Postumus, prefect of the *Augusta*, looked up as his beneficiarius opened the door. At Isca, the rain still poured, and the men of Legio II *Augusta* huddled inside and cursed the Tempestates.

"Yes? What?"

"A courier from the governor, sir."

"Send him in."

The beneficiarius turned and beckoned. A cavalryman entered.

Poenius scowled. Rain dripped from the man's stained cloak to the floor. Mud spattered his legs and uniform and fell in globs.

"What have you?"

"This, sir." The cavalryman held out a message board.

Poenius took it. "Go and bathe. Use the officers' baths if you wish."

"Thank you, sir."

Poenius opened the tablet.

He read quickly, then dropped the tablet onto the table.

"Bad news, sir?" his beneficiarius asked.

"Very bad, Decimus. The Iceni have risen in revolt, and the Trinovantes have joined them. Queen Boudicca has sacked Camulodunum."

"A disaster!"

"To be attacked by a woman, no less! The governor is marching from Mona to engage Queen Boudicca. He orders us to send as many cohorts as we can spare."

"But can we, sir?" the aide asked.

Poenius tapped with a stylus on the table. "We have hostile tribes on either side of us."

"If we strip the fortress of men," Decimus guessed, "the Dumnonii will take advantage of our weakness."

"Exactly. And if we took less than a full legion, and the Durotriges opposed us, could we cut our way through nearly two hundred miles of hostiles?"

"It's all or nothing, sir."

Poenius smacked the table. "All my life I've waited for a chance to command a legion in battle, Decimus! And now the chance is held before me, but I cannot take it."

He paced around the room. "My task is to maintain the peace here. If we leave and rebellion flares behind us, what then? I'll have failed in my duty."

"It means disobeying an order, sir," Decimus recognized.

"Something I have never done," Poenius said. "But what if we fail to reach the governor? Then we've lost this corner of the province. What if the governor has already met Boudicca and been defeated?" He tapped the tablet. "This says that her forces number over a hundred thousand. Should we march to annihilation also?"

"It is a difficult decision, sir."

"By Mars, what have I done to deserve this? Is this how the gods treat me after my years of faithfulness?"

Poenius strode to the door and stared into the sleeting rain that turned the hills into slumping green mounds. "I am no coward, Decimus. But the governor doesn't know our situation. He'd expect me to use common sense. Should we risk ambush and disaster as happened to Valens?"

He swung around. "The legion will remain here, Decimus. If the Dumnonii or Durotriges rise to join Boudicca, we'll be ready for them."

"Will you tell that to the governor, sir?"

Poenius felt cold inside and his knee ached. He had visions of what would happen if he decided wrongly—there would be no recourse other than suicide. He said, "Call me a clerk to draft a reply."

Ailidh made her way through Boudicca's camp as daylight faded. Warriors bedded down under trees, on grass, or on bare ground if necessary, spreading cloaks for cushioning.

Cooking fires blazed in hollows, and the scent of roasting meat mixed with those of wine and beer.

A day of pillage, raping, and killing had created hearty appetites. Warriors laughed, drank, cleaned swords, and divided their spoils: gold and silver coins; torques, rings, brooches and armbands; bolts of dyed and embroidered linen; swords and daggers; and silver goblets and jewels.

A warrior carried a bronze head of Claudius broken from a statue in one of Londinium's temples. To the delight of his companions he passed his water on it and threw it into the river. It splashed in the darkness.

A woman's shrill scream pierced the night.

Ailidh cringed.

A Roman matron was being used by the warriors, or being sacrificed; they screamed the same.

She'd heard screams today until they blended together into one long death-cry of agony.

The lucky inhabitants of Londinium—she stifled a thought of Egomas—had died clean deaths by the sword. The less fortunate were crucified on buildings and trees, used as human torches, or garotted. The least fortunate of all vanished into groves where their shrieks ascended to the gods. If female, they were impaled and mutilated as punishment for bearing Roman offspring.

Another scream wafted from across the river and faded into a whimper.

Ailidh shuddered.

The air reeked with evil—an evil composed of smoke and ash, blood and pain, hatred and revenge.

"Please, God," she whispered, "help me."

On one hand lay the life of the man she loved, on the other, her faith.

How could she choose between them?

Nothing in all her years of training to become anruth gave her a hint of what to do. She'd left Lovernios by the river and wandered, thinking and praying.

Two impossible choices.

Whichever she chose, she couldn't live with herself.

She came to a Roman-style building with a light chariot and a team of horses tethered outside.

A muscled warrior regarded her with obvious desire.

A thought quickened her.

Perhaps . . .could there be a third way?

Ailidh reached under her cloak and withdrew a slender silver wand from her criss. She took a breath to steady the racing of her heart and stepped toward the guard.

"I am Ailidh, daughter of Cathair, and anruth. I crave audience with Queen Boudicca."

Veturius Longinus lay on his couch, staring at the timber rafters of the barracks in Durocobrivis, where Suetonius's party bedded for the night. A spider crawled across the beams, then drifted high overhead on a strand of silk. Veturius watched its delicate movements.

A low whine disturbed his thoughts, and a hard nose nudged his arm.

He rolled onto his side and reached out to ruffle the brown fur between Cara's ears. "I know."

The wolfhound stretched out beside him, muzzle cradled on paws, brown eyes regarding him for an answer he couldn't give.

Veturius sighed. "I suppose you're mine now, girl."

He rolled back to a supine position, his hand resting on the wolfhound's flanks.

"Trust Lysias. I want a girl and he leaves me a dog."

But even to him, the attempt at humor lacked mirth.

TWENTY-FOUR

Annaeus Seneca paused outside the emperor's personal chamber and placed his ear close to the gilded door. The sounds he thought he'd heard in the corridor grew clearer—the strumming of a lyre, and a man's breathy, high-pitched singing. Seneca waited until the song had finished, then knocked and pushed the door open.

Supported by a cushion, Nero reclined on a couch, a lyre propped beside him. Glowing lamps fended off the dark of the Italian night. A small basin of smoldering incense filled the room with fragrance. Cloying, Seneca thought; not a manly scent at all.

The emperor looked up. "Seneca. Good. You're just in time to hear my new song."

The advisor tried not to allow his face to register emotion. "Delighted, Caesar," he murmured.

Nero peered past him. "Where's Burrus?"

"A sore throat, Caesar."

Nero scowled. "You'll have to do." He strummed a chord, then launched into the song Seneca had heard through the door.

Seneca made an effort to pay attention to rhymes about love, wine, and pomegranates.

"What do you think?" Nero asked when he'd finished.

Seneca tilted his head to one side. "Your gift for melody is improving, Caesar, and your poetry shows promise."

Nero looked petulant. "But not as good as yours, is that what you're afraid to say?"

"One is ill-advised to expound the worth of one's own work," Seneca demurred. "That is for others to decide."

"Why are you here?" Nero demanded.

Seneca held up papyri. "Dispatches from Britannia that I thought might interest you, Caesar."

"At this time of night?"

"Suetonius reports that all is prepared for the invasion of Mona. He says that in his next communication he will report the destruction of the Druidae."

"His bravery thrills us. Next."

"The next is from Decianus Catus dated three weeks ago. He says that he was forced to take stern measures with the Iceni, but he confiscated considerable quantities of gold and other valuables from Prasutagus's estate. He sends his respects and a treasury report."

Nero perked. "Good news, Seneca. Give him our thanks. Perhaps now Britannia will become an asset instead of a drain."

"Catus states he was forced to punish Queen Boudicca."

"Then perhaps that's the last we'll hear of the troublemaker. Women always cause trouble, don't you agree?" Nero reached for his lyre. "Would you like to hear another song?"

Seneca bowed. "With respect, Caesar, I'm quite fatigued, and I doubt I could give it the appreciation it deserves." He backed toward the door. "Perhaps in the morning?"

Nero strummed a chord. "Your absence would displease us."

Seneca sighed and halted. "As you wish, Caesar."

Night had filled the tiny window with black when the scrape of wood on wood interrupted Sergius's reverie. Somebody was raising the bar that secured the door to his prison. The door banged open. Sergius picked himself off the dusty floor.

A woman entered followed by an armed warrior. Both held torches; the wavering light accented shadows and facial lines and enhanced the foreignness of their features and dress. The woman scrutinized him, much as, Sergius thought, one would study a particularly disgusting insect before stamping the life out of it.

She fitted her torch into a sconce on the wall and gestured to the guard. "Wait outside."

When the man had left, she moved to within a few feet of Sergius. "So. This is what crawls out of Londinium's sewers," she said in a voice as harsh and gritty as horseflesh against saddle sores.

She topped his height by a head or more. Her tawny hair touched the waistband of her multicolored trousers and the jeweled hilt of a longsword thrust through her criss. Her blouse rippled across a figure that no man could ignore. Her face possessed a regal bearing. Sergius thought she could have been beautiful but for the ferocity of her green eyes. He guessed her to be in the midthirties.

Based on Veturius's flawless description, Sergius had no doubt that he stood in the presence of the Iceni ruler.

"Queen Boudicca," he addressed.

"Ha! You call me 'Queen,' Roman?"

"It is your title."

"Not according to your emperor, the loathsome Nero."

Sergius winced at the insult and half-opened his mouth but said nothing.

Boudicca's sneer twisted her face. "Don't you rush to defend him?"

"Your opinion is your own business."

She cocked an eyebrow. "Is it so? Tell me, Roman, what do you think of me?"

Sergius considered. "You have been wronged."

"I have been *greatly* wronged!" Boudicca startled him with her outburst. "I have been beaten and insulted by the slaves of the animal Catus. My daughters became the playthings of soldiers. My people lament the loss of their lands. What have you to say to that?"

"What can I say? Your grievances are just."

"They are more than just. Catus violated my daughters—in my hearing—and I was powerless to prevent him. Can you understand *that*, Roman?"

Sergius shook his head.

"Well, I am helpless no longer. Catus has escaped me, more's the pity. But this so-called province of Britannia of yours trembles at the sound of my name."

Boudicca circled him.

Sergius felt as if a great jungle cat measured him, toying with him before the final, fatal spring.

"The Druí says you will be a fitting sacrifice. One able to assuage the thirst of the gods."

"Do you say the same?"

Her shoulders lifted. "You're a puny specimen of manhood."

"I bested Culhwch."

Boudicca gave a mirthless laugh. "You have courage, I'll grant you that." She resumed her pacing. "You will die in the morning, Roman."

"I'm not afraid of death."

"Good. Do you hope there's yet a woman's heart that beats within me? I tell you, Roman, that my heart has turned to stone."

"I'll not beg for mercy."

Boudicca reached out to touch the gold torque around his neck. "I have vowed to Andraste that all Romans in Londinium will die."

She dropped her hand. "Still, one has come to me to plead for your life."

"One to plead?" Sergius started. "Ailidh?"

"The daughter of Cathair. She says you saved her when Catus would have had her as he had my daughters." Her lips twisted. "Concern for a Briton, Roman?"

"I love her," Sergius declared.

"Love? A woman of the Britons? Am I to believe that there's a Roman who feels something other than contempt for a conquered people?"

"I bear no ill will toward the people of Britannia. If it lay within my power to reverse the wrongs done you, I would."

Boudicca sighed and leaned her shoulders against the wall. The fierceness of her eyes faded, to be replaced by a faraway wistfulness. "I remember Cathair. He was a man to make any woman burn with desire. And a warrior—such skill! How we young women used to try to attract his attention. When he died, selling his life dearly against the Catuvellauni, we knew not whether to celebrate his rebirth in the otherworld or mourn for what had been taken from us."

"You loved him," Sergius said.

Boudicca stiffened, as if Sergius had struck a nerve. "I admired him, with the passion of a young girl. He served Prasutagus well in the days before I became queen."

She pushed off the wall and again paced the room. "You remind me of Prasutagus, when he was young."

"I accept that as a compliment."

"You're not ashamed to be compared to a Briton?"

"Not one as upright and respected as the late king. Ailidh has told me of him."

"Don't jest with me!" Boudicca snapped.

"My words were truthful," Sergius replied. He met the intensity of her gaze.

After a long moment, Boudicca nodded. She strode to stand behind him. "It has been known to happen that occasionally a warrior is lax in his guard duty."

It took a moment for Boudicca's words to register.

He spun to front her. "I am no coward that I should slink away as a dog in the night!"

Boudicca shrugged. "It is no shame to live to fight again. But stay if you will and die. It matters not to me."

She turned to the door. "Don't think I do this for you, Roman, but for the daughter of Cathair. I, who am now old, whose heart lies in the grave, remember what it was to be young and in love."

She halted and pivoted around to face him. Her eyes regained their brightness. "If, perchance, you are not here in the morning, then I will not have broken my vow. But mark this, Roman, if we meet again, in battle or otherwise, there will be none to stay my hand."

"I am grateful."

Her gaze held him a moment longer, then she pushed open the door and was gone.

Sergius sank back to the floor and studied the scarred wooden panels of the door.

Boudicca—the terrifying queen herself—offered him a chance at escape? Could it be an answer to prayer—his own, Ailidh's, or Paullus's?

He'd spent hours preparing for the inevitability of his death. In his heart, he'd said good-bye to his loved ones.

And now, which was worth more—honor or life? Or was that even a valid comparison? No one would hold a nighttime escape against him; not if he returned to the governor with information about Boudicca's army.

Ailidh had dared much for him. He couldn't refuse to accept the hope of life she gave him.

He couldn't have slept even if he'd wanted to. He sat awake, listening to the scratching and scrabblings of mice in the darkness.

Sergius waited until long after all human sound and movement in the house had ceased and only the settling and creak of timbers disturbed the night. Then he rose, crossed to the door, and listened. The door had been hinged to swing out. Sergius pushed gently. Earlier, when he'd tried it, the door hadn't budged. This time, it edged open.

Slowly, by inches so as not to create noise, he opened it farther.

When it was wide enough, he poked his head through the opening.

A lamp, guttering low, cast fitful gleams through the vestibule. He saw no sign of movement, pushed the door wider, and made to step through.

The door stopped.

His foot hit something soft and yielding.

He looked down.

The guard posted outside lay on his side in front of the door, mouth open. Dead or alive, Sergius couldn't tell.

He caught movement in the shadows. The flicker crossed Sergius's peripheral vision, and he ducked back inside his makeshift prison.

Footfalls: they came so softly he could barely hear them.

He pressed himself into the angle of the wall, wishing the door opened inward so as to provide a modicum of concealment.

He reached for his baldric before remembering he had no sword.

The footfalls stopped outside his room. Someone tapped on the door.

He held his breath.

Boudicca had said that the guard might be lax, not absent. Yet these steps sounded furtive, as if someone tiptoed through the night, not confident like the walk of a guard.

A Druid?

Or an assassin, come by stealth to take private vengeance on the Roman prisoner?

The door inched open.

Sergius tensed.

A cloaked figure sidled inside, one arm extended, testing the darkness.

Sergius leaped—one hand reaching for arms, another to cover the mouth.

A started squeak was quickly muffled.

And then an elbow to his gut sent him lurching back. He hit the wall with a grunt.

"Quiet!" the figure hissed. "Do you want to wake everyone?"

"Ailidh!" Sergius gasped.

She pushed back her hood. "Whom else would you be expecting?" She held out a cloth draped over her arm. "Put this on."

"What is it?" he whispered.

"A brat. You can't get out of here looking like a Roman."

Sergius shook out the long woolen cloak and arranged it to cover his own shorter cloak and armor.

Ailidh pulled a gladius from her criss. "Your sword."

"How—?"

"I took it from Bairrfhionn as he slept. Your dagger too. Quickly, there's no time for questions."

Sergius noted that Ailidh still carried the longer Celtae blade. He slid the gladius into his scabbard.

Ailidh peered out the door and took a step. "Come."

When he hesitated, she said, "Why are you waiting?"

"What . . . ," he began, "I don't—"

"You don't think I could leave you here for Lovernios to sacrifice?"

She stepped over the guard's body.

Sergius followed. "Is he dead?"

"Hardly. But a preparation added to his beer will give him a good night's rest and a sore head in the morning."

She moved lithely through the deserted vestibule.

Another pair of guards snored in the courtyard.

"Did you drug everyone?" he asked.

"They were glad for a drink." She rested a hand on his arm. "Put your arm around my waist."

"Here?"

She cuffed him lightly. "If you see anyone moving, stagger and pretend to be drunk."

"Good idea." His hand slid around her.

"And keep quiet! One hint of a Roman accent and we're caught."

He nodded.

The campfires that had blazed earlier had subsided to glowing embers that crackled and popped. Warriors, flung everywhere on a battlefield of sleep, snored.

Sergius had to watch where he placed every step. Once he kicked into a man, who snorted and rolled over.

Sergius froze.

After an agonizing moment, the man resumed his snoring.

Stars twinkled in a sky finally free of smoke.

Sergius leaned close to Ailidh to whisper, "How long until dawn?"

"Four hours." Even the darkness couldn't hide her scathing glance. "Don't you Romans look at the stars?"

He declined comment. Plenty of time to escape before daylight aroused Boudicca's slumbering horde. The fields of sleeping warriors seemed as if they would never end.

If I had an army, he thought, *I could end the rebellion right now.*

Finally, in a copse of trees, away from the mass of Iceni, Ailidh halted beside a horse.

His horse, Sergius noted.

"The road is that way," Ailidh pointed. "Ride quickly."

And then it struck him. There was only one horse. "You're coming with me, aren't you?"

She shook her head. "No."

"Why not? You can't stay here."

She smiled, her teeth white in the darkness. "We've had this conversation before."

He held her hand. "Before, it was Egomas. This time it's different. There's a war."

"Even more reason. Will the Roman Army welcome me? You'll be preparing for battle. Is there room for a woman in your ranks?"

"I wouldn't want you there."

"Exactly. Women of the Britons fight alongside their men. Roman women don't."

"But you could flee south," Sergius protested. "Join Paullus."

"Is there a surety that hostility won't spread south?"

"No, but—"

"Would you flee with me?"

Sergius hesitated only a moment, but it was long enough.

"I thought not," Ailidh verified.

"You should know me better than that."

"There speaks the proud Roman." Ailidh squeezed his hand. "I'm safer here, among my own people. I'm an anruth. They won't harm me."

Sergius frowned. "You used that word before, *anruth*. What does it mean?"

She turned half away, her face in deeper shadow. "I didn't want you to know. I shouldn't have spoken."

"Why? Tell me, Ailidh."

She turned back to face him, her eyes searching his. "Anruth is the sixth of the seven levels of study. Lovernios has reached the seventh, ollamh."

"You're . . . you're a Druidess?"

She nodded. "Before I learned of the Way, yes. My noble father sent his daughter to learn knowledge."

"Were you . . . a priestess?"

She chuckled. "Do you see me offering sacrifices, Marcus?"

"No."

"I was a scholar. A historian. Only some Druid are priests. Others are physicians, astrologers, judges, like Lovernios."

He relaxed.

Her voice dropped. "But I lost that when I joined the Way. I wasn't welcome any longer."

She slumped against a tree trunk. "Hadn't you wondered why I, a noble's daughter, remained unmarried?"

"I thought . . . you just didn't want to."

"Or why I lived apart, with only Egomas for company?"

He shook his head.

"When I joined the Way, I lost my sacrificial standing. I cut myself off from the rituals, from honor and normal society. I remained free, but that was it. Of all my kin, Egomas was the only one who would have anything to do with me. And that only because of my skill with dogs."

Her voice broke. "I became as a dead person among the living."

"I'm sorry."

"I have no regrets," Ailidh said.

Sergius groped for words. "But, Bairrfhionn . . . the others . . . they think—"

"That I'm still anruth, yes. So does Queen Boudicca. Only Lovernios among those I've met here knows otherwise. And he . . . he could have had me killed for pretending I still had rank—"

"You took a big risk."

She nodded, mutely.

"Why didn't you tell me earlier?"

"What kind of a Roman would want a dishonored druidess?"

He wrapped his arms around her and pulled her close. Her hair brushed against his cheek. "Your status means nothing to me. I fell in love with a dog-seller's niece. Not a Druidess."

She clung to him for a moment. Then she said, "And if you love this dog-seller's niece, you'd best ride. You need to be well away by dawn." Her eyes glinted in the starlight.

He said, "Paullus said something to me. I think he was quoting. He promised me a posterity."

She tried to laugh. "There you are. If Paullus says it, it must be true."

"But it's impossible. Suetonius will bring Boudicca to battle. If she wins, she'll hunt down and kill all Romans. If Suetonius wins, he'll have no mercy on the Britons. Whichever, one of us will be in danger of life."

"Then pray that God spares us both." She pushed him gently toward his horse. "Ride."

He swung into the saddle. "What about Lovernios? He'll be angry you deprived him of a sacrifice."

"He won't do anything. Lovernios will keep my secret."

"Are you certain?"

"I know Lovernios. Go quickly."

"I love you, Ailidh."

"And I love you."

He cantered the horse from the copse. He looked back to where she stood, a graceful figure in the shadows.

She waved.

He returned the wave, then urged the horse on into the night.

Ailidh waited until the hoofbeats had vanished into the distance. Then she wrapped herself in her cloak and reclined with her back against the trunk of an ancient tree.

Despite her words to Sergius, she felt cold inside. Lovernios was kin, yes. But ties of kinship only held so long. Technically, she had broken them already. Only Lovernios's good nature had kept her alive to this point.

Would it last? Or this time, had she presumed too far?

She remembered days—long gone, now—when she'd been a young girl. And Lovernios, a good ten years older than she, had held her on his knee and told her stories. He'd been the one to create in her the desire to be a scholar. His first gift to her had been the desire for learning.

His second had been the lives of Paullus and his companions, and her own.

She pillowed her forehead against her knees. If he chose to expose her deception now and put an end to her life, she couldn't complain. It would only be just.

She fell into a fitful sleep.

Just after dawn Boudicca strode through the armed camp outside Londinium. Whenever she came to a prone figure, she stopped to identify it. Finally, she spied a familiar man snoring on the ground and planted her foot in his ribs. He grunted and rolled away. She kicked him again. He cursed and groped for his sword. Boudicca thrust the blade of her own weapon in the ground before his face.

The man started, rubbed his eyes and squinted.

"Get up," Boudicca commanded.

"Queen?" Bairrfhionn mumbled.

"Up!"

He scrambled to his feet, blinking in the light.

She barked, "The Roman is gone!"

His brow furrowed. "Roman?"

"Do you need the flat of my sword against your thick head to wake you up? The Roman tribune!"

"Gone? But his guards—"

"Are as besotted as you, fool!"

Bairrfhionn spread his hands. "It can't be! When I looked, he was secure in his room in your dwelling."

"Well, he isn't now."

Bairrfhionn straightened. "I'll slay the guards."

"You will not," Boudicca countermanded. "Not unless you want to join them."

Bairrfhionn glowered.

Boudicca continued, "I'll need every man for when we meet the Romans. There are enough who died quarreling in the night."

"Then I'll track the Roman down."

"He'll be long gone. He won't have waited around for you to regain your feeble senses."

A flicker of white in the distance caught her attention. A robed Druí hurried to her. "Get out of my sight," she said to Bairrfhionn.

The chieftain hustled toward a knot of breakfasting warriors.

Boudicca faced the oncoming figure.

"Where's the Roman?" Lovernios demanded. "Your house is empty."

Boudicca's breath whistled, "Escaped in the night."

"Escaped?" Lovernios halted. His dark, burning eyes stared at her.

Boudicca met the gaze.

"What aren't you telling me?" he finally asked, quietly.

"*I?* What do you imply, Druí?" She leaned closer, to glare down at him.

"Nothing," he said, "and perhaps everything."

"My vows stand unbroken," Boudicca claimed.

"Perhaps." Lovernios stroked his chin. "But are those vows the highest you hold?"

"Explain yourself!"

"Sometimes," Lovernios implied, "a heart or a house is divided."

"My heart is set on the extermination of the Romans."

"But does that include all Romans?"

"Yes!"

"I wonder." Lovernios spun on his heel.

"Where are you going?" Boudicca called after him.

The Druí didn't break stride. "To find one who knows."

"You won't learn anything."

"Nothing, also, is learning."

Boudicca bit her lip.

Lovernios disappeared from sight.

Boudicca swung her sword with both hands and brought it down on a stripped corpse. The body bounced as the blade bit into it.

"Curse you, Romans! Curse every one of you!"

She jerked the sword free.

"Bairrfhionn!" she bellowed at the group of warriors. "Bring my chariot!"

Ailidh woke as sunshine dappled the copse, with her neck stiff and sore. She massaged the knotted muscles, then wiped sleep crusted in the corners of her eyes. After stretching her cramped legs, she ambled through the aftermath of pillage. She skirted warriors still in slumber, others waking, groggy, and a few on their feet.

Some, whose greed had led to argument, and argument to brawls, would never wake again. She passed one man with a dagger buried to its hilt in his chest, another whose throat had been cut, and a pair locked in deadly embrace, neither of whom would ever rise again.

A number of Roman women, used and cast aside, would also never wake to the morning.

She stepped carefully to avoid piles of excrement and puddles of vomit.

In a ransacked building she found bread and a flagon of wine over-looked by carousing warriors. A large jar held water, and this she used to wash.

As she exited the building, a low moan arrested her. She stopped and peered into the shadows behind the building.

"Help." The voice was feminine, hushed, and Roman.

A form, sprawled on the ground, stirred weakly.

Ailidh crossed quickly.

The young woman's face was a solid mass of red and purple bruises, her features battered and swollen. Blood drenched the shreds of her tunic. The skin of her arms and chest showed a deadly white against her dirty linen tunic.

Ailidh hurried to the building and brought the last of the water. She dropped to her haunches and held the jar to the girl's split lips.

The girl sipped. "Thank you."

Then her breath whispered away, her eyes fixed, and her body slumped.

Ailidh reached a hand to close the girl's puffy eyelids. She appeared no older than Ailidh herself.

She straightened, to find Lovernios standing across from the girl's body.

"She's dead," Ailidh said.

The Druí didn't glance down. "The Roman is gone. His guards were drugged. I think you helped him escape."

"I did."

Lovernios clenched his teeth. "Do you know what you've done?"

Ailidh looked down at the dead girl. "Saved a life."

"Condemned us all," Lovernios opposed.

"You exaggerate."

"Not at all." Lovernios crossed his arms over his chest. "By your action you've doomed not only the Iceni, but every Briton."

"I have not!" Ailidh flared. She stabbed a finger at his chest. "Whatever may come of this—," and she waved her other hand to encompass Boudicca's camp, "it is none of my doing."

Gently but firmly, he lowered her finger. "It is well you left. Anruth you may have been, but ollamh, never. You cannot see beyond your own desires."

"I see more clearly than you think. If this savagery is the result of bargaining with the gods, then I am glad to have no part in it."

The Druí shook his head. "You dream, Cousin. In your Way you dream too much of love."

"It is a good dream, Lovernios. Join me."

"I cannot. As long as we groan under the Roman foot and darkness hovers over us, I cannot."

Ailidh questioned, "What will you do? Take me?"

Again, Lovernios shook his head. "No. Even though you have abrogated your rights, you are kin to me. Yet despite the blood we share, you cast my mercy into my face and trample on my kindness."

"Lovernios," Ailidh whispered, shaken, "I wish you could understand . . ."

He raised a hand to rub his cheek. "You think me a monster. This face, you think, conceals the heart of a demon."

"No, I—"

"Go, Cousin. Go your way, while I go mine. Your life is in my hands, but I give it to you." He turned away. "But let me never lay eyes on you again."

Tears streamed down Ailidh's cheeks. "What will you do?" she repeated.

Lovernios paused. "Mourn for the death of my people."

Sergius rode slowly until daylight crept above the horizon and illuminated the road. The more distance he gained from Boudicca's camp, the more he relaxed. He'd expected at any moment to hear the sounds of pursuit, but they never came.

At Verulamium, he found the same confusion that had existed at Londinium. As he rode through the panicked town—smaller than Londinium and with no more defenses—the air of desperation clutched at him.

"Has the governor been here?" he asked a man, a retired soldier by the look of him.

"Been and gone." The man made a rude gesture. "Took all the active troops and left us to fend for ourselves."

"Don't fend." Sergius urged, "If you value your life, run."

"Run?" the man sneered. "From barbarians?"

"Barbarian blades are just as sharp as any other."

The fort at Durocobrivis lay deserted. Sergius kept on riding, taking frequent short rests to spare his horse.

He spent the night inside the timber walls of a deserted way station at Lactodurum. He ate of rations that Ailidh had thoughtfully packed in a bag attached to his saddle. He hadn't discovered them until he was well on his way.

The next day he rose early and set out at a steady pace, to cover ground without overtiring his horse. Again, he rested frequently, both for his benefit and the horse's, and the moon had risen by the time he reached Letocetum.

He hailed the guard, gained admission, and cantered slowly along the via praetoria. He dismounted outside the tribune's quarters and entered.

A handful of tali clattered to the floor.

Agricola jerked to his feet.

Veturius stared, wide-eyed. "Jupiter! Do I see a ghost, Agricola?"

"An ugly one," Agricola confirmed.

"It's no woman, more's the pity."

"I hope not," Sergius said tartly. "But I'll be a ghost unless I have a good meal and a bath."

Cara bounded across the room, planted her paws on his chest, and slathered her tongue across his face.

Agricola clapped him on the shoulder. "We'd given you up for dead."

"I nearly had, too," Sergius said.

He collapsed onto a chair and fondled Cara's ears.

"But how'd you get away?" Veturius asked. "Your decurio told us that bloodthirsty she-wolf had captured you."

"She did. But believe it or not, there's a shred of humanity in the wolf's heart." He told them what happened.

Veturius frowned. "So where's Ailidh?"

"After helping me escape, she stayed behind," Sergius said. A leadlike lassitude settled over him. He ran a hand across his forehead.

"We'll put Boudicca in her place soon," Agricola assessed. "Then you'll have all the time in the world for love."

"Boudicca's army is huge," Sergius expounded. "Has the *Augusta* arrived from Isca?"

Agricola pursed his lips. "We expect them any day. And when they arrive, we'll be ready for that Iceni tigress."

"There are so many Iceni." Sergius repeated, "So many . . . ."

TWENTY-FIVE

Conversation at the morning staff meeting arrested in midsentence as Sergius trailed Veturius and Agricola into the plainly furnished, square room in the fort at Letocetum that Suetonius Paulinus had adopted as his office. Bright sunlight shafted cheerily through open windows and birdcalls wafted in from outside.

Had the situation been less critical, he might have enjoyed the effect he created. It wasn't every day that senior officers looked as if they'd seen a man rise from the grave. Sergius wondered, for a fleeting moment, if this was similar to how Christus felt meeting his disciples on the day he rose from the dead.

Suetonius Paulinus stood on the far side of a table, the room's only piece of furniture, flanked by his officers. The governor noted Sergius's arrival with only a momentary flicker of surprise before his face resumed its normal composure. Gellius Marcianus, however, after a moment of initial shock, gave him a welcoming smile and murmured, "Tribune," while Titus goggled.

"Look who's back!" Pertinax exclaimed.

Even Adventus acknowledged him with a friendly nod. Legates Crispus and Falco appeared perplexed, obviously unaware of the reason for Sergius's prior absence.

"Tribune Lysias reporting as ordered, sir," Sergius said to the governor. "I apologize for my delay."

In a matter-of-fact tone, as if Sergius had returned from a routine reconnaissance, Suetonius said, "You've seen Boudicca's camp from the inside, Lysias?"

Sergius nodded. Trust the commander to be interested in military details. He didn't ask how Sergius had been captured or managed to escape, or how he was feeling. Adapt to the unexpected—that had been Caesar's motto, and Suetonius adopted it too. The arrival of a tribune presumed lost wouldn't affect the commander's gravitas.

"I have, sir." Sergius suddenly felt isolated in a rectangle of sunshine on the floor. Tersely, he described what he had observed. The officers listened without interruption. "Her warriors appear to behave as if at an orgy," he concluded.

Marcianus snorted. "Boudicca has a rabble, not an army. She may command some of the nobles, but for the most part each man does as he wills."

"Typical barbarian behavior," Falco scoffed. "No central command."

Suetonius's eyes narrowed, and his gray brows drew together. He scrutinized first Falco, then Marcianus. "Is that what you think?" The chill gaze focused on Sergius. "Do you agree, Tribune?"

Sergius glanced at Marcianus, then back to the commander.

"With respect, sir, not entirely."

"Why not?"

"Because of her actions, sir."

"Explain."

"She's gathered a huge army. Sacking Camulodunum required little effort. After that, Londinium would have been easy prey. But instead, Boudicca anticipated Legate Cerialis's response, lay in wait, and destroyed him. Only then did she turn to Londinium. Yes, her warriors loot and rape, but I think she has more control over her army than we realize."

Titus snorted from his position leaning against a wall. "Did you indulge in looted wine yourself, Lysias?"

"Mind your tongue!" Sergius snapped. "Boudicca's not a milkmaid in a pique. She is a queen who has suffered a great insult, and who commands the loyalty of her people. More than that, she's close to a Druid—perhaps one herself."

"How do you know that?" Titus sneered. "Did she tell you?"

"I saw him. And maybe being a queen makes Boudicca a Druidess."

Marcianus fondled his jowls. "Druidic involvement could account for her ability to raise so many warriors in so short a time."

"It would indeed," Suetonius concurred. "Your estimate of what she'll do, Lysias?"

Sergius thought. "Turn north, sir. With the *Hispana* out of commission, her warriors will be seeking more easy plunder. Cogidubnus poses no threat, whereas Verulamium is ripe for the taking."

While Camulodunum had preened itself as the capitol, and Londinium throve as a rough and cocky trade center, Verulamium turned its nose up at both. Though the smallest city of the three, Verulamium prided itself on the quality of its citizens and the nobility of its villas. Verulamium was rich.

Suetonius nodded, "Agreed."

"Or," Agricola offered, "she could turn east, destroy Rutupiae, and cut us off from all support."

Suetonius digested the comment. "She's already between us and Rutupiae. A pity we haven't the troops there to catch her in a pincer movement."

Sergius theorized, "Boudicca knows that we're the real threat. At the moment, her warriors want loot, and plenty of it. They'll sack Verulamium first. After that, she'll track us. Rutupiae's garrison can be dealt with later."

Porcius Crispus suggested, "We can march and intercept her. Meet the Britons while they're sated. You know what barbarians are like. They'll be fighting among themselves before long."

"They are already," Sergius revealed. "They've been drinking, gorging, and squabbling."

"Boudicca's numbers grow daily," *Valeria*'s Virius Falco countered, picking at his fingernails. "If we delay, we'll find ourselves outnumbered more than we are already."

"There's the problem of food, too," Marcianus added. "Since we're cut off from Rutupiae, if we delay, we'll run short. Pity we destroyed the granaries on Mona."

Suetonius scowled, then nodded. "With the *Hispana* immobilized, *Gemina* and *Valeria* will have to bear the weight of glory until *Augusta* arrives," he responded. "But it would be suicide to fight Boudicca on her terms and her ground. If we're on the march, then we're vulnerable."

"We could send to Rome for reinforcements, sir," Agricola suggested. "Wait Boudicca out. Maybe her army would fall apart of its own accord—*somebody* needs to plant crops."

Sergius regarded, "It might not fall apart if she's a Druidess. The warriors wouldn't dare desert."

Veturius cut in. "Surely even a Druid's influence will wane with time. The necessity for the fundamentals of life would assert itself."

"We can't count on that," Sergius stated.

Suetonius tapped a finger on the table, signaling silence. "It would take too long for a messenger to reach Rome, reinforcements to be approved, and legions to be transported here—although Rome will have to be notified of the situation. By that time, other tribes, sensing a weakness, will join Boudicca's forces."

"Would that be bad?" Agricola offered. "We'd know who were enemies and who were truly allies."

"We'd also have the entire province in flames," Suetonius replied.

"Cartimandua might keep the Brigantes in line," Marcianus said.

"Or she might not. The Dumnonii, the Silures, or the Ordovices might rise. No. It's up to us. We must strike quickly, but not in haste."

"What's your plan, sir?" Marcianus asked.

"Bring Boudicca to us," Suetonius stated. "Let *her* army do the marching, not ours. Choose the ground where we will stand, and make Boudicca take the offensive."

Sergius said, "The Britons will be overconfident, sir. After sacking Camulodunum and Londinium and bloodying *Hispana*, they won't believe they can be stopped. They'll expect another easy victory."

Veturius snarled, "Their victory over us wasn't easy."

"No offense," Sergius consoled, touching Veturius on the shoulder. "I know you fought hard. But they caught you by surprise in an unfavorable location."

"They may expect an easy victory, but they won't get one," Suetonius growled.

Falco proposed, "What if Boudicca chooses not to fight?"

"Lysias is correct. She'll fight. And we'll give her no choice," Suetonius announced. "We'll make it so Boudicca can't ignore us. She'll come for us. And when she does, we'll be ready."

"Excuse me, sir," Sergius asked, "but how do you propose to make Boudicca come to us?"

"A good question," Falco concurred. "If they have easy plunder, why face battle?"

Suetonius's lips curved into a grim smile. "Because we'll make them angry. So angry that they'll forget about plunder and discipline."

"Great," Veturius muttered in Sergius's ear, "just what we need. Bloodthirsty barbarians aren't enough—let's have angry bloodthirsty barbarians."

"So far, Boudicca's warriors have obeyed her," Suetonius continued, pacing across the room and back to his original position. "But what if they don't? Men who desire plunder may obey if they believe it to be in their best interests, but angry men are hard to control."

Marcianus held up a hand. "I agree that it would be beneficial to disorganize Boudicca's army, but how? How do we anger them?"

"What else do the Britons prize besides plunder?" Suetonius asked. "What lies near Letocetum?"

Sergius glanced around the officers, noting blank looks. He too, shook his head in ignorance.

"Sacred sites," Suetonius disclosed. "The centers of their religion." He jammed a finger on the table for each name. "Vernemeton, Manduessedum, Ratae." His voice hardened, "We put them to the torch."

Four cohorts of infantry with accompanying auxiliaries and cavalry set out from Letocetum's fort that afternoon. Suetonius divided the honors. A cohort of the *Valeria* tramped toward Ratae while one of *Augusta's* was dispatched for Manduessedum. The cohort from *Gemina* targeted the major sanctuary at Vernemeton. The final cohort, also of the *Gemina*, marched the scant ten miles to Pennocrucium, to despoil the grove of Cenn Croich. Sacred to Crom Dubh, the dark destroying one, Agricola informed Sergius.

Chief Centurion Helvius Adventus commanded the main *Gemina* detachment, but Sergius requested and received permission from Gellius Marcianus to accompany it. Veturius also, with no legionary duties to concern him, joined the expedition.

Glumly, Agricola announced his intention not to accompany *Augusta's* cohort. "What's at Manduessedum?" he moaned. "The Anker, a sacred river. What are we going to do—pee in it?"

"There's more than the river, surely," Sergius countered.

"Not much. A ceremonial center, apparently. Some circular structure where the Britons race horses. So I'm going to supervise the weapons inventory." Agricola turned and walked away.

Titus, however, embraced the opportunity for further action. His eyes glittered as the two cohorts—*Valeria's* and *Gemina's*—marched in company.

He remarked on Ratae, "The goddess Anu wants sacrifices, does she? We'll sacrifice the Britons themselves on her altars and see how she likes it."

"Agreed," Veturius remarked. "The more the better. If this doesn't anger the Britons, I don't know what will."

The cohorts followed the road that led to Londinium, the same road the legions had driven cross-country to Mona the previous fall. Sergius wondered if perhaps the road itself was a source of Briton hostility, penetrating as it did through a network of sacred sites. But until the attack on Mona, the Britons' sacred sites had been left alone.

The regular thump-thump of hundreds of caligae on the stone road seemed to Sergius to be a reassuring sound, a symbol of Roman solidity. The jingle of weapons and armor and the swish of leather kilts added to the familiar, martial tramp.

Reassuring. Solid. That was the strength of a legion. Not the dark mysticism of the Druidae or the disorganized tactics of the Britons. Rather, the strength of hundreds and thousands of men acting as one.

With such strength, it was hard to believe that the Roman presence in Britannia was threatened. If he hadn't seen Londinium and Boudicca's horde for himself, Sergius wouldn't have credited the stories.

Eventually, the cohorts left the road and followed native paths and tracks into wilder country where thick loam and dense grass cushioned the footsteps.

Adventus avoided the darker forests and tried to steer the cohorts to open ground. Adventus rode confidently, but Sergius noticed the chief centurion kept alert at all times and spread out a wide screen of pickets.

But the landscape seemed curiously deserted. Fields, where farmers should have been planting crops, stood unattended. For the most part, the occasional house lay empty.

"They've probably gone to join Boudicca's plunderers," Veturius commented on the lack of inhabitants.

"They won't be able to eat gold plates," Sergius said.

"Then they'll starve, won't they?" Titus said.

But there were, after all, inhabitants—huts occupied by elderly, or women and children.

"Put them to death," Adventus ordered at the first of such, as the troops razed a motley collection of huts, hacking the supports until the thatched roofs collapsed into shapeless piles of straw.

Sergius drew the chief centurion aside. "Must you kill everyone?"

"We're at war, Tribune," Adventus replied, stony faced, as an elderly couple and their two daughters were dispatched with the sword.

"Do we war with *these?*"

"Everyone," Adventus emphasized.

"What are you complaining about?" Titus interrupted as he wiped the blade of his gladius clean. "The Britons slew everyone in Camulodunum and Londinium—and they will in Verulamium, too, if they haven't already. Did you see them spare *our* women and elderly?"

Sergius shivered at the remembrance of the mutilated women and the murdered men he'd seen. "Does one atrocity warrant another?"

"Have you got flowers for guts?" Titus sneered.

Sergius gritted his teeth.

"The governor's order stands," Adventus closed the discussion.

The cohorts left the pitiful remains to molder—mute warnings for the women's absent menfolk. Sergius rode in silence beside Veturius.

After a few miles, Veturius asked, "What's crawled under your kilt?"

Sergius gestured behind him. "This. All the killing. Was that old couple or were those women any threat to us?"

"Maybe not now," Veturius replied. "But they'd have sons. And their sons would fight ours. Better slay them now."

"That's ridiculous! Who can predict what will happen in twenty years?"

"No one. That's the idea."

"You sound more like Titus every day," Sergius said.

"Thanks for the compliment," Veturius replied. He massaged his wounded arm. "Those savages almost did me in. I have no love for them."

"I don't believe you."

"Then start."

Sergius pursed his lips. Once, during his service in Aquileia, he'd had to arrest a man accused of murder. The man had been an Armenian, a craftsman reduced to poverty by the loss of his stock at sea. He'd been caught stealing food for his family by a homeowner. While trying to escape, he'd pushed the homeowner who'd fallen awkwardly and broken his neck.

Veturius had been slightly acquainted with the accused and had pleaded passionately before the praetor on his behalf. The man's uncivilized origins hadn't mattered to Veturius then. Not that the praetor had listened.

After midday, the cohorts parted. Titus left with his division to devastate the shrines of Anu, while *Gemina's* men marched toward Vernemeton.

Adventus called a halt in late afternoon, and the cohort pitched camp. Sergius moved absently through the familiar routine. As night fell, the gloomy forests closed around. Men shivered at the whooing of owls, and sentries stiffened at every whisper of leaf or underbrush.

The same thoughts and sensations that he'd had at Mona closed in on Sergius as he lay in his tent. Did Druidae live in Vernemeton? If so, were they sacrificing? Was some unfortunate wretch even now shedding his entrails in an unspeakably loathsome ceremony?

He shuddered at the thought.

Such practices *ought* to be exterminated. After all, Rome had outlawed human sacrifice over a hundred and fifty years ago. This was their duty, to drag the barbarians into civilization.

But the people? The ones who lived in the poor huts? They rated less than animals to hear Titus, and Adventus, and Veturius talk. Mild, pleasure-loving Veturius—whom Sergius hadn't thought possessed a solid bone in his body!

And yet, these people were Ailidh's people. They were her blood, her kin. These people, these inhabitants of Britannia, with their crude customs, their atrocious beliefs, their resistance to things Roman, had produced Ailidh. Good came out of the most unlikely sources.

And again, as at Mona, he wondered, *Is this right?*

You're Roman, a voice whispered. *Of course it's right.*

There is neither Jew nor Greek, whispered a counter. And it added, *Nor Roman nor Briton.*

Even Boudicca, priestess of a fearsome alien goddess, had found it in her heart to give him a chance for life.

"Quit mumbling," Veturius grumbled in a drowsy voice from the dark. "Go to sleep."

"Sorry," Sergius apologized.

Eventually, sleep claimed him, but morning came too soon.

From a distance, Vernemeton appeared no different from a thousand other forested hills in Britannia.

Sergius exhaled. He'd expected something—a chill inside, a prickle at the nape of his neck, an uneasiness of spirit—but he felt nothing. He sniffed and inhaled only the fragrance of dew on growing things.

As the cohort approached the western slope of the hill, an irregularity appeared in the trees. If he squinted, the irregularity developed straighter lines than the surrounding woods—lines that betokened the presence of human activity. A shrine, certainly, hid within the trees.

As the legionaries closed to within a few hundred feet, figures streamed from the shrine, and ranged themselves in an arc before the grove.

Veturius snorted. "They'd do better to remain in the trees. Out here, they might just as well kneel and bare their necks."

Chief Centurion Adventus barked orders. "Ready!"

Gladii rasped from scabbards. Shields raised to defensive positions.

From his mounted position at the rear of the cohort, Sergius studied the two-dozen-odd defenders. A mere handful of warriors bolstered the ranks. As at Mona, the defenders comprised Druidae, including priests and women.

But here, there were no hordes screaming curses, waving blazing brands, calling down the wrath of the gods. Only a pitiful few, determined to give their lives for a hopeless cause.

"Forward!" Adventus yelled.

With a jingle of metal loricae, the cohort surged into a jog. Sandaled feet slapped the ground.

As they closed with the Britons, the Romans shouted battle cries.

The cohort swept over the Britons as a wave swept over the shore, washing sand and detritus before it. In moments the Britons were reduced to immobile, bleeding bodies strewn across the ground.

"Not even a fight," Veturius said, disgust in his voice. He stared at his unbloodied sword and shoved it back into his scabbard.

The shrine stood before them: a long, rectangular building, timber-framed wattle with a thatched roof.

"Burn it," Adventus said.

Sergius clenched his fists. "There may be more people inside."

The chief centurion placed his hands on his hips. He didn't look at Sergius. "Then they can stay inside and roast, or come out and die quickly."

Legionaries hurried to light torches and cast the burning brands onto the roof. The dry thatch ignited. Hissing and smoking, the flames raced from one end of the shrine to another, until the entire building erupted into a single huge pyre.

Screams came from inside, and then the roof collapsed in a gout of flame, silencing them.

Adventus gestured to other legionaries, "Cut down the trees."

Ax blows reverberated through the forest, and one by one the oaks of the sacred grove plunged to the earth, entwining their branches in embrace as if sorrowful for their end.

You're being overly imaginative, Sergius told himself. *The trees don't feel anything.* Yet it seemed as if each ax blow was itself a cry from the oaken giants.

All day long the legionaries labored, until by nightfall the hillside looked as bare and desolate as any ruin Boudicca had left in her wake.

Grim faced, Adventus surveyed the rubble. "Boudicca won't ignore this," he asserted. "Even if she wants to, her warriors won't let her."

He swung away. "Tomorrow, we'll rejoin the legions."

Sergius turned his back on the remnants of the Britons' worship center.

Granted, Briton beliefs were as unreal as the Roman gods he no longer believed in; and granted, too, that Suetonius was a general to be reckoned with, who knew how to gain the advantage over an enemy even before battle lines were drawn, but . . .

He closed his eyes.

What would Ailidh say to one who desecrated her land and country?

Suetonius Paulinus accepted Adventus's report with scarcely a flicker of emotion when the troops returned to Letocetum the next day.

"Good. The other cohorts were equally successful." He spoke to Sergius, "Post scouts along the road to Londinium. The moment Boudicca's forces move, I want to know about it."

"Yes, sir," Sergius said, making notes to draft orders to a cohors equitatae. "Where are we to meet the Britons, sir?"

Suetonius swung a map around to him and pointed.

"Near Manduessedum. When Boudicca's army comes close enough, we'll move to new positions."

Sergius realized abruptly that Suetonius's cross-country expedition hadn't been simply to examine the conditions in Londinium. The commander had been assessing the entire stretch of country. A good general possessed foresight; Suetonius had used his to decide where he wanted to meet Boudicca.

"Until then, sir?" Sergius asked.

Suetonius regarded him, then moved his gaze to stare into the distance. "Until then, we wait."

TWENTY-SIX

"They've done what?" Boudicca's high-pitched exclamation matched the ripping of fabric as her clenched hands tore a gaping rent in her léine. Around her, the ruins of Verulamium smoked, and those people of the Catuvellauni who'd taken to Roman ways and built themselves a Roman city lay dead upon the ground. Verulamium's destruction had been a repeat of Londinium and Camulodunum; Boudicca had wondered if her warriors would become complacent. It hadn't happened. The more her warriors spread destruction, the more it seemed as if blood-lust gripped them.

Bairrfhionn took a step back and glanced to Weylyn for support.

The younger man spoke nervously. "The Romans have desecrated Vernemeton."

"As well as Manduessedum, Pennocrucium, and Ratae," Bairrfhionn added.

"Morrigan curse them, they've gone too far!" Boudicca shouted. "Our money, our lands, and now our gods!"

She smacked a hand against a wheel of her chariot. One of the horses snorted and reared.

Warriors crowded around, drawn by the shouts. Boudicca's eyes flashed over the sea of angry faces.

"Enough pillage," Bairrfhionn roared. "Let's destroy the Roman scourge once and for all!"

"Now," Weylyn added.

Boudicca spun away and stalked around the chariot. She gripped the frightened horse's halter and quieted the animal. She took several deep breaths herself, and slowly her initial burst of outrage subsided.

The warriors waited for her to speak.

"Why?" she mused.

Bairrfhionn gaped as if he couldn't believe his ears. "Why? You ask that?"

Boudicca waved a hand. "I wonder why they destroyed those places."

"It's obvious," Weylyn scoffed. "Mona wasn't sufficient. They mean to destroy everything."

"It's more than that," Boudicca reasoned. "Suetonius is a smart man. He plans something. The Romans have never before violated a sacred place merely for itself."

"They violate the entire country!" Bairrfhionn raged. His mustache bristled. "They slaughter the leaders of the people."

"Who cares *why* they did it?" Weylyn demanded. He faced the assembled warriors. "Who's with me? Who will slay the Roman swine?"

"*We will!*" the warriors shouted.

"We mustn't underestimate Suetonius," Boudicca cautioned.

"Look around," Weylyn gestured. "We have twenty times his men! We'll slay them as we would a chicken." His teeth flashed. "This is no time for words. This is a time for action!"

Swords flickered in the air. "*Slay the Romans!*"

Boudicca ran her eyes over the shouting horde.

"*Death to the sons of swine!*"

The blood rose within her. Her heart hammered with the words.

Vernemeton was one of the most sacred of all sites. A people without gods was no people.

Her own sword raised above her head.

"Death to Rome!" she shouted, again, and again, and again.

Ailidh heard the shouts from a distance, from the outskirts of Verulamium. She sat in the shadow of a crumbling villa, eating pillaged bread and drinking stolen wine—or was it stolen? Could one steal from the dead? She'd entered Verulamium after Boudicca's horde had wreaked destruction and satisfied herself with whatever foodstuffs the warriors left.

She'd avoided Lovernios and kept far away from Boudicca. She didn't want to be with Boudicca's horde, but with the country in flames, where could she go? No, as a single woman she was safer following them.

No one paid attention to a solitary figure seated in the shadows. She remained apart as warriors by the thousand took to the road—on foot, on horseback, or by chariot. Wagons of family members rumbled away from the ruins of Britannia's third city. Queen Boudicca's twin-horsed chariot swept through the army, the queen's harsh voice a strident call to action.

Ailidh laid her hand to her chest, where unseen fingers gripped like a terror in the night.

Somewhere, at the end of that road, Sergius waited with his legion.

The swarm of Iceni warriors and their allies seemed endless, as numerous as the stars. Ailidh had never seen so many Britons gathered together. Not even Caratacus had wielded such an army. What chance did the Romans have against them?

Never before had Iceni, Trinovantes, Coritani, and even some Catuvellauni fought together, united against a common foe.

She raised her eyes to the sky. A flock of geese flew in V-formation high overhead, paralleling the course of the warriors. They flew straight: as Druid taught the souls of the departed flew straight.

She laid aside the stale bread and flat wine and rose to her feet. She watched until the geese became black specks in the sky and finally disappeared. Then she mounted her horse and joined the trailers of the vast throng of Boudicca's army.

"You're right to be worried."

Boudicca started, her hand reflexively searching for her sword. Then she relaxed. "You startled me, Druí."

Lovernios fell into step beside her.

Deep in thought, Boudicca had been walking aimlessly amongst her horde. The night seemed quiet. Perhaps the warriors were exhausted from pillage and rapine, for tonight no screams pierced the air. Few warriors caroused. Here and there a knot of men talked or gambled or boasted, or a man and woman lay intertwined, but the drunken revelry had passed. Perhaps anger had banished the spirit of pleasure.

"What makes you think I'm worried?"

Lovernios gestured. "I see a woman walking without speech, without smiling, without seeming to watch where she goes. Her daughters are with a serving woman. There are no Romans near, but her hand never strays far from her sword."

Boudicca gave a harsh laugh. "Why should I worry, Druí?"

"Because you have made a mistake. You know this, but don't admit it."

"Mistake?" Boudicca kicked at a cast-off cloak on the ground. "In a few days, I shall be avenged. The Romans will have paid for the insult to the line of Prasutagus with their lives. We shall be free, Lovernios—free."

"Suetonius prepares a trap."

Boudicca snorted. "He hasn't the men."

"But he has the skill." Lovernios traced in the air with his finger. "Better to destroy Rutupiae. Cut the Romans off from their supplies. Let them hunger and thirst. Let time prey on their nerves until their hands shake and their knees knock and their bowels cramp. Let them come to us."

Boudicca rationalized, "The people want vengeance now, not in the future. Already the nobles itch to see the destruction of the Romans. How can I persuade them otherwise? And what is Rutupiae? It is nothing, an insignificance to be crushed at leisure."

She snuggled her cloak tighter. "It has gone too far, Druí. The Romans attack our gods. That can't continue."

"If Cartimandua were to assist—"

"No!" Boudicca slashed a hand to cut Lovernios off. "I will not share my triumph with that traitorous vixen. She betrayed Caratacus to Rome. She would do the same to me."

"The Brigantes are powerful."

"No," Boudicca repeated, quieter. "We must walk the path we have begun, Druí."

"That is why you worry," Lovernios concluded, but Boudicca ignored him and stalked into the darkness.

Waiting took a week, but finally a scout brought word that Boudicca's army had stirred from Londinium, sacked Verulamium, and advanced westward. For a week, the legions had sat and waited, leaving camp only to forage, their numbers growing each day as auxiliary troops arrived from some outlying fort.

But their numbers didn't swell quickly enough, and the *Augusta* didn't come.

The strain of waiting showed itself in the officers' jerky movements and irritable moods. Veturius seemed as tight as a drawn bowstring—enough so that Sergius hesitated to speak to him, friends though they were. Titus had raised himself to a pitch of fighting fury that needed only the sight of a Briton to touch him off. Agricola forgot to talk philosophy. The normally placid Pertinax neglected to smile.

Whispers and impossible-to-ignore rumors ran rampant among legionaries who weren't privy to official policy and reasoning. Why had the Britons rebelled, men wondered?

The rebellion was only to be expected from barbarians, ran one reply. It was a futile, doomed effort by those who didn't comprehend the benefits of civilization.

Or ran a counteropinion, it was the result of offending the Britons' gods. As punishment for desecrating the shrines of Mona, the gods had raised up Boudicca to punish the Romans.

The second interpretation proved stronger than the first, and men worried. The officers, who knew otherwise, couldn't malign government policies and had little with which to counter the rumors. Disaffection ran high, despite the efforts of the augurs who sought to reassure the troops by consulting the cages of sacred chickens on a daily basis.

At long last a courier arrived from Isca.

Sergius pitied the man, who shivered in his boots as he delivered his message.

The *Augusta* hadn't budged. It wasn't coming.

Poenius Postumus sent his regrets, but he thought it best to remain on guard in the southwest.

Sergius anticipated Suetonius's gravitas would crack under the shock.

Augusta's legate's composure did. Porcius Crispus's face went from white to scarlet to purple. "That sniveling coward! If Poenius hasn't fallen on his sword, I'll personally hold it for him."

"That alters the whole complexion of the situation," Marcianus remarked. "We were counting on the *Augusta*."

"I don't believe it," Crispus moaned. "What man worth his salt would refuse command of a legion?"

"What do we do?" Falco worried. "Withdraw and delay battle while we send more messages to Isca?"

Sergius studied Suetonius. The governor's initial surprise had yielded to an intense concentration. Flexibility was Julius Caesar's secret, Suetonius had told Sergius. What could the commander come up with to replace the loss of a legion?

"No delay," Suetonius said. "That would only play into Boudicca's hands—give her chance to regroup her warriors and restrain their impetuosity." His gaze shifted to Crispus. "Nor do we send messages to the *Augusta*. Poenius may not be the only one hesitant to fight. I don't trust the *Augusta* anymore."

Crispus seemed to wilt. Sergius snuck a glance at Agricola, who seemed equally crestfallen, as if he'd taken a fist in the gut. He felt a pang of sympathy for his friend. He tried to imagine how he'd feel if the *Gemina* fled in the face of adversity. For an entire legion to refuse to fight strained the bounds of credulity.

Suetonius would be justified in ordering the decimation of *Augusta*—the death of every tenth man as punishment for cowardice. But that was unlikely. Despite Suetonius's comment that he no longer trusted the *Augusta*, blame for the legion's failure lay with the man in command—Poenius Postumus. The rank and file probably never heard Suetonius's order or had no idea that they were called to the defense of Britannia.

Suetonius concluded, "We fight as we are."

Manduessedum, where Suetonius Paulinus had chosen to face Boudicca, lay only thirteen miles from Letocetum, but to Sergius they seemed the longest miles of his life. Beside him, Veturius rode silently, as disinclined to conversation as Sergius himself or the brooding hills that flanked the columns.

Long miles.

Longer than the dusty road from Corinth to Aquileia, when joy from his newfound faith crossed swords with anxiety over his parents' reaction.

Longer than the voyage from Rome to Britannia, when eager novelty warred with the knowledge that he was leaving behind everyone he knew and loved.

Longer than . . . longer than the winter miles that separated Deva from Camulodunum, that had separated him from Ailidh.

Now, though each mile brought him physically closer to her, paradoxically, each step also took him farther away.

Was Ailidh still among the vast horde that had risen to Boudicca's banner, the army that scouts tracked as it tramped the road toward them? Or had she abandoned the vengeful queen and sought refuge elsewhere?

He gnawed on a knuckle. She wouldn't have fled. Ailidh was no Roman woman who would do as he had told her. What an independent spirit she possessed! She'd claimed she'd be safe among the followers of Boudicca, that her status as anruth—suspect as it was—still cloaked her with respect.

He prayed she was right.

Despite the brave clamor made by more than ten thousand marching men, the Romans were hideously, almost hopelessly, outnumbered. Boudicca's forces had mushroomed. The scouts who braved death to bring report claimed the warriors numbered beyond counting.

Maybe his mother was correct. Parthia *would* have been better.

Perhaps the scouts overestimated.

But if not . . .

"Cheer up," Agricola's voice broke into his thoughts. "I see black thoughts ruminating in your mind."

Sergius glanced to his left. His friend had brought his horse into line beside him. Beyond Agricola, Titus waved a hand.

Agricola had taken the news of *Augusta's* defalcation hard, but he seemed to be making a conscious effort to retrieve his normal insouciance.

"I'm lost in a world of 'perhaps,'" Sergius confessed.

"'Perhaps' may never come," Agricola replied. "Glory will."

"Glory?"

"Of course. You don't seriously think these savages can beat us? No matter how many of them there are."

"They've made a good showing so far."

"So what? Hey Titus!" Agricola shouted, "What would your father say to being outnumbered twenty to one?"

The younger Flavius bared his teeth. "The worse the odds, the greater the glory."

"See?" Agricola said. "Titus agrees with me. And Vespasian never lost a battle."

Sergius grimaced. "Now he's got you saying it."

Agricola grinned. "I bet your father never faced so many barbarians."

Despite himself, Sergius smiled. "Not all at once anyway."

"So you'll be a leg up on him."

Sergius tensed, realized Agricola meant no disrespect for his father's disability—probably didn't even know about his father's lost leg—and responded, "I am already."

"There you have it."

A voice spoke so quietly that for a second Sergius didn't realize it belonged to Veturius. "It's not a game."

His friend's gaze was fixed straight ahead.

"What did he say?" Agricola leaned over in his saddle.

"It's not a game!" Veturius lashed, his voice suddenly brittle.

Agricola spread a palm. "Nobody said it was."

"Everybody acts as if we're going to a mock battle at training camp!"

"I don't see the commander smiling," Sergius defended.

Agricola followed Sergius's indication of where Suetonius rode, flanked by Marcianus, Crispus, and Falco. "He has both the chance for greater glory and the risk of greater failure."

Sergius gravely reflected, "If we lose, then Britannia is lost."

"Then we mustn't lose." Agricola looked at Veturius until the other man returned his gaze. "I'll do my part."

"Agricola!" Titus called. "Let's shed these gloomy comrades of ours and ride ahead."

Agricola raised a hand in salute to Sergius. "We'll win." He and Titus rode ahead.

Sergius studied the unwavering ranks of armed men. "Perhaps he's right."

Veturius said nothing.

A new voice said, "Do we really have a chance, sir?" Septimus Justus drew alongside.

Sergius hesitated, thrown off stride by the hopeful expression on the young tribune's face. An officer's job was to inspire, he reminded himself—not only the enlisted men, but junior officers too.

He nodded with as much conviction as he could muster. "Yes. We have a fighting chance."

Justus seemed to relax.

A fighting chance.

That's exactly what it would be.

"Manduessedum, Queen," Bairrfhionn reported, reining his horse to match pace with Boudicca's chariot. "The Romans have halted their march."

Boudicca swayed as the chariot bumped over uneven ground. She nodded. "Manduessedum it shall be, then." She gripped the shaft of her lance. "By all the gods and goddesses, this will be a great victory! What the great Caratacus couldn't accomplish, I, a woman, shall."

"Right in the heart of our sacred country," Bairrfhionn added. "The gods will have to listen."

"They'll listen, all right."

Boudicca glanced at a silent figure who rode alongside her chariot. For some reason, the man's presence—his hooded eyes seeming to see beyond what normal eyes could perceive and his laconic speech when he deemed to speak at all—unnerved her. He seemed less a man and more a spirit. "Do you agree, Druí?"

Lovernios shook himself from a reverie in which he saw a wren struggle against death and a woman fall from a horse at an eagle's stoop.

Boudicca stood as tall as the goddess Epona herself, her long tawny hair streamed over her multicolored léine, and the sun sparkled on her torques and rings. Her aggressive posture and bright eyes demanded an answer of him.

He spoke over the rumble of chariot wheels, "If victory went always to the just, then our cause could not fail."

She frowned. "It shall *not* fail, Druí! I have sworn."

"Yes," he said. "You have."

Her eyes held his a moment longer, then she turned to Bairrfhionn. "Find us a place to rest. Tonight we shall gather strength. In the morning we shall crush the Romans."

Lovernios allowed Boudicca's chariot to pull ahead of him.

He pillowed his chin on his chest and thought.

He thought of injustices that needed to be righted, of an enemy to be repelled, and of a people that couldn't quite grasp the nature of the threat that hung over them. He thought of a sacrifice that had escaped him.

Most of all he pondered a dream he wished he'd never had.

The morn would bring death or glory, Sergius thought, as the legions camped for the night. And yet he felt no fear, only a kind of vague emotion that he couldn't name. Resignation? Not quite. Perhaps a calm certainty that all would be well.

But why should he feel that? Maybe it was nothing more than the self-delusion of a man clinging to a faint hope rather than facing a stark reality.

Outside his tent men laughed and boasted of the feats they'd accomplish, trying to bolster spirits. The centurions—experienced at before-battle vigils—cracked lewd jokes, banishing fear of the morrow with a veneer of humor.

Sergius heard the jokes, but he didn't laugh at them.

Some men, he knew—like Justus—would never sleep but lie awake in paroxysms of unconquerable dread.

He repeated to himself the soldier words of Paullus, saying them over and over—the lorica of righteousness, the scutum of faith, the gladius of the word of God. . . .

Weapons for a different battle, surely.

A different battle. . . .

What had Paullus written so many months ago?

"The Lord expected justice, but saw bloodshed; righteousness, but heard a cry."

Paullus was a visionary, a prophet.

He'd also encouraged Sergius to let the Spirit direct his life.

But could it matter now, when perhaps none of them would be alive tomorrow?

A wet nuzzle thrust itself against his cheek.

"I should have left you with your mistress," Sergius said to the big wolfhound. "She has a better chance of escaping this than I do."

Ailidh camped alone under the stars, wrapped in a snug cloak, her head pillowed on another, her breath misting in the cool night air.

A broad band of white crested the sky, extending farther than she could see. The stars invited her, called to her, but she was no cailleoir, a reader of the stars, that she could understand what they said.

She could understand the time of night, yes, and the seasons; but nothing more.

Tonight the stars seemed as distant and unknowable as God.

Since her pleading with Boudicca, she'd steered clear of the queen. And Lovernios went about as a man possessed by demons of despair that he couldn't exorcize.

And she?

She bore her sword, but despite the blood of Cathair that flowed through her veins, she wouldn't fight. She carried her silver staff of an-ruth that had been presented years ago, when she still had dreams of becoming ollamh.

There was no place for love in Boudicca's army, and yet that was what she wanted to offer.

Her mind played dreamily among the stars.

Manduessedum.

Camulodunum and Londinium and Verulamium.

Egomas. She blinked away a vision of his head bouncing on Londinium's cobblestones.

Airell, whom she'd known when she was a little girl.

Followers of Christus, and followers of the old gods.

Briton and Roman.

Herself and Sergius.

Sergius.

Somewhere perhaps he gazed at the same stars that teased her mind with their uninterpretable messages.

She whispered to the stars, "Tell him that I love him."

Boudicca stooped to gaze at her daughters. Aife and Cinnia slept wrapped beneath a tree, sheltered by Boudicca's chariot.

They were so pretty, Boudicca thought, as the light from her torch wavered over the girls. So pretty until the Romans despoiled them.

But come the morrow, and they'd have a future again.

They would be pretty again.

They would marry, and their sons would lead the Iceni.

Careful to make no noise to disturb her daughters, Boudicca turned aside. The girls would sleep, but there would be no sleep for her this night. In the forest, with only her torch and her sword—the sword that was the twin of Prasutagus's blade—Boudicca would pray.

And tomorrow she'd fight.

TWENTY-SEVEN

Sergius awoke before the instruments roused the legionaries from their slumbers. In his tent, with Cara beside him, nose cradled on her paws, he perched on the edge of his lectus and watched her breathe.

A dog couldn't envisage the future. Cara didn't know that he might not outlive the day.

Up and down her sides moved. In and out the breath rumbled through her broad muzzle.

He ought to pray. But a prebattle prayer seemed as difficult as a pre-battle exhortation to the troops. He could pray for victory, but did God take sides? Did it matter to God who won this conflict?

To pray for Ailidh's safety, that was easier. And for his family. For Veturius and Agricola, Paullus, Lucanus, and Aristarchus.

Up and down, in and out.

No worries for a dog.

The tent flap whispered open. Cara's ears pricked forward.

"Good morning, sir," Quintus greeted briskly.

"You're early," Sergius commented.

The beneficiarius set a plate and a cup beside Sergius.

"I'm not hungry."

"Best eat anyway, sir."

Sergius picked up a hunk of bread and studied it. Perhaps Quintus was right. Most Romans didn't eat a morning meal, but today everyone needed strength for battle. He bit into the bread. The sweetness of honey dripped off his tongue. Trust Quintus to find a delicacy like honey somewhere.

Quintus stood watching him. "To tell the truth, sir, I couldn't sleep."

"Sleepless? An old soldier like you?"

"Even old soldiers have fears, sir."

"There's no shame in being afraid," Sergius said and promptly wished he hadn't spoken. An experienced campaigner like Quintus didn't need a tribune young enough to be his grandson to spout platitudes at him.

Quintus stepped outside the tent and returned with his arms full. "Your uniform and armor are cleaned, sir."

Sergius chuckled. "Some poor footslogger had to stay up cleaning my armor?"

Quintus shrugged. "It kept his mind off other things."

Sergius stood and brushed crumbs off his tunic. "If we're to face death, we will face it as Romans." *With gravitas*, he added to himself.

"Exactly, sir."

Quintus wound Sergius's scarf around his neck.

Sergius extended his arms. Quintus lowered his lorica into place and fastened the hooks. The worn leather belt secured his kilt and his metal-tipped apron. Quintus slung the baldric across Sergius's shoulder and then adjusted his dress cloak. The dog's head brooch held it in place. Sergius tucked his dagger and gladius into their sheaths. Lastly, Quintus laced his caligae. Sergius flexed his calf muscles to make sure the laces weren't too tight.

Sergius picked up his torque and fitted it around his neck.

Quintus snapped the plume crosswise into its socket on Sergius's helmet and passed it to him. Sergius wedged it under his arm.

"Thank you." He paused. "See that Cara is placed in the rear with the baggage animals." He bent down to ruffle the dog's head. "Battle is no place for a wolfhound."

On the battlefield, the risk of Cara's being trampled ran high. She'd be safer with the baggage animals. If—God forbid—the Romans lost, some Briton would add her to his spoils.

Quintus showed uneven teeth. "I'll take care of it, sir." He held the tent flap, and Sergius strode into the morning.

Behind him, Quintus called for soldiers to roll up the tent.

Sergius spotted Veturius emerging from his own tent and waved to him. Veturius hitched his belt.

"Seen Agricola and Titus?" Sergius asked.

Veturius pointed. "Over there."

Together, they walked out onto the field where Agricola and Titus stood side by side.

Sergius studied the terrain. In daylight, the advantages of the site Suetonius Paulinus had chosen for the battle became obvious.

An escarpment running in a northwesterly direction intersected the road from Londinium to Deva. Far below, broken into fragments by overhanging bushes, trickled the silver blue line of the Anker—the river Agricola had mockingly declined to pollute. Plains and fields crested to forests on the hills.

The rising sun came from the Romans' right, picking out the multitude of greens, yellows, and browns in the valley. Past midday, though, and the full rays would shine in the Britons' eyes.

Suetonius had selected a site on the flank of the escarpment, in the entrance to a narrow defile. Sergius nodded in agreement. The Briton forward lines would crush together as they tried to advance, which would hinder their movements and present a better target. The ground shelved gently away from the army's position, meaning the Britons would have to charge uphill.

To the rear and on either side, dense forest provided protection and prevented outflanking maneuvers. In front of the army, a grassy plain afforded the Britons no cover.

The Roman legions lay in a compact, orderly, battle formation. With the full strength of Legio XIV *Gemina*, the substantial presence of Legio XX *Valeria*, and the two cohorts of the disgraced II *Augusta*, eight thousand legionaries shifted feet, checked weapons, and followed the barked orders of centurions.

The lightly armed auxiliaries and the cavalry stationed on the wings added another five thousand.

Thirteen thousand men: "Not many," Sergius said out loud.

Agricola cocked an eyelid. "But each one worth at least five Britons."

That still didn't even the odds, Sergius thought. "With the *Augusta* and the *Hispana*, we wouldn't have had to worry."

Agricola's face darkened.

"But their representatives will have to uphold their name," Sergius covered quickly, glancing at Veturius.

Titus stepped forward. "We'll cut the barbarians' hearts out anyway." He extended an arm. "Here come the fools now."

Down the hillside, a string of black dots straggled into view along the plain. Behind them flowed a dark flood of men, chariots, and horses and wagons.

"Tribunes? This is no time to be admiring the view," Gellius Marcianus lashed out.

Sergius whirled. The legate stood behind him, his purple cloak hanging loosely over his shoulder.

Sergius cleared his throat. "We were studying the commander's choice of battlefield, sir."

Marcianus narrowed his eyes against the sun. "I hope it meets with your approval."

Sergius blinked at the sarcasm in Marcianus's voice. Nerves.

"Join your legions," Marcianus ordered, and Agricola and Titus hurried away.

"Requesting permission to join the *Gemina*, sir," Veturius said.

"Granted," Marcianus replied curtly. "Follow me."

He strode toward the cohorts of the *Gemina*.

Sergius gripped Veturius's arm. "Guard my back, Gaius, and I'll guard yours."

For the first time in days, he saw a sparkle of his old friend in Veturius's eyes.

"Always," Veturius concurred. "A luckless task given me by the Fates."

Sergius glanced at the ground. "If anything happens to me, make sure Ailidh's all right."

"If anything happens to you, the same will undoubtedly be my lot. But you have my word. Not that I'll be much good at it, no thanks to Venus."

Sergius grinned. "My mind is at ease, then."

Marcianus had mounted his horse. Sergius and Veturius located their horses and did likewise.

Above the heads of the troops, the standards gleamed. Sergius gazed at the capricorn insignia of the *Gemina*, mounted beneath the gold eagle on its pole of silver. Farther around the arc of men, to his left, the aquilifer of the *Valeria* held high the running boar.

Suetonius Paulinus, scarlet cloak rippling, cantered to join them. "A fine day for a battle, Gellius," he hailed.

"It is that, sir," Legate Marcianus replied.

Sergius studied the commander's face. Despite the tension Suetonius must be feeling, he gave no indication that the day would bring anything more than another minor skirmish. Though the fate of the province rested on his shoulders, he held them stiffly erect.

A nervous general would create nervous troops; Suetonius radiated calm assurance. *He must have nerves of steel,* Sergius thought, conscious of his heart flip-flopping like a landed fish.

Suetonius looked around. "Where's the chief centurion?"

"Here, sir," Helvius Adventus pushed his way into sight.

"Are the troops ready?"

"Ready and eager for battle, sir."

"Good." Suetonius beckoned to Marcianus, the two other legionary commanders, and Sergius. "I will address the troops."

He turned his horse tightly and cantered onto the plain before the army, riding in review along the ranks. Sergius allowed the legates to precede him.

The troops stood at ease, shields resting on the ground, javelins held in light grips. Sergius tried to imagine himself as a Briton, facing that solid, unbroken front of red and blue shields, punctuated with the wicked points of sword blades. Roman legions such as these had rolled over the known world from Hispana to Armenia, Britannia to the Atlas Mountains.

A light breeze ruffled the officers' plumes and tugged at the scarlet and purple cavalry vexilla. The breeze also brought cries and shouts from the advancing Britons. The plain darkened as Boudicca's army formed, gathering into tribes and families. The more adventurous crept to within earshot of the legions. Sergius spared a glance; the leaders had reached the entrance to the shallow valley. One warrior, braver than the rest, rode his horse to within javelin range, hurling taunts and epithets, waving his sword.

Suetonius must have heard the cries, but he kept his back to the enemy. He halted at the center of the Roman line and waited for the troops to quieten to attentiveness.

"Ignore the empty threats of these barbarians!" he shouted. "Look at them—there are more women than fighting men in their ranks!"

Men close at hand relayed the governor's words to those farther away.

Laughter rippled through the legions.

"They'll break when they see your courage," Suetonius continued. "We'll rout them as we've routed them before. Even when a force contains many legions, few among them win the battles. A special glory awaits for our small numbers to win the renown due a whole army!"

One of the centurions raised a cheer, and the legionaries joined in.

Suetonius held up his hand for silence. "Keep in close formation! Wait for the order to throw your javelins. When the order to advance sounds, use your shield bosses to fell the Britons, your swords to kill them. Don't think of plunder; think of victory. When you've won, you'll have everything!"

A wave of sound washed over Sergius. He joined the cheers until his ears rang.

"Think of the tortures these Britons inflicted on the inhabitants of Camulodunum. Think of the veterans whose years of retirement were cut off. Think of your brothers in arms, the men of the *Hispana*, who perished on this foreign soil. Let us conquer the Britons or die on the spot!"

More cheers.

"What if Boudicca won't give battle?" Marcianus asked Suetonius quietly.

"She will," Suetonius assured. "She won't be able to hold her warriors back."

Sergius followed the senior officers to their position behind the troops. Agricola waved as they circled past *Valeria*'s cohorts. Sergius returned one.

He took his station next to Veturius in the rear of the legions, to the side of Suetonius, Marcianus, and the governor's bodyguard.

The legions waited as the Briton horde swelled.

Sergius had thought that the Britons might rush to the attack as soon as they arrived, but except for a few horsemen and charioteers who rode close to the Roman lines and turned away, the Britons kept their distance. If they thought to impress the legionaries by their skill at charioteering, they failed. The light, two-wheeled chariots of the Britons hardly matched Roman four-wheeled racing quadrigae.

"Boudicca must have some control over them," Sergius observed.

Veturius shrugged, "They know we're trapped. Gather together, and then fall on us—that's what they'll do."

Sergius looked to where the sun had risen well in the sky. "How much longer?"

Veturius gave a tight smile. "It's you that's eager now, is it?"

Sergius snorted. He pointed out a line of wagons behind the Briton forces. "Look at that. They brought their wives and children to watch."

"Just like a circus," Veturius compared. "Chariot racing, and then a bloody battle. They're having fun." He ran his finger along the blade of his sword. "And well may they have it."

Britons poured along the plain toward the valley opening, in their lead, a twin-horsed chariot held a woman and two girls.

Sergius gazed at the tawny-haired woman he'd seen once before. "The queen herself," he said.

Veturius spared only the briefest of glances. "Good."

The chariot wheels bumped over uneven ground. The horses' manes blew in the wind. Boudicca gripped her lance with one hand, and the reins with the other. Legs spread, she braced her feet on either side of the chariot. In front of her, Aife and Cinnia held themselves erect.

Aife seemed confident, Boudicca noted. It was a good sign for her elder daughter. Cinnia trembled. Perhaps seeing the Romans crushed would help Cinnia.

Boudicca stared up the gentle slope at the waiting legions. She'd been watching them from a distance as her army approached. They hadn't moved. For their lack of mobility, they could have been statues carved of marble or cast in bronze, instead of living men. The sun picked out highlights in their ranks.

Soon they would be dead men.

Boudicca bit her lip. The Romans weren't spread out as the Ninth Legion had been, easy pickings for her eager warriors. Instead, they'd lined up in compact divisions—the red- and blue-shielded legions in the center, with auxiliary troops on either side and cavalry on the wings.

These legions would be tougher to crack.

But they *would* crack.

The wheels churned dirt as she turned the chariot. Mounted, Bairrfhionn flanked her on one side, Weylyn on the other. A train of Iceni nobles followed in her wake, some in chariots, others on horses. Behind them came thousands on thousands of warriors, men and women both.

And in the rear, wagons bearing wives and children and elders came to watch the battle and the victory.

Bairrfhionn gave a low whistle. "They're ready for us."

"Ready?" Weylyn scoffed. "They're cowering, like the others in their camps. They'll crumple when we hit them."

One of the nobles in the train grumbled, "Why do we fight when there are other towns to be plundered?"

Boudicca whirled. She shouted over the other nobles who heaped invective on the dissenter. "Why? For the defilement of the sacred places! For my lost freedom, my scarred back, and my raped daughters—that's why! What is kingdom and wealth when Roman rapacity doesn't even spare our bodies?"

She held her lance high and shouted so those in the front of the army could hear her. "Hear me! I'm a woman—but we Britons are used to women commanders in war! The blood of warriors flows in my veins! The gods will grant us the vengeance we deserve! We annihilated one legion, and we'll do the same to these. Look how few of them there are! Win this battle or perish—that is what I, a woman, plan to do! You men live in slavery if you will!"

"Follow the Queen!" Weylyn shouted.

"Follow the Queen!"

Boudicca stooped, and from between her daughters scooped a struggling animal. She held the hare by the scruff of its neck.

"Andraste, remember my vow!"

She dropped the hare to the ground. The animal darted away, jerking first one direction and then another as it sighted men or horses.

"Vengeance is ours!" Boudicca yelled.

A roar erupted from the warriors.

They plunged toward the Roman ranks.

"Here they come," somebody said near Sergius.

Sergius watched Boudicca release the hare, although he was too far distant to make out her words. Her chariot disappeared among the rabble.

"A rabbit?" Veturius scoffed. "That's the best they can do?"

Sergius thought of the sacred chickens carried by every legion but said nothing. He searched the field of combatants for a familiar figure. But out of so many, if Ailidh was present, could he even distinguish her?

He gripped the hilt of his gladius.

A seething horde of enraged warriors thundered into the defile. Swords flashed, cloaks swirled, naked chests shone with sweat, and what seemed like two hundred thousand throats screamed and shrieked.

The legionaries stirred, but not a man broke ranks.

Sergius looked at Suetonius. The commander sat immobile, watching the oncoming Britons.

"Prepare to cast!" Suetonius shouted.

Centurions relayed the order.

Each legionary slid his left foot forward into position, balanced his javelin in his right hand—the army accepted only right-handed men— and tensed.

The gap narrowed to a hundred yards, and the shouts reverberated in the valley, seemingly flung at the legions by the trees.

Eighty, and mustaches flowed, legs pumped, and muscular arms bulged.

Suetonius made no move.

Seventy, and a wild-eyed woman pitched a spear at the legions. It fell short and clattered to the ground.

Sixty, and the narrowing defile crowded the Britons together, packing them so that bodies bumped and legs and arms tangled.

Some tripped and fell. Those following trampled them.

Fifty, and when was Suetonius going to order?

A Briton's spear clattered off a legionary's shield.

Sergius's throat tightened. In a moment the Britons would be upon them.

Sweat trickled down his back between his shoulder blades. The tips of his fingers tingled. His cheek itched beneath his cheek plate, and he wished he could scratch it.

No matter that he waited in the rear, with nearly ten thousand trained legionaries in front of him.

Forty yards . . .

"Cast!" Suetonius yelled, and the bright notes of the tuba sounded the command.

From the Roman ranks ten thousand javelins rose into the air. The iron points glittered like a flock of birds. At the crest of their arcs they seemed to pause, hanging over the heads of the densely packed Britons.

And then they fell.

The line of charging warriors staggered. Britons screamed and pitched headlong to the ground. The fortunate ones took the javelins on their small, round shields. But the soft iron tips were designed to bend on impact. Unable to withdraw the javelins, and hampered by the useless shields, the warriors cast them aside.

But the Britons didn't falter. Pushed by the weight of those behind, Boudicca's forces surged ahead, trampling the bodies of the fallen into the ground.

"Cast!" Suetonius shouted again, and each legionary threw his second pilum.

The barrage of deadly projectiles ascended and plunged. Thousands of Britons perished, their death howls mingling with war cries.

"Draw! Stand fast!"

Gladii scraped from scabbards. The legionaries tucked their shields together and braced themselves.

Slipping and staggering over ground already slick with blood and tumbled with bodies, the Britons slammed into the Roman formation.

The roar of iron on iron deafened Sergius.

His horse shied, and Sergius leaned over to quieten it. From his position on horseback, slightly upslope from the main body of troops, he had a clear vantage point.

The screaming Briton ranks lashed against the Roman front lines and broke upon it like a wave against a rocky shore. The Roman line trembled but held fast. Pushing and shoving, warriors and legionaries sought to fell each other.

Vignettes of action clustered within Sergius's vision.

A shield boss caught a Briton who dropped to his knees, where a legionary's gladius impaled him.

A heavy spear slipped past a Roman shield, pierced a lorica, and felled a soldier.

A jab with a gladius slew a screaming Briton.

Blood, sweat, and dust blew on the breeze.

A howling woman tried to leap over the interlocked shields, but gladii reached up to change her war cry to a death shriek of agony.

To reach the Romans, the Britons had to clamber over the bodies of their slain comrades. As they climbed, their guard lowered, and they exposed themselves to Roman counterblows.

Longswords beat against shields, and Roman blades reached below upraised arms to send Briton after Briton to the otherworld.

The tubas blared: Tighten ranks!

Sergius glanced at Suetonius. The governor's eyes were everywhere, weighing, assessing, seeing where the Roman line was strong, where weak.

Tersely, he ordered reserve cohorts to move to the front lines to relieve the tiring men who faced the brunt of the Briton attack. The practiced troops completed the maneuver smoothly, without mishap.

Sergius's horse stepped restlessly. His hand ached from gripping his gladius, and he hadn't even struck a blow yet.

"Relax," Marcianus said from beside him. "Your turn will come."

Sergius nodded.

To his eyes, the Briton forces seemed hardly dented by the loss of the thousands who had perished.

Once, Sergius caught sight of Boudicca. Her chariot wheels flashed as she circled her army. If she was trying to instill discipline or issue orders, Sergius thought she was doomed to failure. The enraged Britons were past all listening.

Women stood on the wagons behind the Briton army, waving their arms, adding their yells to the ferocious din.

And then, for a moment, the battle lulled. The Britons staggered away from the mounds of dead and dying.

The legionaries drew breath, wiped sweat from their eyes.

"Do we charge?" Marcianus asked Suetonius.

Sergius leaned to hear the calm reply.

"Not yet. Let them spend themselves."

"They're not breaking!" Boudicca raged. She had her chariot to herself now, having sent her daughters to safer positions on the far side of the Anker. "By Andraste, they're holding!"

"They've taken casualties," Bairrfhionn replied.

"Not enough!" Boudicca gritted her teeth. "If we could only outflank them."

"We can't."

"We must overwhelm them." Boudicca laid down her lance. She shrugged off her cloak and then tore away her multicolored léine, bearing her scarred back.

"Are there no men among the Britons?" she yelled, whipping her horses to a gallop. "Are there none brave enough to avenge these scars?"

A renewed wave of screaming Britons launched themselves up the slope and exploded against the Roman lines.

The *Gemina*'s second cohort, one of the two weaker cohorts in the front line, buckled.

The Britons seized the momentary advantage and pressed into the gap.

Sergius froze. If the second crumpled, the Britons could tear into the flanks of the first and third cohorts on either side. If the Roman formation collapsed, then every man would have to fend for himself. And against those odds—

Marcianus wheeled his horse. "Form up!" he yelled.

A figure raced past, burly legs pumping.

Chief Centurion Adventus shouted orders, "Seventh cohort advance!"

Tubas blared. The standard-bearer of the seventh leaped forward.

The seventh—the recruits, the fresh-faced boys from the towns and cities, many of them seeing their first real action other than the slaughter on Mona—stepped into the gap to brace the second.

The inward bulge in the line halted, firmed, and then reversed. Thrusting shields forward, the seventh flung the Britons away.

The Roman line reformed as men took the place of fallen comrades.

"A close call."

It took a moment for Sergius to realize that Suetonius had spoken to him.

The governor continued, "A single action can win or lose a battle. Adventus just won it for us."

Won it? Sergius wondered but dared not ask. The battle certainly didn't appear to have been won.

The legionaries repulsed another barrage of Britons.

But still they came.

More and more, like a swarm of flies around a carcass, they came: men and women, youthful warriors and graybeards, skilled nobles handling their swords expertly, and farmers waving hoes and axes; clothed, naked, painted; yelling, cursing, boasting.

They came; they fought; they died.

Sergius held his scarf to his nose. The stench of blood sickened him. The screams rang in his ears like the wails of the damned. Iron sparked on iron like fragments of the flames of hell.

And Romans fell too. A spear or a sword found its mark, and another son of Rome spilled his life on foreign soil.

Veturius had paled bone white—whether from anger or sickening, Sergius couldn't tell.

The sun blazed from a brittle blue sky, and dust streams fragmented sunbeams.

And still they came.

"By the gods, will it never end?" Veturius swore.

A spear flickered through the air, and Sergius ducked reflexively.

Marcianus related to Suetonius, "The men are tiring, sir."

Suetonius nodded. "So are the Britons." He shaded his eyes and scanned the battlefield. "Prepare to charge. The *Gemina* will lead."

Marcianus relayed the order.

Ailidh started at a touch on her shoulder. Absorbed in watching the conflict that raged on the farther bank of the Anker, she thought she'd had this hillside to herself. She spun and found herself returning the gaze of a pair of dark gray eyes.

"Lovernios!" She jerked herself free.

The Druí lowered his hand. "The daughter of Cathair avoids battle?"

Ailidh hesitated. Lovernios's voice was taut and grated in a way she'd never heard before. But his eyes seemed sunken and tired, as if the fires that fueled his fervor had burned low.

She said, "The daughter of Cathair has no need to wield a sword."

Lovernios's gaze passed over her, down the hillside on which they stood, across the river, and to the opposite hill. "Your friend fights."

"You've seen him?" Her heart skipped a beat.

Lovernios shook his head. "No. But I know."

A trick of wind carried shouts and screams. Ailidh focused on the two struggling armies. Boudicca's followers raged against the still intact Roman ranks. Motionless figures littered the plain.

She prayed Sergius wasn't among the fallen. . . .

"How do you feel," Lovernios asked, "seeing your people cut down?"

She shook her head. "Surely there could have been some other way."

"To beat the Romans from our shores?"

"An Albu without Romans is one I've never known."

"Whereas I remember it as yesterday, when we were truly free."

"We are none of us free. We only serve different masters."

Lovernios raised an eyebrow. "Perhaps, could you have controlled your feelings, you might have become a Druí after all, Cousin."

"Instead, I'm an outcast."

"As am I." A flash of emotion overcame the weariness of Lovernios's previous conversation. "As are all Druí whom the Romans hunt down and kill as beasts. As are the Celtae, driven from their lands."

"The Gauls survive. The Galatians live."

"As minions of Rome. When freedom perishes, valor dies with it."

The piercing sound of Roman instruments carried across the valley.

"What is freedom," Ailidh asked, "when the whole world belongs to Rome?" She indicated the hillside. "If we win today, then what? Will the Romans rest? Will Nero consent to being beaten by a woman? They'll come back, stronger than ever, and if we thought we were slaves before, we'll be even more so then."

Lovernios shook his head slowly. "You speak like Prasutagus. And where is he now? To preserve our way of life, we *must* fight."

"And I think we seal our fate by doing so." Ailidh gave a brittle laugh. "One of us is right, Lovernios, and one wrong. But which is it?"

His face darkened. "If you hadn't interfered, the outcome would have been sure."

"If I hadn't interfered, you would have had more blood on your hands than you do already."

Lovernios extended an arm.

Ailidh flinched to avoid a blow, but the Druí merely pointed.

He said, "The Romans are charging."

The note of the cornu had barely faded when the standard-bearers of the *Gemina* and *Valeria* yelled, "For the eagles!" and hurled themselves to the forefront of the legions.

The lines of the legion shifted, into a wedge led by *Gemina's* elite first, third, and fifth cohorts. The auxiliaries swung into place on the flanks.

A slow trot gained speed, lurching over the fallen, and then the legionaries were running—helmet plumes waving, scabbards bouncing against thighs—a solid wall of shields and swords.

The surprised Britons fell back, tripping over bodies and each other, falling back until there was nowhere to go, and their wagons blocked further retreat.

The wedge tore into them, gouging a huge hole in the confused rabble.

Suetonius chopped a hand at the waiting cavalry. "Go!"

Didius Pertinax saluted, shouted a command, and the two cavalry detachments waiting on either wing burst into a gallop.

Sergius's horse strained at its bit.

Without warning, Veturius took off.

"Gaius!" Sergius shouted. "Come back!"

Veturius didn't acknowledge.

Sergius glanced at the commander for permission. Suetonius shook his head.

Sergius reigned back his horse and fought down the urge to follow his friend. They had a commitment to each other.

But he couldn't break rank.

Then the decision was taken from him. A stray spear sliced along his mount's flank. The horse reared and bolted, nearly throwing Sergius to the ground. All he could do was hang on and try to get his horse to fall in with the cavalry.

Lances lowered, the cavalry thundered past the running legionaries. The Britons saw them coming but had nowhere to flee.

The leading horses swept over the foot warriors. Warriors fell beneath the flashing, iron-shod hooves and the lances of the cavalrymen.

Veturius rode hard ahead of Sergius, his gladius carving a gleaming arc as it fell and rose and fell again.

Sergius swung his own sword to fend off thrusts. "Veturius, you idiot! Come back!"

Hands grabbed a cavalryman and hauled him from his horse.

Sergius hacked a Briton away.

He could see Veturius's helmet plume bobbing above the melee, but too many bodies intervened for him to be able to reach his friend. His horse made little headway against the dense mass of struggling humanity.

What could he do if he succeeded in reaching Veturius?

But they were sworn to help each other. He had to try.

The wagons that the confident Britons had arranged to provide a view of victory turned into their death trap. Crushed between the Romans in front and the wagons in the rear, the Britons' sheer weight of numbers worked against them. Pressed together, there was no way to wield a sword, maneuver a spear, or turn and flee.

The battle had turned, and the legionaries knew it.

Rout became slaughter.

Swords flickered like snakes' tongues from between shields as the legionaries pressed forward, slaying and slaying.

The mounds of Briton dead and dying grew higher and higher.

"We've lost!" Boudicca wailed from a vantage position that she'd taken behind the wagons. "How can it be?"

Bairrfhionn, his face smudged with dirt and sweat, said, "Truly the gods have deserted us."

"I swore!" Boudicca yelled, "and this is how they repay me—with false auguries and defeat! Andraste, I curse you! I spit on your name!"

"What are you going to do?" Bairrfhionn asked.

"What *can* I do? The battle is lost, the house of Prasutagus disgraced. There is nothing left for me. Curse it! Curse the day I first heard the name of Rome!"

The warrior's face paled as he took her meaning. "I'll come too."

"No." Boudicca shook her head. She held her lance crosswise, before Bairrfhionn's chest. "Fight or flee, as you will. But I go alone."

Lovernios's hands knotted in his cloak. His voice choked. "They're slaughtering us! Cutting us down like animals." He spread his arms. "Kill us all! Let none be spared! Let the Celtae be wiped from the face of the earth!"

Ailidh recoiled from the Druí's vehemence.

Lovernios spun away. "Go and celebrate, daughter of Cathair," he hurled. "Celebrate the victory of the Romans."

Before Ailidh could reply, the Druí vanished into the trees. She studied the way he had gone, then picked her way slowly down the slope, the river, toward the conflict that raged on the opposite bank.

Sergius wouldn't have wanted her to. But she had to find him.

He couldn't reach Veturius. For every step Sergius's horse took, Veturius's animal seemed to take one also. And the din was so loud, there was no way to make his voice heard.

Why didn't Veturius look back? But his friend didn't, and his gladius didn't rest.

Sergius gave up and contented himself with casting an occasional glance to make sure Veturius remained in the saddle.

A cavalryman beside him took a spear in the neck. He cried out and fell sideways against Sergius's horse. The startled animal reared, and another spear—that should have impaled Sergius—plunged into the horse's forefront. The horse's front legs buckled, and Sergius pitched forward.

He rolled as he hit, and the dying horse crumpled beside him. A flailing hoof struck him in the flank, and pain shot through his ribs.

He gasped for breath and blinked back tears. Feet, booted and naked, pounded the earth.

He couldn't remain on the ground, or he'd be trampled.

His gladius lay within reach. Sergius grabbed it and struggled to his feet.

He danced away from a frenzied animal and nearly tripped over a fallen legionary. He yanked the shield from the dead man's hand and took his place in the line that faced the Britons.

He matched the deadly rhythm of the men on either side—thrust, withdraw, advance.

Each movement stabbed pain through his chest.

Britons raised their arms to wield their long, cumbersome, slashing swords, which left their armpits exposed. With each thrust, another yelling barbarian went down in his or her death throes.

The number of female warriors startled Sergius. But it didn't matter to the legionaries.

He tried and failed to imagine Ailidh among the raging crowd. She couldn't possibly be here. This wasn't the place for a gentle spirit.

He slipped in a puddle of blood but regained his balance.

The Britons were beaten—why didn't Suetonius halt the slaughter?

A glance at the man next to him revealed the answer. Blood-lust suffused the legionary's face. He was enjoying the battle. The Romans had seen three cities destroyed, their women tortured, their comrades slain, and themselves pushed to the brink of defeat. Revenge was sweet. Suetonius probably couldn't halt the massacre even if he wanted to.

And maybe he didn't.

Sergius imagined a cold light of satisfaction on the commander's face. The Britons had rebelled, they'd desired war—well, let them reap the harvest they'd sown.

Suetonius wouldn't show mercy. And besides, dead rebels couldn't fight again.

Sergius's sword arm tired from the repetitive motion. His chest throbbed.

He longed to throw his sword down and quit the scene of destruction, to turn his back on the blood and sweat and vomit, on the noise and confusion, on the hatred and the death. But he couldn't.

To flee meant disgrace. More than disgrace. Desertion meant execution.

Desertion meant he'd betrayed the men on either side of him. The Roman Army hung together by mutual devotion to duty. You guarded your comrades, and they guarded you. These men—maddened though they be by blood-lust—were still his soldiers-in-arms.

And he, an officer, couldn't desert.

Let the battle end, he prayed. *Please God, let it end.*

His arm ached, a gnawing ache that crescendoed into sharp pains from his wrist to his shoulder, and his shoulder to his neck. His left arm throbbed also, from the weight of the shield and the blows the Britons thundered upon it.

Thrust, withdraw, advance.

His nose and throat burned with the reek of battle. His lungs dissolved into a vat of fire that flamed worse with every breath. He tasted blood and didn't know if it was in the air or if he bled.

Water. He needed a drink.

But there could be neither rest nor drink until the battle ended.

The Roman legions reached the wagons.

As the Britons in front of him melted away, Sergius found his way blocked by one of the Briton's carts.

Gladii reached up to snatch screaming women and terrified children into the jaws of death.

Troops vaulted onto the wagons, slashing and stabbing at everyone they found. Horses and oxen snorted and tore at their halters and were hacked to the ground.

Sergius froze, horrified, as a legionary decapitated a pair of children huddled together. Neither looked more than five or six.

He tried to shout, to yell, "No, this is wrong! Enough is enough! Not the children!" But his voice wouldn't come. His parched throat refused to utter sound, and the childrens' bodies crashed to the ground.

Sergius's vision blurred.

His mind refused to work, numbed by the enormity of the slaughter.

What had happened to them? The legions didn't fight unarmed women and children.

Where was the governor?

"Agricola," he wanted to call, "is this your glory? Is this the honor you want to receive? Is this the honor and glory of Rome?"

Somebody pushed him from behind, and he clambered onto the wagon, avoided the corpses that filled it, and jumped to the ground on the other side.

Is this supposed glory what you want to die for? an inner voice asked. He turned the question around. *Is this what you want to live for, to be a part of?*

Everywhere he looked, Britons fled the scene of battle, running to the hills, the river, the forests—anywhere that offered a promise of safety. And legionaries pursued them, cutting them down from behind.

Shouldn't a follower of the Way desire to bring life?

To defend others, to defend your country was one thing, but to slaughter every living person in sight?

Hadn't Christus said to love your enemy?

He stumbled away from the carnage, his feet moving of their own accord.

Paullus had once been a man of blood, a man who persecuted the followers of Christus. Now he proclaimed the sacrifice of Christus, who'd shed his blood for the salvation of men.

Sergius stepped over a mustached corpse, and his mind, amazingly, yielded a name—Bairffhionn.

He felt as if the life had been sucked out of him, as if everything he'd ever learned about life, about society, about civilization, had been stripped away.

The world blurred as though he wandered through the desert where hallucinations waited over every sand-softened hill.

As in a dream he meandered through a dusty land where faceless people appeared before him and then fell away, and a river twinkled in the distance, but he couldn't reach it.

He knew he held a sword, but he didn't know what he did with it.

He glanced at his feet and wondered dully why they kept moving when he didn't want them to.

Blood covered him to the knees. His cloak hung limply.

Where was he going?

Someone called his name. He knew the voice, but whose was it? And why did he call?

He didn't look around.

Veturius?

The voice took on a note of warning, and he knew he should listen and obey, but he couldn't.

A lance flashed from out of the dust, and he heard horse breath and a rattle and a swirling of iron hooves and iron wheels.

He saw color—a bright, multicolored shirt, a mass of long, tawny hair wreathing a full figure, a cloak.

A face full of anguish and despair.

"You!" the figure screeched.

And the lance point, shining silver, reached out for him.

Of its own accord, his sword arm extended to deflect the blow. The lance point grated off the sword and kept coming. It hit his lorica, slid between the plates, and seared along his side.

His sword dropped.

And then the chariot passed, the churning wheels disappearing into the dust and the distance.

His knees gave way.

He saw the ground coming up to meet him, and his mind didn't care, and his body rushed to embrace the hard earth.

TWENTY-EIGHT

Wetness.

Against his ear, his cheek, his neck.

Insistent. Warm.

Irritating.

Sound. A low, intense whining.

From farther away, sobs. A woman's sobs.

A scream: plaintive, weak, that wavered and died.

Death, yes.

But where was the promise of life? If he was dead—and he must be—why did he hear whines and sobs and screams?

Surely, it should be otherwise. Hadn't Christus promised?

Paradise. Where was paradise?

He remembered a flicker of bright light . . . and . . .

He'd fallen. That was it. The ground had blotted out the light.

But . . . shouldn't there have been more light?

Wasn't death more than this?

His ribs hurt. A lancinating pain radiated across his chest.

A lance.

Boudicca.

The memory returned. Boudicca had speared him as her chariot passed him by.

He'd seen death on her lance point, and been powerless to avert it.

Again, wetness across his face and ear.

Whines.

He tried to open his eyes, but they remained fast, something sticking his eyelids together.

And he couldn't speak. His tongue was a swollen, dry lump in his mouth.

But he must have made some croak, for the wetness rasped across his face, over his eyelids. Suddenly his eyes cracked opened.

Light. Bright light.

He squinted.

White teeth. Dark brown eyes. A hairy muzzle. A long pink tongue. A . . . dog? But Cara . . . he'd left her with the baggage animals. How had she gotten free?

From somewhere, his mouth worked free a dribble of spit.

"Cara?"

A shriek, "He spoke!"

A man's voice said, "Give him a drink, woman."

"Sit, Cara," said a woman's voice that brought a tremble to Sergius's heart. "Lie down."

Acid, sour. Old vinegar and water. Posca. From a centurion's wine-skin. He gulped, and the liquid spilled out of his mouth and down his chin.

"Not too much! Don't drown him."

Hands behind his back, raising him. A woman's scent. And finally, his eyes focused.

"Ailidh? Is it you?"

Tears flowed down her cheeks. She laughed and cried at the same time, "What other woman would you be expecting?"

She wrapped her arms around him. For a long moment his world became the softness of her neck, the wild beating of her heart, her breath rustling his hair.

She said, "I was sure . . . you were dead."

Then she held him at arm's length.

He drank in the familiar lines of her face, her twinkling green eyes, auburn hair. "I thought I was too."

He struggled to sit, and winced as pain skewered his chest.

"You're hurt." She instructed, "Don't move."

"Scratched."

The man spoke, dryly. "A moment ago, you were as good as dead, my friend. See what miracles Venus works."

Sergius looked past Ailidh's shoulder. "Veturius! You're alive."

"I should hope so." Helmetless, blood and dust stained, his lorica dented, his face creased with tired lines, his friend leaned on the broken shaft of a spear.

"It was God, Gaius, not Venus," Sergius corrected.

Ailidh said, "Hold still." Her hands moved over Sergius. She removed his cloak, unbuckled his lorica, lifted it over his head and dropped it to the ground. He tried to assist, but his arms seemed leaden, and his shoulders stiff.

He watched her gentle fingers work. Matted blood plastered his tunic to his chest. She wet the area with posca, and worked the fabric free.

Sergius gritted his teeth as the vinegar stung and clotted blood pulled from the torn flesh. She gripped the tunic and enlarged the rent to examine the wound.

"It's deep," she noted.

"I think the blade glanced off a rib," Sergius speculated.

She cleansed the ragged skin.

Veturius said, "I'll find a medicus." He turned and shambled away.

"You don't have to," Sergius began. "It's not that bad—"

"Shhh." Ailidh touched his lips to stop him. She tore a clean piece of cloth from her own tunic and padded the gash.

Sergius patted Cara while Ailidh worked.

He took a deep breath, fighting the pain. "You're not a bad medicus for a scholar."

Ailidh didn't answer.

Another thought rushed into his mind, followed by alarm. He struggled to reach for his gladius. "I'm a fool! You shouldn't be here. The legionaries are killing every Briton they can find. It's not safe for you."

"I spotted Veturius from a distance. He's been guarding me. He told me he saw you fall. He didn't want to let me come to you, but I insisted."

Sergius struggled to rise.

"Don't." Ailidh protested, but he persisted, "Help me stand," and she held his arm to support him.

Cara leaned against his legs, her head nearly waist-level.

The dust had settled, and the sun drooped toward the western horizon. The forest extended shadows across the plain.

Bodies lay heaped as far as he could see. Some moaned; most lay still. The wagons had been overturned, and the bodies of women, children, and draft animals lay in ungainly heaps bristling with spears and javelins. The overwhelming majority of the dead were Britons, but legionaries and auxiliaries lay among them.

The Roman losses seemed scant compared to the Britons'.

Legionaries tramped through the carnage, finishing off those that still breathed and were too wounded to survive. He saw Pertinax, and Agricola, and Titus on their feet. Farther off, he glimpsed Suetonius's scarlet cloak.

Sergius sighed.

He slid his arm around Ailidh's waist. "God knows how glad I am to see you safe. But this was a day that nobody won."

He searched the ground, this time found his gladius, and stooped to pick it up. He rotated the crusted blade in his hands. "This saved my life, but it has taken life, too."

The gladius was a symbol. A symbol of what it meant to be a Roman patrician. Keep the sword, follow the cursus honorus, and he'd become a praetor, a legate, a governor, or a senator.

He'd have money, power, influence. A fine villa. Social standing. Respect.

Without it, he'd be nothing.

Shunned by his family.

A nameless nonentity. An outcast. A plebeian.

Paullus had once held a sword. He'd given it up.

Christus had never had need of one.

And Ailidh . . . Ailidh too had chosen the path of the outcast.

With a violent motion, Sergius stabbed the blade into the ground, so the weapon stood upright.

He straightened and met Ailidh's eyes, inches from his own.

Her green eyes were wide. She looked from him to the sword. "What are you doing?"

"Sacrificing."

She stooped, and before he could stop her, jerked the gladius from the earth. "You need this."

"No, I don't. Not any longer."

"But . . . without it . . . "

"I don't need it," he repeated.

"You can't just walk away from the army," she protested.

"The rebellion isn't over," Sergius said, sweeping a hand over the battlefield. Not thirty feet away, a legionary skewered a still-breathing Briton.

He continued, "Suetonius is a hard man. He'll make certain the Iceni never rise again. I'm not going to be a part of any more killing. This isn't the life I want to live. If I'm to be a soldier, it will be a soldier of the Way."

Her face cleared. "Like Paullus."

He grimaced. "Well, not *quite.*" He thought of his parents and Veturius who didn't understand the way of Christus, who didn't know what it was like to be freed from the old traditions.

Ailidh still held the gladius. "What happens if you desert?" she asked softly.

"I—," He broke off as new images flooded his mind: A court-martial, the fustuarium, death or dishonor.

Strangely, the thought of dishonor didn't bother him. And death? He could die for Christus's sake.

"Take it." Ailidh's eyes pleaded.

She handed the gladius hilt first to him.

Take it, an inner voice whispered. *The sacrifice is sufficient.*

He remembered a story he'd heard from Apollos. As Abraham, a Jewish patriarch, prepared to offer his son Isaac on an altar, he was stopped by God just as his knife was about to descend. The offer was enough. The action wasn't needed.

And Paullus. The old apostle was prepared to die but continued to live for Christus. And Paullus's work in Britannia . . . that couldn't be allowed to crumble.

Numbly, Sergius reached for his gladius.

"Finish your service," Ailidh said. "Then resign with honor." She looked to the ground. "If you care about me—about my people—"

The gladius slipped into the scabbard.

"I do," he said hoarsely. He tipped her chin. "I'll do what I can to ease Suetonius's anger."

He rested his hands on her shoulders. "But only if you're with me, Ailidh."

She moved into his embrace. "An ex-Druidess?"

"And a newly humbled Roman."

Her lips parted.

His own, cracked and dry, moved toward them.

"Sergius! Here's the medicus," Veturius called.

Sergius groaned and dropped his forehead onto Ailidh's shoulder. "Not now."

He broke the embrace and glared at his friend.

"Sorry." Veturius spread his hands. "And the commander wants to know why you deserted your post."

"I didn't," Sergius said sharply. He gazed at Ailidh and sighed. "Just what I need. One more mishap to attempt to explain."

EPILOGUE

The Festival of Beltain
Maius 1, 803 A.U.C.
(May 1, A.D. 60)

Albu (Britain)

In the heart of an oak grove, Lovernios shivered in a cool May breeze that rustled his hair about his ears and plucked at his beard. He wore a fox fur band around his left forearm and a fox fur cape over his shoulders. Otherwise, he was naked.

The oaks stood silently as night descended through branches cloaked with the green leaves of spring. Shadows stretched across the ground, undulating in long dragon tails that writhed and contorted and clutched for Lovernios's ankles. The tree branches waved leafy fingers that beckoned him to the otherworld.

Beyond the grove lay the stagnant black waters of Llyndu, a treacherous bog of dark soil and lank grasses, depthless, unfathomable. In summer and fall, so men said, colors brightened the bog: the white and yellow of myrtle; and the light green of grass, moss, and reeds. The reflection of blue sky in the motionless ponds invited the unwary to meander through its trackless course. But in winter, or when clouds blotted out the face of the sun, boggarts and demons peered with wrinkled and rippled faces from mist-draped pools.

Lovernios's stomach growled. His last meal lay heavy and cold within him—blackened barley bread baked upon a ceremonial lambskin washed down with mistletoe-intincted water from a sacred well. He had chosen a piece of blackened bread with a black mark resembling a thumbprint, deliberately.

Because, and he knew it now, *he* was the appointed victim.

Other, human-shaped shadows stood among the trees. The Druid priesthood.

On this ridge in the territory of the Cornovii, a tiny enclave where Roman sandals had not yet trod, the great Beltain bonfires should have blazed. There ought to have been throngs of people drawn from all classes, commoners and nobles alike. There should have been singers and musicians. There should have been herds of cattle waiting to be guided between a pair of fires in order to protect them from disease.

But this Beltain, there were no singers, no musicians, no animals. The people hid in forests and caves.

And the only fire was a pitiful handful of sticks set in a hollow so that the flickering light couldn't be seen by the Roman troops camped not far away.

Lovernios pulled his cape tighter.

Awaiting him was the triple death, to the three great gods: Taranis, the thunder god; Esus, lord and master; and all-god Teutates.

Lovernios knew the form his death would take. The ax; the garotte; the knife.

Three blows to his skull from an ax, the thunderbolt of Taranis. After the first, he'd be unconscious. Then the garrote of Esus, a thin cord of gut knotted three times, choking him quickly. Then a knife to the jugular and the draining of his blood into a bronze cauldron. And finally the cold embrace of Llyndu, when the chill waters closed over his inert form and carried him to Teutates, to become the consort of the earth mother.

He squared his shoulders. He was Lovernios, the fox, prince of the Iceni, Druí.

And his death was ordained.

He understood that now.

As he understood the full meaning of his dream.

The wren was *druí-en*, the bird of the Druid. The eagle with the raven's cry was Rome, lusting for battle.

On the devastated shore of Mona, in the bodies of men and women he had known and loved, in the remnant who gathered here and in Ériu, he had seen the wren struggle for life.

The woman on the horse was Boudicca, riding like the goddess Epona. But Boudicca lay dead by her own hand, her army defeated, her warriors slain, her daughters vanished. And the Roman heel ground into those who'd escaped death in battle.

The conquered would never rise again.

The gods had deserted the Celtae. From every battle, Rome emerged victorious. Caratacus had failed, Vercingetorix had failed, Boudicca had failed. The people who had once ruled from Ériu to Galatia, who had held sway from the river of Danu into Italia itself, were defeated.

The horse withering was the people starving. Because of the rebellion, farmers hadn't planted spring crops. Bellies would ache, breasts dry, limbs weaken.

This year, the Black Year, the year of three disasters, hung over the Britons like the thunderbolt of Taranis. And there was no end in sight.

What was to stop the Romans from invading Ériu itself? Could the narrow stretch of sea that separated Albu from Ériu hold back the might of Rome?

Lovernios shivered again. When so many had died, what was his life that he should shrink from death? If his sacrifice could avert disaster, then he would meet death gladly.

Even the triple death for triple disaster.

The ceremonies, the dances, and the prayers had been completed. All that remained was the final offering.

The speakers to the gods and the seers stood in a circle. Inside the circle the sacerdotes waited, standing beside a stool and the bronze cauldron. One held an ax, a second the garrote, a third, the knife. Outside the circle rested a chariot, drawn by a white horse whose snorting breath misted in the night air.

If his sacrifice was rejected, then he would be forgotten, another nameless casualty of war. If successful, the hated Romans would be halted, the Britons would survive, and his sacrifice be remembered.

Lovernios removed his fox fur cloak and handed it to one of the attendants. Naked but for the armband, he stood in the starlight.

Would Taranis accept his death? Would Esus accept his blood? Would Teutates accept his body?

Would destruction be averted from the Britons?

He spared a fleeting thought for Ailidh, her Way of love, and the sacrifice of one who claimed to be divine. Perhaps, in a different time . . .

He entered the circle of silent Druid.

He knelt on the ground.

✠ ✠ ✠

GLOSSARY

Roman

Terms

acetum. Sour wine.

amphorae. Large pottery vessels for storage.

annona. Grain levy.

apodyterium. Changing room.

armatura. Drill instructor.

arretine ware. Preconquest pottery from Arretium in Tuscany.

auspira oblativa. An unrequested portent.

balneator. Bathhouse attendant.

balneum. Bathhouse.

basilica. Town hall.

birrus. Hooded cloak of goat's hair.

bracae. Knee-length leather trousers.

bucellata. Baked cornmeal biscuits.

caldarium. The hot pool.

caligae. Boots.

caligatae. "Foot-sloggers." Slang for legionaries (infantry).

canabae. Civilian settlement.

cohortes urbanae. City police.

curia. Council chamber.

decurio. Town councillor; also a cavalry troop commander.

dormitoria. Bedroom.

fabrica. Workshop.

frigidarium. The cold pool.

fustuarium. Punishment for dereliction of duty.

gladius. Short sword.

incolae. Native residents of a provincial town.

liburna (pl. liburnae). A fast, light galley; liburnian ship.

lorica segmentata. Breastplate of overlapping plates.

macellum. Market hall.

mansio. Official "hotel."

mortaria. Mixing bowl.

numen. Spirit.

ocreae. Greaves (shin guards).

oppidum (pl. *oppida*). Tribal towns.

ordo. Town council.

papilio. Leather tent large enough for eight men.

pecuarii. Animal attendants.

phalerae. Circular honors worn on the uniform.

pila muralia. Palisade stakes.

pilum. Javelin.

portoria. Port tax.

posca. Sour vinegar and water carried by centurions.

praetor. State legal officer.

praetorium. Commander's house or tent.

principia. Headquarters.

pugio. Dagger.

quadrigae. Four-horse racing chariot.

religio licta. State-approved religion.

rhyton. Drinking horn.

sacramentum. Recruitment oath of loyalty and obedience.

sagum. Military cape.

samian ware. Red pottery made in Gaul.

scutum. Shield.

strigil. Bath scraper for cleaning the skin.

tabularium. Treasury office.

tali. Knuckle bones used as gaming pieces.

tapete. Wool rug or blanket.

tepidarium. The lukewarm pool.

tributum soli & tributum capitis. Property and poll taxes.

triumvir capitalis. Three men in charge of capital crimes police.

via praetoria; via principalis. The main streets in a fortress.

vinum. Vintage wine (such as Falernian, Aminian).

vitis. A twisted vine stick, a centurion's staff of office.

Provinces

Britannia. Britain.
Gallia. Gaul; roughly modern France and Belgium.
Germania. Germany.
Hibernia. Ireland.
Hispania. Spain.
Italia. Italy.

Towns

Aquileia. In Italy.
Bannaventa. Whilton Lodge.
Caesaromagus. Chelmsford.
Calleva. Silchester.
Camulodunum. Colchester.
Canonium. Kelvedon.
Deva. Chester.
Dubris. Dover.
Durobrivae. Rochester.
Durocobrivis. Dunstable.
Durovernum. Canterbury.
Gesoriacum. Boulogne.
Glevum. Gloucester.
Isca. Exeter.
Lactodurum. Towcester.
Lemanis. Lympne.
Letocetum. Lichfield/Wall.
Lindum. Lincoln.
Londinium. London.
Magiovinium. Dropshort.
Manduessedum. Mancetter.
Mediolanum. Whitchurch.
Moguntiacum. Mainz.
Noviomagus. Chichester.
Pennocrucium. Water Eaton.
Pontes. Staines.
Rutupiae. Richborough.
Tripontium. Cave's Inn.

Vagniacis. Springhead.

Venonis. High Cross.

Venta Icenorum. Caistor St. Edmunds.

Verulamium. St. Alban's.

Viroconium. Wroxeter.

Distances

All distances are given in Roman miles. 1 Roman mile = 1.1 modern mile.

Currency

1 aureus (gold piece) = 25 denarii (silver pieces) = 100 sestercii (brass) = 400 as (bronze).

The sestercius was the ordinary coin for reckoning, although rarely minted due to its insignificant value.

Briton

Terms

Anruth. The second rank (below ollamh) in druidic school.

Brat. Long woolen cloak.

Cailleoir. Astrologer.

Clad. Longsword.

Criss. Belt or girdle.

Druí (pl. *Druid*). The Celtic intelligentsia.

F'athi. (pl. *fáith*). Druid priests, diviners.

Fochluc. Novice in druidic school.

gutuatros (pl. *gutuatri*). Druid priest; "speaker to the gods."

léine. Linen tunic.

neledoir. Cloud diviner.

nemeton. Sacred enclosure.

óenach. Assembly of the túath.

ollamh. Professor in druidic school.

rí. King.

sacerdote. Druid sacrificial priest.

túath. People, territory.

torque. Gold, silver, or bronze neckpiece.

Places
Ériu. Ireland.
Albu. Britain.

Dates

43. Claudian invasion of Britain.
49. Colonia Claudia at Camulodunum founded.
50. Londinium founded.
52. Defeat of Caratacus.
54. Death of Claudius and ascension of Nero (age 17).
55. Temple of Claudius begun.
58/59–61. Suetonius Paulinus, governor of Britannia.
60. Boudiccan Rebellion.

Roman Army

Organization

Legion: 5,000–6,000 men.

> 8 men = one contubernium.
> 10 contubernii = one century of 80 men.
> 2 centuries = one maniple.
> 6 centuries = one cohort of 480 men.
> 10 cohorts = one legion of 5,280 (one cohort of 960 men; 9 cohorts of 480 men).
> Horsemen: 120 per legion. Scouts and dispatch riders allocated to specific centuries.

Alae. Cavalry regiments.
Auxiliaries. Foreign troops.
Infantrymen. Peditae.
Horsemen. Equitate.
Governor's bodyguard. Equites and pedites singulares.

Ranks: Roman army ranks do not have strict equivalents with contemporary ranks. Accordingly, I have retained Roman terms. For ease of reference, though, the following rough approximations may be adopted.

Legatus Augusti pro praetore. Governor and commander in chief of a province.

Legatus legionis (pl. legati), Legate. Commander of a legion: "Major General."

Tribunus legionis (*tribunus militum*), Military Tribune. "Colonel," "aide de camp," administrative.

> 6 tribunes per legion.
>> Senior: Tribunus laticlavius, senatorial rank; second in command of legion.
>> Junior: Tribunus augusticlavii, equestrian rank, often assigned to auxiliary troops.

Praefectus castrorum, camp prefect. "Lt. Colonel." Administrative. 3rd in command.

Primus Pilus, chief centurion. "Major." Field command.

Centurions (various grades). Commander of a century (80 men). 60 per legion: "Captains."

> Primus pilus. Chief centurion, commanded first century of first cohort.

> Princeps. HQ responsible for staff and training. The other centurion of 1st cohort in order of seniority: Hastatus, princeps posterior, hastatus posterior. In other cohorts, the centurions were of equal status, but ranked by seniority: Pilus prior, pilus posterior, princept prior princeps posterior, hastatus prior, hastatus posterior.

optio. Second to a centurion: "lieutenant."

tesserarius. "Sergeant," in charge of sentry pickets, fatigue parties.

Standard-bearers. *Signifers, aquilifers,* and *principales,* ranked as sergeants.

> The aquilifer carried the legion's eagle standard.

> The signifer carried the signa of the cohort.

> The imaginifer carried the imago of the emperor.

> A cavalry ala had a vexillum (flag) carried by a vexillarius.

'Immunes.' Privates excused from more onerous duties.

> *custos armorum.* Weapons officer.

> *agrimensories.* Surveyors.

> *metatores.* Camp site selectors.

> armament workers.

> musicians.

miles gregarius. Private.

Haruspices (s. haruspex) and Augures. Priests.

Cavalry regiments:

praefectus alae (prefect). Regimental commander.

decurio. Troop (*turmae*) commander. (32 men).

Each senior officer had an aide (*beneficiarius*) whose rank depended on that of the officer he served.

Headquarters Staff:

Centurion. Princeps praetorii.

Cornicularius. "Adjutant."

Commentarienses. Registrars.

Adiutors. Assistants.

Speculatores. Judicial officers in charge of prisoner custody.

Beneficiarii. In charge of security of supply routes.

Stratores. Equerries (duties unclear).

tabularium legionis. Clerks and orderlies.

librarii horroreum. Clerk in charge of granary records.

librarii depositorum. Clerk in charge of soldier's savings bank.

librarii caducorum. Clerk in charge of property of men killed.

Cursus Honorum: The Honorable Way.

triumvir capitis (age 18–20)—in charge of capital crimes police.

　　or (for lower classes) praefectus cohortis of auxiliary infantry.

military tribune.

quaestor (age 25). Financial officer.

　　or (lower class) praefectus alae of auxiliary cavalry.

tribune of plebs (honorary).

　　or

aedile. Civil office responsible for shopkeepers and temple order.

curator. In charge of roads.

praetor (age 30). Judge, legal officer.

legatus legionis (age 33–35).

proconsul of province.

　　or

legate of province.

consul (army commands/governorships).

HISTORICAL NOTE

The historian R. G. Collingwood pointed out that the past exists in three aspects: the past as it actually was, the past as it is known today, and the past as it is wished for. In this novel, I have tried to present accurately the events of A.D. 59/60 in a novelized manner, avoiding wishing events and people were different. Of course, moderns cannot penetrate the minds, attitudes, and worldviews of vanished peoples. No matter how we might wish otherwise, we can never know them as they truly were. I have tried to recreate historical personages realistically, given the limitations of historical accounts.

When sifting through fragmentary and contradictory historical and archaelogical details, I have chosen the alternatives that seemed most reasonable to me or that fit in best with the story. For historical accounts of the Boudiccan rebellion, we have only the *Annals* of Tacitus (about A.D. 120) and the *Roman Histories* of Dio Cassius (about A.D. 220). I have gleaned other insights from archaeology and from accounts of life in Roman Britain. Any errors of fact or interpretation are, of course, mine. I have adapted some dialogue from the accounts of Tacitus's *Annals of Imperial Rome,* translated by Michael Grant (Penguin Books, 1956) and Cassius Dio's *Roman History,* translated by Ernest Cary (Cambridge, Mass.: Harvard University Press, 1925).

Concerning names, Cerialis was the only legionary commander during the Boudiccan rebellion whose name has come down to us. Some authorities prefer the spelling "Boudica" for the queen of the Iceni. "Boadicea" is an inaccurate rendition. While it is known that Prasutagus and Boudicca had two daughters, their names have not survived.

Chronology presents certain problems. Tacitus dates the rebellion to A.D. 61. Modern historians have vacillated between 61 and 60, with opinion perhaps leaning toward 60.

Pauline chronology is even more problematic. One tradition dates Paul's first imprisonment in Rome to 57–59, the other 60–62. (See, for example, the *International Standard Bible Encyclopedia* for options.) Obviously the second would preclude his presence in Britain during the Boudiccan rebellion. Donald Selby (*Toward the Understanding of St. Paul* [Englewood Cliffs, N. J.: Prentice-Hall, 1962]) concludes, "Any chronological scheme for the life of St. Paul must be tentative." Since there have been legends from earliest Christian days that Paul *did* visit Britain, I have adopted the first dating. For examination of these legends, see R. W. Morgan's Victorian work, *Did the Apostle Paul Visit Britain?* (reprinted by Dolores Press, 1984) or *The Origin and Early History of Christianity in Britain* by Andrew Gray (1897; reprint, Thousand Oaks, Calif.: Artisan Publishers, 1991).

The events in the story, then, could occur either in fall 59 to spring 60, or fall 60 to spring 61. I have chosen the former.

The Druids have been the victims of romanticization. (In Irish, *Druí* (s), *Druid* (pl); in Latin *Druid* (s), *Druidae* (pl.). The little we know comes from from hostile Greek and Roman sources and from excavations. The romantic accretions of centuries have presented a popular, though unlikely, view of Druids. I have adopted the opinion of leading scholars that the Druids comprised the intellectual strata of Celtic society. Druidism was not so much a religion as, in the words of Peter Beresford Ellis, "an organization which made religion a means to political power." The issue of human sacrifice among the Druids is contentious. Most likely it occurred only in the context of unusual or critical events.

We don't know, either, whether the dialects of the Celtic language were mutually intelligible between the Irish and British branches. For story purposes I have assumed they were.

Many anecdotes in this novel are true. Julius Caesar's tent mosaic, Claudius and Caratacus, the death of Agrippina, the centurion "Fetch me Another." The incident of Vespasian and the scented officer probably occurred when Vespasian was emperor and not legionary commander in Britain.

Regarding Decianus Catus and the rape of Boudicca's daughters: Lest it be thought that I have been too hard on the procurator, here's the conclusion of historian Ian Andrews: "Even as we look back over 1900 years we can find nothing good in the man: the best that can be said of him is that he was not the only one to blame for the rebellion of Boudicca and that his friends and officials were as bad as he was" (*Boudicca's Revolt*, Cambridge University Press, 1972: 22).

Tacitus says simply, "Kingdom and household alike were plundered like prizes of war, the one by Roman officers, the other by Roman slaves. As a beginning, [Prasutagus'] widow Boudicca was flogged and their daughters raped." And also, "It was [Catus's] rapacity which had driven the province to war."

Catus himself may or may not have committed atrocities, but for dramatic purposes I have placed the blame squarely on his shoulders.

Archaeology hasn't revealed details of the Roman invasion route to Anglesey. It has generally been proposed that the Romans built boats at Chester and sailed them around the coast (an arduous undertaking to cross a narrow channel) or appropriated boats they found (which seems problematical). The use of prefabricated craft assembled on location is my idea.

The Boudiccan Rebellion was a violent incident in Britain's history, costing the lives of perhaps as many as 150,000 people. I have tried neither to dwell on the violence nor to gloss over the human suffering. Tacitus states that 80,000 Britons died in the final battle to only 400 Romans—figures that may well have been exaggerated. The death toll in Camulodunum, Verulamium, and Londinium may have approached 70,000.

In 1984, the well-preserved body of a man was discovered during peat-cutting operations in Lindow Moss, a bog near Manchester. The man was a first-century Celt. Celtic scholar Anne Ross proposed that he was a Druid prince, offered as a human sacrifice in the wake of the Boudiccan rebellion. She named him Lovernios. I am indebted to her imaginative reconstruction of his death in *The Life and Death of a Druid Prince* (coauthored with Don Robins, Summit, 1989). The fictional character Lovernios is mine.

The poem "I Am a Salmon" is adapted from a poem by Taliesin, quoted in Peter Beresford Ellis, *The Druids* (reprint; Grand Rapids: Eerdmans, 1998), 71. The Morrighan's prophecy is taken from Caitlin Matthews, *Elements of the Celtic Tradition*, Element Books, 22. "I am the son of Poetry" (adapted) from page 47. The quotations from Vergil's *Georgics,* translated by T. C. Williams (Cambridge, Mass.: Harvard University Press, 1915) and Seneca's *Agamemnon,* translated by F. J. Miller in *The Complete Roman Drama* (London: G. E. Duckworth, 1942) can be found in *Imperial Rome* by Moses Hadas (New York: Time-Life Books, 1965).

The head of a woman and the partial remains of another man have since been discovered in Lindow Moss. Were they too, Druids? Secrets remain in Lindow Moss.

SOURCES

Roman and Christian

Tacitus, Cornelius. *The Annals of Imperial Rome*. Translated by Michael Grant. Harmsworth, England: Penguin Books, 1956.

Cassius Dio. *The Roman History*. Translated by Ernest Cary. Cambridge, Mass.: Harvard University Press, 1925.

Cottrell, Leonard. *The Roman Invasion of Britain*. New York: Barnes & Noble Books, 1992. A readable volume that covers the period from Julius Caesar's landing in 55 B.C. to the final battles of the invasion, A.D. 84.

Webster, Graham. *The Roman Imperial Army* (New York: Barnes & Noble Books, 1969). A detailed description of the structure and practices of the Roman Army.

Adkins, Lesley, and Adkins, Roy A. *Handbook to Life in Imperial Rome*. New York: Facts on File, 1994. An indispensible guide to the details of Roman life.

Frere, Sheppard. *Britannia. A History of Roman Britain*. London: Routledge & Kegan Paul, 1967. A well-written and informative history of Roman Britain.

Scullard, H. H. *Roman Britain, Outpost of the Empire*. London: Thames & Hudson, 1979. A lucid history of life in Roman Britain, with details not found elsewhere.

Salway, Peter. *The Oxford Illustrated History of Roman Britain*. Oxford: Oxford University Press, 1993. Covers all aspects of Roman Britain.

Burke, John. *Roman England*. New York: W. W. Norton, 1983. A handy guide to places and artifacts.

Brunson, Matthew, ed. *Dictionary of the Roman Empire*. Oxford: Oxford University Press, 1991. Covers many people, places, and items of the Roman Empire.

Salway, Peter. *Roman Britain*. Oxford: Oxford University Press, 1981. Covers the entire occupation of Roman Britain.

Grant, Michael. *The Twelve Caesars.* New York: Barnes & Noble, 1975. The lives of the men who ruled the known world.

Benko, Stephen. *Pagan Rome and the Early Christians.* Bloomington: Indiana University Press, 1984. The relationship between Christians and Romans.

Hadas, Moses. *Imperial Rome.* New York: Time-Life Books, 1965. An overview of Roman History.

Watson, G. R. *The Roman Soldier.* Ithaca: Cornell University Press, 1969. Life for the man in the ranks.

Petrie, A. *Roman History, Literature, and Antiquities.* Oxford: Oxford University Press, 1952. A helpful guide to things Roman.

Miller, Martin. *Roman Britain.* London: B. T. Batsford, 1995. Another worthwhile guide.

Roman Invasions, videotape, Cromwell films, 1994. Brings the invasion to life.

Ordnance Survey Map of Roman Britain. Southhampton: Ordnance Surrey, n.d. Indispensible for place names and locations in Roman Britain.

Special mention should be made of English Heritage, which maintains custody of many Roman sites in Britain, publishes excellent brochures and guidebooks, and whose people are uniformly informative, helpful, and friendly.

Celtic

Ellis, Peter Beresford. *The Druids.* Grand Rapids: Eerdmans, 1998. A scholarly examination of the Druids that strips away myths to reveal the historical society.

Webster, Graham. *Boudicca.* London: B. T. Batsford, 1978. An examination of the Boudiccan rebellion by a respected scholar.

Piggott, Stuart. *The Druids.* London: Thames & Hudson, 1968. A critical examination of what is really known of the Druids.

Powell, T. G. E. *The Celts.* London: Thames & Hudson, 1958. An overview of the Celtic peoples.

Ross, Anne and Robins, Don. *The Life and Death of a Druid Prince.* New York: Summit Books, 1989. An imaginative recreation of Lindow Man.

Norman-Taylor, Duncan. *The Celts*. New York: Time-Life Books, 1974. The life of the Celtic peoples.

Kruta, Venceslas, and Forman, Werner. *The Celts*. Translated by Alan Sheridan. London: Golden, Orbis Pub., Ltd., 1985. An illustrated overview of Celtic culture.

Andrew, Ian. *Boudicca's Revolt*. Cambridge: Cambridge University Press, 1972. Brief, but informative.

Morgan, R. W. *Did the Apostle Paul Visit Britain?* London: Dolores Press, 1984.